"You owe me a Christmas!"

Arthur Chakrabarti Watercress stared at me with dark brown eyes that radiated fury and indignation far beyond what one would imagine possible from a boy who stood five foot nine and weighed less than a year-old Great Dane. That's a guess, by the way; I hadn't actually weighed either Arthur or a Great Dane, but you get the point. And his ever-precise British accent coupled with a tiny speck of spittle in the lower left corner of his mouth further undermined whatever intimidation factor he was going for. He was lucky I didn't laugh in his flushed face.

Or maybe because a part of me was still reeling from the surreal fact that he was *here*. In Oklahoma. In my hometown. And specifically, in the courtyard of my Grandma Jo's inn, where, I now knew, he and his aunt were staying over the holidays.

Awesome. Just freakin' awesome.

OTHER BOOKS BY TRACY ANDREEN

So, This Is Love

So, This Is Christmas

TRACY ANDREEN

Viking

VIKING

An imprint of Penguin Random House LLC, New York

First published in the United States of America by Viking,
an imprint of Penguin Random House LLC, 2021
First paperback edition published 2022

Visit us online at penguinrandomhouse.com.

THE LIBRARY OF CONGRESS HAS CATALOGED THE HARDCOVER EDITION AS FOLLOWS:
Names: Andreen, Tracy, 1967– author.
Title: So, this is Christmas / Tracy Andreen.
Description: New York : Viking, 2021. | Audience: Ages 14 and up |
Audience: Grades 10–12 | Summary: When Finley Brown returns to her
hometown of Christmas, Oklahoma, from boarding school, she finds things
have changed everywhere and looks to find her own place at home.
Identifiers: LCCN 2021027306 (print) | LCCN 2021027307 (ebook) |
ISBN 9780593353127 (hardcover) | ISBN 9780593353141 (ebook)
Subjects: CYAC: Self-realization—Fiction. | Christmas—Fiction. | Love—Fiction.
Classification: LCC PZ7.1.A53212 So 2021 (print) |
LCC PZ7.1.A53212 (ebook) | DDC [Fic]—dc23
LC record available at https://lccn.loc.gov/2021027306
LC ebook record available at https://lccn.loc.gov/2021027307

Paperback ISBN 9780593353134

Printed in the United States of America

1st Printing

LSCH

Design by Kate Renner
Text set in Sabon LT Std

To Mary and Mayo Andreen

So, This Is Christmas

Prologue

Perhaps it was because it had been an unusually warm early-December evening. Perhaps that's why the bee left its hive to go exploring. Tired of being cooped up with the other bees, it broke free to stretch its bee wings and see a different part of the world. Or perhaps it just needed to get away for a while, finding the other bees to be annoying and wanting some space before it returned.

Whatever the reason, it was a very poor decision.

I saw it out of the corner of my eye as I walked back down the pathway from the campus store in the early evening, a tiny, frantic motion barely visible in the otherwise stagnant water of the decorative pond positioned between the girls' dorm, Charity House, and the one that housed the boys, Waller Hall.

I stopped to stare until I realized what I was seeing: the bee was upside down in the water. Struggling.

My hesitation lasted a few seconds, then I couldn't stand it anymore—poor thing—and stepped off the path.

The bee was about four feet out from the pond's edge, and,

despite it being warm out, this was still Connecticut and it was still December 9th.

My sixteenth birthday, as it so happened. And an early Saturday evening. Which meant I should be in the middle of getting ready for a fantastic party designed to celebrate the wonders of all things me.

Instead, I was contemplating the rescue of a bee.

I took off my black Converse, followed by my red-and-green Christmas socks, rolled my jeans over the skinny, pale-white lumps that were my calf muscles, grabbed a fallen leaf, and waded into the water.

Holy hell! It was cold! And slimy. Jesus, what was I stepping on? Was that moss? I *really* hoped that was moss.

Of course, it was at this exact moment I was found by Arthur Chakrabarti Watercress, who, if not the last person I would want to encounter in this position, was definitely in the Top Five.

"Finley? What on earth are you doing?" he demanded, because Arthur always seemed to demand. I was convinced "haughty" was his default.

I glanced back to see him frowning at me from the stone bridge that arched across the pond, linking the main campus of Barrington Academy—our mutual coed boarding school—and our respective dorms. His straight, inky-black hair was covered by a plain blue knit cap and the earthy green of his puffy jacket stood out against the light coming from the bridge's faux-old-timey lampposts.

"I'm saving that bee," I answered, as if this was a sane course of action.

I pointed at the tiny creature, which was now about two feet away.

Problem was, I wasn't sure I could take another step closer to save the bee without losing my balance on the slippery rocks and falling ass-first into the water.

So I stood there, in over a foot of water cold enough to make me shiver, trying to figure out how to get to the bee and bring it back to dry land, without getting myself soaked in the process. Not exactly how I thought my quick trip from my dorm room to the campus store for a supply of self-pity-party candy was gonna go.

I waited for him to mock me. Which would be understandable. This was a situation ripe for mockery.

Instead, he asked, "So why aren't you saving it?" His British voice was clipped and precise, like he was a fifty-year-old member of Parliament. Which was one of the many reasons he got shit from our classmates for whom a New England boarding school education wasn't something to be achieved as much as a birthright.

"Because I can't move."

"What?" He cupped his ear. To be fair, he was about fifteen feet away and I had mumbled.

I raised my voice. "I can't move!"

He seemed puzzled. "Just step back."

"I can't."

The lampposts along the pathway and bridge cast shadows in a way that I couldn't fully see his face. Not that I needed to. He was clearly looking from the land surrounding the pond, which was two feet behind me, back to me and finding the gap to be undaunting.

But I was daunted.

He shook his head and continued across the bridge. I assumed he'd gone on to wherever it was he was headed. Which was a relief, because I was feeling like a huge dork and no one needed an audience for that.

I glanced back at the bee, now closer to me than a few moments earlier, but also still out of my reach, and wondered, *What the hell am I doing . . . ?*

"Here."

My head whipped around to find Arthur on the edge of the pond, extending a long, reedy tree branch toward me.

"Use this," he continued, nodding in the direction of the water.

I stared at him, surprised and uncertain. In the six months since I arrived at Barrington, we hadn't had many interactions outside of occasional classroom activity and one tipsy conversation at the Halloween party thrown by Bronwyn Campbell. But he'd never struck me as the sort of person who would give a second's consideration to the welfare of a bee. It felt beneath Arthur Chakrabarti Watercress, whose British Indian mother was a world-renowned scientist of some kind (don't ask me the field) and whose white, London-businessman father's lineage could be traced back to the Wars of the Roses.

He frowned in irritation and waggled the branch. "Do you want to save it or not? Because it's not going to last forever, given the circumstances."

Okay. *That* felt more like Arthur.

I took the branch then turned to look back at the bee, whose movements were slowing. But there was still the matter of the slippery rocks beneath my bare and numbing feet.

"Give me your hand," he said, as he reached out his own glove-covered right hand toward me. I took it and it did provide balance, even if he had to lean forward, because while seventeen-year-old Arthur wasn't short, he also was never going to be the tallest member of anyone's basketball team.

I focused on the bee in the pond, stretching out the stick until it was beneath the struggling insect, providing something solid on to which its pudgy legs could grab hold.

"Got him," I said. Then I straightened, one hand holding the stick with the wobbly bee and the other still in Arthur's grasp.

"I see that," he said. "Perhaps you'd like to step back? Onto land, if I'm in any way being vague."

It took every ounce of self-restraint to not hit him with an equally snarky comeback, but since he was my main source of stability, I bit my tongue.

I tightened my hold on his hand then brought the stick with our rescued bee over for him to take. Once done, I leapt back in the same direction.

My landing was . . . inelegant. I hit the ground on my ass and my red cap slipped off my head, but I didn't take out Arthur or the bee and I didn't fall backward into the pond, so, all things considered, I counted it as a win.

Arthur barely spared me a glance. He was focused on the bee. Of course.

The cool, damp earth seeped into my favorite jeans and I knew I'd be spending a couple of dollars' worth of quarters in the laundry room later tonight.

Which was also not how I'd always envisioned my sixteenth birthday.

None of this was.

And then it got worse.

The laughter reached me first and I immediately thought it was aimed at me.

It wasn't.

Instead, it came from four classmates headed along the path in the direction of the stone bridge. The shadows hid Arthur and me from them, which was good since the chief giggler was my roommate, Thea Selsky, who only a half hour earlier had told me she couldn't hang out tonight for my birthday because she was studying with her boyfriend, Beaux. I'd assumed "study" was a euphemism, but I did think they'd be hanging out in his dorm room. Clearly that wasn't true, either. But where were—

"They're probably going to Bronwyn's party," Arthur said, as if reading my thoughts.

I looked from Thea and Beaux—whom I now recognized was one of the four—back to Arthur, who had transferred the bee from the stick to a sturdy leaf.

Arthur nodded his head in the direction of the retreating quartet.

"What party?" I asked before I could stop myself, already feeling awash in dread.

"For Josie Sutton. Today's her birthday. Didn't you get the invite?"

I hadn't. And I knew it wasn't an oversight. My classmate Bronwyn was many things but most of all she was precise. Like a laser. And for some reason she did not like me. Especially lately. The first two months of our infrequent interactions were annoying, but the past six weeks her viciousness seemed focused on me to the point that I searched my brain for some way in which I may have wronged her, but came up empty. Sure, I wasn't the traditional popular girl, but I had never before considered myself the type to get picked on, either. Overall, I was fairly . . . basic, really. Which made her overt dislike of me such a mystery.

"Is everyone going?" I asked. My voice sounded tight even to my own ears.

"I'm not."

"But you were invited."

He shrugged, bored. "Everyone was."

Not everyone.

I grabbed my cap off the ground, stood, then whacked it against my thigh to dislodge flecks of dead grass, and shoved it back on my head, tucking my long blonde hair beneath with more force than was necessary. My brain felt like it was boiling.

I took my phone out of my coat pocket and pulled up Instagram. It only took a few seconds for me to see the first Insta Story from what were the beginnings of a banging party on the rooftop of La Belle's, a nearby restaurant owned by Bronwyn's family, which made it easier for the underage to be served.

I hit refresh twice and both times new posts from different classmates appeared. Smiling faces in selfies. All celebrating a sixteenth birthday. Just not mine.

"Are you going back to Oklahoma for Christmas?" Arthur asked.

The question jolted me out of the vortex of misery I could feel building in the center of my chest. If it had come even twenty seconds earlier, my answer would have been "Nope," because I had already told everyone as much. My parents, my grandmother, and my best friend, Mia. Since the moment I'd been accepted, I'd had fanciful visions of me wandering the snowy private campus in solitude, reading a book, feeling independent. Like Barrington was my own private retreat.

But that was twenty seconds ago. And a lot had changed

in those twenty seconds. So even though I opened my mouth with the intention of saying no, what came out was a very firm "Yes."

Because I meant it. Bronwyn's snub tonight was the last straw on what was already a hay barn full of snits and jabs and overall bitchiness. And it was enough. I was done with these people and this place. It had once held so much hope for me, but that was now gone.

It was at that moment the bee suddenly zoomed off the leaf in Arthur's hand and disappeared up into the darkened skies of early evening.

Headed home.

I was rude to Arthur. That wasn't my intention when I walked away from him without so much as a "thanks for helping save the bee" or even the bare minimum of "bye," but that was the end result. Rudeness.

It didn't occur to me that I'd abruptly left him by the pond until I was back in the empty dorm room I shared with Thea, scrolling "find cheap flights" websites, the emergency credit card given to me by my parents in my right hand, tapping against the wooden desk.

Tap, tap, tap, tap.

I hadn't bothered to turn on the lights when I entered, instead going straight to the laptop, which was next to the window overlooking the pond.

And that was when I glanced over to see Arthur standing where I'd left him.

A wave of guilt came over me. Grandma Jo would not be pleased; she was big on manners.

My first instinct was to tell him sorry when I saw him next, even as a part of me recognized he probably wouldn't care. Arthur was *not* big on manners, at least not that I'd experienced.

I'd met him on my first day of classes in Advanced Calculus. My mistake was having taken the first seat in the second row, which turned out to have been his favorite. He'd scowled at me then sat in the first seat of the first row to my left with an annoyed huff and refused to look at or acknowledge me for the next month.

That had pretty much set the tone between us.

As I waited for the airline-finder website to settle on a list of possible flights, I watched him pick up an object from the ground then toss it into the water, and I wondered what Arthur was doing for Christmas.

I supposed I should've asked. Was he staying here at Barrington? Or going back to England? The thing about boarding schools was you could stay there when school wasn't in session if you made arrangements ahead of time.

When I first arrived on campus, I thought that's what I'd do, envisioning the experience would be like the middle chapters in the Harry Potter books when all sorts of fun and mischief took place as Harry and the gang stayed at Hogwarts over the holidays. In fact, I blame Harry Potter for many of my woeful misperceptions about what it would be like to be a student at Barrington Academy. Not that I expected magic or epic battles with fantastical creatures that could decide the Fate of the World. It was more like a subtle yearning for the extraordinary. In hindsight, I probably should've read more Salinger.

At first things had gone fairly well.

I'd enrolled in summer school with the idea of getting my bearings with a few classes before the real work of the fall semester began in earnest. I'd even had my dorm room to myself until Thea's arrival in mid-August.

The whole experience was so different from my life back in Oklahoma I might as well have landed on Venus. I thought it was cool.

Then fall classes started and I quickly realized things were going to be a whole different level of difficult. Which I'd anticipated. In theory. But the reality?

Yeah, it was a *lot*.

I'd always been smart. That wasn't bragging, it was the truth. Even as a baby I'd been what the doctors my parents took me to called "advanced for her age." A source of great pride for Mom and Dad, but especially Mom, who had always possessed a deep yearning to be extraordinary. Much like a stage mother shoving her child into the spotlight whether they wanted it or not, she decided I would be the one to fulfill that dream.

I would be extraordinary.

For the first fifteen and a half years, I did my part. I met and exceeded every milestone early and my grades reflected that sense of "special." Which was why I could skip fourth grade and apply to a prestigious boarding school in Connecticut when I was fifteen. I hadn't gotten in right away and that had been a blow. But a few days after learning I was first on the waitlist, Barrington Academy notified me that a space had opened up, and was I still interested?

Why, yes. Yes, I was.

Mom had run around the house, jumping up and down. Dad looked puzzled by her, but proud of me. Over the years,

Mom had kept shelf after shelf in the den filled with my academic honors in a kind of shrine that I found embarrassing, but also secretly pleasing. Because that was who I was: Finley Brown, Brainiac.

And then I arrived at Barrington and I wasn't special anymore.

I was average.

Average.

It was a shock! I'd never been average before. The first time I saw "C" on my paper I was convinced the teacher had been mistaken.

But she hadn't. It was real and I didn't quite know what to do with that.

The obvious solution was to study harder. And I did. And my grades improved to a respectable B-, which was still a gut punch, but I also recognized that I wasn't in a small pond anymore. I was in Lake Huron and I had better learn how to swim against the waves or I was going to drown.

Spoiler alert: I didn't drown. But I didn't *thrive*, either. And maybe that would've been enough for me had I found some sort of accomplishment elsewhere, in sports or Debate Club or any form of extracurricular activity, but I was average there, too. However, there was one place where I wasn't average: socializing. When it came to making friends and fitting in, I would give myself a D+.

Sure, I'd gone to Bronwyn's Halloween party, but she'd invited everyone, including Arthur. That didn't mean either one of us were part of the Cool Kids Club.

Hardly.

I was of the Studies Too Hard All the Time variety and Arthur was . . . well, Arthur. He never fit into any particular category. In a way we were both social satellites, launched from opposite parts of the world, him from London and me from Oklahoma, landing in the same improbable orbit.

A movement in the corner of my eye caught my attention.

I glanced out the window to see Arthur look up toward Charity House. My dorm room was on the second floor, so I couldn't be sure what he was seeing. Was I visible? Probably not. It was a new moon and there weren't many lights by the pond. Still, a part of me wondered . . .

Arthur turned and walked away from the pond.

And another part of me couldn't help thinking this was probably the last time I would ever see Arthur Chakrabarti Watercress, the odd boy from the school where I had bombed. Because I was growing certain that when I got home, I would convince my parents to let me stay in Oklahoma. And while there might be a chance I would encounter Arthur when I returned to Barrington to retrieve my stuff, I knew it was unlikely.

I'm not sure why that struck me right in that moment, why I kept my eyes glued to the blue knit cap and green puffy jacket as they were absorbed by the evening shadows before disappearing around the corner.

But I did. I watched him go. Certain I would never see him again.

Turns out, I could not have been more wrong.

One

"You owe me a Christmas!"

Arthur Chakrabarti Watercress stared at me with dark brown eyes that radiated fury and indignation far beyond what one would imagine possible from a boy who stood five foot nine and weighed less than a year-old Great Dane. That's a guess, by the way; I hadn't actually weighed either Arthur or a Great Dane, but you get the point. And his ever-precise British accent coupled with a tiny speck of spittle in the lower left corner of his mouth further undermined whatever intimidation factor he was going for. He was lucky I didn't laugh in his flushed face.

Or maybe because a part of me was still reeling from the surreal fact that he was *here*. In Oklahoma. In my hometown. And specifically, in the courtyard of my Grandma Jo's inn, where, I now knew, he and his aunt were staying over the holidays.

Awesome. Just freakin' awesome.

And here's another thing—Arthur wasn't wrong. I *did* owe him. Not necessarily a "Christmas," whatever that meant, but I owed him at least an apology, and not about snubbing him post–bee incident. Which I would have gotten to, eventually, if he hadn't gone off like a rage rooster.

"Arthur—" I tried.

That was as far as I made it.

"No!" He held up a single finger. The index one. Arthur would never stoop so low as to flip anyone the bird. That was for imbeciles and sports fans, I'd overheard him say once back when we were at school, and I was pretty sure he considered the two synonymous.

"My aunt and I would not be trapped in this godforsaken town for the next week for what should have been a perfect American Christmas were it not for your pack of lies that led us here."

Yeah, okay. He had another point. I hated it when he was actually right, as opposed to when he felt he was right, which was always. Still, "pack of lies" was a *lit*tle overdramatic, even for him.

I tapped the now-empty plastic cup against my leg. It'd been full of birdseed, which I'd just finished pouring into the bird-feeder when I was accosted by Arthur, who had waited until after brunch before cornering me.

I tried again. "I really am sor—"

"Apologies aren't going to cut it, Finley Brown."

Full name. The universal sign for being in trouble. Delightful. It would appear whatever goodwill we may have created ten days ago in our mutual efforts to save the bee had evaporated.

"What do you want me to do?" I asked, helpless and increasingly annoyed.

"I want a proper American Christmas and I want you to show it to me. You owe me that. You owe me and my auntie a proper American Christmas. Like on that *sham* of a website you showed everyone."

"It's not a sham—"

His eyes widened as he held up his phone, where the screen clearly reflected the image of an idyllic Main-Street-at-Christmas tableau straight out of a movie.

Because, okay, I'll admit, it *was* straight out of a movie, as opposed to representing my actual hometown. And since it appeared on the town's official website, this was a serious breach of protocol. Not that anyone in charge would care.

And, okay, fine. As a former city hall intern who still had the passwords, I *was* responsible for putting that photo there—along with several others that ran the spectrum from kinda misleading to blatant bullshit—but in my defense I never thought anyone would do what Arthur and his aunt did: actually believe it enough to fly all the way from Connecticut to Oklahoma in the hopes of experiencing a Christmas the likes of which, in reality, were an illusion manufactured by a relentless system of capitalism devised to churn nostalgia into profits and create expectations impossible to fulfill. Besides, there were Yelp reviews they could've consulted, and they weren't pretty.

I wasn't going to point out any of that to him. I bit my lower lip instead.

"Well?" he asked. "What have you to say?"

Nothing polite.

"Can you get a refund?"

"No. We cannot."

I sighed, the condensation around my breath visible in the cold, and glanced around, more to avoid his attempted death stare than to orient myself.

As if I could ever not know exactly where I was at all times in the place where I grew up. It wasn't that big, either in population or geography.

And where we were at the moment, the back courtyard of the Hoyden Inn, Grandma Jo's pride and joy, was the one location I knew better than anywhere else. I'd spent countless hours here growing up, being babysat while Dad and Mom worked, and later as an unofficial assistant to Grandma Jo, which was what I was doing when Arthur cornered me about ten minutes ago to let me have it about the result of my truly unintentional misdeeds.

Now, you're probably wondering how posting some fake photos on a tiny Oklahoma town's website could lead to this particular egregious holiday snafu. Which would be fair. There's one piece of information that will help shed some light on the situation:

My hometown's name was Christmas.

That's right—Christmas, Oklahoma.

More on the origins of that in a bit, but you could see how it might evoke a certain expectation among visitors whose excitement at coming here invariably faded once they saw the real thing. Usually that had meant folks got back in their cars and kept driving with little more than slight annoyance and kitschy pics.

Then again, those people also hadn't flown here because of a high school student hoping to impress her new classmates with her *charming* hometown, only to find dilapidated storefronts and a twenty-five-foot wooden Santa sign that lost its head about two years ago after being used for target practice so many times it finally broke off in a spring storm.

No one ever found the head, which was disconcerting. It didn't seem easy to hide.

I looked back at Arthur.

"How would this work?" I asked.

"Well, according to this website of lies you altered to present to everyone in school as some sort of middle-American Christmas Shangri-la—"

"Move on, Arthur."

"—this town affords a multitude of opportunities for visitors to partake in Christmas-related excursions and experiences. Like"—he swiped his phone screen—"building a snowman."

I frowned, looking around at the flat, freezing landscape covered by dead, yellowed grass and not a lot else.

"There's no snow."

"Find some." He swiped again. "A sleigh ride."

"Again, no snow."

"Then you shouldn't have put that on there." Another swipe. "Chestnuts roasting on an open fire."

Lord. Why had I added that? Oh, right. The song had started playing over the all-holiday satellite radio station when I was manipulating the website back in mid-November. Now I had to somehow locate chestnuts in under a week. What the hell were chestnuts, anyhow? Were they like hazelnuts? Would Arthur be able to tell the difference? Knowing him, he probably would.

Maybe Amazon had some.

Another swipe.

"Reindeer."

I frowned. "Reindeer?"

"Reindeer."

He showed me a photo of a reindeer staring back at me with the caption *Feed reindeer corn to actual reindeer!*

And that was when I remembered I was eating "reindeer

corn" (basically Halloween candy corn, except with red and green instead of orange and yellow) at the time of my great deception and apparently got inspired.

Lovely.

Problem was, reindeer weren't exactly indigenous to Oklahoma, and while I didn't know much about them, I was pretty sure they didn't eat candy corn. Not that I'd ever find out.

"Ah," he said, his eyes lighting up. "An important one: a tour of magical Christmas lights."

Thank God, something I could do! Not here in Christmas, but in Chickasha, a nearby town that had an awesome lights festival—and, not coincidentally, where I had borrowed the photo from for Christmas's web page.

"Done," I said with confidence.

His eyes narrowed in doubt, but he continued. "I also want to go to a party."

"That's not on the website."

"Nonetheless, I'm quite sure a town this size hasn't much else for its teenagers to do other than congregate and drink, particularly over Christmas break, and you seem to have enough social skills to have at least one friend here—"

"Thanks?"

"So you should be able to find a holiday soiree, and I would like to attend. With you as my entree, of course."

The thought of bringing a guy who said "holiday soiree" unironically to meet the small-town Oklahoma friends I'd grown up with held very little appeal, but my options were few. Besides, with enough alcohol even Arthur had the potential to be somewhat bearable. Our one previous notable interaction before the Incident with the Bee had been at Bronwyn Campbell's Halloween party. Arthur had brought his own chianti (because, of course) and after a couple of glasses had been passably decent in our conversation about the possibility the Universe was a simulation and we were all sentient programs acting out predetermined stories for the amusement of godlike supercreatures. It made sense after the wine.

"I could maybe ask around," I said.

He nodded, satisfied. Swipe! Swipe! Swipe!

"There's a great deal more here. Review it and we'll discuss later. But you should know there is one element that is non-negotiable: snow. There has to be snow on Christmas Day."

"Seriously, Arthur, we've covered this. There is no snow." I indicated our still-snowless surroundings but he wasn't to be deterred.

"All perfect American Christmases have snow. It's common knowledge. Your website of deceit even promises snow *every* Christmas Day." He pointed. "It says so, right here. And I know for a fact that snow was one of the things Auntie Esha was most looking forward to in coming here."

"If you wanted snow then you should've stayed in Connecticut for Christmas."

"Well, we didn't, did we?"

Nope.

Arthur eyed me a moment before he continued. "You will show both of us each of these Christmas experiences reflected on the aforementioned website"—he held up his phone again, for effect—"and make certain they're idyllic, perfect, and, most important, memorable."

"Why?"

"Because you owe me."

"Because of the bee?"

"No. But I'll add that."

"Your reaction is way outta proportion."

"The reasons for my reaction are my own." His sudden discomfort told me there was more to this.

But I wasn't ready to capitulate.

"And if I don't do everything?"

He was prepared for that question.

"Then I will spend all my time here taking as many photos and videos of this charmless hellscape as possible, interviewing your friends and fellow towns-members, and I will bring all this information back to Barrington, where I will make absolute certain it is seen by everyone, so your image of growing up as some sort of Midwestern princess will be revealed as the lie it truly is. And you know what the likes of Bronwyn Campbell and Josie Sutton and the rest of their ilk will do with *that*."

Yeah, I knew. A part of me was still hurting from Bronwyn's snub ten days ago.

But I also felt, deep down, that Arthur was bluffing. It didn't matter anyhow because he didn't know I didn't intend to return to Barrington, which made his threats to destroy my reputation there toothless.

That didn't stop the guilt, though.

Not for Arthur—he could pound rocks—but for his aunt Esha, whom I'd met at brunch. That was when I'd also seen Arthur here for the first time, which led to me nearly dropping the plate of pancakes I'd been carrying to Mr. and Mrs. Yablonski's table.

I liked Aunt Esha immediately, despite her having an eerily effective poker face that left me with no clue if the sentiment was mutual.

Grandma Jo had introduced us earlier since Aunt Esha was aware that I was one of her nephew's classmates and had expressed to my grandmother the desire to meet me. She had grace and poise, like the international diplomat she was.

It was equal parts intimidating and fascinating.

The thought of her being disappointed by her stay here over the holidays upset me, especially because I knew Grandma Jo had been so looking forward to having a different set of holiday guests from the usual. She'd even gone so far as to practice cooking biryani with chicken, samosas, and kheer so they'd feel welcome. It was always important to her that guests felt at home when they stayed here and I didn't want to be the one to mess that up.

Plus, there were more than a few other personal issues I'd learned since my return. Like my best friend, Mia, dating my ex-boyfriend, Brody, while I was away. And my parents' surprise separation they'd forgotten to mention during our weekly phone calls. Both were issues I wanted to avoid, and taking Arthur around town in some sort of warped "best of" holiday tour would help accomplish that.

So there was a lot more upside for me in this besides avoiding his attempts at blackmail and for that reason I said, "Okay."

Arthur's eyes narrowed yet again. "What does that mean?"

"Well, Arthur, it's a term that has its origins in nineteenth-century Boston and was one of the first words to go what today we'd call 'viral' when an editor—"

His face flushed deeper. "I am quite aware of what 'okay' means in the general sense—*and* its etymological origins, thank you—I'm asking about the context here, now, with you."

"Okay means . . . okay. I will help you—"

"And Auntie Esha, if she wants?"

"And your aunt Esha, if she wants, experience a"—I made quotation marks—"'proper American Christmas.'"

That should have satisfied him.

Naturally, it didn't.

"You have to be enthusiastic about it."

"What?"

"It won't work if you drag us around this"—he waved his hand to indicate the entirety of my hometown with the same gesture one used for shooing flies—"forgotten flyover with that perpetually sullen expression of yours."

"My expression is not perpetually sullen!"

"As one who has the better perspective on your face, I can assure you it is."

"Maybe *you're* the common factor. Maybe every time you're around I feel sullen."

"Regardless, put a lid on it for the duration of our holiday enterprise."

I couldn't take it anymore. "Jesus, Arthur. You sound seventy."

"It's called speaking properly. You should consider trying it sometime."

"You should try not being a dick."

Wow, that was a terrible comeback, which Arthur also recognized.

He smirked. "Impossible." He flicked back the sleeve of his now-familiar puffy green jacket to look at his watch—a Rolex, of course, because while Arthur Chakrabarti Watercress ranked highly among the pantheon of annoying people, he was also disgustingly rich, or at least his parents were—then back at me.

"It's half past noon on this, our first full day here. Auntie Esha and I will be having our dinner in the dining room at six. We can talk before then to plan tomorrow."

"I won't be able to get anything ready by that time; I have to work until four. I'm Grandma Jo's Assistant Manager of Guest Actualization Services."

"That title is clearly made-up."

"Aren't all titles made-up, if you think about it?"

He thought about it. Then half nodded. "Fair enough. But we'll still pursue this further tonight."

He walked away before I could muster any response, which was undoubtedly his intent. Dramatic Exit 101, thy name was Arthur.

Though, who was I to talk? Hadn't I done pretty much the exact same thing to him back at the pond? Minus the flourish, of course.

I watched him stride across the small courtyard to the inn's back entrance, the only sound being the swish of his sleeves as they brushed against the sides of his jacket, his spine ramrod straight like he had been in some accident and had all his vertebrae fused together in a line that allowed for no bending whatsoever.

He stopped at the back patio and turned abruptly to meet my eyes. Then tapped his phone once again to emphasize his demands before entering the inn, letting the door slam shut behind him with an impressive reverberation that echoed in the otherwise quiet afternoon.

God, this Christmas was going to suck.

Two

I waited in the back courtyard for a full five minutes to make sure I wouldn't run into Arthur again before I went back inside the inn and headed straight to the kitchen.

The Hoyden Inn was built in the late 1990s in the traditional American Craftsman style, with a redbrick base, a wide front porch complete with narrow white vertical railing, and white siding.

I loved this inn.

The back part of the property, beyond the courtyard, had four cottages, but Grandma Jo had been trying for a while to get approval for a fifth from the local zoning board so she could move the spa from inside the main house to create a fuller guest experience. That had been her dream for a while now, convinced it would give the Hoyden its own identity to draw tourists to town for something other than the quirky Christmas factor.

But the board kept denying her requests. Their reasons were flimsy and she was convinced it was their way to try to strong-arm her into changing the inn's name so it was thematically consistent with the rest of the town.

But she wouldn't give in. And I admired her for that.

When I entered the kitchen, I found my dad standing beside the white marble–topped island, in the process of making a pimento cheese sandwich on white bread.

Which was bad.

And not just for his digestion.

Pimento cheese on white bread was a very clear sign that Dad was feeling like crap and in need of comfort food, and sadly, this was his go-to.

Had the situation been different, I would have given him grief for his poor meal choice. But I couldn't do that to him now. Not after learning about his and Mom's separation, the reason he was now living in one of the cottages behind his own mother's inn, and not at the house across town he had bought twelve years ago.

Mom was "taking some time for herself," which was Dad's way of explaining why she wasn't home when I arrived a week ago. She was at some kind of retreat in Branson, Missouri, with Aunt Jennifer.

And not returning home despite my arrival. We hadn't spoken yet, only exchanged a few brief and wholly unsatisfying texts.

It was weird. Everything was weird.

"Hey, sport," Dad said while chewing. He leaned his hip against the counter and slouched.

My dad—Vernon Lee "Skip" Brown, for the record—was pretty good-looking, as far as dads go. Had all his hair and he didn't have a growing tire around his middle like so many of my friends' fathers. But at thirty-four, Dad was also younger than most of my friends' dads, so he still had that going for him. Thankfully he didn't use his relative youth as an excuse to try to be my buddy instead of my parent. That would be the worst.

"Hey," I said back, then set down the empty plastic bird-seed cup.

I removed my coat and took one of the blue-and-white-vertical-striped aprons off the peg in the corner, put it on, then grabbed the non-latex gloves, putting them on, too, and started the hot water as I prepared to wash the impressive stack of pots and pans waiting for me in the sink. It was part of my job as Assistant Manager of Guest Actualization Services. There was no Manager of Guest Actualization Services, or any titles, really. Arthur was right, I'd made it up, but now that I had, I kind of liked it. Maybe I'd add that to my college résumé.

"Who were you talking to?" Dad asked.

I frowned at him. "When?"

"Just now."

He nodded to the kitchen window that overlooked the back of the inn.

"Oh. That's Arthur. He and his aunt checked in last night."

"Chakrabarti?"

We all had the habit of referring to guests by their last names when we talked to each other and even though Dad didn't officially work here—he was an insurance salesman—he followed suit.

I nodded. "Though Arthur's last name is actually Water-cress, like the plant. His dad's white."

"You know him?"

"Uh, yeah."

I kept scrubbing the rosemary-potato residue from the side of the stainless-steel eight-quart pot, hoping he'd leave it alone but there was exactly zero chance of that. When it came to dads, there were the ones who wanted to know every aspect of your life at all times and there were those who were satisfied with the basic headlines. Dad was absolutely the former.

"How?"

"Barrington."

"He goes to Barrington?"

"Yep."

"Did you know he was coming to Christmas?"

"God, no."

Dad chewed a little more. Thoughtful.

"Are you . . . dating?"

I almost dropped the pot.

"What? No! Ugh. Gross."

He held up both hands, one still holding the sandwich. "Just asking."

I returned to the pot, scrubbing harder. Tried to get the idea of dating Arthur out of my mind.

Dad continued. "You both seemed animated is all."

"That's how Arthur is."

"You were, too."

"Was I?"

Ayisha Lewis said, "You totally were."

I looked back as Ayisha entered the kitchen and, apparently, my conversation with my father.

Her long black box braids were worn in a high ponytail up top and left loose on the bottom, which was her typical style, but I noticed the tips were a bright burgundy and that was new since I'd left town. Also new? Seeing her in the same light blue button-down shirt, navy crew neck sweater, and khaki pants that I was wearing, which was as close to a uniform as Grandma Jo wanted for folks working at the inn.

Because Ayisha Lewis, the prettiest girl in my old high school, was working at the Hoyden Inn.

Another surprise for me. Who knew so much could happen in six months?

She smiled and nodded to my dad. "Hey, Mr. Brown."

He smiled and nodded in return. "'Lo, Ayisha."

Then Ayisha turned and her dark brown eyes landed on me.

And she smirked. She always smirked. When she was born and placed in her mother's arms, I would bet real money she opened her tiny baby eyes, looked at the woman who created her, and smirked. But she especially liked to smirk whenever she looked at me. There were reasons.

"You were blushing, too," she added deliberately, knowing it would irk me.

Which it did.

"I was cold. It's cold outside. My cheeks were getting beat up by the wind, which made them red." A total exaggeration; the notorious Oklahoma wind had been behaving, but it *was* cold. I was absolutely not blushing.

"Uh-huh," Ayisha said in a way that made her disbelief quite clear.

I turned away from her and set the now-very-well-scrubbed pot on the drying rack then grabbed another and began scrubbing anew.

Ayisha didn't offer to help. Instead, she began making cinnamon tea in a teapot with a poinsettia design. Her hands were slender and elegant. She took care of them in a way I never did of my own. Especially her nails. They were always epic; their long acrylic designs changed often. The theme this week was red and green and they stood out in beautiful relief against the dark brown of her skin. There was no way I would be able to pull off a look that effortlessly cool. Ever.

She caught me staring at her tea-making and raised a single perfectly sculpted dark eyebrow. She didn't offer an explanation since it obviously was for one of the inn's guests—we had about six at the moment, which, along with Dad and me staying here, was a full house.

Dad finished his sandwich then smiled at me and Ayisha before turning his full attention to me.

"You want to come by later for a match?" he asked.

He meant chess. Dad and I had been playing chess since I was able to move the pieces around the board. It was our thing. And while we didn't always have big talks when we played, it was an opportunity if either of us wanted to engage.

I guessed this was his way of setting us up for "a talk," specifically about "the situation" with him and Mom. We hadn't actually done that yet. You'd think we would have by now, but if there was one thing my family could do well it was avoid confronting difficult topics. We could win medals at it.

"Sure. After dinner's done," I replied. Maybe this would also turn out to be a good time to float the idea of me not going back to Barrington, too.

He nodded then left the kitchen.

I looked after him for a moment, feeling a tightening in my chest at the thought of broaching either subject, but especially the one about him and Mom. At sixteen, I really thought I'd avoided the Child of Divorce identity, but that was looking like premature optimism.

The kettle started to whine, but Ayisha didn't take it off the gas stove. She let it keep getting louder as she scrolled through whatever it was she was looking at on her phone.

"Pretty sure it's ready," I said.

She slowly glanced up at me then made no move toward the screeching kettle.

I rolled my eyes and went back to scrubbing.

Things weren't always like this between me and Ayisha. In elementary school we had been almost friendly, back when she was still a grade above me, before I jumped from fourth to fifth.

I was nine years old at the time and the move put me in a peer group that was older and more mature, even if only by a year or so. As an adult that didn't mean a lot, but when you were a kid it impacted everything, especially interpersonal relationships. Because as it turned out, Ayisha Lewis wasn't merely the prettiest girl in her grade, she had also been accustomed to being the smartest.

Until I arrived. Suddenly she had real competition at every turn, from English to math to history. She beat me in art, though. I couldn't draw or mold or craft papier-mâché to save my life, but Ayisha could and did. Her mild annoyance at my academic challenges steadily devolved into a much deeper resentment I never before understood.

I did now.

Six months at Barrington being shown up by everyone there was eye-opening to say the least. And I might have broached the subject with Ayisha except academic rivalry wasn't what really torpedoed our tenuous relationship. That happened because of one Mr. Brody Tuck. The same Brody Tuck who was now dating my former best friend, Mia.

Were all small towns and high schools such a toxic cocktail? As if summoned by some unseen cosmic force that called forth the one person you least wanted to talk with, the phone in my back pocket buzzed.

There on the front screen was the name and profile photo of none other than Mia Gurdowitz. The photo where we were smiling, our faces pressed close together, was from last Memorial Day weekend, at my farewell party before I departed for Barrington. I wondered if she was planning to go after Brody at that time or if the idea came later.

"Bold of her," Ayisha said.

She was looking with seeming disinterest at my screen before she moved to take the kettle off the stove. Guess that meant Ayisha was aware of the Mia/Brody situation.

Who was I kidding? In a town this size, it was a given that everyone was aware of the Mia/Brody situation, even though neither had posted any photos of them together in romantic poses. Believe me, I checked. In hindsight the vibe between them in pics was there, but they were clever about disguising it.

Hitting decline, I slipped the phone into my back pocket. Then I set a clean pot aside. Grabbed a skillet. Began the process anew.

"Guess what goes around comes around, huh?" Ayisha said.

I was glad I wasn't facing her so she missed my flush of anger. This was an old, sore subject. But I couldn't let her know she'd gotten to me. So, in a tone of such calm reason I almost fooled myself, I said, "Brody and I are broken up. When two people are broken up, neither party has the right to dictate who the other can date. Right?"

I glanced back to see Ayisha's eyes flash with annoyance. But only for a second. Then she took the wooden tray with the cups and poinsettia teapot and walked out of the room.

So yeah. Ayisha was who Brody dated right before he and I started dating.

There was no overlap, to be clear, but that didn't stop the tsunami of Ayisha's resentment that washed over me from the moment Brody and I went public. It wasn't logical, but by now I'd come to realize emotions rarely were.

Which was why I had declined every attempt at communication from Mia since I'd arrived at the Sonic seven days ago hoping for a hamburger and cherry-limeade slush but instead getting the sight of her and Brody in the truck parked opposite my dad's Jeep. Making out like it was an Olympic sport.

So gross.

And I immediately lost my appetite.

Fortunately, Dad didn't bug me when I asked if we could go despite having just arrived. Maybe he'd seen my expression, or even Brody and Mia, and decided to leave it alone. Whichever reason, I was grateful.

I managed to get a picture of Brody and Mia before we left, and texted it to her without a message. Yes, it was passive-aggressive bitchy, but I'd only learned about Mom and Dad having issues the day before, so I was already on edge.

But did I have the right to be mad at Mia and Brody?

That was the question that wiggled below the surface. After all, *I'd* been the one to instigate the breakup with Brody. I was leaving Oklahoma for Connecticut, where I would spend the next two years far away from Brody Tuck, the boy with the magnificent floppy hair and sparkly blue eyes, and that hadn't seemed fair to him. I had felt noble at the time. Mature. Even when he cried and I cried and we both wished things could be different.

Mia had been very comforting when it went down.

She'd held me as we sat on the bed in my room and told me I was doing the right thing by "setting him free." That I shouldn't return any of his texts or calls while I was away. "To give you both time to heal."

What bullshit.

A movement out the window over the inn's kitchen sink drew my attention and I looked up to see the back door to the inn's patio swing open.

Out stepped Arthur's aunt Esha followed by my grandma Jo, talking as they strolled around the courtyard's wrought iron tables and chairs.

Their conversation seemed to be going well if the smile on my grandma's face was any indication. And at least Arthur's aunt wasn't raging at my grandmother like her nephew had raged at me. She seemed far nicer. Somewhere in her forties, with short dark hair, her angular face made it clear Arthur inherited a lot of his looks from the Chakrabarti side of the family.

I wasn't a fashionista by any stretch, but I was pretty sure that was the classic Burberry pattern on the scarf tucked inside the flipped-up collar of her cashmere trench coat. She carried herself with a sense of propriety and reserve that tipped you off that she'd been raised elsewhere, even before her English accent gave her away. But she had faint lines around the corners of her dark brown eyes that deepened easily when she smiled, which I got the impression she did often.

However, it was my grandma's expression that caught me. Grandma Jo hadn't looked like that, bright-eyed and happy, in a long time and I didn't realize it until that moment. The last few years she'd seemed to carry an unspoken, invisible weight around. I wondered at the reason, though I doubted I'd ever find out. Again, as good as my family was about loving each other, we were equally good about avoiding the truly hard conversations.

I had a sneaking suspicion I was going to have plenty of those in the days ahead, which was going to make this Christmas break especially interesting.

Three

Okay, so, more about Christmas. Not the holiday, everyone knows about that.

About the town. *My* town.

Which wasn't always called Christmas. When it was formed, after the Land Run in 1893, it was christened Springfield and left alone for the century-plus that followed.

Until 2004, when Ralph Tater-Hall came up with a master plan to set our town apart by changing its name to something related to the world's most popular holiday and then promoting the crap out of it to bring in tourists. And revenue. Good ol' Ralph was the mayor at the time and folks liked him enough to go along with the idea, so the name change became official in 2005.

The crazy thing was it worked. For a while.

Ten years of Christmas, Oklahoma's tourist trappings helped bring the town back from the depression it'd fallen into when Chandler Chickens closed down. The grand plan was for everything to reference Christmas: Mitzi's Café & Pie Shop became the Gingerbread Café, the Springfield Grocery Store became Claus Kitchen, Buddy's Repairs became Santa's Sleigh Repair, and so on.

But then Ralph Tater-Hall embezzled several million dollars from the city's flush coffers and absconded to parts unknown before he could be arrested.

Christmas never really recovered.

It was six years since then. Six long and increasingly lackluster years. You wouldn't think a town could go to seed in less time than the entire run of the TV series *Lost*, but you'd be wrong. It could and it did.

I was there.

Which contributed to why I wanted to leave.

To be fair, Mom probably helped foster that longing, too. For as long as I could recall she talked about how she had always planned to leave Christmas when she graduated from high school and make her mark on the world, but "life got in the way." That was a nice, if not subtle, way of referring to the fact my dad knocked her up their senior year (with me) and from that point on all thoughts of her leaving were tucked away.

But I was starting to think those plans were merely dormant and not forgotten.

She'd never said anything. Directly. More like she'd use me as an example of someone who "had the whole world ahead of her," could go anywhere, be anything if I played my cards right. And I would sometimes catch a faraway longing in her blue eyes as she watched me, especially after I achieved something. I think she considered my scholastic achievements as a sort of escape pod.

She was the one who brought up Barrington to me.

By the time I reached my freshman year at Christmas HS—home of the Sonic Santas!—the seeds had already been planted that getting into an elite, out-of-state boarding school would be a real coup. It's possible I would have wanted to go without Mom's influence, but there's no way to know for certain.

Chicken/egg. Mom/me. Same/same.

I remember I was in the middle of studying for my AP US History exam when she came into my bedroom and set the catalog for Barrington on my desk. It had been shiny and almost book-sized, like the Restoration Hardware megacatalog, with a photo of the school grounds and the main deep-red brick administration building I now know was Remington Hall.

She'd brought many other schools to my attention before, but I knew right away this one was different.

"Here," Mom had said, still in the skirt suit she favored for work. "This is the place."

I looked up from my laptop. "Place for what?" I asked, feeling study-drunk woozy.

"For you to take the next step. Barrington Academy." She tapped the cover and smiled, but I saw her blue eyes flash with a steely determination that meant business.

See, for Mom, school *was* business. She was the executive assistant to the president of Utica Junior College, which was located about twenty minutes outside of Christmas, hence the blessedly secular name. That meant she had insider access and she utilized each and every bit for my benefit.

I was aware there was a fair bit of projection at work.

Had I not come along and blown up her plans, Mom would have studied her way all the way through the school system and become an astronaut or journalist sitting opposite the president, or maybe the CEO of her own company. Whatever that may have been, whatever she wanted to be.

But I *had* come along and she never pursued the education she'd viewed as her Get Out of Jail Free card.

I asked her once why she didn't take classes herself, but she smiled and shook her head and said, "What for? I'm not going anywhere."

Which might have been the saddest thing I'd ever heard her say.

Her parents—Nonna and Big Pa, no longer with us—were not the type who encouraged further education for their daughters, at least not like they did for Uncle Lonnie, who was a pediatrician and lived somewhere in east Florida with his wife, Carole, and their three kids, none of whom I could pick out of a four-person lineup. So when Mom lost her momentum for leaving town, it stayed lost.

She only regained it through me. And through Barrington, which was her ideal of what a good education offered. And as I thumbed through the catalog for the first time, I had felt sure she was right. This was where I was supposed to be. This would be my ticket to a life outside of Christmas.

Yeah. Hindsight, huh?

My phone in my back pocket buzzed with an incoming text. I almost didn't check it but the Pavlovian reflexes were too hard to resist.

hey

Brody.

I felt my body tighten up with a combination of surprise, habitual pleasure, dread, and finally anger. About forty potential responses zip-zoomed around but I settled on the easiest: nothing.

I put the phone back and resumed my dish cleaning and tried not to think about him or how it felt when I saw him kissing Mia.

But that was impossible.

Because the truth was, Brody Tuck was my first love. I hoped to have more in my life, but, like it or not, the first person who got your heart would always hold a special place, and for me that was Brody.

By all rights of the universally acknowledged teenage social pecking order, a guy like Brody should never have thought about going out with a "nice girl" like me. He was made for someone pretty and perfect.

Like Ayisha.

But date we did.

The two of us lasted for almost a year, and I'm not sure we would have if not for the fact that Brody Tuck was dyslexic. A monumental fact you'd think someone would have noticed before I came around, but they didn't. Maybe they were distracted by his overall Brody-ness, because here's the thing—Brody was so gorgeous he came dangerously close to being beautiful, with thick, light brown, wavy hair that meant the most natural instinct was to want to reach out and grab hold of it and go to town. He also had beautiful blue eyes with thick eyelashes that were ridiculous. Add to that the fact he had reached six foot one by the time he was in the eighth grade. It was a wonder he didn't spend all of his free time either fending off girls who wanted to date him or other guys who wanted to beat him up *because* every girl wanted to date him. Instead, he was the quarterback, star pitcher, captain of the basketball team, regardless of the grade or who else might have been around him.

Though Brody had his fair share of flaws, too.

One of the biggest being he approached studying like a cat being forced to do tricks. Having to repeat his sophomore year had been humiliating for him and he confessed later that he'd considered joining the army, but he was still too young. What his having to repeat a grade and my having skipped a grade meant, though, was that we wound up in several of the same classes, otherwise I probably would have had to settle for admiring him from afar.

But when he failed his first two tests in our English class, Mr. Kritchinger threatened to give him an F, which meant Brody was at risk of not being able to play on the varsity football team. That simply would not do.

Now, normally when an athlete wasn't doing well in their studies the end result was coach intervention, but there were always a few teachers for whom any kind of pressure to help a jock was ineffective and Mr. Kritchinger was one. When that happened, the services of a guy like Carson Pettibone were usually called upon. Carson was the smart kid with enough athletic ability to be kept on various sports rosters to function as the team tutor, but unfortunately for Brody, Carson had graduated early from Christmas High School to pursue a premed degree up in Nebraska and was thus no longer available.

Enter me.

When Mr. Kritchinger first asked me to stay after class, I'd been nervous. But then he asked if I was interested in tutoring Brody and my nervousness transformed into awe. Two days later I was walking into the library and sitting down at the back table opposite the most popular boy in school and trying to be cool while not spilling the can of sugar-free Red Bull or word-vomiting all over him.

I only accomplished one of those goals.

The last thing I would have ever believed was that *I* would wind up being the one to break *his* heart.

Four

An hour after my Arthur encounter, I was manning the inn's oak-paneled front desk. The main staircase that led to the second floor was directly behind me. There was no third floor, unless you counted the attic where Grandma Jo stored things. Such as the multitude of Christmas decorations occupying the lobby. Because even though Grandma Jo fought off the town's pressure to rename the inn so it was thematically in alignment with the other businesses, she loved Christmas with a fierceness usually reserved for the fans of K-pop stars.

Everyone knew it, which was one of the reasons her annual Christmas Eve party was such a draw. Folks from all around dropped by from five p.m. to eight p.m. for a variety of hors d'oeuvres and socializing and to bask in the unabashed holiday ambience.

And there was plenty of holiday ambience. Sometimes the place felt like ground zero for the Christmas bomb.

The two back corners of the lobby were guarded by five-foot-tall wooden nutcracker soldiers that Grandma Jo found several years ago on one of her excursions to Dallas—where "too big" was regarded as a starting point—and had shipped up here. Much to my father's dismay, since he was the one who had to haul those suckers up and down the stairs each year.

The corner closest to the window overlooking the front yard was hidden by an ornament-covered, plump blue spruce Christmas tree with a tendency to lean that was hidden by some cedar blocks and a red felt skirt with green swirl piping.

And the last corner had a permanent beverage station, which, as soon as Thanksgiving concluded, was turned into a hot chocolate hangout that lasted through Valentine's Day.

It was very popular.

The mantel over the fireplace was camouflaged by pine boughs with red ribbons and silver bells, and the logs burned in the fireplace were, I could attest, 100 percent real. Yours truly brought in a new batch every morning from the log pile located out back in a spot not nearly close enough to the main house.

I kept an eye on the flames from my position at the front desk because another part of my job was to make sure the fire didn't die out. It was part of the guest-actualization holiday ambience.

As was the crystal dish of peppermint candies that were for guests but were also a regular element of my daily diet this time of year.

I popped another in my mouth.

The front door opened and in walked Dr. Dean Raymond, the town's only resident dentist. His gleaming-white teeth were almost as shiny as the top of his hairless head, which was revealed once he slipped off his neon-orange knit hunting cap.

He smiled politely at me. "'Lo, Finley."

I smiled politely in return. "Afternoon, Dr. Raymond."

Then his glance began dancing around the lobby and I knew who he was looking for.

"Is, ah, your gramma around?" he asked.

"Yes, sir. She's somewhere," I said, giving away no specifics. I'd learned quickly not to give out any intel on anyone at the inn, especially the owner.

Dr. Raymond scratched his pointy chin. "You, ah, expect her soon?"

"Probably, though I make no guarantees."

"Well, ah, I'll mosey over here"—he gestured to the area by the fireplace—"and have a wait."

"Yes, sir."

Then Dr. Raymond proceeded to do exactly that, positioning himself on one of the two floral-print sofas that gave him the best vantage point of the comings and goings of the lobby.

Lying in wait for Grandma Jo, like a short, bald, pale-white cheetah.

Ever since his wife left him two years ago for the local male dance teacher who—surprise!—turned out not to be gay after all, Dr. Raymond had had his eye on my grandmother, as did quite a few other area fellas. Because my grandmother was beautiful, and I didn't mean "for her age." I mean Grandma Jo had always been a babe. Tall and trim, she sported hazel eyes and movie star cheekbones (that I wish I'd inherited). It was unexpected. If you heard a name like "Grandma Jo," you would be forgiven when a certain type of image followed: white hair in a bob, glasses, twinkling eyes, rosy cheeks, and a tendency to dress in bulky cardigans with colorful quilt-like patches.

That's what I would've pictured.

But that wasn't Grandma Jo.

For one thing, she was the first in our family to get

unexpectedly pregnant far too young. Specifically in her first year in college at Wellesley, which was impressive given it was an all-women's school. Alas, Dad wasn't a virgin birth. His very real father was a guy by the name of Lester Colon who was a business student at Babson College. He'd almost married Grandma Jo but she went into labor early on the day they had planned to drive over to the justice of the peace, and after Dad arrived, the idea of marrying was forgotten. Which made it much easier when Lester left for Cleveland six months later and never returned. Grandma Jo liked to say she was glad she'd never bothered to give Dad the last name Colon. Dad was pretty pleased about that, too. Skip Brown was enough of a hurdle.

All this meant that despite the fact she had a sixteen-year-old granddaughter, Grandma Jo was only fifty-three and blessed with the kind of skin that repelled all but the most insistent wrinkles. Like the one between her eyebrows.

Which was on display the moment she walked through the front doors with Arthur's aunt Esha and spotted Dr. Raymond perched on the sofa.

"Shit," she said under her breath.

For a fraction of a second I could tell she was calculating whether it was possible to pivot and go right back out the doors, unseen. But that fraction of a second was all Dr. Raymond needed.

He sprang to his feet, his face beaming with excitement and shiny with too much skin oil.

"Hiya, Jo!"

In an instant my grandmother affected a smile so perfectly affable she could have run for office. Operating a business in a small town required the same amount of political acuity.

"Dean, how lovely to see you."

I moved the peppermint candy around the inside of my mouth and watched.

He went in for a hug but Grandma Jo intercepted him with a firm yet cordial one-handed upper-shoulder squeeze while simultaneously turning them both to face Aunt Esha in a move so smooth it could've been ballet.

"Dean, I'd like to introduce you to one of the inn's newest guests, Ms. Esha Chakrabarti, a barrister from London who has arrived here by way of Connecticut with her nephew for the holidays. Esha, this is Dean Raymond, our town's finest dentist."

Only dentist, I corrected in my head.

"Hiya!" He even waved.

Aunt Esha smiled vaguely and nodded once in Dr. Raymond's direction.

Despite being younger than my grandmother, they seemed to share a similar kind of equanimity. Maybe Aunt Esha's came from being a barrister, aka a lawyer (which I only knew because I spent what little free time I had at Barrington streaming British murder shows on my laptop), though Arthur had once bragged that she was a powerful diplomat. There was probably overlap. All I did know was if I was in the witness box and she was asking me questions—"Where were you on the night of . . . ?"—I would confess everything even if I was nowhere near wherever it was. She was that intense.

There was something to that Chakrabarti DNA.

Dr. Raymond gave her a quick once-over, from her stylish haircut to the expensive if unassuming dark leather ankle boots, then redirected the full force of his attention to Grandma Jo.

"How're the fillings holdin' up?"

"Perfect. Thank you."

He explained to Aunt Esha, "Last month I swapped out the dental amalgam in Jo's back lower-right second molar for composite. That's another way of sayin' white. Can't see 'em. Stealth!"

He waved his hand, palm down, smooth.

Aunt Esha glanced at Grandma Jo. "Congratulations," she murmured, her accent fully English. She and Grandma Jo held each other's gaze a beat longer, each with seemingly blank expressions. But I could tell they were both a shimmering instant from cracking up. I really hoped they would.

Dr. Raymond kept going, nodding to the decorations.

"Place sure looks great! Love those nutcrackers!"

Aunt Esha dropped her gaze to the floor and rubbed the side of her nose while Grandma Jo looked back to him.

"Thank you, Dean. You know how much I adore this time of the year."

"I sure do! And funny you should mention that, because I went out toward Blanchard the other day to pay a visit to Mrs. Greely and as I was drivin' back I passed by the ol' Sedgewick ranch and you will not believe what they're advertisin'."

Grandma Jo played along. "What?"

"Reindeer!"

I bolted to full attention. "Reindeer?"

Dr. Raymond turned his big smile to me. "Reindeer!"

Arthur said, "Reindeer?" as he came down the stairs behind me.

Dr. Raymond smiled at Arthur. "Reindeer!"

Ayisha appeared behind Arthur, also on the stairs, and frowned. "Why's everyone saying 'reindeer'?"

I frowned at Ayisha as she moved to stand beside Arthur, because when the hell had *those* two met? It was like a Marvel movie sequel where villains from previous films unexpectedly unite with nefarious intent.

Ayisha caught my scowl before I could quickly look back to the still-delighted Dr. Raymond, who, loving being the center of attention, was fairly bouncing on the balls of his feet.

"The Sedgewicks got themselves a few real reindeer from a fella over in Bristow and now they got 'em on display for Christmas—the holiday," he clarified unnecessarily. "And folks can come by to see 'em if they want."

"Really?" Arthur said, the wheels in his brain clearly spinning.

Dr. Raymond nodded. "Yep. They've even got 'em to pull a sleigh!"

I locked eyes with a triumphant Arthur then looked back to Dr. Raymond.

"What about the snow? Or, you know, lack thereof?" I asked him.

"They got a doodad that makes snow. How cool is that?"

"Super cool." Though my brain was fervently trying to picture how that could work. I was a sleigh-riding novice but I had seen enough films and advertisements with it to know sleighs would require a *serious* amount of snow. Could the Snow Doodad make enough?

Arthur turned to his aunt. "Mashi, what do you think?"

"About reindeer?"

"About seeing them. That was on our list of things to do." His aunt appeared momentarily perplexed and a tiny glimmer of distress flickered in his dark eyes. "Remember? I emailed it to you when we were discussing coming to Christmas for

Christmas, and then after we made the arrangements, as well as right before we caught our flight."

"Oh, yes. It was exceptionally thorough."

Arthur puffed. "Thank you."

"And wasn't there something on the town's website about feeding them reindeer corn? That sounded so charming."

I hurriedly piped up, "That should probably be verified."

Grandma Jo must have detected something in my tone because she shifted her gaze onto me like a spotlight hits an escaping prisoner not yet over the wall.

I tried to act cool, despite the tiny trickle of sweat that was about to make its way down the center of my back, and smiled.

It was a mistake. She cocked a single brow, which roughly translated to: "You've done something and we're going to discuss whatever it is later when we're not in front of guests, and don't even try to get out of it." I'd experienced that eyebrow before.

Arthur asked his aunt, "Would you like to go there tomorrow? Finley has volunteered to take us around to see and do as many Christmas-related activities and events as we'd like."

Ayisha snorted and murmured, "Good luck."

Before I could get annoyed at either Arthur or Ayisha, Aunt Esha turned her attention to me and smiled. "How kind of you, Finley."

I blushed, like I often did when adults who weren't my relative or I didn't know well focused on me. "Happy to," I lied, and avoided glancing at Arthur.

"What about joining us, Jo?" Aunt Esha asked of my grandmother.

But before she could answer, Dr. Raymond interjected, "That was why I comin' by, to see if Jo wanted to come with me." I couldn't quite tell if he was annoyed at Aunt Esha's spontaneous invitation or if he welcomed the segue to his own.

Either way, Grandma Jo said, "We should all go together," like it was the most normal thing in the world.

"That's a great idea! A group trip!" Dr. Raymond said, his attention reserved for one member of that group in particular.

In the back of my mind I was attempting to figure out how this would work out when Arthur then did the unthinkable.

"What about you, Ayisha? Would you like to join us?"

My head exploded. What the actual—? Seriously, *when* did they meet? Were they buddies now? Or—dear God, no—did they *like* each other? Why did that possibility cause a blossom of heated anger to form in the center of my chest?

Fortunately, Ayisha recoiled at the notion. "No, thank you." I felt a tiny sliver of relief. Then she reached out and briefly touched his arm and smiled sweetly. "But that was very kind of you to include me, Arthur."

I could feel my face go red and I couldn't even blame the wind.

"Perhaps another excursion," he said. "We'll be here for the week."

Was that flirting? Were Arthur and Ayisha *flirting*? Because it looked *a lot* like flirting.

Ayisha caught my eye and ever so slightly—yep—smirked. "That sounds awesome," she replied to him.

I bit what was left of the peppermint candy in two. Crunched it right up.

Dr. Raymond bounced on the tips of his toes, one, two, three times. "This'll be a lotta fun! Reindeer, by golly! I'll swing by tomorrow after my nine-a.m. extraction with poor Barb Malloy. Shouldn't take more than an hour and a half."

He looked at me, Arthur, and Ayisha. "Don't eat candy, kids. Sugar corrodes your enamel like battery acid!"

And with that, he was gone.

I slowly lowered my hand from its automatic reach for the next peppermint.

Five

"Are you serious?" I stared at my grandmother in disbelief. We were in the alcove near the kitchen and I'd just taken off my apron, my thoughts firmly on the idea of going upstairs to take a nap. It'd been a long day and it was still only four in the afternoon.

Instead, my grandmother found me and asked me a favor.

"Yes," she said. "Arthur wants to buy some appropriate attire for the reindeer farm."

"What's appropriate for a reindeer farm?"

"Jeans, I suppose."

"He doesn't have *jeans*?" I asked, incredulous.

"Not here, apparently."

Actually, I could totally see that. But still. "Why do *I* have to go with him, though? What about his aunt?"

"Esha is feeling the effects of jet lag and wants to take a quick nap"—*Me too*, I silently shouted—"before dinner, but she also doesn't want Arthur to go by himself."

"He's seventeen," I tried to reason.

"He's our guest." Grandma Jo hit me with yet another look. "And it will ease the mind of his aunt. Who is *also* our guest."

My lips pressed together tightly. I tried another angle. "But I can't drive."

I was less than two weeks into being sixteen and didn't have my driver's license yet. Sure, most kids rush out to get their permit the first moment they can, but the truth was, driving always made me nervous. Especially after my mother's lone, white-knuckled attempt to teach me last spring that left us both perfectly fine with never trying *that* again.

"You can walk," Grandma Jo assured. "There are shops two blocks up the street. Getting outside will do you good."

Damn. Thwarted. Dad might be the chess player in the family, but Grandma Jo was the one always three moves ahead.

I was about to raise the possibility/likelihood that Arthur didn't want to go with *me* when Grandma Jo glanced over my shoulder and smiled brightly.

"Hello, Arthur."

I turned to see the subject of our debate appear from around the corner, already dressed to head outside. He smiled at my grandmother in return and even gave the slightest bow. Guess he did have manners after all. Just not for me.

"Ms. Brown, hello."

"So Finley here will go with you on your shopping trip."

Arthur blinked. Twice. "Oh?"

He was obviously caught off guard by the idea and I saw my opening. "Unless you want to go by yourself," I said quickly.

"Finley knows exactly where to go," Grandma Jo said before he could respond, her hand on my elbow. "She'll make sure you get what you're looking for. And it'll make your aunt feel so much better knowing you have company."

His dark eyes finally met mine.

I tried to telegraph, *Not my idea!*

This earned a straightening of shoulders and a forced smile. But, like me, he was no match for my grandmother, so he wisely said, "Wonderful . . ."

And five minutes later, I was bundled against the cold in my coat, scarf, and knit hat and walking beside Arthur up the residential block where the inn was located. Our destination was Boots Boulevard, a commercial street with a string of '80s strip malls that contained about a third of the active stores from its heyday. The rest were left with FOR LEASE signs in the windows.

Neither of us said a word.

To my surprise, he let me lead. My goal was to get this over with as fast as humanly possible. I marched us past the empty shops and Deck the Bagel until we were standing in front of the town's western wear clothing store: Wrapped Yule Up.

Arthur stared at the sign. "I can't tell if that pun is terrible or impressive."

I squinted up at it, too. "I've always thought it was impressively terrible."

His lips quirked, bemused. "Which is terribly impressive."

"Either way, they have Wranglers."

He frowned. "Aren't we on a quest for jeans?"

"In Oklahoma, they're the same thing."

"It's a slang term?"

"No, it's a brand. But it's the brand everybody wears."

"Is that a requirement?"

"Not officially. It's kind of the same idea for Coke. Around here, it doesn't matter what kind of pop you order, everyone calls it a Coke."

"Seems restrictive. And what's a 'pop'?"

"Same as a soda, as in 'soda pop.' But that's another story and we're here to get you jeans."

"Wranglers."

I snorted. "Look at you, learning."

He gave a half shrug, but I caught the hint of self-satisfaction.

The door to the store opened and an older man I didn't recognize stepped out. Probably a tourist. He held the door for Arthur and me to enter, and smiled politely at both of us as we passed by. Only I smiled back. Arthur seemed puzzled.

"Do you know him?" Arthur asked, glancing back in the direction of the man who was already out of sight.

"No."

"Oh."

"Why?"

"He seemed . . . friendly."

I laughed at his confusion. "That's how people are in this part of the world," I assured him. Part of the culture shock I went through when I arrived at Barrington was realizing that the aggressively friendly demeanor I took for granted growing up in Oklahoma did not translate well to an East Coast boarding school. I'd been called chipper more times than I could count and it was never a compliment.

Once inside, Arthur's attention turned to the surroundings.

Despite the terrible store name, the space was remarkably well organized. It would never compete with Langston's in Oklahoma City or any of the major brand stores, obviously. But it did all right. Red brick on one wall. Pine floors and shelving that held all manner of western wear and anything else that struck the owner's fancy. Saddles, ropes, horseshoes, stirrups, etc., hung on the walls like art.

Men's attire was in the back, which is where I tried to lead Arthur but he was suddenly hit by a case of tourist ADD. He touched every Christmas, OK-stamped souvenir and knickknack on the tables between the door and our destination. Cowboy hats, T-shirts, sweatshirts, trucker hats, shot glasses, cowboy boots galore, plaid shirts, turquoise belt buckles, and on and on.

I tried to be patient, reminding myself this was probably as foreign to him as Harrods would be for me if I ever made it to London. But when he picked up the Christmas bacon lip balm I had to intervene.

"Jeans are this way." I pointed.

He ignored me and uncapped the tube of balm. Sniffed and winced.

"That's not bacon."

Dammit. Now I was curious.

I stepped closer. "What is it, then?"

He held it out for me to sniff. Which, despite knowing this wouldn't end well, I did. And promptly tried not to gag. It was definitely *not* bacon.

"Right?" That was as close to gleeful as I'd seen him get. Figures.

I capped the balm and put it back where he found it among the other random impulse gifts. Then I grabbed him by the jacket sleeve and tugged him after me until we were in the men's attire section. The wall was dominated by floor-to-ceiling cubbies filled with jeans, most of which were Wranglers, but there were Levi's and other brands, too.

Arthur stood before them all, arms crossed as if sizing up the situation. Then he looked around.

"Are there no people here to assist?"

"Mr. Liberati is by the checkout register."

He looked over to the corner where Mr. Liberati, the store's longtime manager, was leaning against the counter, staring intently up at the flatscreen TV mounted on the wall and clearly not planning to help anyone anytime soon.

Arthur turned back to me. "I thought you said people here were friendly."

"They are. But there's college football going on." He stared at me, not understanding. "Football's like a religion here," I explained. "Especially college football."

I pointed to the TV screen, where players from Alabama and Florida were visible. We were lucky it was an SEC conference game; if it had been the Sooners, chances were good Mr. Liberati would've closed the store early.

Arthur shook his head and muttered, "Sports." Then turned back to the wall of jeans.

"What's your size?" I asked, scanning the selections.

"You don't have to help me," he said, reverting back to the overly uptight boy I was used to seeing. "I know your grandmother is forcing you to be here."

"Yeah, well. I'm here, so might as well make the most of it."

He looked like he was about to object, so I grabbed a pair of neatly folded dark Wranglers that I guessed were his size and tossed them to him.

"Here," I said, as he caught the jeans.

We loaded him up with options—light stretch, vintage, straight leg, relaxed, etc.—then he spent the next fifteen minutes in the changing room by himself. I heard him make noises of dissatisfaction, but he didn't walk the catwalk for me. Not that I was disappointed, just bored. What I wouldn't give for a good nap. When things grew quiet, I knocked on the door to the dressing room.

"How's it going in there?" I asked.

To my surprise the door opened and Arthur stepped out,

still wearing his green puffy jacket but no longer in black pants. Instead, he wore the faded, retro boot-cut Wranglers and I realized in that moment I had never seen him in jeans before. It was always pants. Always pressed. Always hitting the top of his burnished leather shoes, not too long, not too short.

But there he was, in jeans, and they looked good on him. Surprisingly good. Fitting all the right places.

He walked out into the small area where there was a floor-to-near-ceiling mirror. His expression was hesitant with a twinge of self-conscious, another new look for him.

"I feel uncertain," he said, frowning at his own reflection.

"Why?"

"The bottoms." He waved at his black sock-covered feet. "They seem far too wide."

"That's because they're boot cut."

"They're what?"

"Oh, come on, Arthur. You've heard of boot cut."

"If I had I wouldn't have said 'They're what?'"

"Are you from this planet?"

"Depends on who you ask."

He half turned, checking himself out. But the jacket was in the way.

"Here," I said. "Take that off so you can get a better view."

He did as instructed and I held the jacket against my chest as he continued his appraisal. And I did, too, assessing the shape and fit on him, until all at once I became aware that I was staring at Arthur's ass.

A blush came over me out of nowhere and I glanced away. *What the . . . ?*

The image of Arthur at the Halloween party—where he'd come dressed in a black tuxedo with his hair slicked back and an unlit cigarette dangling from his lip, informing everyone he was "Sean Connery James Bond" as opposed to any other version—popped into my head. He had looked suave at the time, which I would never have pictured if I hadn't seen it for myself. I don't know why I was thinking about that. Seemed silly.

Arthur's eyes met mine in the mirror and for one absurd moment I thought he could read my mind. But of course he couldn't. Thank God.

"You're the Wrangler expert. What do you think?" he asked.

"Um," was my extremely articulate reply. "Good."

He arched a brow. "Could you be a tad more specific?"

"They fit well." *Please don't make me look at your ass.*

He turned back. Frowned. "Do you think so?"

"Mmmm-hmm." Oh, no. Was I starting to sweat? This was bonkers. I swallowed and changed the direction of my thoughts, pointing to his light gray sweater. "What are you planning to wear on top?"

"Jumper," he said. I frowned, which he saw and rolled his eyes in mild exasperation. "A sweater," he clarified in an impressive flat, mid-Atlantic American accent.

I snorted. Then, in a strategic effort to avoid further conversation about the fit of his jeans, I grabbed a medium shirt from one of the racks. Long sleeved, blue plaid, pearl snaps for buttons. Classic.

"Here. If you're going to go Full Okie, you should have at least one flannel shirt."

A disdainful grimace was his response. "I do not wear flannel." He turned back to the mirror.

His superiority made me want to push the matter. "C'mon, you'd look cute." As soon as the word—*cute*—left my lips, I cringed in searing mortification. *Cute??* Good Lord! I should've just kept looking at his butt.

Out of the corner of my eye, I saw Arthur go still, but I refused to look at him directly. Instead, I returned the shirt to the rack and nervously tightened my hold on his jacket. His phone slipped from the pocket. It was a miracle of reflexes that I managed to catch it before it crashed against the pine floor. But when my thumb hit the front screen, it lit up.

And I saw the banner text notification for him from Bronwyn. Not that I was snooping. But it was right there and it took a millisecond to read: Hey.

A chill shot through me. "You're friends with Bronwyn?" I asked before I could stop myself.

"Do you mean Bronwyn Campbell?"

"How many Bronwyns do you know?" I snarked.

"Four."

Oh. "Seriously?"

"It's going through a resurgence, particularly in England. Why are you asking?"

"She texted you," I said calmly and held out his phone. "I didn't mean to read it."

He took his phone. "Ah." And after a quick glance, he cleared the notification and turned back to his own reflection.

I bit my lower lip. "So, like . . . are you? Friends with her?"

"I wouldn't call us that."

"What would you call her?"

"A schoolmate." His eyes met mine again through the reflection. "We had three classes together last term," he said, as if to explain. "And she has an affinity for texting."

"Oh." I gripped his jacket harder, wondering if somehow Arthur was reporting back to her about how shitty things were in Christmas. My breathing started to grow shallow. "Why 'Hey'?"

"It's a form of greeting? One favored by Americans, I've found."

My brain started to get away from me. "It's super familiar, though. Are you telling her about Christmas?" To my dismay, anxiousness permeated my voice. Which was stupid since I wasn't going back there and wouldn't see Bronwyn again, so why did I care?

I wished I didn't care.

Arthur slowly turned back to face me. "If you're referring to the fact you lied, no. I've made no mention of it to anyone. As per our agreement. Which I'm going to presume *you've* not yet worked on."

I clenched my jaw. "You're going to the reindeer farm tomorrow."

"That required no effort. It dropped in your lap."

"So? You're still going," I shot back, petulant.

He stared at me for a long beat, his expression hooded, and my heartbeat picked up its rhythm, thudding against my chest.

Then he reached for his jacket.

"I think these jeans will work," he said, his voice neutral. "Thank you. I'll be sure to also express my gratitude for your assistance to your grandmother, so she knows you did as she requested."

With that he turned and walked back into the dressing room.

Six

That evening, Dad and I had the library to ourselves.

It was a small room at the back of the inn and no one's idea of a real library, but it did the trick. There were four bookshelves, including the stand-alone bookcase made of walnut that Grandma Jo found on one of her trips to Dallas. It held the most books. Hardbacks. The leather-bound types with gold lettering that no one ever opened but made for nice décor.

Dad and I sat across from each other at the round Maitland-Smith chess table with its sepia-colored leather board. The black and white pieces were made entirely of wood, not ivory. Grandma Jo made sure of that before she had it shipped up from Texas for Dad's thirtieth birthday a few years ago. Because one of the few things my low-key father loved was playing a game of chess. While Grandma Jo couldn't be accused of spoiling anyone, she tried to find the little things that brought joy to those she loved and made sure they had them.

Dad almost cried when he saw it. He decided to keep it at the inn, though, because he liked it the way it looked here better than our own house. I think he also liked to use it as an excuse to come over to the inn and hang out. He and his mom were close.

I was already losing tonight, but at least it was starting to take him longer to accomplish. It was the twelfth move and he had been staring at the board for five minutes. Normally when he took this long to decide which piece to move, I'd have to tamp down my frustration.

But not tonight.

The longer we stretched out the game, the more time I had to psych myself into bringing up the big topic. Either of them.

Dad finally moved his white bishop to D5.

"Have you talked to your mother?" he asked, his manner casual, as if he wanted to know whether I'd remembered to fill up the gas tank after borrowing his Jeep Cherokee.

I felt my chest constrict. Okay. Here it was: the Mom Talk.

"We've texted," I answered with an equal degree of casual, like my heart hadn't started beating hummingbird fast. "She said she was with Aunt Jennifer and they were seeing the sights."

Aunt Jennifer was Mom's older sister who lived in Springfield, Missouri, with her second husband, Colby, who had sky-blue eyes and dimples, fancied himself a musician, and, according to Mom, had "zero job prospects anywhere on the horizon." Aunt Jennifer was crazy about him.

Dad kept his eyes on the board. "Did she say anything you want to talk about?" His voice remained neutral.

I countered with a one-shoulder shrug. "Not really."

He moved a piece and tapped his finger against his chin. Several moments of nothing followed before Dad said, "Mamma mentioned a group of you are going to see the reindeer ranch tomorrow."

And that was that for the Mom Talk.

Won't lie, I was relieved. And, yeah, that made me a chicken-shit but the last thing I wanted was to hear the words "We're getting a divorce" said aloud. They hadn't been. Yet. Maybe I'd get lucky and they wouldn't ever be. Deep down, I knew the odds were against me.

"Yep." I moved a piece. A pawn. A2 to A4. Basic.

"Your friend from school and his aunt are going, too."

"He's not my friend. We just go to the same school."

Now Dad looked up at me. "Didn't you two go shopping together earlier?"

"Because Grandma Jo asked me to go with him. His aunt was sleeping off jet lag."

Dad frowned. "If you're not friends then what's he doing here?" he asked, moving one of his pawns up two squares.

Another shrug. I looked at the board and moved my rook up to A2.

"That seems odd." I glanced up to see him watching me with concern. "He's not . . . giving you trouble, is he?"

I laughed when I realized what Dad meant. It was sweet to see him get protective, but "No." *Not like that* was what I wanted to add, but refrained. Arthur was many things but I had a hard time envisioning him stalking anyone. For some reason it was important for me that Dad didn't let his thoughts go in that direction. "He and his aunt Esha wanted to go some-where nice for an American Christmas, and, you know, he heard about our town's name, so . . ." I let the rest roll unsaid.

Dad relaxed and nodded. "How disappointing for them," he murmured, a wry tug at the corner of his mouth. His focus was back on the board, so he missed seeing my eyes widen for a second at the understatement.

"I'm going to take them around town," I added. "Show them some of the less embarrassing parts so it's not, you know, a total bust."

"Got it. Hence the reindeer ranch."

"Yep."

"That's nice of you."

I chose not to correct him.

Dad moved his bishop to my A2, took my rook, and I frowned, realizing I needed to pay more attention.

"Are you okay with him being here?"

"Sure."

Suddenly the image of Arthur trying on the jeans earlier today sprang to mind and I felt momentarily distracted . . . But thoughts of Arthur also reminded me of my need to raise the subject with Dad about not returning to Barrington, which filled me with dread.

It had to be done, though.

My brain buzzed with potential ideas for a first sentence ("Speaking of Arthur and Barrington Academy . . ." or "It's funny you mentioned my school" or "I'm okay with him being here because I don't think I'll ever see him again after Christmas is over and here's why . . .").

I took a breath . . . and nothing came out. Not even air.

My throat closed and I bit my lip.

Dad was oblivious.

"Have you talked to Mia since you've been back?" he asked instead.

My grip on my knight tightened. "Nope," I said, moving the piece out of harm's way and letting the opportunity to broach the Barrington subject fall by the wayside. At least for now.

"That's unusual. You two've been like peas in a pod since you were in second grade."

"Yeah, well. Things change." One of the vaguest comments possible. It failed to fool him.

"This have anything to do with that boy?" he asked.

Dad always had a way of not remembering Brody's name, partially to tease me but also to let me know that Brody wasn't his favorite person. It annoyed me when we were going out, but not anymore.

Before I could conjure up a reply as vague as my previous one, Arthur entered the library and inadvertently saved me. I hadn't seen him since we returned from our shopping excursion, which had ended with him buying four pairs of Wranglers in various styles.

He stopped when he saw me and Dad, his back somehow straightening further, which I wasn't sure was possible.

"Oh. My apologies. Ms. Brown said there were books in here I could . . ." His words trailed off as his glance flitted around to the shelves of books before he took a step backward as if to exit. "Excuse me."

"It's Arthur, right?" Dad said.

This caught both Arthur and me by surprise.

Arthur stopped in place.

"Yes, sir."

Now I looked back at Arthur. He was almost at attention as he faced Dad. One lock of straight dark hair fell over his forehead and bounced.

"Finley tells me you came here looking for a good Christmas."

"Yes, sir."

Dad grinned. "It's the name, right? Christmas has to be a great place to spend Christmas? That happens a lot."

Arthur's glance landed on me for a hot second before returning to Dad and I held my breath. Not that changing the town's website without permission was the worst action imaginable but the chances of it being illegal were—now that I thought about it—probably higher than I'd like and that's not something I wanted to explain to Dad. Now or ever.

So I was hugely relieved when Arthur replied, "Yes, sir," and then added nothing else.

"You came in here looking for a book?" Dad continued.

"I did, yes. Finley's grandmother said there were some I could borrow? And to have a look around. But I don't want to disturb your game."

"It's fine," Dad said. Then he brought his queen to D2 with my king blocked in at E1 and announced, "Checkmate."

Usually I at least made it to a minimum of a half hour before he beat me.

Dad stood and smiled at Arthur.

"What kind of books do you like?"

"Normally I'm drawn to biographies"—of course he was—"like Chernow's *Alexander Hamilton*, but we've had quite a few of them assigned to us lately, so I was rather hoping to find something more on the entertaining side."

Dad politely didn't comment on Arthur's way of speaking as if he was recently retired from the royal guard and waved to the room. "Then you've come to the right place. There are some good ones. Ever read Jasper Fforde?"

Arthur's expression lit up and he came close to relaxing. "Indeed! I'm quite the fan of the entire Thursday Next series."

Uh-oh. This was totally Dad's wheelhouse. He could talk satiric sci-fi until the person opposite him pitched forward and hit her forehead on the table with a resounding thud, which I had done at least twice.

I began to put the chess pieces away, preparing to bolt the moment they made it to Douglas Adams, but to my surprise

Dad only managed, "I wish he'd hurry up with the sequel to *Shades of Grey*," before he checked his phone and announced, "Gotta return this—see you around, Arthur," followed by a distracted "Good game, sport," aimed at me.

Then he was out the door. Leaving me and Arthur alone.

Again.

There was an awkward beat. There was *always* an awkward beat with us.

"Did you show your aunt the jeans?" I asked.

"Not as yet. I figured she'd see them tomorrow."

I nodded, kept putting the pieces in their green felt spaces.

Arthur nodded at them. "I didn't realize you played."

"Just with Dad. Though it's more like he lets me think I'm going to win for a while before kicking my ass. Kinda like you saw."

He smirked. That word again. Because it suited him. Maybe he really was meant for Ayisha. They could fall in love and get married and have a brood of smirking babies.

That thought alone reminded me of earlier and before I could think I asked, "How did you meet Ayisha?"

"She brought me a cup of cinnamon tea and we got chatting. She's quite lovely."

I worked very hard not to scowl as I put away the last chess piece and shut the drawer.

"Are you going to ask her out? You know, have a holiday romance?" I tried to lace the question with lighthearted teasing, but it came out with a bit more edge.

He stared at me for a long moment then turned to the bookcase with the leather-bound books.

"It hadn't occurred to me," he replied, keeping his focus on the book spines before him. He selected one, took it out, and opened it. I got the impression he was pretending to read the first page.

"You two seemed friendly," I continued, not able to help myself. It bugged me. A lot. Almost as much as seeing Bronwyn's text earlier.

"Should I not have been friendly?" he countered.

"I don't care."

He glanced up. "I didn't ask if you cared. I asked if I shouldn't have been friendly with Ayisha."

"Do whatever you want."

"Don't you like her?"

"It's complicated."

"A clear evasion."

"Yep."

"Which I'll take to mean no, you don't like her."

I hesitated. Because that wasn't entirely true. There was a time I *had* liked Ayisha. I'd thought she was the coolest person in the whole town. And I thought she'd liked me as well, at least a little, despite the year between us. That felt like forever ago.

Arthur tipped his head to one side in curiosity. "Did she date someone you liked?"

I was surprised at the directness. It was like he was boring a hole right through me.

"Other way around."

Arthur leaned back. "I see." He dragged out the "see" in a way only the British could, followed by a moment of silence. "And are you still dating . . . him? Her? Them?"

"Brody Tuck. Him. And no, we're not dating." Before he could come up with another uncomfortable question, I pointed to the open book in his hand. "Which one'd you choose?"

For a second I wasn't sure he was going to let me get away with that unsubtle change of subject, but then he glanced at the title. "*Reader's Digest's Condensed—Volume 4, 1957.*"

I laughed, relieved. "Classic."

He seemed mildly amused, too. "How can I go wrong? There are five stories from which to choose, one of which is entitled 'Warm Bodies.'"

"I'll bet that's not as fun as it sounds."

I regretted that the second it came out of my mouth. Because it was borderline flirtatious and there was *no* reason for anything flirtatious between me and Arthur Chakrabarti Watercress, thank you very much. Especially in light of my earlier reaction to watching him try on jeans.

Maybe he didn't notice.

But then I saw his olive skin darken with a blush and he returned the book to the shelf and, yeah, he'd noticed. Shit.

I could feel myself grow warmer, too, and knew from experience it was likely making my cheeks redden. I may have a smidgen of Cherokee in my DNA thanks to Grandma Jo's branch of the genetic tree, but Mom's Nordic/Irish ancestors won out in the most overt ways, which meant I had blue eyes, light blonde hair, and my future was destined to be filled with lots of sunscreen and blushes I could never hide. Like now.

It was then I got a divine Hail Mary in the form of a phone call from the one person I least wanted to talk with: Mia.

The buzz of the incoming call from my former bestie shattered the silence in the library.

I flinched.

Arthur didn't.

Make no mistake, I absolutely did *not* want to talk with

Mia, but this was the only distraction I had available. So before I could second-guess myself, I hit the phone's green button.

"Hey," I said, as if I hadn't been dodging every form of outreach from Mia for the past few days.

"Finley?" She sounded as surprised as I felt.

"Yeah, hold on." I put the phone against my shoulder and stood, facing Arthur. "Sorry, I have to take this."

He nodded then turned away from me, his back once again straight and formal as he resumed his focus on the books. His shoulders were broader than I remembered. Had they always been like that?

I blinked at myself. *What the hell was* wrong *with me lately?*

"Finley?" Mia's voice was muffled against my sweater.

I fled the library, happy to be away from Arthur as fast as possible.

Seven

The spa for the Hoyden Inn was tucked away on a first-floor corner of the main building. Grandma Jo was always looking to make additions or improvements, so she'd added the spa a few years ago, but it was very small for her overall vision.

However, when it was closed, it was a great place to have a private conversation.

Thankfully it was closed and I ducked inside.

"Finley?" I heard Mia say again.

"Hold on," I answered, with no effort to disguise my irritation.

The spa wasn't much more than four rooms: a check-in area, a changing room, a massage room big enough for two tables if couples ever wanted to go together, a sauna that I was pretty sure had originally been a storage closet.

I wound up in the massage room.

The lights were off but enough moonlight streamed in through the double floor-to-ceiling windows that I could see where I was going.

I stood by a window and took a deep breath to calm my nerves.

"Hey," I said, and Arthur's earlier commentary on the greeting echoed in my memory.

"Hey," was Mia's response.

A long silence followed.

I didn't need a FaceTime call to know Mia was probably biting her thumbnail. That was her go-to anxiety move ever since we met in elementary school.

"You called me," I reminded her once the silence had stretched on.

"Yeah. Uh . . . I didn't think you were coming home for Christmas."

"I changed my mind."

"Yeah, I got that. Why didn't you tell me first?" There was a hint of accusation in her voice, which got my back up.

"Did I need your permission?"

"No, that's not what I meant. I meant . . . I mean, why . . . why did you change your mind?"

"I have my reasons," I replied.

"Did somebody tell you? About me and Brody?"

I huffed out a laugh. "No. No one told me about you and Brody. Not even *you*, my supposed best friend."

"Oh, *now* I'm your best friend," she snapped, her voice rising, and I knew the gloves had officially come off. "That's messed up."

"How?"

"Because you left, Finley. And you barely talked to me at all for the last, like, three months!"

"Because I was in *school*, and studying!"

And trying not to be a total failure, something at which I had failed. Not that I'd told Mia—or anyone here at home—about that part. It was humiliating.

"And hanging out with your new friends," she continued, sounding hurt.

That jab threw me for a moment. Between the two of us, Mia was definitely the more sensitive. There were probably as many stars in the Milky Way as there were times I'd apologized to her for saying something that accidentally hurt her feelings over the years.

And a part of me started to automatically fall back into my pattern with her, to tell her that wasn't true and try to make her feel better.

Except the words wouldn't come out.

"You're totally not even denying it," she accused when I failed to respond.

I felt her anger starting to boil over, but when I opened my mouth a second time to speak, my brain went blank. It's like there was a white wall where words and feelings should be. I closed my mouth and continued to say nothing. "Whatever." She spat the word out at me. "Yeah, I'm dating Brody. Why do you care? You left him, too. You left everyone to go be someone better than the rest of us, so don't get mad if *we* move on, too!"

The phone went dead then, and I didn't bother to try to call her back.

I knew what would come later tonight: a flurry of text messages, because when Mia got hurt, she got angry.

And Mia was hurt. What kind of friend was I that I hadn't noticed?

I sighed, knowing I should go get ready for bed. Tomorrow was going to be a long, weird day, filled with Chakrabartis and a chatty dentist and reindeer.

But I stayed by the window. It wasn't as if my room here

was truly *my* room anyhow; it was where I was staying over the holiday. My real bedroom was in the empty house across town.

However, Dad was staying here and Mom was in Missouri, and I was helping out at the Hoyden.

When I showed up out of the blue last week, Grandma Jo directed me to one of the "just in case" rooms at the back of the inn she kept unoccupied for emergencies. They weren't great rooms. Big enough for a twin bed, wooden desk and chair, dresser, closet complete with foldout ironing board, and a "full" bathroom that would've been better suited to a camper.

There was a reason she didn't rent those out to the public. But beggars/choosers and all that.

Grandma Jo lived in one of the cottages because, as she liked to say, she needed at least the semblance of separation from the inn so she didn't lose her mind. She usually rented out the other three, but Dad occupied one now.

It was weird how I learned about him and Mom.

I had spent the days leading up to my travel envisioning a scene of me knocking on the front door and one of my parents—probably Mom—opening the door and seeing me standing there with my luggage and me smiling and saying "Surprise!"

Then Mom's face would light up and she'd hug me and then Dad would hug me and once they got over the surprise, they'd ask me what I was doing there.

That would be the perfect lead-in for my desire to come home permanently and they'd be so happy I was there with them that they'd be receptive. I would move back into my room on the second floor with its bay window overlooking the front yard and everything would go back to how it was when I left six months ago.

None of that happened.

Instead, I had arrived at the house early in the evening to find it was quiet. Even the front porch light had been off, which was odd.

I'd knocked on the front door before using my house key to enter, pulling my luggage behind me into the foyer.

No one answered when I called out and by that point I knew something was off. The air was stagnant and every murdery *Dateline* episode I'd ever watched flashed before my eyes.

I stepped back outside and called Grandma Jo.

Once she got over the surprise, she sent Dad to fetch me.

"Whatcha doin' here, sport?" he'd asked, as we stood in the living room where I'd grown up.

That had been my first opportunity to tell him about Barrington Academy and my plan to never again darken its doors. But I didn't. All I really wanted to know was, "Where's Mom?"

"Your mom's taking some time for herself" is how he phrased it.

He explained that she had gone to see Aunt Jennifer in November and decided to stay through Thanksgiving.

Which led to her telling him she intended to remain "a little bit longer."

Which then led to her telling Dad in early December that she was going to stay there "indefinitely."

And that was about as much explanation as I was given. The rest I had to fill in on my own, which of course meant I chose to color with the "doom" crayon and did my best to avoid the situation for the following week, though even *I* knew that would only last so long.

I sighed, feeling tired to my bones.

I finally left the spa to make my way through the first-floor hallways, intending to go up the back stairs to the second floor, where my tiny room was located.

But when I passed by one of the hallway windows overlooking the pathway to where the cottages were located, I caught sight of Dad on his phone, wearing his winter coat and pacing beneath the light of the moon.

He talked and gestured and gestured and talked.

I stopped to watch.

Gut instinct and common sense merged to make me certain Mom was on the other side of that call. His expression was tight and he ran his hand through his short chocolate-brown hair.

My parents weren't arguers; that wasn't their style. Or at least they weren't when I was around. Which made the whole situation that much more difficult for me to fathom.

Then he ended the call and his body slumped in what seemed like defeat.

I wanted to go to him but my feet were rooted. Fortunately, I wasn't the only one who had been watching. Grandma Jo approached him from the direction of the inn, slipping on her down coat before she reached him.

I couldn't hear what they said, but I watched her pull him into a comforting hug and, equally unusual, he let her.

Then she rubbed his back as they turned together, her arm looped through his, and continued on down the path toward their cottages.

Right then I felt the phone in my pocket buzz, alerting me to an incoming message. Sure enough, when I checked I found a voicemail waiting for me.

From Mom.

It must've come in when I was walking through the hallways or maybe even when I was in the library. I played her voicemail.

Hi, honey, it's Mom. I love you so much. I know things are . . . really weird right now. I was hoping to talk with you, not just text . . . I didn't know you were coming home for Christmas. I wouldn't have . . . (She sighed.) *I would have made sure to be there if I had.* (A long pause.) *Anyhow, I'm going to try to call again tomorrow. Maybe in the evening? If that works for you. I love you and I miss you . . . Bye.*

The voicemail ended.

For a moment I thought about calling her back. I knew she was still awake; the message was from only fifteen minutes ago. I didn't.

Between that message and now, she probably had talked with Dad, and it didn't look like that had gone well.

Which was the excuse I gave myself for putting my phone back in my pocket and continuing on up the stairs, to my temporary room.

Where, at least for the night, I could try to sleep, and hide.

Eight

Grandma Jo was at her hostess best when she told me and the others that Dad would be joining our merry band of reindeer sightseers on the day's adventure, thus bringing the group's total to an even six: Grandma Jo, Dr. Raymond, Dad, Aunt Esha, Arthur, and me.

We all met in the lobby.

Arthur wore his dark Wranglers and every few minutes he'd covertly bend at the knees to stretch the stiff material. I probably should've advised him to wash them at least once before wearing them, but he was old enough to figure that out. Besides, watching him was oddly adorable.

I was as surreptitious as possible in my attempts to read Dad's expression. He seemed like his normal self, though the dark circles under his eyes were new and I spotted the first glint of gray hair at the back of his head.

Which I definitely would *not* point out.

Ayisha was manning the front desk when we'd gathered to leave in the late morning. If there was any part of her that felt the smallest longing to join us, she covered it extremely well.

Grandma Jo smiled. "Thank you for coming in on short notice, Ayisha."

"Sure thing, Ms. Brown. Happy for the extra hours."

"Val called a while ago. She'll be in at twelve thirty to relieve you instead of noon. That won't cause you any trouble, will it?"

Val Limekiller was one of the half dozen other employees who worked at the Hoyden and she hadn't been on time to anything starting with when she showed up two weeks past the due date for her birth.

Ayisha, who was always punctual, maintained her smile. "No, that's fine."

Grandma turned to the rest of us. "Looks like we're going to have to take two cars. Skip, do you want to drive?"

Dad nodded. "Sure."

Before Grandma Jo got any further, Dr. Raymond pounced. "Then that leaves me and Jo in the other car! We'll get there first and add Skippy to the reservations, which I made yesterday."

Dad's eyes narrowed at the never-used nickname of his nickname.

Dr. Raymond was already onto getting Grandma Jo to himself. He waved his hand in the direction of the front doors. "After you, m'lady."

A slightly stricken look flashed in my grandmother's hazel eyes but she mustered up a smile. "Of course." To the rest of us, "We'll see you there."

Pretty sure I read a *Please hurry* hostage energy off her before she and Dr. Raymond exited the lobby.

Which left Dad, Aunt Esha, Arthur, and me.

"Have fun, y'all," Ayisha said to us, with a big smile that could have lingered on Arthur longer than was necessary.

Arthur returned her smile until he caught sight of me and

then he looked momentarily uncertain whether he'd breached some unknown protocol.

Not that I cared. He could do what he wanted. Date Ayisha, not date Ayisha, it was no skin off my nose.

I grabbed a peppermint for the road.

The four of us bundled into Dad's Jeep Cherokee, adults up front, and me in the back with Arthur.

Last night I'd found it hard to sleep, so I scribbled down some ideas for what to do while he and his aunt were in town. I'd even managed to order three pounds of fresh chestnuts from a farm in Michigan. Ha! Take that, just "dropped in your lap."

As Dad pulled the Jeep out of the inn's parking, I was about to reach in my coat pocket to retrieve the paper when Dad glanced in the rearview mirror.

"Arthur? Did you find a book?" he asked.

"Yes, sir. *A Spell for Chameleon.*"

"Love that one. Starts the whole Xanth series. Kinda heavy on the bosom talk and the guy never met a pun he didn't like, but it's pretty fun. Let me know what you think."

"I will indeed."

Aunt Esha shifted in her seat as we drove down Merry Street, the town's main thoroughfare. I saw her peer out the window at the storefronts as we passed, most of which had been painted either red, green, or white since the town's name change. Though they weren't maintained equally and the whole strip bore little resemblance to the photos on the website.

Dad must have noticed the direction of her gaze, too. "This your first look around Christmas?" he asked.

Aunt Esha turned a polite smile in his direction. "No. Arthur and I went for a walk not long after we checked in two days ago. Such an interesting town."

Dad's laugh was a borderline guffaw.

Arthur tossed me a pointed look as we passed the headless Santa sign that marked the end—or beginning, depending on the direction of your travel—of Merry Street.

I quickly took out the sheet of paper to redirect this line of conversation.

"I came up with some ideas of things we can do while you're here, after the reindeer."

"How thoughtful of you, Finley," said Aunt Esha.

"Such as?" Arthur pressed, not as easily swayed.

"Okay, so tomorrow is the town's Christmas Parade. It starts right after dusk so the lights can be seen. All the local businesses from the surrounding counties participate, and, you know, not to give anything away, but Santa shows up at the end."

Arthur arched an eyebrow. "Is the parade on the street we just drove down?"

"It is."

"Does it last three minutes? Because that wasn't a long drive."

"Be kinder, Arthur," was the gentle reprimand from up front. "Your friend is doing us a great favor."

Arthur's reaction was immediate. "Sorry, Mashi," he said contritely.

My eyes about bugged out. When had Arthur ever been *contrite*?

He avoided my gaze but I could tell by his clenched jaw it required effort.

"Please continue, Finley," Aunt Esha urged.

I looked back at the paper. "I was also thinking we could maybe do some Christmas baking before the parade."

"Cookies or gingerbread? It seems most of your American Christmas films have one aspect of that or another," said Aunt Esha.

"Cookies?" I ventured because there was zero chance I'd be able to do anything with gingerbread. Not that my cookie-baking efforts went beyond a single tutorial from my grandmother when I was ten.

"Christmas cookies are delightful," she said.

I was relieved. "Also, there's an indoor ice-skating rink we could try."

Dad shook his head. "Not anymore. Micky's Winter Wonderland burned down three months ago."

That was news. "What happened? Faulty wiring? Lightning?"

"Insurance scam. Micky was a little too fond of the casinos for his bank account's liking. They arrested him after Thanksgiving."

Merry Christmas, Micky.

"What about the one in Norman?" I asked, referring to the nearest big small town where the University of Oklahoma was located, a thirty-minute drive away. "There's one there, right?"

Dad hit the turn signal and got us on the road to Sedgewicks'. "Pretty sure."

As I was making mental note to check, Arthur piped up.

"There is indeed an ice rink called—" He squinted at his phone and frowned. "Sizzling Iceplex? Seems a bit contradictory. It is outdoors, though, and is presently offering a free fruitcake for every thirty-fifth visitor. Odd. Why do you suppose it's thirty-fifth?"

I shrugged.

Dad glanced at Aunt Esha. "Do you skate?"

"Not since I was a young girl. Which was a very long time ago."

"Hardly." Dad smiled then glanced back at me. "I can drive everyone, if you'd like."

"Cool. Do you want to drive us to Chickasha for the lights, too?" I asked.

"I'd love that," Dad said. I noticed his energy was starting to pick up.

"What lights?" Arthur asked, nodding to the paper in my hand.

"The Chickasha Festival of Light. It's actually awesome." I leaned closer to Arthur and whispered, "There was a picture on the website. The light bridge?"

"That was real?"

I stared daggers at him a moment. But I also couldn't help noticing he smelled really nice, like a woodsy amber, maybe. Was that cologne or soap?

Aunt Esha said, "All of those sound like excellent options, Finley. My nephew and I appreciate your kindness and hospitality. Is that not so, Arthur?"

"Indeed," said nephew murmured, though his expression was less convincing.

I looked back out the window, deciding not to dwell on anything woodsy or amber.

We drove past a large white sign proclaiming SEDGEWICKS' RANCH in red letters at the top of a long dirt road.

We had arrived.

The land leading up to and including Sedgewicks' was as yellowed and dead as everywhere else. Which was going to make for an interesting sleigh ride.

The first impression was that it looked like a typical Oklahoma ranch.

Buildings were big and functional, yet lacked TLC. Someone had attempted to repaint the main barn a fresh red, but only got about ten feet up, probably as tall as their ladder would reach, then quit. The effect was a bright red ring around the barn base with the other twenty feet a weather-beaten gray.

The whole thing felt like its roots were showing after too long away from the salon.

Semi-rusted discarded farm equipment sat in batches and there were animal pens, though the only animals visible were cows.

We parked in the graveled section with a half dozen other cars and once I got out of the Jeep, it didn't take long to realize where this place diverged from a regular ranch: everything that could possibly be stamped with the likeness of a reindeer had been.

The parking sign, the trash can, the front door, the building itself, a flag (below the Stars and Stripes), even the concrete stops had a goofy reindeer's face smiling up to greet each car.

Arthur stood next to me, surveying the surroundings. "Well. They certainly embraced the theme."

A theme that carried over to the interior of the converted house, which was the greeting area/gift shop/café, except jacked up to eleven. Welcome mats, antler light fixtures, reindeer upholstery on the sofa and chairs. The Christmas tree in the center of the lobby had only reindeer ornaments and its branches drooped from the sheer volume. It was a lot.

And yet the mounted reindeer head opposite the front door was still unexpected.

Arthur stopped in his tracks when he saw it.

Dad jammed his hands in his coat pockets. "Guess we know how Rudolph *really* got his job."

My eyeballs rolled straight into the back of my head at Dad's dad joke. But Aunt Esha tittered in amusement and Dad beamed, pleased with himself.

Grandma Jo spotted our arrival and quickly joined us, Dr. Raymond hot on her heels.

"You're here!" she beamed.

Dr. Raymond held up a piece of paper with a cartoon reindeer head on the top. "Got your ticket, Skippy!"

Dad tensed. "Skip." He accepted the ticket with two fingers. "Thanks."

Dr. Raymond handed out the rest.

Grandma Jo put her arm around my shoulders and squeezed me a little too tightly. "We're the next tour group. They only have two guides at the moment."

"Drakkar and Axe Moses," Dr. Raymond expanded, then looked at Arthur and Aunt Esha to expand even further. "No relation. To Moses. *They're* related."

Grandma Jo kept her focus. "They're out on a sleigh ride, but the ticket keeper expects them back in fifteen minutes."

Dr. Raymond looked at Arthur and me. "You can feed the free-range chickens if you kids are interested." *Did he think we were five?* "And the hot cocoa is included in the ticket!"

Okay, fine. I did like hot cocoa.

Grandma Jo moved to slip her arms through both Dad's and Aunt Esha's, putting herself between them. "Let's grab ours and wait in the café."

She propelled both in the direction of the adjacent café. Dr. Raymond followed.

I glanced over to where Arthur had been standing only to see him already in the gift shop opposite the café.

More shopping. Okay, then.

But I had to admit even I was curious about was in there.

Turns out, a lot of reindeer things.

The space was compact, about the size of my "just in case" bedroom but with every possible surface crammed with reindeer paraphernalia that ran the gamut from obvious to bizarre. I prayed there wasn't the reindeer equivalent of bacon lip balm.

Arthur moved around the exterior shelves, fascinated in much the same way he had been while jeans shopping.

"Do you have a shopping-addiction problem we should discuss?" I asked, amused.

"Only whilst on vacation to towns named after holidays." His dark brows pulled into a deep frown and he picked up the reindeer-headed kalimba. "Interesting."

He placed it aside then moved to the next section.

I pointed toward the door. "Everyone's over in the café. Do you wanna join?"

"No, thank you. I'm still full from breakfast. Plus, I perused the menu last night off their website. I'd rather not find out if 'reindeer oysters' are what I suspect."

The lady with a reindeer-antlers headband in her skunk-striped hair who stood behind the register volunteered, "They are."

And I never needed to eat again.

Arthur's face lit up. "Christmas crackers!"

Before I could ask if that was another reference to reindeer oysters, skunk-haired lady piped up. "Those're reindeer snappers."

"Reindeer snappers?" He seemed perplexed as he examined a square box with some sort of Christmas-wrapped tubes vaguely shaped like large Tootsie Rolls. I didn't recognize what they were.

"Uh-huh. Snappers."

"That doesn't even make sense," he argued. "Reindeer don't have beaks. Or snap."

Skunk-haired woman shrugged an *I only work here, what do you want from me?* shrug. "They're $39.98 for a pack of eight."

Arthur shook his head. "Outrageous." Then he placed two boxes in his pile before adding a pair of men's socks.

I pointed to the pile. "You're getting all that?"

"I am, yes."

Plop! A small birch-bark reindeer joined the rest.

"Why?"

"Because though I am relatively young with my whole life ahead of me, I can say with complete confidence that I will never come back here ever again." He held up a pea-green sweater with a brown reindeer vomiting Christmas tree ornaments woven onto the front. "Brilliant."

On the pile it went.

"I don't get it," I said, as I examined a coffee mug with a sexy lady reindeer. "Do you have a thing for reindeer?"

"God, no." His back was to me.

"Then why . . . ?"

"I simply find them"—he turned abruptly to face me and said in a voice devoid of humor—"hilarious."

I blinked. Because he had somehow slipped on a red nose. It was incongruous in general, but on Arthur it was baffling.

And then the red nose lit up!

I was startled.

And then—God help me—I let out a deeply unattractive spontaneous giggle/snort that really should have been mortifying.

But then the *most* amazing thing happened—Arthur laughed, too.

He actually *laughed*!

Not at me, either, but with me, and easily, and it changed his whole face. Softened it, made his dark eyes sparkle and emphasized his perfect, straight white teeth.

My attention was drawn to the dimple in his left cheek I hadn't realized existed—I was a longtime sucker for a good cheek dimple—and I noticed the hint of a cleft in his strong chin.

I felt an entirely unexpected and unwelcome *pang* land in the center of my chest.

Blinking a few times, my smile fading quickly as my brain struggled to catch up to . . . something. *Something* that had happened, was still happening?

But that was impossible!

My gaze swung back to Arthur, who, thankfully, had already returned his attention to his task of clearing out half of the gift shop.

I was grateful, because I was spiraling into a borderline meltdown, which I kept neatly tucked away from view. Because no one developed a crush in the middle of a reindeer gift shop.

That—that was bonkers!

No, no. I was clearly reacting to the shitstorm that had rained down on me ever since I came back to Christmas. Maybe even earlier. Maybe since the bee incident, when Arthur had been so helpful and cute and—

No! What? Stop! My brain was not allowed to go anywhere near *there*. Nope, nope. That was a restricted subject I would never, *ever* examine. Lock on door, key thrown away.

"Are you all right?" he asked, suddenly beside me, carrying two large shopping bags, and though the space was small, I was still surprised.

"What?" My voice was sharp, my heart beating far too fast.

"You seem . . . preoccupied."

"Well, I'm not," I countered. "I'm totally present. Very much, you know, in the moment."

And apparently babbling. Great.

Arthur regarded me like I was possibly losing my mind, and I would not disagree.

"Well," he said. "I'm happy for you. Are you getting anything?"

"Huh?"

He arched an eyebrow. "As a reminder, your 'very much in the moment' is taking place in a gift shop and I was inquiring if you were purchasing anything."

"No."

"Then shall we join the others?"

"Yeah, okay."

He shot me a look that could almost be construed as concern. "Are you certain you're all right?"

"Yep!"

To prove it I spun on my heels and walked right out of that reindeer gift shop. After a moment, he followed me.

At that exact second, two identical men with identical ruddy beards entered through the front doors. They looked like former NFL offensive linemen dressed in identical heavy, brown, waxed cotton coats bearing the Sedgewicks' Ranch reindeer emblem.

Ladies and gentlemen, Drakkar and Axe Moses, twin brothers who were about ten years older than me and who had worked at Sedgewicks' for as long as I could remember. They were big and loud and, according to Grandma Jo—who somehow always knew such things—vegan, because they had an abiding love for animals in all forms and that did not allow for consuming them.

"Reindeer wranglers are in da house!" one of them—I'd never been able to tell them apart—announced with a deep, booming voice that required no amplification.

Arthur and I stopped. He looked over at me and raised his eyebrows. It was a simple gesture, one I was sure he had done before. But this time I felt a flutter of butterflies.

I looked away at once.

Grandma Jo, Dr. Raymond, Dad, and Aunt Esha came out of the café together.

One twin took our tickets and shoved them in his coat pocket while the other addressed us with a big smile.

"Howdy, folks! Welcome to the inaugural reindeer season here at Sedgewicks' Ranch. I'm Axe."

"And I'm Drakk."

"And it looks like y'all signed up for the reindeer tour and the group sleigh ride. Now, the reindeer tour lasts about a half hour to an hour—"

"—and y'all get to feed 'em."

"—and pet 'em."

"—and love 'em."

"But when it comes to the sleigh ride," Axe (I think) continued.

"—we're just gonna let y'all know that our sleigh is real cool—"

"*Real* cool."

"But it ain't gonna fit six of ya."

"Nope."

"And that means two of y'all—"

"—are gonna have to hang back—"

"—while the others head out."

I felt dizzy.

"Now, we can do a second sleigh ride—"

"—after the first."

"If y'all want."

"Just let us know."

I lost track of which one was talking by that point. Fortunately, Grandma Jo kept her wits.

"One sleigh ride is enough. And it's only right that our two guests be the ones to go," she said, smiling at Aunt Esha and Arthur.

I was about to volunteer to stay back when Dr. Raymond interjected, "Skippy and Finley can go, too. Jo and I can always have our own sleigh ride another time."

He smiled at my grandmother. His method of wooing clearly was to wear down the object of his affection through sheer persistence.

By looking at her, it might be kinda working. The wearing-down part, not the wooing. She looked resigned, though her nod was noncommittal.

Ten minutes later we were all piled in an EV SUV (those big boys were earning their progressive stripes) and making the puma-quiet ride up the trail to where they kept the reindeer.

They had their own barn, which looked newly constructed, complete with solar panels and an exterior group pen where the animals were gathered. Once the world's quietest SUV was parked, I was stuck in the back row with Dad while we waited for everyone else to exit.

I watched Arthur go then turn around to offer his hand to his aunt, not that she needed help. It was clear by how he did it that the courtesy was something that had been ingrained in him. Brody had done that for me a few times, but that was when we were dating. For Arthur, it seemed . . . natural.

And why was I noticing this?

Dad and I exited last and we followed Arthur, Aunt Esha, Grandma Jo, Dr. Raymond, and the Moses twins across the cold, uneven, snowless ground until we reached the pens.

And there they were.

Reindeer.

It was surreal to finally see them after so much buildup. They were big, but not overwhelming. Four of them had antlers while three did not. When we entered the pen, a couple without the antlers made their way over to us with an air of expectation.

Drakk or Axe handed out small bags of reindeer feed to each of us as Axe or Drakk doled out some basic reindeer trivia, including the fact that "reindeer" were basically what North Americans called caribou, their noses were resplendent with veins, which meant they actually *did* have faintly red noses in the cold, and their milk had more fat than cow's milk. They used that as a pitch for their reindeer cheese, available in the café. Arthur's eyes lit up.

Aunt Esha peered into her bag of reindeer food. "No reindeer corn?"

I started to sweat.

Drakk (I was pretty sure) shook his head. "They don't eat corn."

"What about those red-and-green candies?"

Drakk was polite. "Ma'am, they're herbivores. And 'sides, candy'd rot their teeth."

Dr. Raymond beamed.

Aunt Esha shrugged then she handed grass to a beast.

I relaxed until she added, "Someone should correct the town's website, then."

My dad frowned. "Website?"

I rushed forward. "How come some have antlers and some don't?" I asked of our guides. It was possibly all one word—Howcomesomehaveantlersandsomedon't—I said it so fast.

Grandma Jo's sharp gaze turned back to me.

Arthur shot me a look, which I ignored.

Axe, though, grinned. "Glad ya asked, little lady." *Me too, Axe*, I thought as I saw Aunt Esha and Dad focus on his answer; Grandma Jo took an extra beat. "Male reindeer lose their antlers in November—"

"That means it's the lady reindeer," Drakk said, "who're the ones who pull Santa's sleigh on Christmas."

Axe pumped his fist in the air. "Santa the feminist!"

Drakk whooped and clapped as loud as thunder.

Grandma Jo, Aunt Esha, and Dad joined them, laughing, the reindeer corn forgotten.

Hopefully.

Then I felt an unexpected bump in the center of my back that pushed me forward, nearly colliding with Arthur, which would have been embarrassing under normal circumstances but felt a thousand times worse given my unwelcome gift-shop moment. Fortunately, he seemed not to notice.

I could still feel myself blush, though. *Ugh.*

When I turned around, I found myself eye to eye with one

of the lady reindeer—her antlers *were* impressive—who stared expectantly at me. Clearly, she knew the drill, whereas I was the newbie and needed to get with the program.

Happy to have something to do other than think about Arthur, I took a handful of grass from the bag, which the reindeer wasted no time in taking from me. Pushy.

"That's Calliope," Axe told me, nodding to my reindeer. "She's gonna pull the sleigh along with Erato."

He pointed to the one Arthur was feeding.

Aunt Esha perked up. "You named them after the Muses?"

Drakk shook his head. "That was Mrs. Sedgewick's doin'."

"We were gunnin' for Sooner sports greats."

"Vessels."

"Sims."

"The Boz—"

Thankfully Arthur then asked, "Where *is* the sleigh?" or else that list could've gone on a while.

An excited Axe drew Arthur and me to another side of the pen. Our two reindeer followed.

Axe pointed. "There."

And indeed, there it was, in all its unique sleigh glory.

It was red like Santa's traditional sleigh, with gold trim on the sides, three rows for seating, including the elevated driver's perch, and—

Arthur tipped his head to one side. "Are those . . . wheels?"

Axe grinned. "Yep! Good eye." He slapped Arthur on the shoulder, sending him forward before Arthur caught his balance, if not his breath. To be fair, a whack from either giant Moses twin—even a friendly one—would send most people flying. "They're flotation tires. Me and Drakk put 'em on ourselves. On account there ain't no snow."

Yes!

"Clever," Arthur murmured, while trying to rub his shoulder without being obvious.

"Dr. Raymond said you had a snow-making doodad?" I ventured.

If possible, Axe's smile grew even larger. "That's right!" I made sure to stay out of his friendly-slap radius. "You'll see it on the ride!"

I had to admit, I was intrigued.

Which was about the moment Calliope peed on my boots.

"Aaaaahh!" was an approximation of what came out of my mouth as I leapt aside as fast as possible, which meant the left boot was hit the worst.

Unfortunately, my right boot landed in a fresh pile of reindeer shit, and like that, my nice boots were nice no more.

Drakk didn't look remotely sympathetic. "Life on the ranch," he said with a tiny snicker.

I stared at my boots in dismay. I didn't have a huge supply of decent footwear and only one set of nice outdoor boots. These boots. My favorites.

Axe was either more sympathetic or he didn't want a bad online review.

He hurried forward. "Here, lemme show you where the bathroom is in the barn so you can wash those off."

I glanced in Arthur's direction and saw him biting his lower lip, trying not to crack up, which made everything that much more irksome. Sure, if our roles had been reversed and he was the one with reindeer excrement on his shoes, I would very possibly/entirely likely be outright laughing—however, that was beside the point. The jerk.

But also, what a timely reminder! Now, surely, I would lose

that fleeting, foolish . . . *whatever* it was I was feeling for him. God willing.

I followed Axe.

Growing up in a small town in Oklahoma meant I had been to my fair share of barns over the years and, hands down, this was the most beautiful I had ever seen. It was like a post-renovation reveal from an HGTV show, with everything fresh and new and spacious. There was even shiplap!

Axe pointed to a pine-green door.

"Right in there, Fin. Take yer time. We're gonna be loadin' up to go for our ride in 'bout fifteen minutes or so."

I thanked him and walked gingerly to the ladies' bathroom. It was a single, so I closed the door behind me, locking it out of habit.

There was a knock at the door.

"Finley?"

I stiffened. It was Grandma Jo.

"Yeah?"

"Let me in, I'm going to help you."

I reached over to unlock the door.

She entered and shut it behind her. Her purse always managed to hold whatever obscure item she needed at a moment's notice. Right then it was a pair of disposable gloves and a travel packet of disinfectant wipes.

She set everything out on the white marble counter and took in the bathroom, impressed.

"Goodness. If I wasn't so sure the boys were married to the ranch, I'd hire them to build the spa cottage." Then she placed several paper towels neatly on the counter, slipped on the disposable gloves, and nodded to my boots. "Pull up your jeans." Which I did. She got to work, unzipping the left one—the one with the pee. "Now the other one." She set them on the paper towels and began scrubbing.

But while my grandmother was helpful by nature, I knew instinctively that wasn't why she was here. Which was confirmed in under two minutes of her arrival.

"I noticed your reaction when Esha mentioned reindeer corn and the town's website. That's twice you've seemed uncomfortable." She kept working on the pee boot. "Spill."

I was sock-footed and cornered and we both knew it. Dammit.

"I, uh . . ." I cleared my throat. ". . . kinda . . . changed it last month? Remotely?"

Maybe phrasing it in the form of a question wouldn't make it seem quite as bad?

She frowned, baffled. "Why on earth would you do that?'

I fidgeted. "Make it seem, you know, nicer here. In Christmas. Than it really is."

"For Arthur?"

Now it was my time to frown. Where had *that* come from? "No. I had no idea he was going to see it or show it to his aunt."

"Then for whom?"

I hesitated. This wasn't where I wanted to confess the full extent of my failures to my grandmother. Heck, I wasn't sure I wanted to do that at all.

I shrugged like it was no biggie.

"Just some girls."

"At the school?" she pressed, and I nodded. She glanced up from her task to fix me with a knowing look. "Are they perhaps not appreciative of your Oklahoma background?"

I wasn't sure if this was the full reason behind my social

ostracization but my instinct told me it played a part, if only by the number of times Bronwyn had affected a truly terrible version of what she thought was an Okie accent but would have been better suited for a *Gone with the Wind* revival. They weren't remotely the same.

"I don't think so."

Grandma Jo's scrubbing got harder and she muttered, "I had to deal with that same crap at Wellesley." She shook her head, probably at some memory. Then she stopped her scrubbing and looked at me very firmly. "I'm going to give you some insight into bitchy people that I wish someone had told me when I was your age: Their behavior is *never* about you. It's *always* about them and whatever deficiency *they* harbor."

"Feels like it's about me," I mumbled.

"That's what bullies do, they project. Usually on the person they think will let them get away with it, whether it's because they think they're weak or, more often, because the person doesn't want to stoop to their level."

"So are you saying I *should* stoop to their level?"

"No. But you should stand up for yourself. Which is hard. Believe me, I do understand . . . My mother"—Great Grandma Beryl, aka GGB—"was always on me to be nice to everyone and fit in and not make a scene or embarrass her, and I did as she wanted. Well, mostly. Your dad was a bit of inadvertent rebellion. And buying the inn. She didn't think a young, single mother should have done such a thing, but I went ahead anyhow. But there were other areas when I should have stood my ground, and I didn't. And I regret it to this day." I watched her jaw muscles clench.

"That doesn't sound like you, Grandma," I said in surprise.

"That's because GGB passed when you were six and you've

only really known me since then. Trust me, Finley. No matter how old we are, we're all our own continuous projects in evolution."

Another knock came at the door.

It was Dad this time, informing us to "Hurry up. We're fixing to leave on the sleigh ride."

Nine

I'm not quite sure how it happened, but I wound up beside Arthur in the sleigh's back row.

I don't know what his feelings were about it, but if the return of his Queen's Guard posture was any indication, he was as uncomfortable as I was.

There was enough room for us to have a six-inch gap between our legs if we both hugged the sides, which we did, so there was no touching.

At least while we were stationary.

Happily, Grandma Jo succeeded in ridding my boots of reindeer reminders and even spritzed them with a travel-sized room deodorizer, scented in orange peel and clove. Which contributed nicely to the holiday ambience. Go figure.

Drakk handed out a couple of green-plaid woolen blankets to us. "It's gonna get cold as a witch's tit out there," he explained.

He handed another blanket to Dad and Aunt Esha, then winked at me and Arthur like he was in on some inside scoop and I felt all my internal organs wither in abject mortification. I didn't dare glance at Arthur to gauge his reaction.

Dad and Aunt Esha were in the middle row, with Drakk and Axe in the elevated front, since they were driving, if that's the right word for gently encouraging the two reindeer—Erato and Calliope, my nemesis—to "giddy up."

Grandma Jo and Dr. Raymond waved good-bye like parents sending their kids off to college.

Except we didn't. Move, that is. It seemed Erato and Calliope weren't feeling it.

I gazed ahead through the gap between Dad and Aunt Esha to see the twins engage in a quick twin-versation that consisted of single words from one to the other ("Go." "'Kay." "Got—?" "Yep.") and then Possibly Drakk hopped off to get in front of the beasts and lure them forward, step-by-step, with the promise of food, while Probably Axe held the reins loosely in his massive hands.

It seemed to work. Sorta.

Erato stepped forward but Calliope remained in place, blowing out a breath in a sign of irritation so obvious it crossed species. She bobbed her head, her impressive antlers cracking against Erato's.

Probably Axe frowned. "She's bein' all kindsa moody t'day."

Possibly Drakk nodded. "Spoiled."

"You spoil 'er."

"I sher do." He rubbed Calliope's nose. "Your Uncle Axe loves you, baby."

Okay, I got the which-one's-which wrong. Sue me. They were like a shell game.

Axe reached up to Calliope's harness and loosened it a little. "There. It was too tight," he said.

That seemed to do the trick.

The first tug of the sleigh forward was a bit of a jolt and I grabbed onto the edge to keep from bumping into Arthur, who was entirely too close for comfort.

This time I did sneak a peek in his direction. He was steadfastly staring forward, so I only glimpsed his profile.

Which was, I had to admit, a very nice profile.

The early afternoon sunlight breaking through the clouds gleamed off his shiny black hair, which reminded me of the Halloween party. When he'd slicked it back with a heavy gel à la *Dr. No* (he had been very specific about his Bonds, down to the film), and, I could now admit to myself, it had made him look kinda . . . hot. Especially in the tux he'd worn.

And while his hair was now back to gel-free, a lock fell over his forehead in a way that gave him an almost-rakish air, and, oh Lord, what was happening to me?

This was *Arthur*, for God's sake. The boy who'd been pissy at me because I sat in his favorite chair at school, and felt compelled to try to answer every question in a way that made even the Barrington teachers (with the exception of Ms. Martinez, who seemed to find him amusing) grit their teeth.

And who was theoretically blackmailing me into helping him have a good holiday with his aunt.

I would likely never have to deal with him again once I told my parents I didn't want to go back to boarding school. It wasn't as if our worlds naturally crossed.

My grip on the side of the sleigh tightened.

Axe hopped back up into the sleigh beside his brother as we approached the winter-bare woods.

It was quiet and peaceful.

I started to relax. I noticed Dad and Aunt Esha were also relaxing. I saw Aunt Esha look out at the woodsy surroundings with a gentle smile, which pleased me. Maybe this would tip the balance of her holiday to Christmas into positive territory.

Then Axe stood up and turned to face us, holding a black metal box high above his head: the Snow Doodad.

I found out later its official name was a handheld, portable SnowMAX-Q112 Snow Machine, which, when activated, rivaled a leaf blower in terms of decibels.

To counter the less-than-jolly audio ambience, Drakk tapped a button on his phone, which was when we learned the sleigh came equipped with customized inlaid speakers, one of which was right next to my left ear.

The first notes of "Sleigh Ride" as sung by Johnny Mathis blasted out like a cannonball.

I screamed and jumped, my shoulder slamming into Arthur's, startling him as much as the music shockwave that hit him from the right.

We collided in the middle, the six inches of separation suddenly gone.

"Sorry," I said, though since I hadn't shouted it, he probably had to read my lips over the noise.

He nodded and we did our best to scoot back to our respective sides.

But that now-familiar woodsy amber scent lingered on the right side of my coat and, full disclosure, I wasn't exactly unhappy about it.

Fortunately, distraction found me by way of "snow" shooting from the doodad into the air above us.

Initially, it was pretty.

The white dots arcing high and swirling through the wind really did convey the feeling of being in a snow globe or winter wonderland.

Then they landed, on me, on Arthur, on Dad and Aunt Esha,

and it soon became clear this wasn't snow, this was foam. And the chemicals used to create its effects sting like hell when they land in your naked eyeball. Guess how I know that.

Blinking rapidly, I rubbed my right eye, which made the situation worse. And smeared my mascara.

"Are you all right?" Arthur asked, leaning over close enough that I could hear him as we bounced and jostled along the tree-lined pathway.

I peeked up with my still-open left eye, and somewhere in the back of my mind it occurred to me I probably looked like a pirate.

"Yeah," I muttered, because, really, I was. This was hardly a grievous injury. Merely an irritation. But, damn, it *irritated*.

Arthur unzipped his jacket to reach inside to an interior pocket and withdrew a packet of tissues, which he offered to me.

"Here."

I hesitated then took a sheet.

"Thanks," I told him, then noticed the tissue bore a reindeer pattern. Of course.

It was difficult to imagine Brody carrying a packet of tissues. About the only thing Brody always had at the ready was one of those tiny dispensers of Listerine Cool Mint strips so his breath was fresh in case a spontaneous make-out session opportunity presented itself. Which, with Brody, it often had. Not that I ever complained. He was a good kisser.

The memory of Brody and his handsome face swam into my brain and for a moment I felt a pang of missing him, the way he felt when he held me, the cool spice of his aftershave. Then the image of Brody the last time I saw him, making out with Mia, appeared and the pang of longing vanished.

I wiped my eye until the irritation had diminished and smiled my thanks to Arthur.

He nodded but said nothing, and for a moment, things seemed almost normal.

Until Calliope started honking, which was a sound reindeer made. Along with huffing and grunting. And she started making these noises in rapid succession.

I doubt I would have been concerned—what did I know about reindeer noises?—if I hadn't caught a glimpse of the look between the Moses twins, who seemed a wee bit perplexed.

Things escalated quickly from there.

Being in the third row, with Dad, Aunt Esha, and the twins between me and the reindeer, I didn't exactly have the best vantage point for what sparked what would later become known as the Reindeer Romp, but for reasons known only to Calliope, she started giving attitude to Erato—slamming antlers against hers, hockey-checking her side—who, in turn, wasn't having any of it and gave as good as she got.

And in the blink of a non-irritated eye, they started running.

I don't know if they thought they could escape each other, but the end result was the sleigh suddenly took off flying!

Okay, we never actually *flew*—they weren't those kinds of reindeer—but Calliope and Erato ran like they thought they could.

Everyone in the sleigh was slammed around in varying degrees of "oooomph!" and "aaaaah!" and "shit!"

Sidebar, did you know reindeer can run between thirty-five and fifty miles an hour? It's a fact I learned the hard way. Super fun.

Drakk regained his composure first and pulled hard on the

reins, shouting "Whoa!" in a voice so booming birds in the surrounding trees flew off in a loud fluttering of wings.

The reindeer ignored him.

Our sleigh bumped and jostled and hit ruts in the mud-dried ground that sent us momentarily airborne before we landed with force.

Everything felt rattled and discombobulated and terrifying.

And that was *before* Calliope's newly loosened harness ripped away and she went running off into the woods.

Drakk and Axe exchanged wide-eyed looks before Drakk yelled, "Get 'er!" and shoved his massive hand against Axe's shoulder, propelling his brother off the seat and onto the ground.

Arthur and I turned in unison to look out the back of the sleigh.

Axe bounced up like a basketball and didn't miss a beat before he started running into the trees after Calliope.

Arthur and I turned until our eyes locked, his as wide as I knew mine must have been, both in borderline shock.

Did that just happen??

Then neither of us moved, even as the sleigh started to slow to a more manageable speed.

For several beats we stayed staring at each other and I saw light brown flecks in his dark brown eyes. He truly had amazing eyelashes, even better than Brody's. And then the realization dawned on me that we were close. *Really* close. My breath caught. My heart slammed. I lost complete track of where we were.

He swallowed before his gaze dropped down and it was at that moment I realized we were holding hands. Tightly. Who grabbed whom, I couldn't say, but somewhere along the bumpy ride, it happened. And it felt entirely natural and wonderful and I never wanted to let go.

Which was why I had to let go.

I released his hand and turned to face forward, my mind spinning, feeling out of sorts in a way that had nothing to do with the roller-coaster sleigh ride and everything with the impression of his warm grasp that I experienced like a phantom limb.

Until my gaze landed on something else, something that carried the opposite of the almost-euphoric strumming I felt going through my veins, something that made me instead go cold.

Dad was holding hands with Aunt Esha.

Ten

My head was throbbing.

This was all my fault. If I hadn't applied to a prestigious boarding school as a way to get into an excellent university and create a better life filled with travel to foreign countries, nice clothes, and the peace that comes with financial security then I wouldn't have changed the Christmas website that lured Aunt Esha (and Arthur) here so she could meet my dad, go on a sleigh ride that rivaled something from Mr. Toad's Wild Ride, and wind up holding Dad's hand. Albeit briefly.

They had let go of each other with a nervous laugh about two seconds after I saw them.

But it was long enough. There had been hand-holding and it wasn't between my parents.

My stomach was in knots.

The rest of the sleigh ride passed without further incident, and Axe and an unrepentant Calliope reached the reindeer barn about the same time we did.

I also noted the breathless, laughing way Dad and Aunt Esha tag-team told Grandma Jo and Dr. Raymond what had happened.

"The whole experience was one I shan't forget!" Aunt Esha concluded, practically beaming.

My grandmother seemed almost envious, despite the fact we could've all been killed.

I suppose I should have been pleased that Arthur's aunt had found our near-death experience almost fun. That was, after all, the objective, making sure she (and Arthur) had a good time here in Christmas. But I couldn't get the hand-holding out of my mind, hers with my dad, or mine with Arthur, who, for his part, had been as quiet as I was for the remainder of the outing at Sedgewicks'.

The Moses twins were deeply apologetic about the whole out-of-control-sleigh-ride thing, and when we left, each of us carried a gift bag filled with free reindeer-themed paraphernalia, including some of the smoked cheese, and a coupon for half-off on the next visit.

As we walked to the Jeep in the parking lot, Dad put his arm around my shoulders.

"You okay there, punkin?" he asked. "You're kind of quiet."

"I'm fine," I answered. Then with a glance over my shoulder where Aunt Esha and Grandma Jo were chatting a few feet behind us, I added, "Wish Mom could've been here, though."

Dad's expression barely altered, but I knew him well enough. Hearing mention of Mom wasn't easy.

He nodded once then hit the key fob and moved to get in the driver's seat.

Aunt Esha caught Arthur's attention. "I think I shall ride back with Jo and Dean," she said. "Is that all right, Arthur?"

Arthur nodded. He carried his third gift bag of reindeer stuff (I wonder if he regretted his earlier shopping spree).

I moved to sit in the back seat, knowing that would force

him up front, beside Dad. I needed the time of the drive back
to the inn to regroup. A lot of things were swirling through my
mind, and with a couple of text-notification buzzes from my
phone, I could add one more: a message from Brody.

> hey . . . mias real upset what did yall say 2
> each other?? and why arent you txtng me
> bk?

Staring at his words reminded me how much the punctua-
tion—or lack thereof—in his texts used to bug the crap out of
me. It was one of the things he and I used to bicker over, even
though I knew it was a sore topic for him, given his dyslexia.
I should've been more forgiving. But I wasn't in a forgiving
mood.

I clicked my phone screen off and tossed it on the empty
seat beside me, staring out the window for the remainder of
the drive back to the Hoyden, succeeding in blocking out the
sound of Dad and Arthur discussing books and authors and
whatever else.

They kept it up even after we parked, so I grabbed my own
gift bag, and headed into the inn.

Ayisha was still at the front desk. I frowned at her.

"Aren't you supposed to be gone?" I asked, more harshly
than I'd intended. It earned me a steely-eyed look in return.

"Yes," was all she said back to me and I knew she would
volunteer nothing else.

Grandma Jo entered behind me and was equally surprised to
see Ayisha. But she skipped over curiosity and landed straight
on, "Val didn't show?"

Ayisha shook her head. "Car problems."

Grandma Jo held her tongue. "Thank you for staying, Ayisha. What are the chances I can keep you until five?" She sounded hopeful.

"I already called my mom to tell her I'd be staying longer."

Grandma Jo relaxed. "Thank you," she said with a sigh of relief. "I really appreciate it."

This meant I was going to have a slight overlap with Ayisha since my shift at the inn started at five.

Right then Dad walked into the lobby while chatting with Arthur and Aunt Esha, Dr. Raymond having been ditched at some point.

And I needed to get out of there.

I didn't bother to look in Arthur's direction despite the fact I could feel him watching me head upstairs. I went to my tiny room that wasn't really my room, flopped across the twin bed, and stared up at the ceiling.

At some point, my phone rang, and surprisingly I didn't jump like I had with the Johnny Mathis "Sleigh Ride" blast. I recognized the ringtone at once—the Wicked Witch of the West from *The Wizard of Oz*—which meant my mother was calling. And before you get mad at me at the tune association, Mom was the one who picked it out because *she* thought it was funny.

I answered, but kept staring up at the ceiling tile.

"Hi."

"Finley!" She sounded relieved.

"Hi, Mom."

"I'm so glad to hear your voice. And not on voicemail."

I was having an unexpected emotional reaction to hearing her voice, too, but I kept that to myself.

"What's going on, Mom?" I asked with uncharacteristic

directness. But I could feel my emotions roiling in a way I wasn't used to and I couldn't keep them inside.

"Oh, honey . . ." Her voice was laden with overlapping emotions; I detected hesitation, sadness, maybe some regret, though I may have been wanting to hear that.

I sat up on the bed and pulled my knees to my chest. "Never mind, I don't want to know . . ."

"Finley—"

"No, wait. I *do* want to know. I thought you were going to be here when I got back from Barrington," I said.

"I didn't know you were coming home."

"I didn't know *you* were leaving it."

I could tell that landed. Not that this was a fight, despite the part of me wanting to make it one.

"Sweetie, it's . . . it's complicated."

That word again. I hated it. "Yeah, Dad kinda said the same thing."

"What did he say?"

"Not a lot."

Mom's sigh echoed in my ear and I pictured her rubbing the base of her palm against her forehead like she did when she was spent.

"Listen, Finley. Honey. If I'd known you were coming home for Christmas, I absolutely would have been there to be with you."

"But not Dad. You'd have been here to be with *me*, for me, but not for Dad. Right?" There was a long pause before she sighed a second time and my irritation bubbled inside of me. "How long have you been planning to leave?"

"What—?"

"Is that why you pushed me to go to Barrington? So you could leave as soon as I was gone?"

"No! Finley, I want you to go there so you can learn and grow and have opportunities."

I couldn't help myself, I laughed at her vision, but I wasn't amused.

"Finley? What is it?"

"It's nothing," I said. Maybe now was a good opportunity to spill my guts to my mom about staying here instead of returning, though deep down it didn't feel right. Not when *she* wasn't here and everything felt out of sorts.

"Finley, I don't want you to think any of this is about you, okay? This is between me and your father."

"Does that mean—"

"Does that mean what?"

Before I could stop myself, I asked, "—you're not dating someone else?"

I hadn't been aware this was a concern on any level until the question was already out in the open. But as soon as I heard it, I realized how much it was a fear of mine. I held my breath, my stomach twisted in dread. But Mom's response was quick.

"No, not at all. Neither your dad nor I are seeing anyone."

"How would you know? You're not here. He could be the next contestant on *The Bachelor* for all you'd know."

An uncertainty crept into her tone. "What are you saying?"

"Nothing." I plucked at the handmade quilt that lay folded across the foot of the bed.

"Then why did you . . . ?" There was a long pause. "Is Skip—is he . . . seeing someone?"

For a moment I thought about telling her that he was, if only to gauge her reaction, but that would have been wrong, especially since I wasn't certain it was true. One hand-hold does not a relationship make. If it did then Arthur and I would be in one, and we definitely weren't.

"I don't know, Mom. But he has all his hair and that puts him ahead of most of my friends' dads in the looks department, that's all I'm saying, so I wouldn't be surprised if she does like him maybe a little."

"She?" Her voice went up an octave. "Who's *she*?"

I bit my lip. That "she" had slipped out, I swear, but it was too late now.

Sensing I was walking on eggshells, I hesitantly answered, "Arthur's aunt."

"Who's Arthur?"

"A boy from my school, from Barrington. He and his aunt are here in Christmas and they're staying at the inn and we all went on a reindeer sleigh ride today—"

"Reindeer??" She seemed both dumbfounded and upset.

"Yeah, over at Sedgewicks' Ranch. They have reindeer now and we all went together—"

"Who's 'we'?"

"Me and Dad and Arthur and his aunt—her name's Esha and she's older than you and Dad but not as old as Grandma Jo, who also went to the farm, but she and Dr. Raymond didn't go on the sleigh ride since there wasn't enough room. Anyhow, the reindeer went nuts and we got taken on this crazy ride in the sleigh and everyone's okay, but, you know, it was scary, and I . . ." I swallowed and felt unexpected tears prickle at the back of my eyes. "I really wish you'd been there." I wiped my cheeks where tears had spilled over. "Not to be scared or anything, but . . ." I shrugged even though it wasn't a video call. "Just because . . ."

It took her a long moment before she replied.

"I wish I'd been there, too." Her voice was thick and it took every ounce of self-restraint not to blurt out something about any of the hand-holding, Dad and Aunt Esha's, or mine with Arthur, but another part of me understood it would've been manipulative, even if all I really wanted was her reassurance that everything was going to be all right, no matter what happened.

"I miss you, Mom," I said, my voice quiet and heavy, too, because that wasn't manipulation, it was what was in my heart.

"Oh, Finley. I miss you, too. So very, very much."

Eleven

I made it down to start my shift at the front desk with thirty seconds to spare.

I still got the stink eye from Ayisha, who looked from me as I descended the stairs to the grandfather clock in another part of the lobby.

It'd been my intention to get there earlier, but after I hung up with Mom, I found myself crying into the pillow like a pathetic cliché. It had only lasted a few minutes, but my face was still a puffy, red mess.

I'd spent a half hour with a cold washrag over my eyes, trying to remove all traces of my emotional outburst. The look Ayisha gave me told me I hadn't succeeded.

She almost made it to a minute before she asked, "You . . . okay?"

Her frown told me she didn't so much want to ask that as couldn't stop herself.

I must've looked amazing.

"I'm fine," I muttered, followed by a sniff that was my body basically calling me a liar.

"Uh-huh."

Her obvious disbelief irked me and I snapped, "I am! I'm *fine*." Like a crazy person.

She rolled her eyes. "Whatever." Then turned away from me and took her phone out of her purse, which was on a shelf behind the desk. As she typed out a quick text message to someone, I was hit by a wave of remorse. She hadn't done anything to deserve me acting out like a bitch. Besides, she wasn't who I was mad at, not really.

"I'm sorry," I said quietly.

She turned back to face me and her irritation was plain. "Which is it? Are you fine or are you sorry?"

I took in and breathed out a deep breath. "I'm sorry. Not fine."

She stared at me without blinking and for a moment I forgot she was only a year older than me because it sure felt like I was being sized up by an adult and found lacking. Her putting a hand on one hip and cocking her head only emphasized that impression. But when she finally spoke, her tone was more knowing.

"This about Brody and Mia, or your folks?"

A weight came over my heart and I was grateful there weren't any guests around. "It's just everything," I answered, crossing my arms over my chest. Then I realized, "You know about my parents?"

She raised a single brow. "Your dad's been living here for the past few weeks."

Oh. Right.

I dropped my head and it took everything I had not to start crying again. "I didn't know." My voice was rough. "Not until I got back. About them. Or Brody and Mia."

She was silent for a long moment before she said, "Well, that sucks."

I looked up and saw her watching me closely, but not, thankfully, with pity. And I felt the tiniest bit lighter. Especially when she handed me a tissue from one of the boxes we kept out of sight below the desk. More people handing me tissues.

"It sucks ass," I agreed, and that made Ayisha snort. I wiped my nose and scowled. "What?"

She shrugged a single shoulder. "I don't think I've ever heard you say that before."

"Sucks ass?"

"Yeah."

I grabbed another tissue. "I'm not a prude, you know," I said defiantly.

She shot me a look and, oh, who was I kidding? I was. Sure, not as uptight as some of my Christmas classmates. Kimmy Bunting, for example—whose Evangelical parents kept watch over her and her younger sister, Kayla, like they were the CIA and the girls were a potential terrorist cell—was infamous for telling teachers whenever she heard anyone say "a four-letter word." Which endeared her to no one. I wasn't like that.

Though, since I spent almost all of my spare time studying or accruing extracurricular activities that looked impressive on a future college application and played chess with my insurance-agent father, I shouldn't have been surprised this was how Ayisha, the World's Coolest Person, viewed me.

And to my surprise, I found I didn't like the idea of her seeing me like that.

"You think I'm a prude?" I asked, not able to hide the wounded tremor in my voice.

"You wanna know what I think of you?"

"Yeah," I responded with more conviction than I felt, because there was no way this was going to go well for me.

Her eyes narrowed, then I could almost read an "all right, you asked" in her expression. "I think you're snooty."

I blinked, surprised. "Snooty?"

"That's what I said. Snooty."

Well, that was ridiculous. I was a lot of things but I knew for certain that, "I'm not snooty."

"You asked my opinion and I gave it to you."

"Yeah, but . . . *snooty*?" Maybe she and Arthur were suited for each other, because "snooty" sounded like his kind of word choice.

"Mmmm-hmmm. In that always-had-it-easy kinda way."

The phone at the front desk rang and Ayisha answered it before I could challenge that offensively wrong assessment.

"Hoyden Inn, front desk, this is Ayisha, how may I help you"—she glanced at the readout on the computer where the name of the guest presently checked in was kept next to their room number (105)—"Mrs. Yablonski?"

I had to wait about ninety seconds until the call was completed (yes, we could make sure Mrs. Yablonski and her husband had apple-walnut pancakes for breakfast, and no, there would be no extra charge, happy to help) and she hung up before I could continue.

"You think I'm spoiled?" I demanded the moment the receiver hit the cradle.

"It's not a bad thing."

"It's a *terrible* thing," I countered hotly.

"It means your folks and your grandma care enough to make sure you're protected from the shitty side of things, and that's good. But it also means when shitty things happen, you're not ready. And things always get shitty."

I absorbed her words, acknowledging the threads of truth

that maybe, possibly, were woven throughout. I gripped the back of my neck, sighed heavily, and confessed, "I feel like *everything* got shitty while I was away."

Ayisha raised both hands and affected a lighter tone. "Think of it this way: two more weeks, and you'll be back at Hogwarts and you don't have to think about the shitty everything that's here." Something in my expression must have tipped her off because she looked closer at me. "What?"

If you had told me as early as this morning that Ayisha Lewis would be the first person I told about Barrington, I would have scoffed.

But that was before I'd gone through Arthur, the Reindeer Romp, my dad holding hands with someone other than my mom, and talking with my mom.

The next thing I knew the words were tumbling out: "I don't know if I want to go back to Barrington next term, I think I want to stay in Christmas because I suck at school and have no friends and I don't belong there. I don't belong anywhere . . ."

She stared at me unmoving for ten seconds then shook her head dramatically, a single hand up in a "stop" gesture. "I'm sorry?" Then she pinned me down with her raw incredulity. "Back up. You want to *leave* Barrington? The super-prestigious boarding school you spent all of last year telling everyone that you were soooo excited to get into? It made me wanna punch you!"

She wasn't wrong, I had been pretty locked on about going to Barrington, to the extent I even annoyed myself, so the turnaround from her perspective must seem abrupt.

And I didn't quite know what to say next, it was all so pathetic. I was pathetic.

I rubbed my face with one hand and all I wanted to do was

go back up to my temporary room, crawl under my temporary covers, and fall into a deep sleep that lasted for at least a week. Maybe longer. Maybe forever.

But on the flip side, I felt the powerful urge to unburden myself and tell someone what I was feeling, even if that person had called me snooty and confessed the desire to punch me all in the same conversation. But sometimes we don't choose our confessors.

I drew a breath and—

"Ayisha."

Ayisha and I both turned at the voice coming from the front door and here was Ms. Nicole Lewis, standing just inside the front doors of the lobby. She was not pleased.

"Mamma."

Ms. Lewis gave Ayisha a familiar look of mild annoyance that I had been on the receiving end of at least twice in our conversation over the past ten minutes. The physical resemblance in the Lewis family, which included Ayisha's two younger sisters, Billie and Linda, was strong, though Ms. Lewis always kept her hair ultra-short and natural. I'd never met Mr. Lewis—he was out of their lives by the time Ayisha and I were in the same grade and butting heads—but if you had told me Ayisha's mother had reproduced through cloning, I would have at least considered the possibility.

"You texted me you would be outside and I have been waiting," Ms. Lewis said.

She worked as the head of accounting at the state's second-largest propane distribution company but she always carried herself like the CEO.

Ayisha gathered her purse and emerald-green wool coat, folded neatly on the same shelf. "Sorry," she said.

I felt the need to speak up. "It's my fault, Ms. Lewis. Ayisha was, uh, helping me with some stuff." That was potentially accurate.

Ms. Lewis smiled at me. "Thank you, Finley. Nevertheless . . ." She fixed Ayisha with an expression that filled in the rest of her unspoken sentence and Ayisha quickly buttoned up the front of her coat.

"I'm coming, Mamma." She looked back at me, her voice dropping low. "We'll finish talking about this later."

And as I watched Ayisha join her mother and walk out the front door, I knew for certain that we would, whether I wanted to or not. And I honestly wasn't sure which way I was leaning.

The front desk officially closed at eleven p.m., and at eleven p.m. and fifteen seconds, the phone was forwarded to voicemail, the computer shut off, lobby lights dimmed low, front doors locked, and the sign that read WILL RETURN AT 7 A.M. was placed on the desk ledge for any stray guests who happened to wander by with questions.

By 11:03 p.m., I had taken my tired body into the kitchen and was in the process of nuking a cup of hot water in my new Blixen mug (because while I may have been discombobulated about Dad and Aunt Esha's hand shenanigans, I still had the presence of mind to make sure that particular mug was officially part of my Please Don't Sue or Write a Bad Review gift bag from Drakk and Axe).

Grandma Jo was one of the few people on the planet who

was indifferent to the glorious superpowers of coffee, though her love of all things tea more than made up for it.

I selected a linen bag of lemon-ginger to go with my newly heated water and headed for the library with no intention of reading anything, but at the same time not wanting to go to my tiny room just yet.

Naturally, Arthur was already there.

I made it three whole steps into the library before I realized he was tucked in the window seat, book in hand, beneath the red dragonfly glass Tiffany floor lamp Grandma Jo found on her trip to New Orleans three years ago.

He'd changed out of his Wranglers back into black pants, a heather-gray fisherman's sweater with a two-button collar that revealed a white T-shirt beneath, and ankle-high black men's slippers that looked cozy.

But he could have been sporting head-to-toe raggedy sweats for all I cared because I couldn't stop staring at the black, rectangular-framed glasses he wore and how they made him look nerdy hot. Which I had never before considered my type.

But, as it turned out, it *really* was.

Sensing my presence, he peered up and over the top of the frames and was surprised.

"Oh. Hello." He sat upright, feet flat on the floor, marking his place in the book with a bookmark before automatically reaching with the other for his glasses as if to remove them.

"No!" I said with more force than necessary.

His fingers froze on the frames and I tried to cover.

"I mean, I . . . I didn't know you wore glasses."

"Only at night, when I'm reading."

"They look nice."

"Thank you." He hesitated, uncertain and uncomfortable. "Though I . . . can't actually see you with them on."

"Oh."

He took them off, folded them closed, and set them on the ledge next to the bare window, which had an obscured view of the darkened courtyard.

A glance and I could tell at least two or three people were at a table beneath the red glow of a heat lamp, but the angle and shadows made it impossible for me to see their identities.

Not that they were my focus.

Arthur was.

I took a step closer, tucked a strand of my hair over one ear. I noticed him follow my movement before looking back at me, and a nervous energy shot through me that might as well have been a double shot of espresso.

"So, um . . . checking in," I said because I felt the need to say something and not stand there like a huge dork thinking about how cute he looked. "Are you and your aunt still interested in doing Christmasy stuff? I mean, considering how things went today."

A small smile quirked at the left corner of his mouth. "Considering how things went today, Auntie Esha is even more enthusiastic."

I took another step closer. "Seriously?"

"Quite."

"Huh." So much for me getting out of the agreement. Not that I wanted to. "She must really like Christmas."

"Very much." He scooted over to create more room on the window seat and I interpreted that as an invitation to sit down.

So I did.

And waited for him to continue while mentally steeling

myself to not stare at his mouth. Why had I never noticed his mouth before? Or that he had amazing lips?

I took a sip of tea.

"My maternal grandparents—also Auntie Esha's parents—were among the few Christians in Kolkata, in West Bengal. Well, 'few' by Indian terms. For them, the right to celebrate the holidays was not taken lightly."

"Christianity isn't illegal in India . . ."

"No, of course not. But it is definitely the minority, which was one of the reasons my grandparents immigrated to the UK when Mummy was a little girl. She has no memory of her time there, only growing up in England. And my auntie was born in London. Dadu was the one who loved Christmas the most but he passed when my auntie was ten years old. She said that her love for Christmas came from him, and to this day celebrating it makes her think of her father."

A pang of guilt hit me at the waves of negativity I'd been riding about his aunt all night long. I nudged the discussion elsewhere.

"What about your mom? Your parents? Do they like Christmas?"

He hesitated and I felt him struggling with what to say.

"They do . . ." He tapped his right index finger against the back of the book. "But mostly as a time in which they can go on holiday. The remainder of the year keeps them . . . quite busy. Mummy is a professor of astrophysics at Oxford while my father runs the family business." He glanced at me now out of the corner of his eye. "I suspect you have no idea what that might be."

"Something with trucks?" I made a face that showed he was right about my ignorance even though I recalled him mentioning it approximately a thousand times back at Barrington.

But I hadn't been interested then.

I was now.

"Moderately close," he said. "But also wildly incomplete. Watercress Industrial is one of the world's top four manufacturers of construction equipment. It was started by my grandpapa and his brother after the Second World War and took off about a decade later. Now there are plants on five continents."

He puffed up a bit with pride at the telling, and who could blame him?

When the Hoyden had won "Best Boutique Inn in Oklahoma—2016" from *OK Visitor Magazine*, I'd worn out my welcome in a few places telling everyone about it and making sure they saw the photo of Grandma Jo looking gorgeous that accompanied the article. Later I put the whole thing on the inn's official website's "about us" section.

It was a big deal.

Arthur's familial accomplishments were a much bigger deal.

"So basically what your family does is one of those things no one ever thinks about but everyone needs and uses and makes the person who makes it rich."

Arthur regarded me for a long moment, unable to contain his surprise. "Correct. In a vague, all-encompassing fashion."

"I get that a lot."

He arched a look of mild amusement at me once he realized I wasn't making fun of him, but attempting to joke with him, if anything at my own expense. He relaxed a tiny bit more as he continued.

"Anyhow, for my parents, the final fortnight of the year is less about celebrating a holiday than it is an annual opportunity to explore the far corners of the world."

I felt a tug of envy. Traveling to the far corners of America was something I had on my bucket list, but the idea of being free and able to see the whole world?

Yeah. It was beyond.

"That sounds cool," I said, keeping my envy tempered. "Your passport must be amazing."

"I don't go with them." His voice was devoid of emotion as he stared at the shadows past the halo of the lamplight over my shoulder. "Not anymore. Not since I turned seven. My parents sat me down then to explain that Father Christmas was a society-wide agreed-upon lie told to children and it was best if I learned that directly from them, in theory to foster mutual respect."

I blinked at him as I attempted to process what that must have been like.

And my envy evaporated.

"Holy shit, Arthur," I said softly. Inarticulate, yes, but it was the only thing I could think to say.

Suddenly parts of him were starting to make a lot more sense. It hurt my heart to think about Arthur going through something so callous from the two people most expected to protect him.

He continued on in the same flat tone that carried the faint undercurrent of grievance I was sure he'd considered hidden. "From that point on they saw no reason to make more of the occasion, apart from the necessary efforts to keep up appearances amongst their friends. Which typically means extravagant parties and the proper amount of décor. What it does not mean, however, is feeling obligated to bring me along on their various travels."

"Who did you stay with, then?"

But the second I asked the question, I knew. And he confirmed.

"Auntie Esha took me in every Christmas. At first, we spent the holidays at her flat in London where she would go absolutely mental decorating every square inch. Not unlike the lobby of your grandmother's inn." For a flash, I wondered if there were overly large nutcrackers there, too. "As I got older, however, we started venturing out to places that were especially Christmas-oriented. Dublin. Quebec. Vienna is a particular favorite. And though I'm obviously not a little boy anymore, we still spend it together. She usually plans out everything for the both of us. Except this year." He met my eyes with a piercing look. "When I did."

Well. Shit.

Twelve

DECEMBER 21

Today was going to be a good day. I was determined.

I woke up before seven despite having gone to bed later than usual. I'd lost sleep because my mind replayed every nuance and inflection from what had proven to be a very long yesterday.

But it was my interaction with Arthur that dominated my thoughts.

Every few minutes I circled back to the moment when we accidentally held hands in the sleigh and then later our conversation in the library when I finally understood why Arthur had basically gone full bonkers upon realizing Christmas the town *maaaybe* wasn't quite the idealized holiday experience he'd been counting on when he had convinced his beloved aunt to change their plans at the last moment.

From Leipzig to Oklahoma. Which was a big-ass change.

I was going to make up for it.

I was going to do everything in my power to create Christmas Christmas Magic for Arthur and Aunt Esha, whom I also succeeded in convincing myself was *not* flirting with my father and had only clutched his hand on the sleigh ride as a way of anchoring herself amid the chaos.

It made sense. And it made me feel better.

One of the first things I did when I opened my eyes was close them again and craft a mental vision board of how today was going to play out.

The most important thing was to keep it simple. I had a limited number of decent Christmas-related options to present to them that held the opportunity for a positive experience, including my grandmother's Christmas Eve party. I needed to space those suckers out.

Today would be two: baking Christmas cookies and then later going to the Christmas Parade. Super basic, but hard to mess up. I hoped.

And maybe later I could ask Ayisha if she knew about any non-grandmotherly parties taking place so I could fulfill Arthur's request to go to one while he was here. Not that my growing crush on him changed my reluctance to introduce him to my peers. He was still Arthur and, feelings or no feelings, that had the potential to be problematic. He'd probably try to wear an ascot.

After I showered, I spent longer than normal getting ready. My hair had chosen today to lean into the static electricity that came with winter and it was all I could do not to look like a Nikola Tesla experiment.

Once I got it under control, and did extra primping, I slipped into my favorite jeans and dark red sweater, since I wasn't working and it complemented my fair complexion.

Then I headed down to the kitchen, where I immediately got in the way of Mrs. Buzzard.

Mrs. Buzzard had worked in the kitchen of the Hoyden Inn

since its beginning and, as far as I'd been able to figure, was around the same age as Methuselah. And even though over the years her tiny frame had shrunk, making her now clock in under five feet, and she only had passable hearing in her right ear, that woman was terrifying. Because while Grandma Jo owned the inn, from five to ten a.m. every day (except Tuesday), the kitchen was Mrs. Buzzard's domain.

One entered at their own peril.

The two other cooks (Reggie and Lloyd, both women) who rotated in the afternoons and evenings weren't nearly as temperamental. They also weren't breakfast savants, which despite all of her drawbacks, Mrs. Buzzard unquestionably was. Her French toast should probably come with a warning from the FDA for potential addiction.

A few years ago, Grandma Jo had gently informed Mrs. Buzzard that if she *were* so inclined to retire, it would be understandable and there would be *no* concern about income because my grandmother was prepared to keep paying her in full.

Mrs. Buzzard had declined.

She cooked at the Hoyden Inn not because she needed the money—a life lived frugally had made certain of that—but because it got her out of the house and away from her retired husband of sixty-three years who drove her insane by being underfoot.

She didn't like underfoot.

That morning, I was underfoot.

"What are you doing?!" she yelled at me, more because of her poor hearing than actual anger. I think.

I'd snuck in while her back was turned as she minded the stove and had been standing in front of the open refrigerator long enough to trigger the soft beeping of the door alarm. And though Mrs. Buzzard could hear almost nothing (especially when a guest made a special request for their meal that she didn't agree with), apparently that sound got through.

"I'm taking stock—" I started.

"What?!"

I tried again, louder. "I said I'm taking stock of some supplies."

"Why?!"

"Because I'm going to be baking Christmas cookies later."

"You?!" She slammed the handle of the long wooden spoon against the side of the stainless-steel pot containing rosemary new potatoes, which I was sincerely grateful I wouldn't be cleaning later today. That would be Val Limekiller's job, if she managed to show up.

"Yes, ma'am."

"You don't cook!"

"It's baking," I pointed out.

"Baking is cooking!"

"It'll be simple baking."

"What?!"

"Simple baking!"

"You don't do that, neither!"

Grandma Jo entered, unfazed by the yelling. "Good morning, Finley. What brings you down so early?"

I noticed she was dressed in her best royal-blue sweater and dark wool slacks with shiny black boots. She'd even put on more makeup than usual, eyeliner and blush. She looked especially pretty and I wondered if it was *for* someone. Was she going to meet Dr. Raymond later?

I wasn't sure how I felt about that idea, not that it was any of my business.

But yeesh.

Mrs. Buzzard pointed the spoon in my direction. "She wants to bake!"

Grandma Jo couldn't contain her surprise. "Bake?" Then she couldn't contain her amusement. "You don't bake."

"That's what I said!" Mrs. Buzzard pointed at the refrigerator. "Close the door! It ain't summer an' we ain't coolin' off the whole place!"

With a sigh, I shut the refrigerator door then turned to Grandma Jo and held up a paper with the recipe I'd found earlier this morning after searching a hundred baking sites.

"I can follow a recipe," was my defense.

"Ha!" Mrs. Buzzard banged the wooden spoon again before stirring the contents.

Grandma Jo reached her hand out to me. "Let me see." I gave her the paper and she scanned the recipe. "This seems simple enough." Votes of confidence were clearly going to be hard to come by in this kitchen. Then she frowned. "The portions are too big, though."

"I thought Arthur and his aunt would like to make Christmas cookies, too." Even saying his name aloud gave me a warm, fuzzy feeling.

Grandma Jo looked up at me while Mrs. Buzzard banged the spoon twice. "Who are they?!"

"Guests," Grandma Jo clarified.

"They'll burn my pans! Novices always burn pans!"

"What time were you planning to have this cookie class?" Grandma Jo asked, ignoring Mrs. Buzzard with practiced grace.

I turned my body slightly away from Mrs. Buzzard and lowered my voice. "After she leaves."

"I heard that!"

I spun on the tiny woman in disbelief. "Seriously?"

Grandma Jo cleared her throat. "This is a fine idea, Finley." I returned my attention to my grandmother. "But we're missing a few items you'll need." She handed me back the recipe. "We're low on butter and nutmeg and out of icing bags. And maybe you could pick up some supplies for the Christmas Eve party."

"Oh, okay." But I frowned. This was where being newly sixteen without either a driver's license or learner's permit became problematic. I bit my lip. "I don't suppose you could run me over to CK?" That stood for Claus Kitchen, the local grocery store.

But my grandmother shook her head. "I have to finish writing my proposal for the zoning board—again." She rolled her eyes. "Then I have a meeting at ten with a couple who may book the inn for their wedding this June."

Well, that explained why she looked nice. I was relieved it wasn't because of Dr. Raymond, though it left me in something of a pickle.

I was about to see if Dad was around when Arthur strolled into the kitchen, hands tucked into the pockets of his Wranglers and sporting his newly purchased vomiting-reindeer sweater. My heart fluttered like a traitor.

He stopped and his gaze pinballed off the three of us.

"Oh. I'm terribly sorry. I heard Finley's voice—"

Mrs. Buzzard scowled at him. "Who are you?!"

"I'm . . . Arthur?" His dubious appraisal of Mrs. Buzzard practically screamed: *I've somehow made a terrible mistake.*

Mrs. Buzzard scowled at me. "Cookie boy?"

I started, "Ye—"

Mrs. Buzzard scowled back at Arthur. "Don't burn my pans!"

Arthur stared at her, baffled.

I intervened. "Hey, Arthur. Didn't you and your aunt get a rental car?" I'd recalled them reserving one of the inn's guest parking spots.

He kept his wary eyes on Mrs. Buzzard. "We did, yes."

"Are you super busy right now?"

"Not even slightly busy."

"Can you run me over to the grocery store?"

"Certainly."

Grandma Jo turned to Arthur. "Would you mind also swinging by the Gingerbread Café? Mitzi has some pies waiting for me to pick up."

"Of course," he said.

Grandma Jo smiled at him. "Thank you, Arthur."

He blushed and beamed at her. Most men did, regardless of age.

Before I got jealous of my fifty-three-year-old grandmother, I grabbed Arthur by the elbow and tugged him out of the kitchen.

We agreed that I would run up to grab my coat and he would locate his aunt to get the keys to their rental and let her know of our mission.

Five minutes later we met back in the inn's open-air parking lot.

I was standing at the edge since I wasn't sure which was his car when the lock-lights of a black GMC Hummer H2 blinked on and off. Then *I* blinked in astonishment because of all the cars I would have envisioned associated with Arthur, none were of the borderline-tank variety.

Before I could utter a word, Arthur explained, "It was the only car the airport rental company had left. To be clear, I'd reserved a Land Rover." He moved around to the passenger's door and, to my surprise, opened it. For me. I stared at him until he grew uncomfortable. "Has no one opened a car door for you before?" he said.

I had to think about that. Had Brody ever held the car door for me? I couldn't recall.

Arthur rolled his eyes and jerked his head for me to get in and that made me feel better. Snippy Arthur was in my comfort zone.

I climbed (and it was a climb) up into the passenger's seat—which was made of a bright red leather with some black trim, on the off chance it wasn't already aggressively macho enough—and he closed the door.

He sauntered around to the driver's side, where he, too, had a bit of a climb to get inside. This thing was made for giants like the Moses twins, not mere mortals.

Have you ever seen the interior of a Hummer H2? I'm sure, as conceived by the US military, the ginormous transport was the model of efficiency. But I was confident that driving down the streets of a small Oklahoma town to run errands was not what its creators had in mind.

It was absurd.

And the thought of Aunt Esha's face when she first saw it made me chuckle.

"What?" he asked, as he started the monster and eased it out of the parking lot.

"Take a right, then at the next stop sign turn left onto Angel

Avenue," I told him, pointing in the opposite direction of Boots Boulevard from yesterday. "And I was laughing at what your aunt's reaction must've been to seeing this thing." I indicated the car. "Did she freak?"

"Au contraire. She was the one who wouldn't allow me to trade down to a sedan."

My eyes bugged. "Get out!"

"Not whilst I'm driving," he murmured with the barest hint of joking. "Her point being that neither of us are particularly accustomed to driving on the wrong side of the road here in the States, so we might as well hedge our bets in terms of surviving a potential head-on collision by having the superior vehicle."

"Huh. She makes a good case. Grim, but good. Also, maybe don't share that story with Grandma Jo until you're about to leave."

"Ah, yes. Noted."

I pointed ahead. "Turn right here on Dasher Drive and then we'll turn left onto Jolly Lane and stay there for about half a mile."

"These names are absurd." But he turned right as instructed. "And, as it so happens, Auntie Esha has also always wanted to drive one of these."

"Really?"

"Truly."

"Well, she's full of surprises."

"Your father said the same thing."

My whole body tensed and my breath caught like some massive, celestial hand had grabbed me around the torso and squeezed.

"What—when?" I eked out.

"When I went to get the keys. He and Auntie are playing chess and it would seem she has already bested him in two matches. They were gearing up for a third go when I found them in the library."

Breathe in, breathe out. Breathe in, breathe out, I told myself. It didn't mean anything. Games of chess were the antithesis of sexy. They were cerebral. And long. And kind of boring, if you tended to lose often. Trust me on this. But even as I rattled off those indisputable facts, I knew I wasn't as successful in convincing my on-fire brain that there was no flirtation afoot as I had been last night.

A flurry of questions arose and swirled: Was Esha Chakrabarti single? Arthur had never mentioned her having a romantic partner. But had she ever been married? Divorced and was still pining? Considered becoming a nun? She lived in London, I knew that much, which made her hella geographically undesirable—a happy check in the "negative" column—though if someone truly wanted to date another person no amount of distance could stand in their way.

Suddenly I was reminded about Brody Tuck and our breakup conversation as we sat on the picnic tables in Partridge Park. He had made that very point after I had presented what I'd considered to be sound reasoning for why we couldn't continue to date while I was gone.

My head started to fog up like I was coming down with an emotional flu.

"Finley?"

Arthur sounded like he was speaking to me through water and I barely registered him, too caught up in the overwhelming sense that I had screwed everything up with my parents, even if logically I knew better—

"Finley," he said, louder, and this time I snapped out of my mental tailspin. Or at least slowed it down.

I blinked. "What?"

"What is our ultimate destination?"

Death, I wanted to say. But instead: "Claus Kitchen." Then I sighed.

"Bugger. We passed that blocks ago."

A glance around and I realized we were near the end of Jolly Lane, where it left the commercial zone.

Arthur tugged at the wheel because turning a Hummer around was not as deft as, say, a Honda. It required a lot of "turn left . . . turn left . . . turn left . . . turn right" for whole streets until we were headed back toward CK.

"Sorry," I muttered. "I started . . . daydreaming." Technically true.

He glanced at me. "Are you all right?"

"Yeah."

Another glance and I knew he didn't believe me. I was going to have to start thinking of some better answers when people asked me that question. Before Arthur could do exactly that, however, he was thankfully distracted.

"Is that . . . an elf?"

Following the direction of his gaze led to a scrawny man with wiry, unkempt hair sprouting out from under a red-and-green pointed cap, minus the white pom-pom that used to be on top. His pants were baggy red sweats, his coat a bright green with red sleeves, and his black shoes had curls at their tips. He slept, cheek against fist resting on the arm of a fold-out lawn chair on the corner of Santa's Workshop Mall, a red kettle that had no affiliation with the Salvation Army by his feet, with a sign that read HELP GET ME BACK TO THE NORTH

POLE propped up. Though everyone knew the only pole he'd ever seen was two counties over and used as support for dancers named Sugar and Saxxxon.

"That's Steve," I explained. "Christmas's resident homeless person."

"Which is an oxymoron."

I rolled my eyes, though that felt like Arthur's objective. "He *resides* in town, just nowhere specific."

"And he's the only homeless person?"

"We're not that big a town."

"Can't someone find a place for him?" He peered at Steve's retreating image through the driver's-side mirror.

"People have tried, but Steve likes to be outside. Says his spirit cannot be contained. Judge Roddy basically told him he wouldn't be arrested for vagrancy again if he would just dress in Christmas theme."

"Are you quite serious?"

"Yep. The judge said it was a way to have Steve contribute to society by contributing to the town's overall ambience. I'm not sure that's as effective as he envisioned."

"Well, it's a fascinating compromise, I'll give him that."

Arthur turned on the left signal and we carefully pulled into the CK parking lot, which was already packed despite it being still somewhat early in the morning. At the back, we found two empty spots beside each other and Arthur nearly broke a sweat to get the Hummer parked without taking out the cars on either side of us.

Claus Kitchen was like every small-town grocery store except there were painted images of a smiling Santa on one side of the forest-green CLAUS KITCHEN sign and a cheery Mrs. Claus on the other.

The moment we got inside I saw a transformation come over Arthur. He lit up, rubbing his hands together in excited anticipation. That boy sure liked to go shopping.

"Right. What is our objective?"

"We're getting some ingredients to make Christmas cookies since I thought you and your aunt would like that," I said.

It took all my effort but I pushed my growing animus for his possible-homewrecker aunt (who was nowhere near as pretty as my mother and growing less so by the second) out of my thoughts to focus on our goals.

"Brilliant! Auntie was inquiring about that possibility only this morning at breakfast."

Oh, was she? How nice. Whatever.

I scowled at my paper with the recipe.

"Is, ah, that woman going to be part of the experience?" His wariness had returned.

"Which woman?"

"The tiny, frightful one with the large wooden spoon."

"Mrs. Buzzard. And no. I figured it'd just be the three of us."

Though suddenly I wasn't so sure that was a good idea. I was going to have a marble rolling pin at my disposal and every reader of true crime knew that did not mix well with seething resentment.

A blissfully ignorant Arthur relaxed. "I'll let Auntie know of the plan so she doesn't accept another invitation." He took out his phone and shot off a text.

"Like, what other invitation would she get?" I asked, trying and failing not to sound belligerent. "She's supposed to be here with *you*."

"True, but she *is* an adult and she seems to get along well with your father and grandmother. They were all up quite late last night, chatting in the back courtyard."

So *that's* who was in the shadows under the heat lamp! Jesus, Mary, and Joseph, how much interaction had they already had? At least Grandma Jo had been there to chaperone. Though she seemed to like Esha, too.

Was it possible, given whatever was happening between my parents, Grandma Jo was pushing Arthur's aunt toward my father?

Before I was able to plummet too far into that particular rabbit hole, Arthur snapped his fingers twice in front of my eyes. "Earth to Finley."

"Yep, yep." I nodded like I hadn't zoned out into the land of poisonous imaginings. "We, um, need butter, nutmeg, and icing bags."

"Ice bags?"

"*Icing* bags."

"Isn't that what I said?"

"No. You said 'ice.' "

"What are those?"

"You don't know what icing bags are?"

"You act as if they are common knowledge."

"For making cookies, they are."

He crossed his arms. "Do I in any way, shape, or form strike you as the sort of person who has experience making cookies?"

I jabbed my index finger at his chest. "You're wearing a sweater with a reindeer vomiting Christmas tree ornaments in the middle of a town dedicated to that very same holiday, so maybe some, yeah."

His dark eyes narrowed. "Hmmm." Then he dropped his

arms. "You make a logical argument. But no. I've never before made cookies, Christmas or otherwise."

"Fine. Let's find some icing bags."

"And where would they be?"

A singsongy voice behind Arthur said, "Aisle three."

Arthur turned and we both saw another shopper—Mrs. Gowdy, who owned the local nail salon and, as her brightly lacquered talons indicated, was also her own best customer—smiling at us though she and her overflowing cart were clearly blocked by our presence in the aisle.

"Terribly sorry," Arthur said, stepping farther aside to give her free passage.

Mrs. Gowdy smiled and waved off his apology. "It's all right, honey. Y'all were havin' the cutest sweethearts' spat and I didn't wanna interrupt." She nodded at Arthur. "Love the sweater." Smiled sweetly at me. "Good to see ya, Finley. Hope your folks work things out. It'd be a real shame if they split up." Then she continued merrily on her way, the damage done before either Arthur or I could stammer out the requisite dating denials, though I managed to register the full implication of the town's awareness about my parents' marital woes.

We were left with awkward silence.

Arthur cleared his throat. "Aisle three?"

I nodded. And we headed in that direction.

Thirteen

Twenty-five minutes later, we were waiting for Mitzi to retrieve the pies Grandma Jo ordered for today's lunch and dinner meals from the back of the Gingerbread Café. Which looked exactly like a giant gingerbread house, inside and out. Of all the places in town to embrace the Christmas theme, the blatantly tacky really worked here, inching very close to endearing.

But what truly drew people were the baked goods. The owner, Mitzi, was our town's version of Ina Garten and the pre-diabetic Paula Deen. Grandma Jo had long ago wisely handed over the creation of the inn's dessert options to Mitzi.

I glanced at Arthur, who was waiting with his hands linked behind his back, investigating the trays of Mitzi-created cakes, cookies, and slices of pies lined up in the glass-covered display case, and I felt a squeeze in my heart. Even before he spied something in the case and his eyes brightened.

"Jammie Dodgers!" he exclaimed with a level of unbridled joy I'd never before seen from him.

But I didn't have a clue what he was talking about.

"What's a Jammie Dodger?" I asked, thinking this was a

perfectly reasonable question, but the look of stupefaction he directed at me made me reconsider.

"You've never had a Jammie Dodger?"

"Big 'nope' on that."

"They're only the world's greatest biscuit."

I'd watched enough British TV shows on Netflix to know he meant cookie. Sure enough, when he pointed into the display case and I saw a tray of round shortbread cookie sandwiches with a reddish substance I recognized was raspberry jam visible in the heart-shaped cutout in the center. Mitzi had labeled them—

"Christmas Jammies," I said, since that's how I always knew them. While I didn't know diddly about Jammie Dodgers, *these* cookies were freakin' delicious.

"A blatant appropriation of an English staple," he said. "But I don't give a stuff. I've not had them in months."

His longing was so acute it gave me insight as to what Young Arthur must have been like. Which was adorable.

I had the strongest urge to slip my arms through his and snuggle up next to him. But I pushed that urge right back down where it came from, thank you.

Instead, I glanced in the direction of the bell that chimed as the café's front door opened.

And that's when I saw them. Entering together. Laughing.

Or at least Mia was laughing. Brody seemed distracted as he stood behind her, holding the door to let her pass, and I felt a three-pronged stab of envy, resentment, and panic arc across the café's interior and land right in the center of my chest.

I ducked down behind the display case, out of view. That still left me with a partially obscured sightline as Mitzi guided them to the booth with the red table next to the front window.

Which had been *our* spot, once upon a time.

It felt like years ago but my last dinner date here with Brody had only been in late March, a week after my official acceptance letter to Barrington had arrived in the mail. I remember spending our whole meal trying to figure out how I should tell him, and when it was time to go home, wondering why I hadn't found a way to work it into the conversation.

His wavy hair was slightly longer than I remembered. I suppose it had been long when I caught him and Mia making out at the Sonic. But that hadn't exactly been a detail to register then. Unlike the way their dueling tongues were visible from a distance of twenty feet or the fact he was squeezing her right breast through her pale pink sweater like it was a hand-and-arm strengthener. That had definitely registered.

It didn't help that Mia had never looked prettier.

She had always vacillated between pretending not to care how she presented herself to the world (aka the brief goth phase in junior high that lasted only long enough for her to realize she didn't like piercings and black was not her best color) and caring more than anyone else I knew (which was every other time that *wasn't* the goth phase). Her naturally dark hair was cut in a long bob and the ends flared out from beneath the white beanie with two oversized white pom-poms that shimmied as she walked.

Mia had always been cute. I'd told her so a thousand times a day ever since we met on the playground in elementary school and decided to become best friends. Mainly because she needed to be told a thousand times a day. Security in self-image was an area in which she still needed a lot of work. Though being the emotional support person for Mia was no longer my job.

It was Brody's.

"Finley?" I looked up to see Arthur frowning down at me. "Whatever—?"

"Shhh!" I glared at him and put my index finger up to my lips.

His voice lowered the tiniest bit. "—are you doing?"

"Hiding. Obviously," I stage-whispered. "Keep your voice down and don't look like you're talking to me."

He did neither. "You know, of course, what the next logical question is."

"Because I don't want to be seen."

"Could you be a tad more specific?"

"By my ex-boyfriend and my best friend. Who just came in."

"Oh." He glanced around. "Both are here?"

"No, I was thinking they might stop by so I ducked down to test my reflexes. Of course they're here!"

He shot me another look. "You might want to keep *your* voice down," he murmured dryly.

The desire to get the hell out of there was very strong. The question was, how? Going back through the front door was now impossible, but that didn't leave a lot of options. Once again, Arthur read my mind, not, I suppose, that it was particularly difficult.

"Does that door at the end of the hallway lead outside?" he asked, tipping his head toward the short hallway outside the bathrooms a few feet across from where I was crouching and I felt a bloom of hope. I nodded. "How about I stay to retrieve the order while you sneak out that way like a wanted criminal?"

"Perfect!" I whispered.

He discreetly handed me the key fob and I got a tiny jolt as our fingers touched. He didn't seem to notice.

"I'll meet you in a few."

Then he moved slightly to his left to block the space between the display case and the main dining area, giving me cover like the perfect accomplice.

I mouthed a sincere "thank you" and his slight inclination was acknowledgment enough, and if you think my appreciation for all things Arthur grew tenfold with all of this, you're damn right it did.

But now was not the time for crushing.

I popped up the collar of my woolen coat, pulled my knit hat down low, and scurried across the space from the display to the hallway and out the emergency exit so fast I impressed myself. Not that I planned a future life of crime, but it was good to know I had a skill set I could fall back on should the need arise.

Ten minutes later, Arthur and a sizable carryout bag joined me in the warmth of the Hummer, where I was scrunched down below the window in the passenger seat.

I accepted the pies from him and peered into the bag.

"There are three boxes."

"Excellent observation." He started the engine and gave all of his attention to the task of slowly backing out of the parking spaces.

"Did you buy the Jammie Dodgers?"

"Naturally." He put the Hummer into drive. "Keep down. We're passing the front of the café . . . aaaand clear. Safety belt on, please."

I sat up, locking the seat belt into place, and sighed.

He kept his eyes forward, hands on the steering wheel at the ten-and-two position. "I grasp why you're disinclined to meet your ex-paramour," he said. "But not why you wish to avoid your best friend."

My head lolled back against the seat rest. "Because they're dating," I explained dully. "Each other."

"Oh." A long silence followed. "I see." Followed by a longer silence. "And I take it you were unaware of this until recently?"

"Yep." Then I realized, "We're going the wrong direction."

"We are not, actually." He seemed very confident on this point for a guy who had only been down Jolly Lane one other time in his life. But he was still focused on our earlier conversation. "When did you two break up?"

"Right before I left for Barrington."

"And *you* were the instigator, or was he?"

"I was. But that's not the point," I insisted.

"Isn't it?

"It isn't."

"Then what is the point?"

"Friends don't date your exes, and vice versa, without asking permission first, especially best friends. It's a universal code."

"Then why were *you* the one slinking out of the café? If *they* were in violation of this universal code, as you put it, they should be the ones to slink." He tapped the steering wheel with his right index finger and kept his focus forward. "Unless you still harbor feelings for . . ."

"Brody. Brody Tuck."

"Brody Tuck." He repeated it like it tasted bad. "Let me guess, he's exceptional at sports and all the girls throw themselves at his Neanderthal feet."

"Yes, yes, and he is, actually. Neanderthal. Three percent."

That seemed to surprise him. "You know this how?"

"His brother sent off one of those DNA kits and when it came back, Brody was excited to tell me the good news. He

149

said he thought that was why he recovered from injuries faster than the other guys, like he was Wolverine."

"Fascinating." His tone of voice indicated otherwise. "But back to my question: Do you still harbor feelings for Mr. Tuck?"

I shrugged and shifted the takeout bag on my lap, uncertain of the answer. "I mean, doesn't everyone always have some residual feelings for their first love?" I challenged, chancing a look at him in profile.

His expression was impossible to read.

"I wouldn't know. It hasn't yet happened for me."

"Never?" I asked, surprise laced in my voice.

He took longer than I expected before he said simply, "No."

And left it at that.

But I knew there had to be more. As I got to know Arthur, bit by bit, it was becoming apparent there were layers upon layers hidden behind his walls of rigid English propriety and snarkdom. I could feel them. And despite knowing perfectly well that I was playing with emotional fire for so many reasons, but chiefly since I wasn't planning to return to Barrington next term, which made the exercise of getting to know him in all his facets essentially pointless, I still wanted to find out what that "more" entailed.

So I pressed.

"What about a crush? You've had crushes, right?"

Then I held my breath, because what if he answered "Bronwyn Campbell"? What if that was the real reason she texted him? Or maybe it was some other horrible girl from Barrington? Or worse—if possible—what if he announced a secret girlfriend back in England whom he called every night? Or texted? Or both? And planned to marry one day because she was a member of the upper class like he was, and their families would find the situation mutually beneficial for the future of big truck manufacturing?

Her name was probably Poppy. Or Millicent.

When he nodded decisively and said, "I have," I bit my upper lip. But then he said, "Ms. Darby in Year Four." He flipped on the right turn signal and started to ease the Hummer over to the side. "What you Americans would call third grade. Or possibly fourth, I'm never quite sure." He parked the Hummer in an open spot parallel to the sidewalk outside the entrance to Santa's Workshop Mall and turned on the emergency blinkers. "She was plump. With rosy cheeks. A mass of ginger hair that could not be tamed. Truly a vision." He turned to me. "Alas, she failed to see my potential and instead married a wanker named Gerald and moved to Liverpool. My heart still bleeds."

With that, he reached into the carryout bag from the café and extracted what appeared to be two paper-wrapped sandwiches I'd failed to notice, along with a large bottle of water from the door pocket.

He reached over to the radio and turned it on.

Christmas music from one of the many pop stations filled the interior. He hit the preset buttons until he found a song by The Waitresses I recognized. It was one of my favorites.

"Back in a jiff," he said, and hopped out of the Hummer before I had the chance to ask him what he was doing.

From my passenger's seat, I watched him make a dash onto the sidewalk then over to Steve, the Willfully Homeless Elf, who roused himself from his lawn-chair slumber upon Arthur's smiling approach.

I sucked in a sharp breath as I realized what he was doing.

Oh, no. No, no, no . . . This was terrible. Terrible! But what could I do? Other than watch Arthur chat with Steve before offering him the two wrapped sandwiches and bottle of water, all of which Steve accepted with a smile, sitting up in his lawn chair and even straightening his elf coat as he and Arthur engaged in conversation of some nature, and this was unquestionably the worst thing Arthur could have done to me.

Because it was kind.

It was generous.

It was so very, *very* unexpected.

He didn't hand over the food then take a selfie with the funny-looking homeless guy and post it on social media as proof of his awesomeness or the hilarity of it all because (haha!) homeless people are funny. *Woot!*

No. He stayed and listened as Steve started talking (and talking and talking) and he occasionally got a few words in edgewise, at least enough to make Steve laugh until the older guy hacked up and spat out something wet, which was gross, then he recovered and smiled brightly back at Arthur, who miraculously didn't cringe.

For a second or two, I tried to imagine Brody doing something like this, but it didn't mesh. Not that Brody was a bad guy.

But he wasn't . . . Arthur. And what was I supposed to do with *that?*

I sighed to myself in heartfelt misery as Arthur waved to Steve, who was already halfway through the first sandwich, and started back toward the Hummer, with me tracking him every step of the way.

He opened the door and climbed back in, shutting it quickly and rubbing his chilled hands together.

"Right," was all he said, his focus on the process of turning the Hummer around on the narrow, two-lane street to go back in the direction of the inn.

Other than giving him instructions, I didn't utter a word the rest of the ride, but my heart was pounding the entire way.

What to do, what to do, what to do . . .

Fourteen

In the end, I made cookies. Or, at least, put forth my best effort with Arthur and Aunt Esha. Along the way I learned that having an ever-increasing crush on someone whom you cannot be with for a litany of reasons did not make that crush go away.

Quite the opposite.

I also learned I am not good at cooking, or baking, or really anything to do with a kitchen, though I suppose it just confirmed what I already knew.

We also burned the pans. Badly.

Yeah . . .

The three of us stared down at the smoldering disaster that was our first batch of what was supposed to have been a dozen funfetti cookies shaped like stars and Christmas trees that were supposed to be dipped in dark chocolate later and/or iced (the bags of icing at the ready). We also had another couple dozen pfeffernuesse, which were small, spicy Dutch cookies that seemed doable with the barest hint of exotic and thus a change of pace, but were really just me leaning a bit too far over my culinary skis.

It had started well enough.

Once Mrs. Buzzard was out the door, I knew I had the kitchen for the next two hours before Lloyd arrived to begin her dinner prep.

I sent up a text to Arthur that the coast was clear.

When he and his aunt arrived together in the kitchen, I showed them both the recipes I had in mind. My distrust of Aunt Esha was tamped down by her warm smile.

"Thank you so much for taking the time out of your holiday to help Arthur and me have a wonderful experience here in your town," she said, her dark brown eyes (which were shaped differently from her nephew's, wider and softer, but with the same color, right down to the flecks of gold) shimmering with warmth as she squeezed my upper shoulder. She had a deceptively strong grip for someone so slight of build.

And *ugh*. What was with these Chakrabartis and their poorly timed kindness? Didn't she know I was internally and irrationally angry at her? No? Because it was internal?

Details.

I smiled in response. "Sure thing."

Maybe I had some of Grandma Jo's political adroitness after all.

It also probably helped that I found out Dad had gone into work while Arthur and I were tootling around in the Hummer looking for groceries, which somehow made me feel the tiniest bit better.

Though, maybe he just didn't want Aunt Esha to keep beating him at chess.

I had the ingredients for the two different batches laid out on the island with printouts of the respective recipes, having added pfeffernuesse after the trip to CK because I wanted to liven things up.

I'd even managed to scrounge up three aprons, though it took some convincing and an oath that no photos of him in it would be taken before Arthur accepted his.

Aunt Esha took it all in. "What wonderful choices, Finley. Arthur, don't you think these will go well with some of the hot chocolate?"

He perked up. "That's brilliant, Mashi."

I started for the dry pantry. "I think we have some—"

"No!" They said it simultaneously, then she added, "Thank you."

"Auntie brought over our own," Arthur informed me.

"Charbonnel et Walker," she clarified further, as if I would recognize the brand.

"American hot chocolate is little more than chalky brown water," he said.

"Arthur is being tactless. But also accurate." She patted his arm. "I'll make a quick dash upstairs." And smiled at me. "Continue on!"

I flashed her a thumbs-up then cringed because, resentful or not, that was plain goofy on my part, but she was gone before I could moderate my dorkiness.

I turned to Arthur.

"Ready?" I asked.

He gave me a thumbs-up. I flipped him off. He smirked. And I shoved a steel bowl with butter, sugar, and vanilla extract into his midriff with more force than necessary. Crush or no crush, the "ooomph" was worth it.

"That goes with the mixer." I pointed to the aqua Kitchen-Aid mixer on the counter behind him.

He seemed puzzled. "Do you expect me to mix this?"

"Why else are you here? The commentary?"

"I assumed I'd be the taste tester."

"Gotta make something to taste first."

I pointed again and he seemed resigned to being more of an active participant than he'd originally envisioned. After watching him spend more time than I thought possible attempting to figure out the tilt mechanism and flat beater, he flipped the speed knob straight to ten, which, no. Just . . . no.

He caught on quickly, but a good amount of the vanilla hit his apron.

I added some more and he mixed much slower while I warmed some chocolate baking squares on the stove. The amount of concentration showing in his face reminded me of some of the tests we took back in school, and it occurred to me how little I knew of him. On a basic level. His love of James Bond and Jammie Dodgers aside.

"How long have you been at Barrington?" I asked.

He glanced at me. "What?"

"Barrington."

"Oh. Um, a year." He really was focused.

"Why'd you come to America?"

"The cheeseburgers. Americans have the upper hand when it comes to any meal cooked over an open flame."

"I'm serious."

"As am I." He grabbed a scraper spatula out of a utensil jar.

"Do you not want to talk about it?

"Cheeseburgers?"

"Now who's being evasive?"

He kicked up the mixer speed a notch, keeping his eyes on the mixing bowl.

"It's just," I continued, feeling dogged. "Most Americans think the British have the upper hand in education."

"Unquestionably."

"Then why did you come to America? You're rich, or your parents are. And you're annoyingly smart."

"I shall take that as an unintended compliment." He tentatively used the spatula to push some batter away from the sides.

"So I'm thinking you could go anywhere."

"I could have, yes."

"But you chose Barrington."

"I did." Finally he looked up to meet my eyes for a moment. "Barrington is, as you know, exceptional, even by English standards." Back to the bowl. "And Auntie Esha is friends with Sonya Martinez."

"Ms. Martinez?" I asked. "Who teaches Honors Biology?"

"Correct. She is also on the admissions board."

"Oh. That explains it."

Now he frowned at me. "Explains what?"

"Why she finds you amusing."

He raised a single eyebrow. "Amusing."

"Yeah. When you raise your hand at every single question like Hermione." I demonstrated.

He stood straighter, offended. "I am *not* Hermione."

"You totally are." His eyes narrowed and it was all I could do not to laugh because he looked cute when he was annoyed. "What? She's the smartest character in the whole school." He was not mollified. But neither was I. "And you didn't really answer the 'why' you came here."

"Didn't I?" Once again the dough proved engrossing.

"Nope."

"Hmmmm . . ."

I drew in a breath to press on.

Which was when Aunt Esha returned holding a white tin. "Drinking chocolate!" she said in triumph.

Arthur smiled. "Perfect."

And it was then I realized he had effectively filibustered me to avoid answering my question. Which only made me want to know the answer that much more.

Fifteen

Creating British hot chocolate was way more involved than opening a packet of instant cocoa and plopping it in a mug of hot water then adding a marshmallow or, you know, ten, which was my typical modus operandi.

I let Aunt Esha take charge since I was already starting to sweat the cookie dough for the funfetti shortbread with dark chocolate dip, which didn't look like I thought it should. Neither did the pfeffernuesse, one being too mushy and the other lumpy.

But I convinced myself the cookies were in the precooked larva stage, so it was okay.

We shoved four trays of both into the oven, which I then turned on only to realize I should have had it warming up the whole time, so I added about twenty-five degrees to make up for the oversight.

As we three waited in the empty adjacent dining room for the cookies, Aunt Esha handed Arthur and me our mugs of British hot chocolate, keeping one for herself.

Both watched me intently and I felt like a science experiment taking that first sip. The contrarian in me wanted to shrug and say "whatever, Brits." But as much as I hated to admit it, there truly was no comparison.

"That's . . ." I looked at them watching me in expectation. ". . . a lot better."

They smiled at the same time, which highlighted their resemblance. It wasn't always present. Arthur's skin tone was a lighter shade of brown from his auntie's, and though I didn't know what his father looked like, I had a feeling Arthur's jawline came from the Watercress side. But after learning last night the importance of Aunt Esha in his life, I could see the similarity in their mannerisms. Particularly around their eyes when they smiled.

We sat at a table in the dining room, which also had an unused fireplace.

Aunt Esha set her Hoyden Inn mug down on the table, her long, elegant fingers curved around its handle. "I shall send you a tin of Charbonnel et Walker in a care package." Her eyes danced in merriment. "Like I do for Arthur."

I smiled despite myself. "You send Arthur care packages?"

Ignoring Arthur's low hum of annoyance, Aunt Esha nodded. "There are some English things one cannot find in the States."

"Like what?" I pressed, forgetting for a moment that I was secretly mad at her.

"Mashi—" he pleaded.

She ignored him. "Jaffa Cakes. Murdock face scrub and pomade. Oh, and Shrimps & Bananas!"

The latter earned a double take. "Shrimps and bananas?"

Arthur groaned.

"It's a type of candy. I'll add some to your care package." She winked impishly.

I glanced at Arthur, who was deliberately not looking at either of us. "So Arthur likes candy, huh?"

"He does." She reached over to tweak his blushing cheek. "My nephew is very sweet."

Arthur leaned away from her with a deep scowl and I chuckled.

Then she refocused on me. "Have you ever been to England?" she asked.

I shook my head. "No, I've never even left the United States. I hope to, someday."

She eyed me in a way that made me feel like she was seeing everything about me. "I believe you will. Jo has told me some stories."

"She has?" My grandmother hated gossip, though I guess talking about your granddaughter didn't really count. And I was glad Aunt Esha had been talking to Grandma Jo and not my dad.

She nodded. "Indeed. She paints you as a very determined young woman." My heart swelled at that. Aunt Esha turned to her nephew. "Do you think that's accurate, Arthur?"

He weighed his words carefully. "That Finley will get to England? Yes, of course. Travel is considerably more accessible these days." His aunt stared at him without blinking until he shifted uncomfortably in his chair and glanced in my direction. "And, yes, Finley can be very determined."

"I can?" I asked in surprise.

"Can't you?" he challenged back.

"Well, yeah. I just didn't think you noticed."

He took a sip of his hot chocolate before murmuring, "I did."

I felt something in that, in his tone. A charge. But it was ephemeral and elusive and—

"There you are."

We turned toward the dining room's entrance to see Ayisha approaching. She carried a square white package covered in clear tape and a mailing label.

My disappointment at being interrupted before I could try to get Arthur to expand on whatever it was I may or may not have heard in his voice was forgotten when I saw she was looking directly at me.

"This arrived for you," Ayisha said, as she placed the box in my hands.

It was heavy and it took a second for me to remember who and what the sender, "Nutcase," was. But when it clicked, I smiled in excitement.

"The chestnuts!" I exclaimed.

I grabbed a knife from the table's place setting to cut open the tape and withdraw a plastic bag filled with honest-to-goodness shiny, raw, brown chestnuts. Whole and complete.

I took out one and held it up and it really did look like a hazelnut on steroids.

"For roasting on an open fire," I said.

Arthur examined it with interest. "And for conkers."

There was a moment of puzzled silence. Ayisha seemed as baffled as I was.

"What's a conkers?" I asked for the both of us.

"It's a game with chestnuts between two people," Aunt Esha said, clearing up nothing.

"And a bloody brilliant one at that," Arthur said. He held out his hand for the chestnut and I placed it in his palm. "You drill a hole through, from top to bottom." He tapped the chestnut. "Then you thread a string through, tie a knot here at the bottom and at the top, and take turns trying to hit the other person's conker."

"The first chestnut to break loses," Aunt Esha said.

"It's quite well known," he continued. "There are even championships."

Ayisha and I exchanged looks of incredulity.

"For breaking chestnuts?" Ayisha asked.

"On a string?" I continued.

He nodded. "It's fun."

Ayisha was skeptical. "Yeah, I'm gonna take your word on that."

But Arthur shook his head. "I know it's not selfies and social media, but it's far more engaging than one would imagine. I'll make a few conkers and show you both tonight."

"I'm gonna have to pass on that kind offer," Ayisha said. "My younger sisters are in the Christmas Parade tonight."

Aunt Esha slapped her hand on the tabletop in excitement. "That's right! The parade is tonight. I am so looking forward to it."

Ayisha regarded her with suspicion. "Have you *seen* what our Christmas Parade looks like?"

I felt a pang of dread as Aunt Esha nodded. "Indeed I have. There are several photographs on the Christmas website. I am particularly looking forward to the floats, they seem so terribly elaborate."

Oh, crap . . . I really needed to fix that thing.

Arthur deliberately cleared his throat and I did not look in his direction. Instead I decided to mitigate his aunt's expectations through the time-honored tradition of lying.

"Just so you know, I heard the parade's going to be, um, smaller this year." I held up my index and thumb close together.

"Oh?"

"Yeah. There won't be any synchronized dancing troupes.

Dr. Raymond's wife ran off with the local dance teacher and, uh, no one picked up the slack in his absence." At least there was a kernel of truth in there. "So that got eighty-sixed."

"How difficult for Dean," she murmured. "It explains a great deal . . ."

"Also," I cleared my throat. "The light parade part had to be canceled once folks started having seizures."

Arthur rolled his eyes.

Ayisha was confused. "Light par—?"

"Lawsuits galore," I said, cutting her off. "You know how lawyers are."

Aunt Esha's lips curved up at the corners in amusement. "I'm familiar."

Which was when I remembered she was one. Awesome. But I was already in the flow, so I kept going.

"I'm not real sure about the giant snowman balloon, either. Or the trained flock of Christmas goats dressed like elves." (Finding that photo in my internet search had induced a five-minute fit of laughter, so I had to include it on the site. Lotta regrets now.)

Ayisha cocked her head at me. "Are you smokin' something?"

Before I could manufacture the right degree of disingenuous indignation, the first acrid wave of actual smoke reached us.

We turned to the kitchen and my stomach dropped at the sight of an undulating dark gray wave of smoke coming through the doorway.

"Shit!"

I shot out of my chair and was the first one in the kitchen, which was already filling up with smoke.

As fast as possible, I turned off the oven and popped open the door, which was a mistake. A fresh and much larger billow of burned cookie dough rolled out and smacked me in the face.

I coughed and waved my hand. Then I hurriedly grabbed oven mitts and two of the trays. Behind me, Arthur did the same, followed by Ayisha, and soon we four were looking down at the smoldering remains with not a lot to say.

Except for Ayisha, who summed it up with: "Yikes."

Accurate.

Then she looked at the three of us. "Well, I gotta get back to the front. Good luck," she added, before zipping out of there so fast she probably didn't even get the stench of smoke on her clothes.

I, however, bore the stench of another Christmas failure.

I didn't want to look at Arthur, who couldn't have been pleased. No one burned cookies in idealized holiday scenarios. It was a rule. Just like there was always supposed to be snow, another area of failure.

"Might we be able to open the window a bit?" Aunt Esha asked, discreetly clearing her throat. "Lest the smoke alarm activates?"

An excellent and obvious idea. I did just that. The chilly late-morning air whooshed in as the smoke started to go out, but not fast enough.

Grandma Jo entered, her brows drawn into an alarmed frown as soon as she saw the blackened remains of the cookies. "What happened?"

I shrugged, helpless. Hopeless.

She took in the sight of the baking disaster in all its simultaneous charred and undercooked glory then noticed in dismay, "You . . . burned the pans." Her eyes were wide and her lips were thin. I legit gulped. "You're going to be the one to tell Mrs. Buzzard."

"Yes, ma'am."

I knew she was fighting down the urge to be perturbed in front of guests and I felt awash in embarrassment from every direction.

Which was when Aunt Esha stepped forward to hand Grandma Jo a cup of the hot chocolate.

"Here. Sip." Her manner did not allow for debate.

At first Grandma Jo seemed thrown by the overt and obvious distraction. But she accepted the cup because Oklahoma manners were her default.

At Aunt Esha's head bob, my grandmother took a tiny, tentative sip and I could tell it was only to be polite, particularly with guests. A second later, however, the taste seemed to reach the pleasure synapses in her brain as her hazel eyes widened.

"Oh, wow. What *is* that?"

"Not American hot chocolate," Aunt Esha said smugly.

It was like watching Amelia Bedelia save the day with her lemon meringue pie as any degree of annoyance at finding the Christmas cookie calamity in her kitchen was instantly forgotten. My grandmother's shoulders relaxed.

"This is amazing," Grandma Jo said after a second, considerably longer sip.

Aunt Esha's smile was entirely self-satisfied. "It is even better with a splash of bourbon."

Grandma Jo broke into a big grin. "I have a bottle of Blanton's."

Aunt Esha flat-out clapped her hands like she was three years old. "Perfection!"

Grandma Jo turned to me. "Finley, you'll clean this up?" It was absolutely not a question.

I nodded.

Arthur frowned. "Mashi? Are we not going to attempt a second batch?"

Aunt Esha shook her head. "Oh, I think one will suffice," she said dryly. "And you have your Jammie Dodgers. They're more than enough, aren't they?"

"I suppose so—"

"Wonderful!"

Before the two older ladies left, I felt compelled to remind them, "Don't forget the parade starts in a few hours."

But my words were directed at their giggling, retreating figures and I wasn't convinced they heard me.

I looked back to Arthur, who turned his attention to the charred cookies.

"Shall we toss it all, then?" he asked

It was a relief he seemed to be taking it well.

I nodded and that's what we did, including the pans, spending the next fifteen minutes cleaning up the mess with hardly any communication between us. I was convinced he was mad at me.

And why wouldn't he be? I was messing up his Christmas plans, the first of his own design. If I had set about to ruin his holiday with his aunt, I don't think I could have done a better job, which was profoundly disheartening. It was bad enough that my own holiday was a colossal fuck-up, I didn't need to keep ruining his along the way.

When we were done, the last remnants of the misadventure placed in the dishwasher and the countertops wiped clean, I leaned back against the center island and dried my hands with a dishcloth and stared into space at nothing in particular, fighting the overwhelming sense of failure after failure after failure that went far beyond burned baked goods.

I had no idea how long I stayed like that, but it must have been longer than I realized because I didn't hear Arthur leave the kitchen or notice he was gone until he returned.

And broke my thousand-yard stare with a Jammie Dodger.

"Here," was all he said, as he offered it up to me.

I blinked. Blinked again. Frowned.

Then looked up to meet his dark brown eyes, which were still difficult to fully read, but enough concern eked through that I dropped the washcloth, covered my face with my hands, and burst into mortifying tears. Which I was sure wasn't the reaction he was going for.

I ugly-cried like an absolute idiot for several moments, not fully sure why but also unable to stop myself. Also unable to run away to someplace dark and distant where I would be considerably less exposed.

I sensed Arthur lean up against the center island beside me, at a proper distance so as not to be invasive but not so far away as to seem like I was being shunned, which, somewhere deep in my lizard brain, I appreciated, especially because I wasn't a crier. Or at least I hadn't been before the last several weeks got hold of me. And I couldn't even blame this on my period, which had happened two weeks ago.

This was all awkward me.

When my tears began to wane, I felt something lightly pressed against my right hand, and when I instinctively took it, I realized it was a handkerchief this time. A real one. Black cotton with white piping and the scrolled white letters ACW embroidered in the corner. It was almost enough to make me start crying again, but I managed to hold the second emotional wave at bay.

"Thanks." My voice was scratchy and I sniffed a wet,

snobbly sniff that bore no dignity, but I was too tired to care as I wiped my puffy, tear-stained face.

When I stared down at the handkerchief, uncertain what to do with it because this was the first time in my life I'd ever used one, Arthur murmured, "Keep it. I have more."

One final dab and a sniff, then I folded it neatly and pressed it between my palms. Then with a deep breath I gathered my courage to glance over at him.

He half faced me, his left hip and side against the island, with his elbow resting on its top, fingers laced casually together as he watched me without any trace of pity or disdain, just observation.

"I imagine that wasn't merely about the cookies," he said, his voice quieter and softer than I'd heard before.

I swallowed and shook my head. "But I don't know if I'm ready to talk about . . ." I sighed, a headache threatening. ". . . everything right now."

He immediately started to straighten. "Of course—"

My hand instinctively shot out to take hold of his forearm to stay his retreat. "Not that I don't want to talk about stuff with *you*," I said quickly. "Just, just not right now." Our eyes connected and I could feel him slowly relax. "Okay?"

He nodded. "Whatever you wish." Then his glance dropped to where I was practically clutching his arm and I let go at once, a hot wave of embarrassment coming over me.

"So, um . . ." I tucked a strand of my hair over my ear and shifted on my feet, experiencing a pang of anxiety that had nothing to do with my earlier outburst, or, at least, not directly. "Do you still want to go to the parade later?" As soon as the words came out I realized they sounded like I was asking him out, so I hurriedly added, "You know, *all* of us. Me, you, your aunt, and my grandma, too. If they're not—"

"Blotto?"

"—tipsy?"

We said at the same time and then both broke out laughing in a way that felt like fifty pounds sloughed off my back and evaporated into the ether.

After a few moments, he smiled and brought back that cheek dimple that *did* things for me.

"I think," he began, standing straighter, but this time without his usual awkwardness, "Christmas wouldn't be Christmas without a visit to a Christmas parade. Particularly in a town called Christmas."

I felt like I needed to clarify: "You know it's not going to look like the website, right?"

He chuckled and shook his head, but it felt more like himself. "At this point, Finley," he said, sounding both resigned and amused, "it seems prudent for me to surrender *all* of my expectations."

Sixteen

The Christmas Christmas Parade was traditionally an exercise in appreciation for the underwhelming because what it lacked in its low-budget presentation, which was everything, it more than made up for in artless enthusiasm, which was also everything.

Around four p.m., as the winter sun crept toward the horizon, folks started plonking down their lawn chairs and blankets and spare cousins to stake their claim on their spot along Merry Street, and the food kiosks selling hot beverages, bratwursts, and warm pretzels at either end of the parade route did bang-up business. Alcohol was never officially served at any point, a holdover from Oklahoma's conservative history, when it adopted Prohibition in 1907, at the same time it became an official state, twelve years before the 18th Amendment was passed nationally. But that didn't mean most of those gathered didn't bring their own.

Mayor Bobby Jim Slaughter personally set up a portable bar made out of whitewashed pallets that fit in the back of his pickup truck. He mainly used it for tailgating at football games and all the other sports that weren't football, but he also broke it out for the Christmas Parade, which was probably a big factor in his being reelected, despite not actually having accomplished much over his two terms. Still, he hadn't stolen funds from the town and run away, so in that alone he was an improvement on his predecessor.

While Christmas was not big by any measure, when it came to our parade, it was the most crowded the town got. Almost everyone from the directly surrounding counties came out to either watch or participate, or, quite often, both. It was common for members of a particular entrant to wave to the crowd as they passed, disembark at the end of the route, and circle back to where their group of family or friends were holding the space so they could wave to whoever was up next in the procession. It was about as close as folks around here got to recycling.

Grandma Jo always shut down early so everyone who worked at the Hoyden Inn could make their way to Merry Street with enough time to take part in the event. That meant Ayisha was gone before I had a chance to swing by to see . . . what exactly, I wasn't certain. If she was going to be at the parade? I knew she would be. If she wanted to maybe talk later? But did I really want that?

Again, I wasn't certain, though the idea wasn't freaking me out as much as it had the night before and I had to admit a part of me was itching to talk to someone. Six months ago, I would have sought out Mia, but that wasn't possible now.

Obviously.

And I wasn't entirely sure yet about talking with Arthur. Not because I didn't trust him because by this point, I did, but because . . . well, because the idea of telling him I didn't want to return to Barrington felt awkward in a way I wasn't yet willing to fully acknowledge.

I met up with Grandma Jo, Aunt Esha, and Arthur in the lobby to walk over to Merry Street together, much as we had for the reindeer romp, though both Dad and Dr. Raymond were absent this time.

Dad was going to join us directly from his office, while Dr. Raymond had an entry of some nature, so he had told Grandma Jo that he would find her there. I didn't like the sound of that, it felt like a double date with Grandma Jo and Aunt Esha meeting their guys, and my displeasure must have shown.

The air was already cold and the three blocks through the surrounding neighborhood from the inn to Merry Street were shaded with trees. We were headed in the opposite direction from where Arthur and I had walked to Boots Boulevard.

Arthur and Aunt Esha were a few feet ahead and engaged in their own conversation, creating a cloud of their breath in the chill. Both were bundled up, him in his familiar puffy green jacket, her in the trench coat and Burberry scarf.

Grandma Jo looked over at me as we strolled side by side.

"You seem grumpy," she said, her voice low.

I didn't want to talk about it, so I instinctively went for a diversion. "Did you two get tipsy?" I asked. It worked; she seemed caught off guard.

"What? No. We only had a tiny splash of bourbon to go with the hot chocolate. It takes more than that to get a person tipsy."

I shrugged. "Yeah, I know, Grandma."

She shot me a look. "And how do you know?"

"Because I'm sixteen."

She pressed her lips together briefly. "Which is five years below the legal drinking age." At that, *I* shot *her* a look, and to my surprise, she backed down, and even grew a little whimsical. "I sometimes forget you're not a baby anymore. It seems like just yesterday Skip and Dana brought you home from the hospital . . ." She stuffed her hands deeper into her long black coat and looked lost in thought as we crossed the street.

I was glad she brought up Mom, though; it gave me an opening.

"Mom called me last night," I said, keeping my eyes on the back of Aunt Esha's head to see if she had any reaction. There wasn't one. We were about a block and a half from the parade route and I could already hear some distant rumblings of the crowd.

Grandma Jo looked at me as we continued walking. "Oh? And?"

"And she misses us. *All* of us." Yeah, I made that part louder on purpose. Still no reaction from Aunt Esha, who seemed to be in conversation with Arthur. I raised my voice just a tick more as I added, "She also said that she and Dad were *both* not seeing other people."

Instead of being mollified, Grandma Jo's brows drew down in irritation. "She shouldn't be sharing that kind of thing with her daughter."

"Why?" I asked.

"Because it isn't proper."

To my surprise, Grandma Jo stopped in her tracks on the sidewalk. We were on the razor's edge of sundown now and the lights only reached one side of her face, but when I stopped to look back, I could see her eyes were wider and her mouth slightly agape.

"What?" I asked. Despite having my back to Arthur and his aunt, I sensed they had stopped as well.

Grandma Jo shook her head. "I just sounded like GGB," she almost whispered in awe.

And she had. While I had been very young when GGB was

still alive, hers was a presence that left a deep impression, which lingered long after she shuffled off this mortal coil. If there was one thing she liked to do, it was tell people when they weren't being "proper." And she didn't limit her definition to manners, either. Oh, no. Where to place the salad fork or writing "thank you" notes was merely the launching point. For her, propriety encompassed a wide range of potential missteps in society, and though I had been six years old when she passed, which meant my memories of her were fuzzy ten years later, I had gleaned enough about her through family conversations to know that she scared me a thousand times more than Mrs. Buzzard—even *with* the burned pans!—ever could. I was pretty sure Dad would agree. He had never shared a story about GGB that implied affection.

Distracted, Grandma Jo ran a hand through her shoulder-length hair, which had been colored a multitude of subtle shades of blonde to brown for as long as I could remember. There was probably gray underneath it all, but I'd never seen evidence. Then she looked down the block to where it bisected Merry Street. In the gap at the front of the street we could see it was already full of spectators and also hear the music, though we had time before things kicked off.

"Let's find our spot, then get some food," Grandma Jo said, taking over the mantle of the evasive one. I was more than happy to relinquish the title. And though I was very curious what had caused that reaction in her, I didn't press. Chakrabartis were watching.

We secured our spot fifteen minutes after arriving at the parade route, though we had to walk extra blocks to find a space big enough for all of us. "Christmas Here with You" sung by the Four Tops and Aretha Franklin boomed from the various speakers positioned overhead via duct tape on light posts and street signs up and down the route. It was the antithesis of fancy but it got the job done.

We hadn't even settled in when Dad found us in the crowd.

The three adults chatted and I watched for signs of subtle flirting between two of them, but nothing seemed to ping my radar as they discussed the food and beverage options. Scintillating.

I got bored and looked away, my gaze shifting across the street, toward the Christmas Visitor's Center.

And landed on Brody instead.

He stood almost directly opposite me across Merry Street, but I saw him.

And he saw me.

Mia was beside him, of course. Her arm through his and snuggled up to his side, not unlike I'd wanted to do earlier with Arthur at the café, but hadn't because we weren't in that place. While Brody and Mia so clearly were.

Our eyes locked and I felt a stab of so many things at exactly the same time that I couldn't say which was the most prominent. Maybe nervousness. But, full disclosure, there was also awareness and a prickle of pride that he was focused on *me*. Which was a hundred percent shallow, of that I was quite aware. And it reminded me of how I'd spent the first months of being his girlfriend, envisioning how other people saw us rather than recognizing what it was actually like to be *with* him. The overwhelming Brody-ness of it all had taken time to fade. But slowly, slowly it had. Left behind in its once-sizzling place was a boy who didn't have much to say about current events or history (recent or distant), or movies, and definitely *not* books of any kind, or much of anything beyond sports, his own summer lawn-mowing business, his hair (which truly *was* awesome), and his desire to one day be the backup quarterback for the Denver Broncos, mainly to become friendly with John Elway, whom he had once met at a Punt, Pass, and Kick youth camp, where the legendary quarterback told him, "Nice throw, kid."

It all grew . . . excruciating. And when we reached the point where I didn't want to make out anymore, I knew something had to give. Which was almost the exact moment when my acceptance packet to Barrington had arrived.

But now, seeing him again like this, and having him watch me, I felt that familiar sizzle go up my spine. Like a habit. Or maybe more of an ego boost I desperately needed.

My first instinct was to look away and pretend I didn't see him, even if the time for that had long passed. But then I remembered what Arthur had asked earlier: If *they* were the ones in violation of the universal friend code, why was *I* the one running away?

He was right. And so I held my ground.

For a moment, it seemed as if Brody was going to wave to me, but then Mia—who hadn't yet noticed me—said something to draw his attention and he broke eye contact to focus on her.

I glanced away. And met Arthur's hooded brown eyes.

I knew he'd watched my silent exchange with Brody. He was, after all, standing beside me. What I couldn't tell, though, was what he was even thinking about it. *If* he was thinking about it.

"Ladies and gentlemen," the deep male voice boomed over the array of speakers, "please find your positions as the Christmas Christmas Parade is about to begin!"

I glanced back to see only Grandma Jo and Aunt Esha standing behind me and Arthur. Dad had gone solo to grab the snacks. I hadn't been asked what I wanted, but he already knew. Peppermint mocha. It would keep me up late, but the parade had been special for me since I was a kid, when I would sit on my dad's shoulders and watch the people go by, neither knowing nor caring that it was lame by most standards. Now I knew, but there was still a thrill inside me as the first entrant arrived.

Sue me, I loved a parade.

As with every year, the event kicked off with the Christmas Sheriff's Department's SUVs, covered in garlands, with the middle one sporting a big red nose in the center grate. They flashed their lights and hit their sirens, which was the cue for the crowd to start cheering.

And cheer they did.

Much to my relief, Aunt Esha was caught up in the pull of the parade, too, applauding alongside Grandma Jo. Even Arthur seemed moderately engaged, which I counted as a victory.

After the Sheriff's Department SUVs got things rolling, what followed were a half dozen high school marching bands from the surrounding areas, belting out a variety of holiday songs.

I recognized Ayisha's twin sisters—Billie and Linda—on the French horn and clarinet, respectively, in the Christmas Junior High band. At twelve, they were accomplished musicians, which for a French horn and clarinet was a pretty remarkable achievement. Most kids gravitated toward guitars or drums or the piano, but not the Lewis twins. They chose two of the least interesting musical instruments and *still* managed to be outstanding. That was talent.

Next up were three thematically connected Nativity floats, with cutouts of animals on the sides and folks dressed as Jesus, Mary, and Joseph at various points on their journey. Pretty standard Oklahoma stuff.

But after that, things started to get . . . odd. And I don't mean "odd" like the year Mitzi decided to come dressed as a sexy cupcake, tap-dancing around on her own Gingerbread Café float, though that's forever imprinted on many a person's memory.

No. This was more *Twilight Zone* level of peculiar.

My first "huh" moment was with the arrival of a group of dancers in Santa-ish outfits who engaged in a choreographed routine that felt like a synchronized workout, but still came off with moderate success. I was surprised because there had never been organized dancing at any of the Christmas Christmas Parades, even before the departure of the local dance instructor.

And it felt . . . familiar? But I couldn't place how, so I let it go.

Five more floats for local businesses came after. All but one—the motorized Wayne's port-a-potty, which was a perennial—was just someone driving their own car with signs taped to the doors and maybe some extra décor like a pine tree or strings of lights. Everyone associated with each car wore Santa hats, waved to the crowd, and pretended this part wasn't the parade equivalent of the "sponsored by" scroll.

For his part, Arthur seemed bemused by it all, especially the driverless port-a-potty with the Santa cap on top.

"Is that what I think it is?" he asked.

"It is." I leaned and whispered, "Kinda hoping your aunt thinks it's a TARDIS."

He snorted and his eyes crinkled in amusement. And I felt ridiculously proud of myself. Also? He still smelled amazing.

Steve the Deliberately Homeless Elf decided to make an appearance. He didn't always. Here's a tidbit about him: Despite being homeless, he had a car. A 1972 El Camino. Green with personalized touches, such as the words CHRISTMAS ROCKS!!!!! spray-painted (not professionally) in yellow on the passenger-side door. Rumor was, he'd inherited it from a cousin in Pawhuska, and, when it was operational, he used it to deliver grocery supplies on behalf of CK. And if that period of the car's operation coincided with the Christmas Christmas Parade, you could bet it would make an unofficial appearance.

Like tonight.

When Steve spied Arthur in the crowd, he waved excitedly and inadvertently swerved the car in our direction for a few seconds before he corrected with a "yikes!" grin and a shout of "My man, Arthur!! Wooooo!!"

Arthur waved back, not as zealously, but with a genuine smile, complete with dimple.

Arthur glanced over his shoulder to find Aunt Esha looking at him in open curiosity.

"I'll explain later," he told her, then refocused on the next parade entrant, with only a quick glance at me out of the corner of his eye.

I smiled.

What followed was a flatbed pickup truck (decorated, of course), and in the bed itself were what looked like mounted projectors, and Gunner LaRue, the local computer specialist everyone went to for anything technical, in a Santa suit.

Gunner's focus was on what initially appeared to be a keyboard but revealed itself to be a motherboard. He tapped keys, twisted dials, and the streetlights along Merry Street went off.

There was a beat of surprised silence, followed by a blast of techno-ish Christmas music . . . and a laser light show!

A real one, too.

Okay, maybe nothing to rival Disneyland, or even Silver Dollar City, and the music was a millisecond behind in timing, but the effort was downright decent for a town this size. Dancing snowflakes on the side of buildings. A choir of cartoon angels sang along with "Hark! The Herald Angels Sing," which felt too on the nose but no one was quibbling. Then came stars, Christmas trees, more snowflakes, presents with bows, and candy canes.

And lastly an illuminated Santa in his sleigh with eight reindeer flew overhead.

Everyone oohed and aahed in all the right places, and when the streetlamps came back on, Arthur leaned in close to my ear and I held my breath.

"I thought there wasn't going to be a laser show," he said.

I met his eyes, so close, and shrugged, wide-eyed. "There never has been before."

"Curious."

I had to agree.

And when he leaned back, he was just the tiniest bit closer. Maybe a mere half inch. He probably didn't realize.

But I sure did.

A glance over my shoulder and I saw Aunt Esha also seemed bewildered. I put on a full-watt smile.

"So much for the lawyers, huh?" I said at my utmost chipper.

Her smile was indulgent. Which was fine by me.

Returning my attention to the parade, I again caught sight of Brody across the street.

Our eyes met and this time he did manage a small wave when Mia was looking elsewhere. It felt sneaky, which was not cool. This time I felt a stab of annoyance.

Next up was Dr. Raymond in his gold Acura, with him standing half out the sunroof in his white doctor's coat with a green garland around his neck. A large white tooth was affixed to the trunk and the sign on the door that we could see read MOLAR EXPRESS.

He smiled and tossed red-and-green bags of toothbrushes and sample-sized toothpaste to the crowd.

But he grew especially animated when he spied Grandma Jo.

Pointing to her, he reached down to whoever was driving (maybe Ollie, his dental assistant?) and emerged with a special gold bag, which he pitched with Kershaw-esque precision at Grandma Jo.

She caught it out of defensive reflex then opened it as everyone around her watched with blatant curiosity, myself included. She briefly closed her eyes before opening them again to wave at a beaming Dr. Raymond.

"What is it, Grandma?" I asked

With embarrassed reluctance, she withdrew a sample bottle of clear mint mouthwash with a twig of a green plant tied by a red ribbon around its neck.

"Mistletoe," Aunt Esha murmured in barely contained amusement.

Gross.

Grandma Jo shot her a look that only made Arthur's aunt snicker.

I glanced away and spotted Ayisha across the street, several yards down on the same side of the street as Brody. She was with some friends and they looked like they were having fun.

For a flash, I wondered if/when I came back to Christmas to

stay, they would be interested in bringing me into their friend clan because it wasn't as if I could return to BFF-ing with Mia or hanging with Brody and his group. Of course, that would mean befriending Ayisha first, and while that felt ever so slightly less impossible than it did two days ago, it was still a tall order.

Then I noticed an odd expression come over Ayisha as she stared in the direction of the approaching parade entrants. The angle from where she was standing allowed her to see it before I did, but only by a bit.

And when I did see it, my mouth dropped open.

Because there was an honest-to-God twenty-foot SNOW-MAN BALLOON flying above the heads of the dozen handlers—which looked like half of the Christmas varsity hockey team—who valiantly kept it in place via ropes. And the weirdest part was, it looked almost exactly like the one I'd stolen off a random website and placed on our own.

But it had never been one of our own.

Until now.

What the what?

Arthur tipped his head to one side like a perplexed puppy.

I glanced back at Aunt Esha, who was less amazed, because as far as she was concerned this was how a Christmas Christmas Parade always went.

And it wasn't as if I could tell her that it sure as shit *was not*.

By the time the goats in elf outfits showed up, I decided I needed a break from the trippy parade before I tumbled all the way into the Matrix.

Dad hadn't made it back with the snacks yet so I used that as an excuse.

I tugged on Arthur's sleeve.

"I'm going to get something to drink. You want anything?"

"Not now. Perhaps a cider in a bit."

I nodded and slipped away through the crowd without looking back.

I got about thirty yards down the heavily populated sidewalk when I spotted Dad returning, holding a cardboard tray of drinks and paper bags with what appeared to be cinnamon churros sticking out.

He smiled then frowned when he saw me. We stopped and let folks move around us.

"Where you going? I just got your peppermint mocha." He nodded to the green paper to-go cup with the white lid in the tray.

I grabbed it and took a sip. It was hot and heavenly.

"Thanks."

He nodded back in the direction he'd come from and I spotted several food kiosks ahead. "That took longer than I thought. The lines seem extra long this year."

I nodded. "You missed Wayne's port-a-potty."

"Darn it. Did it have the Santa hat or the elf hat?"

"Santa."

"I like the elf hat better. Has more character."

"Yeah." It was my turn to nod. And then, I don't know what came over me, but right there on the sidewalk, which was far from the right place to ask, I asked, "Do you like Arthur's aunt?"

Dad slow-blinked at me. "Do I like her?" he repeated.

"Yeah."

"Esha?"

"Yeah," I said, barely able to contain my irritation. "The only aunt he came here with. Do you like her?"

"Sure. She's great." He laughed. "Kicked my butt in chess. Twice."

"No, I mean . . . Do you *like* her? Like, you know. Like."

I stared at him.

And then he *did* understand what I meant.

My dad was never an especially expressive person, which made him a great balance for my mom, who most definitely *was* expressive. About everything. She felt things and you felt what she felt as she was feeling them. Dad was the opposite. Downright sphinxy.

But right there in that moment, despite the poor lighting and the multitude of other distractions, Dad's face telegraphed a dictionary's worth of thoughts and emotions in rapid succession, all of which he managed to jam-pack into a simple, "Oh."

His hazel eyes went wide and he looked past me, in the direction of where I knew Aunt Esha was presently watching the parade, then back at me, and I could feel him wanting to say things. Lots of things.

But instead he sputtered, "N-not, it's . . . not . . . it's not . . . no. No."

Which, I gotta say, wasn't convincing.

I took a deep breath, though, and nodded. Like I believed him. And smiled tightly.

"I'm gonna go get something to eat," I told him.

He awkwardly held up the tray. "I got snacks here."

"I want my own. I'll be back in a bit."

Then I didn't wait for his answer, but instead kept walking toward the food kiosks that were huddled together at the edge of Partridge Park, and despite the parade being well underway, were surrounded by a ton of people.

My stomach felt like it was tied in knots. I wasn't remotely hungry but I got in the line for Tish's Treats anyhow and vaguely wondered what I would order to justify being there. A multitude of sugary options were scrolled in extra-swirly handwriting on two chalkboards that framed the order window and I was deciding between the peanut butter snowballs and something called holiday crack toffee while trying not to think about my dad's reaction when I heard a familiar voice behind me say,

"Hey, Fin."

I stiffened.

Brody.

Shit.

My heart started beating hard as I turned around to find him standing a few feet away. By himself, no sign of Mia anywhere, and a voice in the back of my mind wondered if he'd ditched her. But I knew Mia well enough to know she couldn't be far. When she liked a guy, she made damn sure not to let him stray from her sight for too long. And it was very clear she liked Brody. A lot.

"Hi, Brody," I said, managing to sound like I was completely unaffected.

He wore the expensive pair of dark jeans I knew he'd gotten for his birthday back in early March and the same vintage brown leather distressed jacket that made him look impossibly hot, with a black sweater and a red-and-black-checked scarf. It was a good look on most guys but felt borderline unfair on him.

"Uh, can I talk to you for a sec?"

He jerked his head away from the line where four people were behind me and two in front, all of whom were now watching us with almost as much interest as they had in ordering the holiday snacks. Such was small-town life.

"Yeah, okay."

I exited the line and together we walked farther into Partridge Park. Near the very same picnic table where we'd broken up six months ago. Great. Nice memory.

We stopped and faced each other. Awkwardness hung between us like the third musketeer.

"Hey," he started.

"We covered that part," I reminded him.

"Oh, yeah." He rubbed the back of his neck, which I knew to be a total tell. "How are ya doin'?"

"Fine."

"Yeah?"

It's entirely possible I may have rolled my eyes. "I'm fan-freakin'-tastic, Brody. What do you want me to say?" I could feel myself scowling at him and his pretty face grew pinched.

"I don't know," he answered, in such a way that was both defensive and unwittingly vulnerable and I felt like I'd swatted a kitten. (To be clear, I do *not* swat kittens.)

"What did you want to talk about?"

"I mean, I guess . . ." He shrugged both shoulders. "I texted you."

"I know."

"A buncha times."

"I know."

"You didn't text back."

"I know."

"Are you, like, mad at me?"

"Why would I be mad at you?" I asked, even as the thought bubble above my head unspooled a long scroll's worth of options.

He kicked the dirt with his black Doc Martens. "Because of me and Mia, you know."

"Well, I know *now*. After I saw you both."

"Yeah. She showed me the picture you sent."

"Maybe she can put it in a scrapbook. You know how she loves scrapbooking."

He frowned. "Yeah."

Oh my God, did Mia love scrapbooking. Anyone in Mia's orbit had been the recipient of at least one scrapbook at some point. I had eight, one for each year we knew each other. They were very thorough.

"But, like, are you?" he persisted. "You know, mad?"

I drew a breath to answer, though I wasn't entirely certain what I was about to say, when Mia came walking toward us at a rapid clip, dark eyes wide.

"There you are," she said, which was likely directed at Brody but her focus was on me.

I smiled. "Perfect timing."

"Why?" She almost didn't stop as she barreled into Brody, wrapping both of her arms around him while facing me.

"We were just talking about you," I continued.

Her eyes narrowed. "What were you saying about me?"

"We were discussing your love of scrapbooking. I was about to tell Brody here that you made a scrapbook for me right before I left for Barrington. It was amazing. And how long after I left before you two started hooking up?"

Brody stood up straighter. "It wasn't like that."

"So you're not hooking up?"

"No, I mean, yeah, we are—"

Mia jerked away from him in indignation. "Baby!"

He was confused. "What? We are."

Her dark eyes turned thunderous. "Oh, okay. I'm just a hookup? That's all I am to you?"

Uh-oh.

Brody realized his error as swiftly as only someone dating a volatile person can. "No!"

"Because that's just bullshit!" she continued, and I knew from my own experience that we were about to be subjected to the Full Mia Treatment.

Brody held up both hands, imploring her to believe him. "No, no, you're not. You're not. Mia, baby, no. You're my girl."

I felt a pang of jealousy shoot through me at that, at "my girl," irrational and stupid, but also very real even if I knew I had no right to it.

But then I caught a motion out of the corner of my eye.

And I turned to see Arthur strolling up to us. Or, more specifically, me.

I was surprised but also relieved.

Arthur held my eyes and smiled.

"The cider here is delicious. Your father purchased a cup for me," he said smoothly, toggling the blue to-go cup he held before he turned to face Brody and Mia. "Hallo."

Brody stiffened and cocked his head, equal parts uncertain and wary. "Who are you?" he demanded of Arthur, who in return half bowed, unfazed.

"Arthur Chakrabarti Watercress. And you are . . . ?"

"Brody."

Arthur's face lit up as if in recognition. "Tuck. Yes, I've heard of you." He glanced at me. "Three percent Neanderthal, wasn't it?" Before I could reply, Arthur looked back at Mia. "Then you must be Mia."

For her part, Mia was clearly confused, which was a thousand percent better than her being on the verge of losing her shit.

"That's right," she said.

Brody zeroed in on me. "You told him about the DNA test?" he demanded, newly pissed.

"Yeah, so?"

"That's not this guy's business." He pointed at Arthur.

I shook my head. "Brody, you tell everyone about being three percent Neanderthal. It's going to be your yearbook caption."

"I tell everyone *I* know." He pointed at Arthur again. "I don't know this guy."

Arthur smiled. "Once again, Arthur."

Brody shot him a look. "I heard it the first time. Who are you and how exactly do you know Finley?"

"Arthur and I go to school together," I said.

Mia rolled her eyes and curled her upper lip. "Christ. It's always about that goddamn school."

"Barrington," Arthur supplied, before taking a sip of his cider.

I watched a surprised thought dart across Brody's face. "Wait, wait. Hold the fuck up. Are you two"—he pointed between us—"like, a thing? Is he your *boyfriend*?"

A long silence followed where neither Arthur nor I answered. And I took Arthur not immediately scoffing in disgust or waving off the notion of us being an item as an invitation for me to be the one to take the lead in replying. Which he probably assumed would be with honesty.

It wasn't.

Instead I impulsively said, "It's early." And let it hang out there, naked and exposed, for Brody and Mia to fill in the implication as they saw fit.

In the four seconds that followed, Arthur had a couple of options about how to respond to what we both knew to be a lie. He could have told the truth to Brody and Mia right then and there, which would have been humiliating for me, but he had no reason to spare my feelings. Or he could have pretended not to hear correctly, though that would take a bit more finesse.

But he didn't do either of those things.

What he did do was put his arm around my shoulders, awkwardly, but there, and said, "I am having a delightful time getting to know Finley's family and charming hometown."

Brody took a step back as if he'd been struck.

He stared at me in barely contained fury. "You told me you couldn't date anyone because you were going to be spending all your time studying. You said that!" He pointed to the nearby cement picnic table. "Right there!"

I unconsciously leaned in closer to Arthur and his puffy green jacket. "Things changed." And I emphasized my point by looking between Brody and Mia. "For both of us."

Mia, for her part, seemed as upset about me and Arthur as Brody was, which I didn't quite understand.

"How long have you two been dating?" she demanded.

"I already told you, it's early."

"Before you came back here, though?" she pushed.

Brody sneered and answered for me, "Why else would he be here, Mia?"

Bad move, Brody, I thought, wincing internally.

Mia shoved against his chest with both hands. "Don't you snap at me!"

He quickly muttered, "Sorry—sorry!"

He'd get shit for that later, but Mia had other questions that took precedence. She turned back to me, eyes flashing.

"So, to be clear, you were totally dating this guy and you never once mentioned it to me even *before* you found out about me and Brody? Is that what I'm hearing?"

Well, I walked right into that one.

I sighed and felt the first stirrings of what had the potential to be a wicked headache. But then I felt Arthur's arm around my shoulders tighten a tiny bit and I felt better. Not alone.

It was nice.

"Yeah," she continued when I didn't say anything. "You've got a lotta nerve, Fin, acting like I did something wrong when you were the one not being a good friend this whole time." She shook her head and took two steps away. "We're outta here," she said, then started walking. When Brody hesitated, she turned on him. "Now, Brody!"

Brody sighed. And hesitated again, his eyes on me and Arthur. But only for a second or two more before he turned and followed Mia out of the park.

Arthur waited until they were out of sight before he lowered his arm from my shoulders. I missed the feeling at once.

"*She* was your best friend?" he asked dubiously.

"We met in elementary school. It was simpler then."

"It would have to have been," he murmured, and took a sip of his cider. Then he shifted to regard me. "I hope you don't mind . . ." He held up his right hand, the one that had been around my shoulders.

I shook my head. "No. In fact, thank you." I could feel myself blushing. "I shouldn't have implied anything was going on between us." I drank my peppermint mocha to cover my mounting embarrassment.

He moved to sit on top of the cement picnic table. "Makes sense why you did, though."

"Does it?"

I followed and sat beside him. Both of our feet were on the seat and we faced in the same direction. Not too close.

Then again, not too far away, either. I could feel him radiating warmth and it took everything in me not to bury my face in his shoulder.

"In a way," he said, oblivious to my longing for a sneaky snuggle. "It's difficult to be the third wheel, especially when you harbor feelings for one of the other two."

"That's just it," I countered, shaking my head. "I don't think I do. Harbor feelings, I mean. For Brody."

He arched an eyebrow. "Might I remind you that earlier today you referred to him as your 'first love.'"

"He is, or, you know, he was."

"Then what is it about this situation that has you upset enough to conjure a relationship with me?"

I sighed. "I think it's just . . . everything."

He watched me for a moment. "Your parents?" His voice was softer now.

"Yeah. Wait. How do *you* know about them, too?"

"The woman at the local grocery with the talons"—he held up one hand to demonstrate—"who was less than discreet."

"Oh, right. Mrs. Gowdy."

"Is it fair to presume that their situation contributed to your tears in the kitchen?"

I nodded.

"I'm sorry," he said, and I knew he meant it. Which was comforting.

"Are your parents still together?" I asked, wanting to shift the focus off me.

"They are." His lips thinned a bit. "I'm not certain anyone else could handle them, except perhaps Polly."

"Who's Polly?"

"My sister."

I blinked in surprise. "You have a sister?"

"I believe I just conveyed that fact, yes."

"You've never mentioned her before."

"I try to mention her as little as possible."

"So, not close?"

"In any respect, chiefly in age. Well, and temperament. As well as life experience, interests, and goals."

"So, not close."

"No."

I looked away, letting my eyes travel unseeing over the bustling kiosks. "I always wanted a sibling," I said wistfully. "But my parents stopped after me."

"I'm fairly certain that was my parents' plan, too, after Polly. Alas . . ." He shrugged as if to keep it light.

"Oops?" I asked.

"Oops," he agreed.

"Me too. Oops."

"I suppose that makes us a pair of oops."

"Is more than one 'oops' an 'oopsie'?" I pondered.

"Like a murder of crows?"

"Or a conspiracy of lemurs."

"Or a zeal of zebras."

"I always liked that one." I held up my to-go cup. "Cheers, Mr. Oops."

He tapped his cup against mine. "And to you, Ms. Oops."

We took a drink from our respective paper cups, and he finished off the rest of his cider.

"How come you're not watching the parade?" I asked.

He grew quiet for a moment, as if choosing his words with care. "I saw that Brody chap leave his side of the parade route as soon as you did and I deduced he was going in search of you."

"So you followed him following me?"

"Essentially. But only after your father returned and said he'd given you your drink and that you were off to secure a snack. I assumed that would make you something of a sitting duck should Neanderthal Man"—I snorted—"find you away from your herd like a defenseless gazelle and pounce. Which it appears was what transpired, with an assist from the girl in the pom-pom cap."

I leaned back and looked at him. "Arthur Chakrabarti Watercress. Did you 'white knight' me?"

"It's entirely possible." He glanced over at me and I couldn't tell exactly what it was he was thinking or feeling, but there was a tiny hint of a smile in his eyes. "But only in the most respectful-of-your-own-feminine-power sort of way."

I laughed. "Why do I feel you got that from your aunt?"

He tapped his nose then smiled, the lines around his eyes crinkling. And I melted.

I would have been perfectly content to sit there for another hour, close to each other, talking, despite my ass growing numb from the freezing-cold cement tabletop. But I also knew we had people waiting for us.

Arthur seemed to realize that, too.

He hopped off the table and reached out his hand to offer me help. Which I took because I'm not an idiot.

And when he didn't immediately release my hand, I felt a powerful shiver go through my chest that had nothing to do with the cold night air.

He squeezed my cold, ungloved fingers twice. "Lest we run into the dynamic duo," he explained.

My chest squeezed. "Good idea," I said, happy for any excuse to hold his hand and not merely because it was so very much warmer than my own, though that was a plus.

Together, we walked back in the direction of our respective family members, only letting go of each other once we arrived.

Seventeen

DECEMBER 22

Arthur decided to take his aunt to the Gingerbread Café for breakfast next morning, a move I thought had as much to do with avoiding any possible interaction with Mrs. Buzzard post–pan fiasco as the "Christmas curiosity factor," as he claimed in his text to me this morning.

Which, yeah. We were texting now.

Take that, Bronwyn.

I wanted to be excited about it—a cute boy texting me!—but the logical section of my brain shut that down tout de suite by pointing out that, duh, of course we'd be texting. We had to coordinate things, which required the ability to communicate, and texting was the most efficient form of communication, move on, nothing to see.

And it wasn't as if there was an iota of flirting in our exchanges, either in word choice or subject or even emoji (though Arthur had yet to use emojis with me).

Nope. Just Arthur being Arthur and letting me know the 411 in the most basic fashion.

I suppose I should've been happy that he thought enough of

the Gingerbread Café to show it to his aunt, that it somehow passed the undercurrent of the Perfect American Christmas test that pervaded everything about their holiday in my hometown.

But it would've been nice to see him. Especially after our brief foray into fake dating last night, which if this had been a rom-com we would have formalized with rules and taken to far greater lengths that included learning everything about the other person so we appeared genuine to the world at large and somehow wound up accidentally kissing because we wanted to prove to the disbelievers we *were* a real couple even though we weren't, even though at least one of us (hi!) secretly wanted to be.

Alas, no.

The duration of our romance was as long as it took to walk back from the park to rejoin Dad and Grandma Jo and Aunt Esha on the parade front lines. Then we morphed back to being just Finley and Arthur. Schoolmates, like him and Bronwyn. And even that had an expiration date, though thus far I was the only one who knew that rather important factoid.

Well, and Ayisha. Kinda. Speaking of . . .

Val Limekiller was late. Again. However, this time I was happy about it because that meant Ayisha was staying later to cover Val's morning shift and thus overlapping with mine, which also meant we could finally have that talk I wasn't initially sure I wanted but now really, *really* did. I wasn't sure how to get the ball rolling or where it might end. I thought maybe Ayisha would bring it up, but she didn't.

Instead, she looked preoccupied all morning.

I spent most of the breakfast/brunch subtly attempting to get her attention as we served the guests, to no avail. There were three factors working against me.

One: Mr. and Mrs. Yablonski were not satisfied with their pre-ordered food substitutions and made a bit of a stink about it, which led me to . . .

Two: An interaction with a cranky (even by her standards) Mrs. Buzzard, who let me know in no uncertain terms that not having the proper pans to make her meals threw off her entire preparation mojo, which was why she had forgotten about the Yablonskis' apple-walnut-pancakes request.

And three: Ayisha ignored me. Though I suppose it was more like she had other things on her mind and failed to let her eye be caught.

Which meant I was going to have to be more assertive.

I had an iffy relationship with assertive.

Sometimes, I had no problem with it.

Like last night with Dad when I asked him about his feelings for Aunt Esha. Boom! On the walk home I noticed he took great pains to keep Grandma Jo between him and Arthur's aunt. He'd zipped off to his cottage instead of joining Grandma Jo and Aunt Esha (minus Dr. Raymond, who was also absent because Mayor Slaughter had cracked his tooth opening a bottle of beer and required emergency surgery in the early a.m.) for post-parade wine by the firepit in the courtyard.

But sometimes assertive was harder.

Like trying to talk to someone I was fairly certain regarded me as barely tolerable about pressing issues that could affect the direction of the rest of my life. Maybe I should have chosen someone else to confide in, but there just wasn't anyone else.

Which probably said a lot about my need to expand my interpersonal horizons.

Ayisha and I managed a brief exchange in the kitchen when

I brought in dirty dishes and she was making an extra pot of coffee from the drip maker.

Mrs. Buzzard was gone by this point, though not without having left me with very detailed instructions on the exact replacement pans she expected me to buy for her. All-Clad stainless steel. She was taking advantage of the situation, but I'd deal with that later.

Instead, I smiled brightly at Ayisha when I entered.

"Hey," I said.

She nodded at me then looked away at the coffee pot because watching the flow of brown water was more interesting.

I tried again. "I saw you at the parade last night."

"Yeah. I saw you, too. With Brody." She smirked.

I bit my tongue and deposited the dishes in the sink.

"Did he invite you to his party?" she asked.

I glanced over my shoulder at her. "Party?"

"Yeah. Tomorrow at his house. Christmas Eve Eve."

I rolled my eyes. "Oh, God. That has to be Mia's doing. Christmas Eve Eve is something she always likes to say every year, like it's clever."

"Makes sense. Brody's never had a party with a theme before. Just beer."

I started filling the right side of the double sink with hot, soapy water for the dishes to soak. "No, he didn't invite me."

Not in the park, and not later in the flurry of texts he sent telling me he thought it was shitty for me to bring a guy home to meet my family and that I'd hurt Mia and him. Oh, and dont tell mia im txting u.

I hadn't responded. What was the point?

Now I looked at Ayisha.

"Are you going?"

She shrugged. "I dunno. Maybe. Not a lot else going on."

She reached into the cupboard and got out two of the Hoyden Inn deep-red stoneware coffee mugs Grandma Jo had had specially made for the inn.

I was trying to think of a way to broach the subject of Barrington and my various emotions around it when she added, "Arthur mentioned he wanted to go to a party while he was here. And not the kind your grandmother hosts."

I stiffened and felt a shot of adrenaline akin to panic go through me. "When did you talk to Arthur about that?" With effort, I managed to keep my voice steady.

"The other day, when I brought him the tea. I didn't know about Brody's then."

"Oh." Well, at least that was before he and I started spending so much time together. I knew I should go back into the dining area to see if any guests needed anything else, but I needed some answers first. "So . . . are you two going together? You and Arthur?"

"I hadn't thought about it."

I dried my hands. Folded the dish towel and set it aside. Neatly. And tried not to let my raging anxiety bleed across my expression. "If he wants to go and you want to go then you should both go."

What the hell am I doing? I legit had no idea. Words were emerging from me as if they had no association with my brain or heart.

Ayisha was dubious. "Really."

"Sure," I said, shrugging one shoulder like I was convinced what I was suggesting was remotely a good idea, even though *it so wasn't*. "Arthur mentioned wanting to go to me, too, so it's obviously something he really wants to do."

She stared at me. "And you'd be okay with that?"

"Totally!" God, I was such a liar and, it seemed, a self-sabotager. But I kept going like an out-of-control boulder tumbling downhill. "There aren't a ton of options for him, party-wise."

"That's true." She seemed about to say more when she looked past me and frowned in confusion. "Is that Dr. Raymond?"

I turned and followed the direction of her gaze out the window overlooking the courtyard, and, sure enough, there was Dr. Raymond, acting suspicious as he approached the juniper hedge trees that formed an evergreen wall on one side of the courtyard.

"What's he doing?" I asked.

"Well, he's not meeting your gramma, she left a half hour ago."

We both watched him reach into his orange deer hunter's jacket and take out an opaque plastic CK shopping bag that appeared to be full. From there, he withdrew something green.

Ayisha frowned. "Looks like he's hanging something?"

But from this angle it wasn't clear what it was.

She shook her head, already done with the matter. "He's so weird." Then she refocused on me. "Can you bring these"—she pointed to the two mugs of coffee—"to the Meacos in dining? I need to head upstairs to turn down the guest rooms."

"Sure. But I thought we'd both do the rooms."

"No, I'll do them. You take the front desk. I'm not in the mood to be around people right now."

Which meant now was not the right time to bug her about Barrington.

"What about these?" I pointed to the dirty dishes soaking in the sink.

"Leave them for Val." She smirked and for once it wasn't aimed at me.

Ten minutes later, I was standing at the front desk, writing up a message for Lloyd, who was thankfully far more easy-going than Mrs. Buzzard about the changes the Yablonskis wanted for their dinner, when Dr. Raymond appeared in the lobby.

I smiled politely. "Hi, Dr. Raymond."

"'Lo, Finley."

I saw him holding the plastic CK bag, though now it seemed less full.

"How'd the surgery on Mayor Slaughter go?" I asked, as I eyed the bag.

"Fine and dandy. Temporary cap in place and I gave him a handheld bottle opener he can hang from his belt."

"That's nice of you. I'm pretty sure my grandmother's out at a meeting."

"Yup. With the planning commission. I'm goin' over there right now. Just had to do a quick errand first."

"Here?"

"Yup." His eyes sparkled. "Jo's great about always making this place look nice for Christmas and 'specially for the Christmas Eve party, but I wanted to add extra fun this year." He bounced on the tips of his toes.

My eyes narrowed. I knew from experience that Grandma Jo liked things to be a certain way, especially when it came to her holiday decorations, so Dr. Raymond making any changes without telling her first struck me as unwise.

Then he took out a sample of what he had in the plastic bag and his grin widened.

I frowned. "Is that an herb?" I asked, at least grateful that it in no way resembled pot leaves. Not that I could for one fraction of a second envision Dr. Raymond high on anything other than nitrous oxide.

But then he explained, "It's mistletoe." And when I peered closer, I saw that it did look like the plant Grandma Jo had held up at the parade. "For kissing," he further explained, and I wished he hadn't because I never needed to have the notion of "kissing" and Dr. Raymond in the same vicinity.

Ever.

"Yes, sir," I said, and wished he would just leave already.

He didn't. He was too proud of himself.

"I put batches 'round here. For a surprise." He smiled that perfect veneer of a shiny white smile. "Fun, huh?"

"Hmmmmmm . . ." was all I could muster.

Thankfully, he checked his watch and his eyed widened. "Yikes! Gotta skedaddle! Don't wanna be late for the meetin'. I'm on the board now, ever since Micky Fleck got kicked off on account of his arson. Here." He tossed me the bag and I caught it right as Arthur entered the lobby. Dr. Raymond glanced at Arthur as he told me, "Use it wisely." Then with a "Howdy, Arty!" he bounded out the front door, headed for the planning commission meeting. And Grandma Jo.

Arthur straightened his shoulders. "For the record, I have never before been called Arty, nor do I ever wish to be again."

"You're in luck," I said. "This is an Arty-free zone."

"Thank God."

I took him in for the first time since we'd parted in the second-floor hallway.

To my surprise, he was wearing the Wranglers again. They'd been washed since the trip to the farm, and the fit was more relaxed. There was no ornament-vomiting reindeer sweater this morning. Though he had managed to sneak in a more traditional reindeer "jumper," one with midnight blue on the sleeves and shoulders, claret red on the lower half, populated by white snowflakes and, of course, white deer and pine trees silhouettes all around.

I hid a smile. As long as I lived, I would forever associate reindeer with Arthur Chakrabarti Watercress.

He noticed the sprig of mistletoe that had spilled out onto the desk and, leaning one arm against the ledge of the front desk, pointed. "You know that's a parasite?"

"Mistletoe?"

"Indeed. It impales its host with its tiny roots, siphoning off water and nutrients to the point of potentially killing the tree."

"I thought it was supposed to be romantic."

"That association came later. The Celts used to bring it indoors during the winter months to help brighten the ambience and it came to represent fertility. And the name itself comes from words in an old dialect that meant 'bird droppings' since its seeds are often spread from, well, bird droppings."

"You're like a walking mistletoe wiki."

"When I study something . . ." He pointed to his temple. ". . . it's a steel trap."

"And you've studied mistletoe?"

His gaze dropped away from mine as if he realized he'd given too much away. "I did."

My curiosity got the better of my mouth. "*For* someone?" I probed, suddenly nervous there really was a Poppy-Millicent after all. Waiting for his return across the pond.

To my dismay he answered with a circumspect, "Possibly."

Which wasn't what I wanted to hear. "I thought you said you've never had crushes."

"No. I said I'd never been in love. There's quite a difference. And I already admitted to having had a crush before."

"Oh, right. Mrs. Darby."

"She was *Ms.* Darby when I knew her. Her new last name is Ramsbottom."

"You made up that name."

"I could never make up a name as magnificent as Ramsbottom." His lips twitched and his eyes danced.

"Was Mrs. Ramsbottom the one who inspired your mistletoe research?"

"She was not."

Silence hung. He showed no inclination to fill it.

"Then who was?" I pressed.

His expression shuttered. "That is a much longer story."

I held out my arms. "Look at me. Standing here. Surrounded by all this time."

"Then now is the perfect opportunity to ask you about tonight."

"Tonight?"

"Yes. Auntie Esha had such a lovely experience at the parade and again this morning at the Gingerbread Café, I was rather hoping to keep this uncharacteristic streak of good fortune going and venture out to that lights experience you said wasn't entirely trumped up."

"It's in Chickasha and it's real."

"Excellent!" He straightened up and tapped the palms of both of his hands against the desktop—*rat tata!*—in satisfied approval. I liked seeing him more chill like this. "What do you think about going there this evening?"

"You, me, and your aunt?"

"And anyone else you can think of. Your grandmother or

father, perhaps." He glanced over at the front doors and lowered his voice, leaning closer. "Though I'd prefer a slight break from the dentist, if that's all right with you."

"A hundred percent."

"Such a relief." He leaned back.

"Yeah, that sounds cool. And don't think I didn't notice how you deflected from telling me about your crush history."

"Is that what I did?"

"Uh-huh. And yesterday you filibustered me about why you're attending an American school."

"You can't possibly find it of interest."

"Why don't you try me?"

He paused, seeming to consider his answer. "Perhaps," was all he said. Then he reached into his pants pocket. "Here." He withdrew a chestnut, now with what appeared to be a white shoelace running dead through a newly created narrow hole in its center, with a knot at the bottom to keep it hanging in place. It kinda resembled an itty-bitty, adorable medieval nut-mace.

"A corker!" I exclaimed, as he handed it to me.

"Conker."

"Same thing."

"It is not. Which you'll know once you've played." He then took out a second conker. "I took the laces from my trainers, so I'll need them back, and I placed both conkers beneath my mattress last night because heat helps get them hard—" He stopped at once.

The double entendre struck both of us at the same time and our eyes met. Then he proceeded to flush so deeply he could have blended with the lower half of his sweater.

I burst out laughing. How could I not? Deep guffaws. And I

didn't stop until Arthur's face cracked and he joined in, not as boisterously, but grinning in embarrassed amusement.

I reached out and grabbed his arm, much like I had in the kitchen yesterday, perhaps naturally seeking connection.

Our eyes met again, both filled with amusement, mine to the point of tears, and they held longer this time.

And that's when I felt it. Undeniably, amazingly. A frisson that reached out from me to him or him to me or both, I wasn't entirely sure. But the origin wasn't the point. Only that it was there. For a moment, I honestly couldn't breathe. I saw the column of his throat move as he swallowed. And our eyes stayed locked as the laughter started to die out . . .

"What's so funny?"

I blinked and pulled back my hand, ending our connection, and looked over to see Val Limekiller lope her long-legged way into the lobby with a puzzled expression in her sleepy eyes as she glanced between Arthur and me. She was about five years older than I was, and if Jeff Spicoli had a baby with Olive Oyl, it would've been Val.

"Nothing," I replied reflexively, my mind and every other part of me still buzzing.

I saw Arthur draw away and blink a few times himself, which I took as confirmation that I wasn't imagining things. There had been *something* there, enough to make his blush somehow deepen and his formal posture return.

"What time would you think would be best to begin our holiday lights excursion?" he asked, hands on hips, back military straight.

"Um, it starts at six p.m., I think, so maybe we leave here at six? It'll take about a half hour to drive there and park and get tickets and everything."

His head bobbed with a tad too much enthusiasm. "Perfect."

I didn't want him to leave yet, so I asked, "What are you doing for the rest of the day?" I suppose I could have mentioned Brody's party, but this felt safer.

"Auntie wanted to do a bit of shopping in town and then your grandmother invited us over to her cottage around three to watch a Christmas movie."

"Which one?"

"It's not yet been decided. Auntie Esha's suggestion was *Love Actually*, which I then countered with *Die Hard*."

"And were shot down."

"Decisively. Your grandmother's suggestion was—"

"*It's a Wonderful Life*," we said in unison.

His smile returned. "I think we shall let a flip of the coin choose for us."

"Probably a good idea."

"Are you perhaps around to join us?"

"I can't." I waved behind me. "I'm here until about three, then I have to nap. And don't you dare make fun of me for napping." I pointed at him with a stern expression to emphasize my seriousness on the matter. He held up his hands in surrender.

"I have nothing but a deep and abiding appreciation for the afternoon nap. Woe that Western civilization fails to properly acknowledge their healing properties."

I smiled. "Totally."

We shared a smile.

Val chuckled behind me. "Y'all are so cute," she drawled, and I bit my upper lip in embarrassment.

Arthur's formality rushed back. "Right. We shall be in touch," he said.

I couldn't help myself, I saluted, which earned an arched eyebrow in return. But there was a hint of a smile, too.

As soon as he exited the lobby, I turned back to find Val leaning against one side of the desk, watching me through hooded, knowing eyes.

"Whatever," I said, then decided to leave her to go tackle the dishes. I did some of my best processing while doing the dishes. Usually.

Eighteen

An hour of dish soap–induced processing later and I was in no better a place than when I started. In fact, I may have been worse. Emotionally, that is. The kitchen looked amazing. But my mind?

A jumble.

Arthur. Cute, annoying, funny, too-serious-for-his-own-good Arthur somehow made me feel like I was caught in a spell.

And I was on the verge of putting events in motion to take me away from him.

Then again, maybe I shouldn't? Maybe I should keep my Barrington-related anxiety to myself and return there and let no one else be the wiser. In a way, that would be the easiest thing to do.

But did I want to return to a place where I was otherwise failing at every turn because I had a huge crush on a boy? Sure, there was the tiniest chance he maybe liked me, too; I was starting to think there was a possibility. At the same time, I adamantly didn't want to be the kind of person who made massive life decisions based on my feelings for a cute boy.

I hadn't done that for Brody. Which had been at the core of our breakup.

There were other factors, of course. Our fundamental in-compatibility, for instance. As far as Brody was concerned, though, I hadn't taken him into consideration when I decided to apply to Barrington and especially once I had accepted admission.

Which wasn't true. I *had* thought about him. I thought of what life would be like if I stayed here in Christmas instead of going to the elite boarding school, and I didn't have to look be-yond my own mother.

But now here I was, six months later, pondering the same decision only in reverse, and once again there was a boy in the mix, muddying my perspective when what I needed most was clarity.

The only thing I knew for certain was I wouldn't find the answers going around in circles in my own head.

Which is why I went upstairs. Not necessarily in search of Ayisha, but not *not* in search of her, either.

My non-search found her in the last room at the end of the second-floor hallway, in the room rented by the Yablonskis. I was grateful to find it wasn't either Chakrabarti room. That would've been too close to boundary-crossing.

Fortunately, the door to the room was propped open by the maid cart and I saw Ayisha in the middle of stripping down the bedding. Her braids hung loose and her movements were slow. Not perpetually on autopilot, like Val. Rather, she seemed exhausted.

I lightly tapped the door then entered, not waiting for her permission as I grabbed a couple of disposable gloves from the cart because there was too good a chance permission wouldn't be forthcoming.

"Hi," I said, as I went to the other side of the bed to help unhook the fitted sheet from the corner. There was a protocol for cleaning a guest's room and it started with removing all the bedding.

She frowned at me. "What are you doing?"

"I thought I'd help."

"I already told you I didn't want help."

I released the sheet and it sprang back at her. She caught it and I caught a glimpse of her drawn expression. Damn, she was tired.

She must have felt it, too, because she held out the old bedding.

"Take these," she said.

Which was what I did.

For a few minutes, neither of us said a word. We just worked. Straightening and sweeping and dumping the tiny wooden wastebaskets that were remarkably full of empty pop cans, sample-sized potato chip bags, and, yikes! I hoped that wasn't a used condom.

Next up was dusting and disinfecting the surfaces. She took the former and I took the latter.

Then I attempted to grease the conversational wheels.

"The parade was really good."

She nodded. Kept dusting.

"Kinda weird how they added all those new parts, huh?" I tried again, as I used a rag to wipe down the desktop.

Nothing.

Well, this is fun. Okay, I'd switch gears. Move into the family angle. "I saw your sisters in the band." That earned at least a glance up. I took this to be encouraging. "They're really good."

She laughed, but it was devoid of humor as she returned her dust cloth to the cart, grabbing the fresh bedding.

I was confused. "What? You don't agree?"

Ayisha's lips curled. "Oh, they're awesome." She tossed the top sheet and pillowcases onto the chair. "Always have been. Mom likes to say that she knew they'd be great musicians even before they were born. Though she thought they'd be singers. That's why she named them Billie and Linda."

I nodded along because I got the Billie Holiday reference. Though the Linda—

"Linda Martell," she supplied, as she shook out the fitted sheet. "First Black woman to sing solo in front of the Grand Ole Opry. I don't expect you to know. Most folks don't. But Mom loved her."

"I guess it's kinda like destiny, huh? Them being into music."

"Yep." She started tucking the fitted sheet into place. "They're gonna be little band superstars. As long as I'm around to stay after school and make them study while Mom's at the office. And I get to tutor them until dinnertime because they'd rather play their stupid instruments than study and they'd probably fail otherwise. But that doesn't matter to some people."

She swiped the flat of her hand down the fitted sheet to smooth out the wrinkles with considerably more force than necessary. Her red-and-green nails were a blur.

"It doesn't?" I placed the disinfectant bottle and old rag into the used bag that hung off the side of the cart.

"Nope."

I crossed to help her get the fresh fitted sheet in place.

"Like who, for instance?" I asked casually. She stopped to stare at me and I felt the heat of discomfort creep up my neck. "Never mind," I muttered. Maybe this wasn't such a good idea.

Another handful of moments passed before she clarified,

"Like the admissions people at Oakengates." The irritation in her voice was no longer an undertone. It was *the* tone.

"Oakengates?"

"That's what I said. They just got accepted this morning."

"Why does that sound so familiar?" I mused aloud, unfolding the top sheet.

She grabbed the other side. "Because it's one of the New England performing arts private schools that feeds into Barrington."

"Oh, right. Oakengates. It's in Massachusetts."

"Yep."

"That's a really good school," I said automatically, and she pressed her lips together tightly. "Which I'm thinking you already know . . ."

"Yeah."

A few moments spent tucking in the top sheet.

"That's weird," I said at last.

"What is?"

"That they're going to a private school in New England, like I am. I mean . . ." I chuckled. "It's not as if there's some sort of long-established educational pipeline from Christmas, Oklahoma, to exclusive New England boarding schools."

"Not weird. Your mom helped Billie and Linda find Oakengates. She helped them secure the musical scholarship, too."

She took up the bedspread.

"Oh. That makes sense, then. She helped me apply to Barrington, too."

"Yeah. I know." She started to smirk, but it didn't hold the same edge. Instead, it felt . . . sad. "And now you wanna throw all that away. Like it's nothing."

"That's not true—"

"It *is* true, Finley!" She gripped the bedspread tightly, anger suddenly coming off her in waves. "Everything comes so god-damn easy for you that you don't appreciate what you got."

"Hey!"

"No!" She pointed her finger at me and I shut up. "Do you have any idea what I would give to be where you are? To have the opportunities you're going to have when you graduate?"

Now I was getting pissed. "Well, maybe you should've applied."

"I *did* apply, you little shit! How do you think your mom found out about Barrington in the first place?"

"She works in education—"

"*I* told her about it! *I* did." She jabbed her own chest for emphasis. "I did the research and I brought her the big shiny catalog and I asked her to help me with my application because she knows about what schools look for."

The big shiny catalog. Shit. A cold dread came over me.

"She . . . didn't help you?"

Maybe she heard the fear in my tone because her voice calmed and she shook her head. "No, she did. She helped. Then she asked me if I was okay with telling you about it, too."

Relief flooded. I wasn't sure how I'd react if my mom had done something to block Ayisha's application. But then I frowned. "Is that why you're so mad at me all the time? Because I got in and you didn't?"

Her eyes pierced me. "Oh, I got in. Full scholarship. Happiest day of my life. But then Mamma found the acceptance package and . . ." She stopped talking and dropped her gaze, the memory clearly upsetting.

My mind was spinning, trying to process. "Your mom didn't know you'd applied?" Ayisha shook her head and I felt something from her I never thought I'd feel—vulnerability. It was heavy. My throat closed and I realized I was teetering on the edge of tears. And I wasn't entirely sure why. I swallowed and asked quietly, "I mean, she was proud of you . . . wasn't she?"

She relaxed her hold on the bedspread but still held on. "She was a lotta things for me. Proud was one. But pragmatic won out." She dropped the bedspread to the mattress. "Someone had to watch the wonder twins while Mamma was at work. And that someone had to be me."

I filled in the blanks. "You withdrew."

"I withdrew." Her eyes met mine, sharp and unyielding. "You're welcome."

I reeled. But before the beginnings of a reply could start to form in my head, she nodded to the bed.

"I have a headache. Finish up, will ya?"

She didn't wait around for me to respond before she walked out, leaving me alone in the room with a swarm of questions that were going to have to wait.

Nineteen

"Are those *camels*?"

Arthur pointed at the small, dimly lit pen where indeed three bored camels were waiting for the tiny humans known as children to be placed on their mighty backs for a small fee as excited parents took photos and videos on their phones.

"Yep," I said, doing my best to keep myself out of the funk that had hit me on and off since my earlier encounter with Ayisha. I didn't want anyone to ask me if I was all right; there had been enough of that already and I didn't have the answer.

But if I kept brooding on the situation, I would wind up being a killjoy for the evening's excursion and that wasn't cool, either. Brody-and-Mia confrontation aside, last night's parade had been very close to successful, helped in part by the freaky synchronicity of the actual experience with my online creation.

So I pulled a card from Grandma Jo's hostess deck and pasted on a smile from the moment our quartet—Arthur, Aunt Esha, Grandma Jo, and me—assembled for our journey to Chickasha.

And it mostly worked. I did feel better.

At least in the moment.

Tonight, however, as I lay in my temporary bed, staring at the ceiling of my temporary room, would likely be another story. Then I could concentrate on what to do with the info bomb Ayisha'd dropped.

But that was hours away.

The air was brisk as the four of us walked around the Chickasha Festival of Light, which was a legitimately cool Christmas experience.

Not long after Thanksgiving was over, millions of colorful lights in all shapes and sizes went up around the forty-three-acre Shannon Springs Park. Visitors could either drive slowly through in bumper-to-bumper traffic or stroll the walkway, past the 172-foot Christmas tree, and the pond where plump ducks and geese lingered.

The main attraction, though, was the long pedestrian bridge that spanned the breadth of the pond and had every inch covered with white lights so bright I wouldn't be surprised if they could be seen from airliners flying high overhead. There were other attractions, too, all covered in lights. A Ferris wheel, carousel, food trucks, photos with Santa.

And camels.

Arthur's expression was almost accusatory. "You never said there would be camels."

"Arthur? There are camels at the lights festival."

His eyes narrowed and I snickered. Then he returned his attention to the incongruous beasts. "Why camels?"

"It's the Jesus part of Christmas. Three camels, Three Wise Men?"

"Of course." He shook his head as if he should have known that.

"Folks are big on Jesus around here," I explained. "Though everyone has their own version."

"There's only the one Jesus."

Grandma Jo spoke up. "But an infinite number of interpretations. Haven't you noticed there's a church on almost every other corner in town?"

"I had, rather." Arthur nodded. "Some are positively massive."

"'Our Jesus is better than your Jesus' is a favorite saying around here," she said wryly.

Arthur turned to his aunt. "Mashi, do you want to go closer to the camels?"

Aunt Esha smiled. "That's quite all right."

"There's a horse-drawn carriage ride if—" Grandma Jo started to offer only to be met by three simultaneous and emphatic "No!" from Aunt Esha, Arthur, and me.

Followed by Aunt Esha's "Thank you, though."

Then Grandma Jo got it. "Oh, right. The sleigh."

"Speaking only for myself, I've been around enough pack animals for this holiday." Aunt Esha rubbed her bare hands together.

Grandma Jo noticed.

"Should we go get a hot drink?" she asked.

Aunt Esha's dark eyes widened. "I like that idea very much."

I assumed Arthur and I would go with them, not that I was in the mood for a beverage. We had only just arrived and the food trucks were on the other side of the festival.

However, Grandma Jo was on a different page. She smiled at me. "Finley, you and Arthur should keep going. We'll meet you back here in an hour?"

I blinked. Surprised. "Um, okay."

Grandma Jo and Aunt Esha wasted no time in leaving Arthur and me as they walked on ahead, branching off to a different pedestrian pathway until the trees and festival-goers blocked them from sight.

I'm not gonna lie, I felt mildly miffed. *Did my grandmother just* ditch *me?* She had been acting weird lately. Maybe she and Arthur's aunt were going to have "girl talk" about Dr. Raymond and Dad and she didn't want "the kids" around, but that didn't mean she had to peel off with her new BFF.

Then again, that also meant Arthur and I were alone.

And a zing of excitement shot through my chest. Not that anything would be done about it. Still, I smiled inside.

For his part, Arthur appeared focused on continuing onward to see as much as possible.

He nodded to the light-strewn pathway. "Shall we? I want to check out the Ferris wheel, the carousel, and then the bridge."

He ticked them off on his fingers with determination.

I gestured to the pathway with a wrist flourish.

As we walked, I noticed the other couples strolling together, cuddled and hand in hand. I wondered what it would've been like to be here on a date with Arthur. Other than the occasional sugar-fed child running away from their parents, the atmosphere was romantic. Whimsical. There was something about the multitude of colorful lights wrapped around the bases of all the trees along the pathways or interwoven through their branches that helped foster a fairy tale–like atmosphere.

Unfortunately, Arthur didn't seem to be with me on this. But at least he appeared to be having a good time.

When we reached the carousel, there was a line of twenty people ahead of us.

I pointed to the towering mobile Ferris wheel, which was nearby and where the line was smaller. "Do you want to ride that first?"

Arthur glanced up at it.

"No."

"Afterwards?"

"No."

"I thought you wanted to see it."

"'See' being the operative word. And I have. It's quite impressive."

The carousel started to slow down and the final bars of Peggy Lee's "Christmas Carousel" played out, which meant it would soon be our turn to board.

"Are you afraid of heights?" I asked.

He unzipped the front of his jacket.

"It's not fear. It's respect." He took out his wallet from his interior pocket. "For gravity."

Before I realized what he was doing, he handed over a twenty to the guy controlling the carousel and held up two fingers.

"No, wait—" I said, reaching for my small purse hanging crossways over my chest.

Arthur held up a hand. "I'm making you endure yet another night of my company, the least I can do is not have you pay for it."

Carousel Guy nodded at us and we went forward to the carousel itself, which was, of course, covered in lights forming a point high above. We had our choice of pastel-colored horses, a giraffe, zebra, possibly a dragon (never could figure it out), and two red benches that too closely resembled sleighs for my comfort level.

Funky horse it was.

Arthur took the maybe-dragon beside me. "Do you want me to snap a picture of you?" he asked, nodding to me on the horse.

"No, that's okay. My hair has too much static." I ran my hand over it and parts of it floated outward to prove my point.

"That's half the fun." He grinned, leaning his cheek against the pole.

"That's okay."

"No one will know who took the photo."

Our eyes met and I realized he was offering to keep himself anonymous. As if I wouldn't want anyone to know the two of us were out socializing.

I felt a twinge in my heart. "I wouldn't care if they did," I said, and caught the barest glimpse of relief in his eyes. I cocked my head. "Did you think I would?"

He shrugged. "I noticed you haven't updated any of your posts anywhere since you've been back home."

I tipped my head to one side. "You follow me?"

"No. I did a virtual drive-by."

"Like a creeper," I teased.

His lips twitched. "Absolutely."

"Well, for the record, I haven't updated anything because . . ." *I've been too up in my own head.* ". . . I've been too busy. Haven't even checked in."

Other than Twitter for basic news purposes, even though that was usually too depressing. Someone somewhere was always doing something to piss off someone else and it gave me a headache. Besides, almost none of my friends used it. I usually checked out the full spectrum of social media, even Facebook, though that was mainly for keeping up with some of the older relatives. But I didn't live on it like most of my peers.

"That explains it," he said, his tone breezy.

"Do *you* want a pic?"

He hesitated and to my amazement I realized he did.

Before he could answer, I hopped off the horse and came over to him, taking out my phone to get a bunch of shots. He was awkward at first, no surprise, but then startled me by throwing out a perfect Blue Steel, which cracked me up and that earned a genuine smile in return. *With* that cheek dimple. Which I caught on camera.

And in the process, lost my funky horse. A small boy with a Where's Waldo red-and-white knit cap jumped on it and his mother moved to help keep him in place. A quick glance around and I realized there were no more open rides.

Which is when the carousel creaked to life.

Arthur pushed himself up as if to give me his spot, but this time I held up my hand.

"Stay," I insisted.

Instead, I grabbed the pole of the dragon (?) with one hand and its nose with the other then planted my feet as the speed started to pick up. Arthur reached down to grab hold of my wrist to help me with balance and I had a flashback to the pond at Barrington.

"It's not endure, you know," I said and our eyes met. His brows drew forward in a slight frown of confusion and I clarified. "Earlier, you said I had to 'endure' your company, but that's not true."

"Isn't it?"

I shook my head.

He stared at me and slowly his dark eyes with those amazing lashes softened while at the same time the air around us crackled.

The treacly music grew louder to the point of overwhelming, and I wasn't in the mood to try to shout over it. Glancing around at everyone else, I didn't recognize anyone in particular, but I felt a connection with the environment. Not the carousel, per se, but the Oklahomaness of it all. There was comfort to being back in surroundings I knew so well. Relief. Oklahoma and Connecticut were two very different states, two very different perspectives and ways of life, and while Chickasha wasn't my hometown, it carried the same familiarity.

The distraction mixed with centrifugal force caused me to wobble.

Arthur's grip on my wrist tightened.

I glanced back up to find him staring down at me, his eyes hooded. Then, keeping his gaze on mine, he relaxed his hold ever so slightly but only so his fingers slipped from my wrist to my hand, and our fingers laced together. My heart beat wildly in my chest.

We stayed that way for the rest of the ride.

Twenty

The pedestrian bridge was always the most popular spot in the lights festival. I didn't know its full length, only that it was long and the white lights extended the whole way over the inky water where its illuminated reflection was captured in mirror-like clarity.

The narrow breadth only allowed for two lines of visitors, going in opposing directions, which caused many a traffic jam.

Standing back from the entrance, Arthur stared at the bridge, his face bathed by its canopy of lights, hands stuffed in the front pockets of his jacket. Both of them. Sadly.

Our hand-holding ended as soon as the carousel ride was over.

But by now, I was more confident there was some unspoken chemistry going on that, much like the bridge itself, went in two directions.

I nudged Arthur's elbow with my own. "We can't leave the lights festival without walking across the bridge."

That seemed to pull him out of whatever it was that was dancing around in his mind.

We started forward.

There wasn't a formal line, like with the carousel or Ferris wheel, so we merged in behind a middle-aged couple who were without kids; they were probably on a date.

I fleetingly wondered if they'd do what so many other couples did and take advantage of the shadows beyond the lights to make out. It was a time-honored tradition. Then I wondered if Arthur and I might do that and I felt a flush of heat go through my body.

About midway across the bridge, the couple paused and turned to ask us to snap their picture with the white lights as background. Arthur accepted their phone and as he was taking his time with the precise framing, the guy withdrew some mistletoe to hold over his wife's (girlfriend's? mistress's?) head, pulling a goofy face as he kissed her cheek.

"Thanks, kid," the guy said, as he accepted his phone back. "Want one of you two?"

"Oh, that's not—" Arthur started.

"Sure," I interrupted, and handed over my phone to the woman. This might be the one chance to sneak in a pic of the two of us and I was not about to let the opportunity slide.

Arthur assumed his usual robot-posture when caught off guard, but I knew he would and took further advantage of the moment to slip my arm through his and smile like a goofball.

As the woman framed the shot, the guy held up the mistletoe. "Wanna borrow . . . ?"

"No, thank you," Arthur said.

"It's a parasite," I added.

The guy frowned at us in confusion, but Arthur looked down at me and we smiled at our own inside joke.

Ten minutes later we were on the other side of the bridge and in yet another line, this one for a hot beverage at one of the food trucks. I kept my eyes peeled for Grandma Jo and Aunt Esha, but neither was around. Which was fine. We were supposed to meet them back over by the camels in twenty minutes anyhow.

Once Arthur had his hot apple cider and I my peppermint tea, we slowly strolled toward the edge of the pond and stood there, side by side, gazing at the lights on the other bank. We were away from the hordes and it was quieter.

The moon shone down from high in the indigo sky, and the sounds of the festival seemed more distant from where we were, so that it felt like we were isolated. The bridge was very much in view still, which made me think of the photo we'd taken, and that reminded me . . .

"So, what was her name?" I asked, not expecting him to know what I meant, which he didn't.

"Whose name?"

"Mistletoe girl."

He returned his gaze out over the water and for a second I wasn't sure he would answer.

But then he said, "Astrid." And sighed heavily, almost a huff, and I saw his breath dance on the cold night air.

"Astrid," I repeated, taking it in, rolling it around in my mind for a moment and deciding it belonged in the same family as Poppy or Millicent. "Is she still around?" I kept my voice casual. I was proud of that.

He shrugged one shoulder. "Somewhere."

"Waiting for you?"

He laughed without humor. "No."

I suppose I should have let the subject drop since it clearly wasn't pleasant. But now that I knew there was a girl he'd liked, I needed to know more.

I decided to keep my tone light. *La-la-la, no big deal, oh, and,* "Does she have as cool a last name as Ramsbottom?"

He snorted. "Blanchard."

"Too bad." I took a sip of my drink and let the hot peppermint sensation warm me from the inside. "How did you two meet?"

He was quiet and I worried I might be going too far. But he seemed to have decided to at least venture into this area of his past.

"We met through my sister, Polly. She works with Astrid's father in finance. Deadly dull."

"I thought you liked finance."

"I do. I meant Lord Blanchard is deadly dull."

I laughed. "Lord Blanchard, huh? Fancy."

"Very."

"When did you meet young Lady Astrid?"

He slowly started walking along the edge of the pond and I fell in step beside him. "It was two summers ago."

Keep it playful, Finley. NBD.

"Ooooh. A summer romance."

"I wouldn't go that far."

I noticed there were more shadowy couples around this area, no doubt attracted by the darkness and surrounding trees.

"Did you and Astrid date all the way from summer to Christmas? Is that how the mistletoe came in?"

Arthur slowly twirled his cup of cider. "It's . . . it's, um . . ." He stopped and sighed. ". . . difficult. Embarrassing." He rubbed the back of his neck before facing me. "Humiliating, really."

Oh. This was different. It was one thing to get a romantic backstory from the boy you liked, it was quite another when that same backstory was the source of humiliation and pain.

I waved him off, taking a step back. "You don't have to tell me."

But it would seem he wanted to. "The short version is I liked her. I thought she liked me. I was wrong." He said it as if stating mere facts disassociated from himself. He resumed walking and I followed.

"Her mistake."

He sent me a wry look. "Isn't that what people say when they're trying to make you feel better?"

"Yes. But it's also the truth."

For what it was worth, he seemed to appreciate that. A cuddly couple approaching us from the opposite direction passed by. We nodded politely to each other as we crossed and continued on our respective ways.

"Actually, it *was* my mistake," he admitted. "Quite a doozy, too."

"You really don't have to tell me."

"I haven't told anyone. Not since it happened."

"Does your family know what happened?"

Resentment flashed across his expression. "Oh, yes. They know. All of them. And Sonya Martinez."

I frowned. "Ms. Martinez?"

He nodded. "At my auntie's behest, Sonya helped me gain admission to Barrington . . ." He cleared his throat. ". . . after I was kicked out of my previous boarding school in the UK."

I felt my eyes widen in surprise and I stopped, catching him by the jacket sleeve. "Kicked *out*?"

A big inhale and exhale. "I should probably start at the beginning," he murmured. I waited as he chose where to begin. "I met Astrid when Polly brought Lord Blanchard and his family to my parents' home in St. George's Hill, which is close enough to London to be convenient but not so close as to be *too* convenient."

"The riffraff are kept out."

"Nearly everyone is kept out."

"But not the Blanchards."

"Oh, no," he murmured dryly. "Definitely *not* the Blanchards."

I searched his face, which was difficult to do in the heavy shadows, but enough of the festival's light made its way over to us from the four huge, white snowflakes marking the far end of the pond that I could see the hint of bitterness.

"Did you crush on her right away?"

"Sadly, yes. But in my defense, she's quite attractive. Superficially. She attended Raleigh School and at the time I was at Jarrow Academy. They're not far from each other, which I took to mean fate. But it didn't. Not in the way I'd hoped. We flirted madly over two weekends in August and exchanged numbers so the flirting continued well into the school year, even though we didn't see each other."

"That must've been difficult."

"Yes. So much so, I decided to take it upon myself to remedy the situation by calling on her at her school."

"Is this where the mistletoe comes in?"

"Not yet. Don't be impatient."

"Sorry. Continue."

"When I arrived at her dormitory at Raleigh, she refused to come down to meet me."

"After you'd come all that way?"

"It wasn't that far, really. Our two schools were affiliated and there was quite a bit of cross-dating between Jarrow and Raleigh."

"Still."

His lips quirked. "Yes. My disappointment was acute. Until she texted her apologies."

"Oh. Didn't see that coming."

"We started texting all the time afterwards."

A terrible thought tickled the back of my mind. "Just texting?"

He wagged his finger. "Ah, look how quickly you caught on." He placed the flat of his palm to his chest. "I, however, was a bit too credulous."

A sense of dread bloomed in my chest. "Oh, no."

"Oh, yes."

"What happened?" I whispered, even though I wasn't entirely sure I wanted to hear.

"Christmas. Raleigh was hosting a Christmas party and Astrid invited me to attend. *With* her."

"This feels ominous."

"Only because you know part of the outcome. Young, blissfully ignorant sixteen-year-old Arthur took the time to research mistletoe—this is where it's finally pertinent—and decided to disregard all the unromantic aspects of its origins to concentrate on the romantic ones. Thus, I secured a bunch, wrapped it in red ribbon, and made my way to Raleigh for the Christmas Dance."

"There was no Christmas dance!" I guessed.

"There was indeed a Christmas dance."

"Oh. Please tell me you didn't end up with a bucket of pig's blood poured on your head."

Arthur stared at me.

"Sorry." I made a zipping motion over my lips. Nodded at him to continue.

He shook his head. "I was not Carrie in this situation." I

gave him a very silent thumbs-up, then he cocked his head to one side. "Although, come to think of it, perhaps I was. To a degree. Though no bodily fluids were dumped at any point."

I rolled my hand for him to get on with it. This was like being in a movie where you knew the main character didn't make it to the end but you're not *quite* sure how that came to be so you're waiting for the proverbial ax to fall or shoe to drop or, in this case, heart to break and it was *torture*.

"At the dance were Cory Goedert and a group of his mates. They attended Jarrow with me and they enjoyed making my life . . . difficult." His eyes darkened and despite his efforts, I heard the underlying pain this caused him. A flurry of awful possibilities caused my stomach to clench.

"I'm sorry, Arthur," I said quietly.

That earned a small but sincere smile. "Thank you," he murmured. "My situation with them was made even more difficult because . . ." His jaw hardened. ". . . Cory was dating Astrid the whole time."

"No!"

"Mmmm. It gets worse."

My hand went over my eyes.

"He delighted in informing me that *he* was the one who'd been sending me the flirty text messages and also the one who invited me to the Christmas Dance. Not Astrid."

God. The mortification he must have felt when he learned. I had a mad urge to fly to England, find this Cory asshole, and . . . I wasn't sure exactly what, but it would be epic. And Astrid, too.

Which raised another question.

"Did she know what was going on?"

"I never fully found out. She knew some of it, I could tell as much by her expression."

"That's awful." I shook my head. "But wait. How did you get kicked out of Jarrow?"

"At the dance, Cory and his pack surrounded me when I went to speak with Astrid. I was sorely outnumbered and, frankly, I was . . . unnerved. And incredibly angry. Not at Astrid, I wasn't thinking like that. But at what had happened, what *was* happening. Cory came at me and I—" He closed his eyes and his shoulders slumped. "I hit him first. Broke his nose. But that wasn't what caused all the problems. Well, not by itself." Arthur's eyes grew pained. "Cory went flying back, into Astrid." I gasped and my hand went to my mouth. "She wound up with a black eye."

"Oh, Arthur."

"Eliminating a considerable amount of back-and-forth, both in the moment and later once our families got involved, Lord Blanchard and Mr. Goedert made certain I was booted from Jarrow and then proceeded to blackball me from every other private school in the UK."

"What about your parents? Didn't they fight for you?"

He stopped walking again, his gaze unseeing over my shoulder. "They did not." His tone was flat. "By the time I got to tell my side, Polly had already reached them and told them what she'd heard from Lord Blanchard, that I was an out-of-control danger who needed to be expelled and sent somewhere far away."

"America?"

"I don't think they particularly cared where, so long as I wasn't anywhere near Astrid or Cory."

Sometimes words failed. And sometimes the simplest were the best. "They suck," I said, and reached out to squeeze his hand.

He squeezed back. "The only person who had my back

throughout was Auntie Esha. She placed her call to Sonya."

Of course. I felt a stab of guilt at all the unkind thoughts I'd silently directed at his aunt over the course of their stay. No matter what was going on between her and my dad, she had been a strong supporter for Arthur at his worst moments and that had to count for something.

"And so you came to Barrington."

"Yes. By that January I was a Barrington Eagle. Rah-rah." He smiled a small smile. "I suppose that means next month will be my anniversary."

"I guess it does."

"Shall we have a party? Not invite Bronwyn?"

I felt like a deer in headlights and released his hand like it suddenly caught fire.

He grew puzzled. "Finley?"

"No, yeah." I bobbed my head and tucked my hair over one ear, both of which were the equivalent of a neon sign that said UNCOMFORTABLE! "That sounds, yeah . . ."

I resumed walking back in the direction we'd come from, toward the festival and escape.

Arthur followed and his eyes bore into me, obviously sensing something was amiss. "What is it?"

For a hot moment I considered spilling about not going back to Barrington. But on the heels of him telling me about his raw and deeply vulnerable experience, it didn't feel like the right moment. However, Ayisha's face popped up in my mind and I went with that.

"Actually, I just learned something about Barrington, and I'm not sure how I feel about it."

"What was it?"

So I stopped walking and told him. Not the part about staying in Christmas, but the part about Ayisha and how, even though I didn't know for certain, I was convinced the only reason I got into Barrington is because she had been forced to withdraw. Which made me feel like a changeling and wish she could have stayed.

When I finished, I gave a helpless shrug. "No wonder she hates me. I'd hate me, too."

He chewed the corner of his lip for a moment, which, truth, was a welcome if fleeting distraction. "I don't think she hates you for that."

"You don't?"

"No. Probably more resentment, I should think. Not hate."

"Oh, much better." I frowned. "Wait. She told you she resented me?"

His eyes widened. "No! Not at all. It was more how her upper lip would curl when she said your name." He demonstrated.

It was familiar.

But, more to the point, "You guys were talking about me?" Then another, deeply unnerving thought occurred. "Did she invite you to Brody's party? Are you two going together?"

"What? No! I only referenced you on the day we met, about our school connection. Which in hindsight could also explain the lip curl." He refocused on me. "And what's this about Brody's party?"

Arthur's own lip curled as he said Brody's name.

"Brody has a party tomorrow night and I thought Ayisha was going to invite you to go with her."

"Oh." He pulled a face. "I know I initially said I wanted to go to a party, but all things considered, I'd rather not go to that one."

"Thank God."

He grew thoughtful again. "Was Ayisha's withdrawal from school temporary or permanent?"

"I didn't ask."

"Because if it's temporary, she could possibly still be admitted. And I'm proof that one can be admitted midway through the year. Most people don't take that into consideration, but there are often openings that pop up each semester. People drop out for all sorts of reasons."

Another stab of guilt hit me. This was Segue City right here. An open invitation from the Universe. *Speaking of that . . .* , was what I could have interjected here. Or *Interesting you should mention people dropping out . . .*

But I didn't.

Instead, I cleared my newly dry throat. "True."

Arthur, oblivious to my personal tumult, continued blithely. "For instance, you'll soon be getting a new roommate," he said.

It took a second for his meaning to compute, then my eyes widened. "What?"

"With Thea leaving."

I shook my head, probably too dramatically, but I was feeling dramatic. "Why is Thea leaving?"

He cocked his head at me. "I gather the two of you aren't close."

"She treats our dorm like a drive-by closet and she spends almost all of her time with Beaux."

"A bond that will likely continue for many years to come."

"You're talking in Arthur-speak again. Why is Thea leaving Barrington?"

He stuffed his hands in his jacket pockets. "This feels dangerously close to gossip."

"Which I'm a hundred percent okay with."

"I'm not."

Great. He drops broad hints then decides to establish moral boundaries.

I took a breath. "Okay, so. Not gossip? But instead think of it like you're providing me with much-needed information about my living situation."

He struck a philosophical pose. "But is it *truly* 'much-needed'—?"

"Arthur!"

"She's pregnant."

I did a double take. And truthfully? The first thought through my mind—after *holy shit!*—was, *Oh, thank God it was* her *and not* me! Not that the possibility was even present, at least without divine intervention. But when both your mother and grandmother got knocked up way too early in their lives, let me tell you, the fear is *ever present*. The few times Brody had tried to go there with me, I dropped the words "pregnant" and "baby" and "diaper changes" and that always did the trick.

But a funny thing happened as I was digesting this latest bit of bombshell news—I glanced away from Arthur. The kind of unconscious glance you do when you're trying to fully comprehend something that's pretty huge.

My eyes just flittered off.

And that's when I saw them.

Over Arthur's shoulder by about twenty yards. Past the lights. In the shadows by one of the trees. Two shapes, clearly a couple, close together in a way that suggested more than friendship. They were walking together, giggling, adjusting clothes and hair and exchanging heavy-lidded looks that lingered and needed no explanation.

Grandma Jo reached over to lightly brush a strand of hair

away from the cheek of Esha Chakrabarti and earned a soft smile as her reward.

And I reeled as my brain exploded. All thoughts of Ayisha's place at Barrington or Thea's pregnancy were banished to the ether.

In that instant, I realized I'd been right all along.

Aunt Esha *had* been having a holiday romance.

It just wasn't with my father.

"Finley," Arthur said, trying to draw my attention back to him. "You're doing that thing again where you look like you're lost in a haze."

I rubbed a hand over my eyes to try to orient myself. "Sorry," I mumbled, my heart slamming against my chest as I dropped my hand to my side. And counted to ten before opening my eyes. "Can we, um . . . head back?"

He flicked his jacket sleeve back to look at his watch. "Right. We're running a bit late. I hope they haven't been waiting long."

Oh, no need to worry about that.

I made a noncommittal sound in the back of my throat and we started toward the festival.

With Arthur beside me, my focus stayed forward in order to keep them in my sight. They were ahead of us by at least a dozen yards, as we all reentered the hyper-illuminated area of the festival. That was when Arthur recognized them from behind.

"Mashi," he called out.

Both women turned around to face us and any scintilla of uncertainty vanished as dual looks of surprise crossed their faces at seeing us. Their red lips and mussed hair could have been dismissed as resulting from the cold.

I knew they weren't.

"Hi, Grandma," I said tightly.

Grandma Jo smiled. "Hello, you two." Then she dipped the lower half of her face into the Burberry scarf wrapped around her neck. I'd never before seen it on her; I had, however, seen it on Esha Chakrabarti.

My mind was popping like fireworks. I didn't know what to say or do. Was there an entry in a manners guide about how to behave when you find your grandmother has been getting frisky with the aunt of the boy you like? Oh, and by the way, you had no idea she was remotely into women? How would you list that in the index? Under Hella Awkward Family Moments?

I clenched my jaw so hard it was a miracle I didn't crack a tooth.

Which reminded me of Dr. Raymond.

Who was probably never gonna get any use out of that mistletoe.

"Did you have fun?" Esha asked, as we reached them.

Arthur nodded. "Yes. It's nice." For him, that was a five-star review.

I stared at my grandmother. "Did *you* have fun?"

She blinked at me, uncertain. "We did." Her eyes darted away and she blew into her hands. "But it's getting cold. Should we head back home?"

Esha smiled at her. "Yes, let's."

The four of us resumed our trek to the parking lot. I watched them exchange fleeting glances and I kicked myself the entire way.

How had I failed to see it? Because now that I knew it was beyond obvious. The looks, their body language and laughter. It was *right there*. I felt like a complete idiot.

As soon as we got back to the Hoyden, I was going to talk . . . with someone.

My father? Did he know? About his mother?

And why did no one tell *me*? I felt excluded from my own family. Again.

I also vowed to corner my grandmother because I *had questions*. Lots and loads and buckets and barrels of questions.

And I would have done exactly that once we returned to the inn and entered the premises from the back way . . .

. . . except when the four of us turned down the flat stone pathway that led from the Hoyden's parking area, we found our path blocked by my father, who was gesturing as he engaged in an intense and highly animated discussion.

With my mother.

Twenty-One

"**M**om!"

I practically launched myself into her arms and hugged her fiercely.

She hugged me back and it wasn't until then that I realized how much I had missed her. How she felt, how she smelled. Everything. The overwhelming number of issues I needed to talk with her about took a back seat to just having her here again. With me. Finally.

"Hi, honey," she whispered against my hair, and the sting of tears pricked at my eyes and throat.

I forgot for a moment that other people were present. But when I drew back to look at her, I caught sight of Arthur and his aunt continuing on in the direction of the inn. He glanced back before turning out of sight and sent me a reassuring smile, which I appreciated.

My lips folded in and I pressed them hard. I wanted to call him back as some sort of reinforcement. I didn't. I sniffed and wiped my face instead.

Grandma Jo and Dad remained.

Mom kept her arms around me. She smelled like vanilla and

sandalwood and looked exactly like she always did. Blonde. Blue-eyed. Pretty. Her hair was cut differently, though. Shorter and with a bit more edge. For as long as I could remember, she went to Nelda Hodge's house for her cut and color, her natural blonde hair having faded into an undeniable brown at the end of her twenties. But now her shoulder-length style had been re-shaped to something trendy, with layers and bangs and it was kinda . . . sexy? I wasn't sure how I felt about that.

"I'm glad you're here," I said. My voice was thick with emo-tion. And exhaustion. It had been another long day and I had already been tired when we left for the lights festival. Now I was wiped, yet also buzzing on an adrenaline hit that too soon would fade.

I glanced between her and Dad, whom I noticed was no lon-ger animated as he watched us.

Grandma Jo nodded to Mom. "Good to see you, Dana," she said, her tone measured, but not cold. I was pretty sure there was a thread of relief mixed in there.

Mom must have heard it, too, because her nod to my grand-mother wasn't perfunctory or stiff, which had been known to happen between them.

Despite being in each other's lives as family members for at least seventeen years—since before I was born—Mom and Grandma Jo were never going to be great friends. They weren't enemies, either. They were two people whose lives would likely never have intermingled in any meaningful way had they not intermingled in the one of the most meaningful ways possible.

Me.

"Hi, Jo," Mom said, her hand unconsciously rubbing small circles in between my shoulder blades.

"Finley and I are just returning from Chickasha," my grandmother continued, as if merely relaying mundane information, as if my mother had been gone only for the day instead of for the past few weeks. "We were at the lights festival."

Mom smiled. "That sounds like fun."

Grandma Jo nodded. "It was."

In the back of my mind, I wanted to hit pause on my life. Go to the kitchen. Get a glass of water, and maybe some leftover pie. Lie on the sofa, watch a movie. Or stare at nothing and let the tsunami of recent life events settle in to the point I could properly digest them, figure out what was important and what wasn't. And once I knew, I'd hit play on the cosmic remote to resume right here in this moment.

Grandma Jo made eye contact with Dad and looked toward Mom. "Do you two want to continue your conversation? In the privacy of your cottage?"

That last part was clearly a hint to my parents to take whatever it was they had been arguing about indoors, away from prying eyes and ears.

Dad shook his head. "I think these two could use some time together." Mom nodded her agreement and added a smile of appreciation. He turned to Grandma Jo. "Do you want to come over?"

"Sure," his mother said.

Dad leaned down and kissed the top of my head. "Night, sport."

"Night, Dad."

The adults said their goodnights to each other in that polite way adults do when things are tense but there are children present, and as much as I was tempted to call them out on it, I was also relieved.

When it was just the two of us, Mom squeezed my shoulder. "Do you want to go back to the house?"

"All my stuff's here at the inn."

"We can get it, bring it with us."

I considered the idea for a moment then shook my head. "I have the breakfast shift. Maybe tomorrow."

"Of course."

I crossed my arms over my chest. "Can we go inside? It's freezing."

She smiled and stroked my hair. "You bet."

The Yablonskis and the Meacos were bundled up and seated around the propane-fueled brick firepit in the courtyard, laughing and drinking as Mom and I passed. They smiled and waved. We did the same in return then entered the inn through the back door.

Right inside there was a standalone restroom and Mom stopped by it.

"Honey, I'm going to take a minute to freshen up," she said. "I'll meet you in the lobby lounge."

She dipped into the restroom and I continued on down the back hallway that goes past the kitchen.

As I passed the open doorway, though, I caught a glimpse of Arthur inside. The overhead lights were off and the only illumination came from the under-cabinet LED lights, but I saw him and immediately made a detour.

He still wore his jacket as he poured hot water from the kettle into one of the Hoyden mugs, a tea-bag string visible over the side.

"Hey. I thought you were going upstairs," I said, inhaling the aroma of cinnamon.

He smiled when he saw me and I couldn't help thinking

how much had changed between us in such a short period.

"In a moment," he said, then nodded to the mug. "Tea helps me decompress at the end of the day."

"Same. Though tonight I may need a gallon."

The corner of his mouth curved up, in sympathy and understanding, not mockery. "You have had quite the holiday so far, haven't you?" he noted, his voice softer, deeper.

I was tempted to laugh at his understatement, but held back. There was something about the lighting and the stillness of our surroundings that invited whispers. He set the kettle aside and leaned his hip against the counter and his focus shifted entirely on me, which sent my heart hammering wildly.

"Thank you," he murmured.

"What for?"

"Listening earlier. Being on my side." His gaze fell away for a moment. "I haven't talked about . . . all that happened with anyone other than my auntie in a long time. And absolutely no one my age. It's a bit freeing, really."

That surprised me, despite knowing how high he tended to keep the walls around himself. I wasn't sure I could've held off telling someone *not* in my family my side of a story like his. But that made me even more aware how big a step this was. For him. For me. For us.

"Thank you for trusting me enough to tell me," I said.

And the way he just looked at me, intensely, it almost felt as if the ground beneath our feet was shifting, tipping us forward toward each other.

"I do, you know," he said, in a voice so soft I almost missed it.

I leaned forward into the space between us, narrowing it. "What?"

He reached out to touch my hair. "Trust y—"

"Finley, there you are."

Arthur and I straightened away from each other in a flash and I turned to see Mom enter the kitchen. Her attention bounced between me and Arthur, curious.

"Hi, hi," I said awkwardly. "Mom, this is Arthur Chakrabarti Watercress. Arthur, this is my mom."

Arthur nodded. "How do you do, ma'am."

Mom smiled. "Arthur, right. Finley mentioned you."

His brow lifted in surprise. "Oh? Good things, I hope."

"Just about the sleigh ride." Her smile thinned. "And that you were here with your aunt. Is she around?"

Crap! I turned my back to Arthur enough that I could widen my eyes at my mother, send her a white-hot "cease and desist" look.

"Auntie is upstairs," he told her.

Mom plastered on a brighter expression that I knew from experience wasn't remotely authentic. "Well, I look forward to meeting her, too."

Taking Mom's hand, I turned back to Arthur. "Okay, so, good talk. Had a lotta fun tonight. Mom and I are going to the lobby. Bye!"

I didn't give either of them a chance to say another word. Which was a shame, really, because there was a lot more I wanted to say to Arthur, but I couldn't risk it.

"He seems nice," Mom said, as we headed down the hall near the lobby.

"He is." I lowered my voice. "And his aunt was never flirting with Dad."

Mom gave me a look that was difficult to read as we walked. "You're sure about that now?"

"So, so, *so* sure." I didn't tell her why I was certain. It felt important to get official verification about Esha's orientation and relationship with Grandma Jo before I blurted out something else misleading to my mother. There were enough messes for me to clean up already, thanks.

When we rounded the corner into the lobby we found it blessedly empty. Except for Val, who was leaning against the interior of the front desk, arms crossed, eyes closed. Yet she still said, "Merry Christmas, Mrs. Brown," when we entered.

Mom smiled in return. "Merry Christmas to you, too, Val."

Val's eyes never moved.

Mom and I continued to the far end of the lounge and sat on the floral sofas, surrounded by the sights and smells of late December. The fire in the fireplace dwindled but still had enough energy left to heat the room.

We sat facing each other, both feet on the floor in a way that was suddenly weirdly formal and I didn't like it.

I stood.

"Do you want something to drink?" I asked Mom, gesturing to the hot chocolate bar in the corner. Arthur had inspired me.

"Some hot water would be nice."

I should have guessed that. After the sun went down in winter, Mom liked to drink hot water only. In summer, it was a big glass of ice water. It was one of her quirks. I preferred to disguise my water with something, which right then was a bag of Harney & Sons holiday black tea and a packet of raw sugar. Which wouldn't necessarily help me decompress from this crazy day, but it tasted good and gave me something to do with my hands.

Once that was accomplished, I sat back down again and faced her, holding the mug in my lap.

"It's good to see you," she said, reaching out to touch my forearm. "How are you?"

Where to begin?

"Fine," I lied.

"Not too busy at the inn?"

"Nope."

"Good."

This was excruciating. I'd never had this much difficulty talking with my mom. Sure, we'd had our issues and there were many times when I'd want her to leave me alone. *Many* times. But that was basic teenager stuff.

This? This felt like I was talking with my Uncle Lonnie in Florida, whom I barely knew.

Mom continued. "Did you and Arthur have any more adventures?" Off my puzzled look, she continued. "You know, like with the sleigh ride? That sounded so fun."

I scoffed. "We nearly died." An exaggeration.

"Oh." She deflated a little. "The way you told it, it sounded like you'd had fun."

"There were some good parts about it," I admitted begrudgingly.

She brightened. "Yeah? Like what?"

Holding Arthur's hand unexpectedly. Seeing him in that red nose and cracking up. Realizing I liked him in all his idiosyncrasies. Were they because he was British or absurdly wealthy and thereby out of touch with normal behavior, or because he was simply Arthur and that was who he was?

I told her none of those things. Rather, "We got reindeer cheese," was what I said. "It's in the refrigerator." I pointed over my shoulder, back in the direction of the kitchen.

"Reindeer cheese?"

"Uh-huh." I nodded. "It's smoked."

"Oh." She appeared to be figuring out what to do with that information. "Is it any good?"

"I haven't tried it."

"Well." She tapped her nails against the side of the mug and I noticed she was still wearing her white gold wedding ring with the tiny diamonds. "Maybe Grandma Jo will put it out for the Christmas Eve party."

"Maybe." I bit my lip. The lights of the lobby Christmas tree danced off her face and for a second she seemed young, like my age. "Are you going to be here for that?" I asked her.

Her brow furrowed slightly. "Sure. I go every year."

"But this . . . isn't like every year," I pointed out. "Is it?"

A silence followed.

She dropped her eyes. "No. It isn't."

More silence. Until I couldn't take it. "I wasn't sure you were coming back," I burst out.

She sighed. "Of course I was, honey." Her tone was placating, which irked me. "Christmas is my home."

"But you were gone for months."

"Five weeks."

"It feels longer."

"You just found out."

A minor detail.

"And about that," I said. "Why didn't you say something? We had calls every week and you never mentioned anything was going on with you and Dad."

She shrugged helplessly. "You were at school. And we . . . we were working it out."

"From Missouri?"

"I came back."

"After five weeks."

"Actually, I tried to come back sooner, but your dad thought it would be good for me to stay gone a while longer."

That surprised me. The impression I'd had was that she was the one who chose to be gone the entire time. Before I could ask "why," though, she rubbed her hand over her forehead, seeming tired again, regardless of her attempt at freshening up.

"Honey, I don't want to have this discussion here." She glanced in Val's direction before refocusing on me. Her forced smile was at least partially genuine. "Why don't you get your things and come home with me tonight?"

"I told you, I have to be here early for my shift."

"You've done early shifts from home before. It's a five-minute drive. I can bring you if you like. Or now that you're sixteen you can drive yourself."

"I don't have my driver's license," I reminded her.

"Oh, right. We should get you your license before you go back. When is that, anyhow? Have you already bought the ticket?"

"No."

"Okay, we'll do that before you go back—"

"I'm not going back."

As soon as I heard the words tumble from my lips out into the world at large, I sat up straighter. Because I hadn't meant to actually say them. And not so definitively.

But I had.

Mom tipped her head in confusion. "What do you mean?"

"I-I . . ." A deep breath. "I don't want to go back to Barrington." *I think. Maybe.*

She carefully set her cup of hot water on the coffee table to focus on me. "Why?"

Her gaze was sharp now, and I knew I wasn't going to get out of this, regardless of how tired either of us was. Still, I made the attempt.

"For a lot of reasons."

"Finley."

"Fine. Because I'm not good at it, Mom." There. I'd said it to her. "My grades are lame and I have no friends and there's nothing for me there. Nothing."

Except Arthur.

That thought slipped in when I wasn't looking and I couldn't deny it. He was my biggest reason to return at this point and the lure was undeniable. My gut told me it wasn't enough. We hadn't even kissed, though maybe we were headed that way a few minutes ago.

Still. We definitely weren't a couple. To make an enormous decision based on a few moments and the feelings of connection that were only now starting to seem real was foolish and risked being self-destructive.

And besides, "I shouldn't be there."

This caught Mom off guard. "What do you mean? Of course you should."

"Ayisha should have that spot, not me."

Mom blinked in surprise. "How did you find out about that?"

Now I blinked in surprise. "So you did know?"

"Well, of course. I helped her apply."

"No, I meant that I took her spot."

"*That* I don't know for sure. No one does."

"But I probably did, right? She withdraws and I get in." Mom remained silent. "Why didn't you tell me? That she was the one who found Barrington? That she's the reason I'm there?"

253

"It wasn't my place, honey. And Ayisha didn't want people to know after Nicole asked her to withdraw."

"It's really messed up that Ms. Lewis did that."

"Finley, I want you to listen to me." That was her deadly serious tone, so I listened. "It's not that simple. There's just one of you and three people looking after you as you grow up. Those numbers are reversed for Nicole. She's had to make some hard choices that your dad and I have never had to do, like about basic childcare, and no one should judge her for that. No one. Do you hear me?"

"Yes, ma'am," I mumbled contritely.

And I felt a ripple of shame for having done exactly that. Judged Ms. Lewis without thinking about things from her perspective. Ayisha was right about me having it easy. Not lately, but overall in life. As pathetic as it sounded, that had never occurred to me before.

Still, I'd seen the pain in Ayisha's eyes as she talked about having to withdraw and the unjustness stuck with me.

"But—and just listen," I hurried when I saw her about to interject. "The numbers aren't reversed anymore. Billie and Linda are going to Oakengates."

Mom's eyes lit up. "They got in?" I nodded. "Oh, good. They're so talented."

"Maybe don't mention that in front of Ayisha."

Mom nodded.

I stood up and crossed to the fireplace. "But the girls getting in there means the whole reason Ayisha couldn't go to Barrington is gone now."

"True . . ."

"Which means she could go."

"Possibly. If there's a spot for her."

I absentmindedly tapped the red glass ornament dangling from the pine bough stretched across the mantel. It swayed precariously. "I think I should give her my spot. It's only fair since it was hers to begin with."

Mom drew a deep breath. I knew she was mentally counting to calm herself. She was the one who taught me that trick. After several moments passed, she stood and joined me at the fireplace.

"First of all," she said evenly, "that's foolish. Second of all, it doesn't work that way."

"Why? My friend Arthur got in there midway through a school year, so if a spot opens up . . ." I pointed to myself.

"What about you? What would you do? Come back here, to Christmas?"

"Would that be so bad?"

She opened her mouth to respond then stopped herself. And seemed to reconsider. After several moments she admitted, "No." And slowly exhaled, as some of the tension she was carrying seemed to fade. "No, it wouldn't." She dropped her gaze and seemed bemused. "Which I'm starting to figure out myself."

I watched her and sensed whatever it was she was thinking right now was part of why she had left in the first place. After several moments where all I could hear was the occasional crack of the firewood and the faint instrumental Christmas tunes Val favored when she was at the front desk, Mom met my eyes. The defensiveness and challenge were missing.

"Let me ask you something, Finley. If I hadn't talked about you leaving Christmas all these years, would you have wanted to? On your own?"

"I don't know," I answered.

"Maybe you should think about it."

"Oh my God!" I threw up my hands in frustration. "That is seriously *all* I've been doing since my birthday!"

She chuckled. "Which sounds exactly like you." Then she smiled gently and reached out to stroke my hair and this time I let her. "You overthink things, Fin. Always have," she said with a quiet affection. "You get that from me." Her mouth twitched knowingly. "Everyone thinks your father is the overthinker, because he's quiet." Her smile turned inward. "Makes him seem like he's brooding. But he's the opposite. He decides something and that's that. No second-guessing, no 'what-if-ing.' But me? I've spent . . ." She sighed deeply. ". . . my whole life 'what-if-ing.'"

"Since you got pregnant with me."

She met my eyes. "I have never, never once regretted you. Not once. And I never will."

"But you could have done so much more," I whispered, feeling my lips start to quiver, which was vaguely mortifying; I had never been this much of a crier.

She put two fingers under my chin and tipped up my face until I met her blue eyes so very like my own.

"But I will never do anything better than be your mom."

I started crying then. Big time. About everything. About Barrington and my grades and not being invited to Bronwyn's party or fitting in, about getting caught lying about my hometown, about Ayisha and Mia and Brody, and thinking badly about Esha and why my grandmother hid such important things from me, and what would happen to my parents. And about Arthur, who was weird and kind and whom I liked more than I thought possible, but who lived in a world where it seemed I could never belong.

And Mom held me.

We didn't talk about much more after that. We were both too spent. She went home to our empty house, and I went up to my tiny room and got in bed with the full intention to do more thinking about everything that had happened today.

And yesterday.

And many more days.

But the second my head hit the pillow and my eyes closed, I tumbled into a deep sleep before a single thought could begin to form. I didn't even dream.

Twenty-Two

Was it possible to have a hangover from family drama? Because when the alarm on my phone went off at six a.m. and I swung my feet to the rug-covered floor, I was pretty sure that was happening to me. My head felt foggy, my eyes were puffy, and my energy levels were in the red.

The breakfast shift began at seven a.m. and I did not want to be late for Mrs. Buzzard. I knew today was her big prep day for tomorrow's Christmas Eve party, which was her biggest event of the year. I prayed the rush delivery of the replacement pans didn't get caught up in the Christmas postal rush. I'd been the recipient of enough stink-eyed looks as it was.

One quick shower and blow-dry later, my hair was up in a ponytail (no time to deal with the hella static) and I was in my khaki slacks and light blue oxford beneath the navy sweater. I was saving the red sweater for the party tomorrow.

I took an extra ten minutes to come up with Christmasy suggestions for Arthur and his aunt to do tonight—ice skating in Norman; going to see a revival of *Miracle on 34th Street* at the Avalon, which was a nearby converted opera house built in 1919; or maybe roasting those chestnuts—then texted them to him and still made it downstairs with five minutes to spare.

Upon arrival, I found I was already the fourth person in the kitchen, including Grandma Jo, Mrs. Buzzard, and Steve the Deliberately Homeless Elf, whose unmistakable car was operational so he was delivering party supplies from CK.

Ayisha had the day off, so there would be no chatting with her. I knew she would be in tomorrow so I resolved to wait until then.

And there was no opportunity for chatting with Grandma Jo, either. By the time I got downstairs, she was already in full Busy Boss Mode as she went over the party's meal lists with Mrs. Buzzard and ducked in and out of her office, which was around the corner from the kitchen.

She seemed everywhere at once. Yet when Esha and Arthur came down for breakfast, I noticed she made a point to slow down and spend extra time at their table.

I also noticed Arthur didn't look at me once.

In the kitchen, I snuck a glance at my phone to find he had responded to my text, but it was with a perfunctory I'll ask my auntie. Then again, perfunctory actually was pretty much SOP for him.

However, a tingle of . . . concern? went up the back of my neck as I worked to help keep the dining area running smoothly (refresh the chafing dishes so the scrambled eggs weren't rubberized, replace the canned heat, tidy up spills, make sure Mrs. Buzzard remembered the latest meal changes from the Yablonskis, etc.) while unsuccessfully attempting to catch his eye.

To be fair, he spent most of the time engaged in conversation with his aunt and I got super busy when all seven members of the Sweeney family stopped by for brunch despite not being guests, which wasn't uncommon, but on this particular morning was inconvenient.

It seemed like I blinked and it was noon.

Mrs. Buzzard would be staying later today to help prepare for tomorrow, along with Reggie and Lloyd, so they booted me from the kitchen. Not that I was complaining.

Another check of my phone showed no follow-up response from Arthur but I had three other texts:

One from Mom. (Loved talking with you last night! I miss you, my baby!)

One from Dad. (Let's play a game of chess soon. Tonight?)

And, to my infinite surprise, one from Mia. (Brodys having a Xmas eve eve party 2night. A bunch of ppl r coming & you & mcarthur can come 2 if u wnt)

I wasn't sure whether she was deliberately getting Arthur's name wrong, but that was incidental to the invitation itself.

Which was obviously a surprise.

The answer was a quick no, we weren't going to stop by, though I didn't text her that response. Even if Arthur hadn't already said he would prefer not to go, I still had plans to be with him and his aunt, whatever those might wind up being. I was kind of hoping for ice skating. More of a chance for hand-holding as a way to keep each other upright. Or maybe one of us might accidentally fall and make the other laugh then fall themselves and we'd wind up in a surprise clinch. Which never really happened, but it sure would be nice if it did.

I decided to go in search of Arthur to ask him in person, which led me down the hallway past my grandmother's office, where I saw she was talking and smiling with Esha.

"Hey," I said, leaning in the doorway.

They jumped. And boy, did I want to say something ("Don't

worry, I kinda already caught you two post-make-out last night so cat's outta the bag!"). But refrained. For now.

"Hi, Finley," Grandma Jo said, standing straighter.

I nodded to her then focused on Esha, whom I likely owed about a hundred silent apologies. "Do you know where Arthur is?"

"I believe he said he was going to the library to do some reading."

"Thank you." I leaned out to leave then leaned right back in. "Did he say anything to you about us all doing something together tonight?"

"He did not. But that could be because he knew we"—she gestured between herself and my grandmother—"would be having dinner tonight."

My eyebrows went up. "Oh? Just the two of you?"

Grandma Jo nodded. "Yep."

She unconsciously tugged on her right ear, which I knew was a nervous tic of hers and as much as I wanted to point and say, "Ha! I already caught you!", another part of me was profoundly disappointed she felt she needed to hide this HUGE part of herself from me.

I said, "Fun." Because what else could I say? *Don't do anything I wouldn't do?* I was pretty sure they already had.

Then I left them alone with a friendly wave.

Sure enough, I found Arthur in the library window seat, reading some paperback book with a centaur on the cover.

Closing the door behind me for privacy purposes, I had initially intended to ask him about tonight's plans, if there were going to be any, which I hoped there would be.

But instead, I did that blurting thing I sometimes do.

"Is your aunt gay?"

Arthur glanced away from his book in surprise and blinked at me. "I'm sorry?"

"Your aunt. Is she gay?"

He sat up straighter and put his bookmark in place. "I believe the preferred term is 'lesbian.' Gay seems to be used more for men, though I don't know if there's any degree of exclusivity on—"

"Arthur!"

"Yes. She is. Lesbian."

I came closer to him. "Why didn't you mention this before?"

"It was never germane to any of our conversations."

Sure, he had a valid point, but I still shook my head in amazement and plopped down beside him on the window seat.

"I thought she had a crush on *my dad*."

That earned a full chortle. "Wrong member of the family."

"Yeah, apparently." Then I realized, "You knew?"

"That my auntie is smitten with your grandmother? Yes. I thought it rather obvious."

"No. Well, I mean, yes. In hindsight."

"It was a contributing factor to why she was amenable to changing our plans so last-minute."

I backhanded his upper arm. "Shut up!"

"Ow!"

"How?"

He rubbed his upper arm and frowned at me. "The inn's website. When I mentioned my suggestion about coming to Christmas, and the Hoyden in particular, she read some article on the site about the inn having won some prestigious award."

"'Best Boutique Inn in Oklahoma—2016' from *OK Visitor Magazine*."

"If you say so. It has photos of your grandmother, who, it

goes without saying, is absurdly pretty." I glared at him and he cocked a brow. "Well, she *is*."

"Okay, but how did your aunt know Grandma Jo would, you know . . . like her back?"

"I don't think she did. Until she got here and they hit it off at the jump. I suppose it was a chance on her part, really. Or she just got lucky." He cleared his throat. "So to speak."

"Huh."

His eyes narrowed at me. "Does that bother you?"

"That your aunt and my grandmother like each other? No. That my grandmother has been hiding this huge secret about herself all my life? Yeah. It really does."

Arthur grew still. Then he leaned back, his eyes newly hooded. "Are . . . you saying that Jo isn't out?"

I shook my head. "Yes. She's, I guess, super in, if that's the right way of saying it. Which makes no sense."

He blinked several times. "No. It doesn't," he murmured quietly, almost to himself. Then a second later he stood abruptly. "Pardon me."

He started for the door.

"Hold up," I called and followed him.

He paused, his hand on the doorknob.

"Where are you going?"

"Quick errand."

"Oh."

He opened the door but I grabbed his black cable knit sweater by the elbow to stop him again.

"What about tonight?" I asked.

"Tonight?"

"Well, I mean, yeah. About Christmasy things. I texted you earlier?"

A nod of recognition. "Ah, yes." But he added nothing further.

"So, your aunt told me that she's going to dinner with Grandma Jo, but did you, um, maybe want to still do one of those Perfect American Christmas activities?"

He gazed at me so long I wondered if he heard me at all. Then he shook his head. "No, thank you."

The curtness caught me by surprise, which he must have seen in my expression because he attempted to soften it with a smile. But it failed to reach his eyes and that earlier tingle of concern became an electric current of dread. Those walls of his that had been down as late as last night were suddenly all the way back.

Something was definitely wrong.

Yet before I could draw in a breath to ask him what was going on, he already had the library door fully open and was gone.

Twenty-Three

Ten minutes after my unnerving library encounter with Arthur, I was standing in the inn's parking lot staring at Mrs. Buzzard's dark blue 2004 Lincoln Town Car. I was trying to determine whether I really had enough knowledge about how to drive because I knew replacing a wrecked car was a whole lot different than replacing burned pans.

My goal upon exiting the library had been to grab a slice of banana nut bread left over from yesterday's lunch then swing by the hot chocolate bar and head up to my room, whereupon I would at long last veg out and process everything that had happened to me. But especially try to determine what the hell was up with Arthur.

None of that happened.

Mrs. Buzzard had pounced on me the second I entered the kitchen and demanded I run an errand for her. She said I owed her since the replacement pans had yet to arrive, which was stretching the idea, but, at the same time, guilt was a magical motivator. She needed me to swing by the Gingerbread Café to pick up her orders for the party, at which point I reminded her about not having my driver's license.

She handed me her car keys anyway.

And thus, there I stood. Staring. Hoping that very large automobile was an automatic because if it was a manual transmission, I had no chance.

Despite the chilly wind, a trickle of sweat went down the center of my back.

"Hey there, sport."

I turned to see my dad regarding me with a quizzical expression from the edge of the lot closest to the inn. Relief flooded.

"Dad! What are you doing *right now*?"

Twenty minutes later, we were seated at the counter of the Gingerbread Café, Dad with a bowl of broccoli cheese soup, and me with a cheeseburger. A slice of freshly made gingerbread waited in the wings for us to share. He had left his office at lunchtime to swing by the inn to grab a bite when he noticed me, so we decided to make a father-daughter meal out of the excursion.

I raised my second cup of coffee. "Merry Christmas Eve Eve," I said to him, which reminded me that I had yet to respond to Mia's text.

He smiled and raised his own mug in return. "You too."

We tapped cups then got back to the business of eating, which, no lie, was much needed. My now-pointless effort to get ideas for Christmas activities to Arthur had cut my arrival to my breakfast shift so close I didn't actually get breakfast. Irony. Which meant by the time Dad and I were eating, I was fast approaching woozy. But once I had half a burger, a plate of fries, and some coffee in my system, I felt human again. Enough so that I noticed more stress-related gray hairs intermingled with the brown on the back of Dad's head.

"How are you doing?" I asked.

He glanced up. "I'm fine." The corners of his hazel eyes crinkled, forming deep lines that seemed to have gotten deeper recently. "Though that's supposed to be my question to you."

"Well, today it's my question to you." I ate a fry. Then another. And another. "Have you talked with Mom?"

He used his spoon to push around a piece of broccoli in his bowl. "We've texted a bit."

"And?"

"And? When did you get so pushy?" He tried to make it sound light, but I knew he was uncomfortable.

"When my parents started living in different states," I countered, and that took a bit out of his bravado. "So? How's it going?"

"You don't need to worry about that."

"Dad. I'm already worried."

This time he met my eyes and I saw genuine concern. "I'm sorry, Fin. 'Course you are. I didn't mean . . ." Then he looked back down at his bowl of soup, but I noticed he didn't eat any. "Your mom and I . . . We're . . ." He sighed.

"Are you going to get a divorce?"

He stiffened at the word then shook his head. "No, Fin. No one's said that."

Yet? Was there a "yet" at the end of that sentence?

"Do you still love each other?"

That was my big question. The most important one. Nothing else really mattered, did it?

Dad set his spoon down on a paper napkin and folded his arms on the countertop. He stared forward.

"I fell in love with your mom when I was around your age. And I've loved her every day since. But that doesn't mean she's obligated to love me back."

I frowned. "What do you mean?"

His head tipped back and forth. "Sometimes, when you truly love someone, you gotta let them go."

"Like *Frozen*?"

That earned a small laugh. "You really did watch that movie too often."

But I was serious. "Dad."

"Your mom, when she was young, she was a force of nature." He gazed off again and I knew he was remembering. "When she was in high school plays, she was always the star. All eyes were on her. You couldn't help it. I used to volunteer to paint sets just so I could be near her in rehearsals."

I smiled. "Like a sweet stalker."

"I'd like to think of it more as a benign admirer."

"Guess it depends on how it's received."

"I suppose it does."

"So you painted sets and admired her from afar."

"Until one day, Dana's mom's car didn't work, so your nonna couldn't pick her up from rehearsals . . ."

I knew this story. "And you swooped in with your Jeep to offer to drive her home and used your time together to woo her."

"By inviting her over to listen to The White Stripes' *Elephant*."

"Super nerdy, Dad."

He grinned a crooked grin. "Hey, you play the leverage you've got. First kiss we ever had was to 'You've Got Her in Your Pocket.'" Then his smile turned wistful. "Seems kinda appropriate now." I made a mental note to look up those lyrics. "She and I have had some really good times together." He smiled at me. "Present company definitely included. But the simple truth is, Fin, we didn't *choose* each other to be our forevers. Fate took care of that."

I dipped a fry in the smear of ketchup at the edge of my plate. "If you hadn't gotten pregnant in high school . . . ?"

"We'll never really know. Who's to say if we'd be each other's happily ever after?"

I knew my dad well enough to know he hadn't meant for that to sting me, but it did. About my own impact on both their young lives, and the terrifying prospect of what the future for our family held.

"Are you saying you don't want to be with Mom anymore?"

"Not at all. I'll always want to be with your mom, that's never changed one bit. But what I mean is . . ." He struggled for a moment. "It's not right for me to keep her to myself. She should be out in the world, exploring. Having all eyes on her again. Not hanging around Christmas with someone who's . . . always been old."

"Did Mom say that?"

"No."

"Then how do you know that's what *she* wants?"

"Look, honey. Dana's the one who decided to go to Missouri."

"She said she tried to come home sooner, but you thought she should stay gone."

This caught him by surprise. "She told you that?" I nodded. He sat back, tapping the tips of his fingers against the Formica. "Only because I thought . . . I thought she might be coming back home out of habit. And I wanted her to come home for me."

At that moment, Dad was about as vulnerable as I'd ever seen him. It moved me and before I realized it, I'd hopped off my counter stool and wrapped my arms around his neck. He hugged me back for several moments. Then he exhaled and we parted and I kissed his scratchy cheek. He smiled at me.

"Mom loves you, Dad," I said with conviction. "I know it."

Dad nodded once, but I saw he wasn't as certain as I was. He turned to signal to Mitzi to bring the check.

As I was standing by the register waiting for Mitzi to ring up the order for Mrs. Buzzard, my attention fell on the tray of Christmas Jammies—which would forever be Jammie Dodgers for me now—and it occurred to me that I didn't have a Christmas present for Arthur. In the spirit of "what do you get the boy who has everything?" I made a separate purchase of every last Christmas Jammie Dodger there was and had them put in one of the café's russet-colored gable boxes. I'd put a red bow on it later, dress it up.

Dad gave me a funny look. "Didn't you just eat?"

"These are for Arthur," I explained with as casual a tone as I could muster. "They're his favorites."

In life, there was possibly no more annoying and uncomfortable look than that from a parent when a potential "young love" romance was involved. Nails-on-a-chalkboard level of awful. I chose to ignore the one my father gave me right then.

Dad dropped me off at the front of the inn and I waved to him from the porch steps as he drove off. Doing my best to balance the two large plastic bags and gable box from the Gingerbread Café, I entered the front lobby.

No one was at the front desk, but that wasn't unusual. The Hoyden wasn't a Hilton. If a person wanted help and no one was around at that given moment, they could ring the bell.

But I spotted three suitcases by the desk itself, one quite large and two others more of the carry-on variety. Odd. I didn't recall anyone scheduled to leave today. Everyone was booked through Christmas.

The tumble of footsteps on the stairs drew my attention and I was surprised to see Arthur coming down, wearing his green jacket and a pair of Wranglers. Looking cute. . .

"Oh, hello," he said, as he crossed to the front desk and set down two room keys. "Is it all right to leave these here?"

I blinked and ignored his question for one of my own. "What's going on?"

"We're checking out."

I did a double take. "Checking out?" I repeated.

He nodded. "Yes." And turned to lift the straps of one of the two overnight cases over his shoulder.

"Now?"

"Yes."

I shook my head and set the plastic bags filled with pie boxes and cakes and whatever else Mrs. Buzzard had ordered down on the desk ledge beside the room keys.

Then turned to face him.

"I don't understand. You're supposed to be here through the twenty-seventh."

"That was the plan, but the plan has changed."

"Why? What about your aunt? Isn't she supposed to be having dinner with Grandma Jo?"

"Not anymore." He picked up the black canvas bag with the sturdy leather handle. "Thank you so very much for all you've done to bring the spirit of Christmas to our stay here. You've truly gone above and beyond."

Of the permutations in Arthur's moods since I'd come to know him—from snobby to rage rooster to goofy to sweet—I had never seen him quite like this. This Arthur was . . . polite.

To *me*.

I scowled at him. "What is wrong with you? Why are you acting so formal all of a sudden?"

"I'm always like this." He shot me a wry look. "Lest you forget, you once accused me of sounding like I was seventy."

"That was days ago."

"Not so many days. Not enough to be . . ." He paused to choose his word with care. ". . . worthwhile."

I could feel the back of my throat start to close up. Though I may not have known what was going on, I knew something awful had happened. "I thought I was going to show you Christmas. For Christmas." My voice was tight.

"And indeed you did. I assure you, Finley, my auntie and I shall never forget our holiday here. Truly."

"What about"—I glanced around and even though whoever else was supposed to be manning the front desk was nowhere in sight, I lowered my voice—"your aunt and my grandmother?"

A flash of irritation streaked across his dark eyes. "That is none of our business."

"But they *like* each other."

"No one truly upends their life for a holiday romance. That's only in the movies." Then he nodded to the larger case that was still by the front desk. "I'll be back for that."

I didn't give two shits about his suitcase.

"Good-bye, Finley."

With that he walked out the back of the inn.

I stood there for several moments, uncertain what was happening, what *had* happened. My mind raced trying to put together any bits or pieces, but came up lacking. Then I remembered the gable box of Jammie Dodgers in my hands.

His Christmas present. Purchased less than a half hour ago, but already pointless.

I looked to the suitcase he was planning to come back for and, without giving it a thought, unzipped the front pocket, pushed the Gingerbread Café box inside, and zipped it back. What the hell else was I going to do with it?

In a daze and on automatic pilot, I grabbed the two plastic bags and went into the kitchen, where all three cooks zipped about in three different directions.

Grandma Jo was nowhere to be seen.

It wasn't until I'd handed over the bags to Mrs. Buzzard—who did not say thank you—that something in what Arthur had said struck me.

My heart started to beat madly.

I ran out the back of the inn through the courtyard and headed for the parking area, where I found Arthur, having already retrieved the final suitcase, on his way to the Hummer. Where Esha sat in the passenger's seat, her expression inscrutable, even for her, as she stared out the side window.

"Arthur!"

He stopped and turned to me.

I caught up, slightly out of breath from my dash. "Goodbye?" He tipped his head to one side, perplexed. "You said . . ." *Deep breaths, calm down.* "You said, 'good-bye.'"

"Yes?"

"Why?"

His eyes narrowed. "It's what one says? Or are there different parting phrases here in Oklahoma?"

"Don't you mean, 'see you back at school'?"

Recognition dawned then. His back slowly stiffened and it

was then he reminded me of the Arthur I knew from the beginning. The Queen's Guard posture.

"I think we both know that's not happening," he said coolly, walls up, moat dug, alligators and dragons installed.

Which meant he knew.

Somehow.

"Did Ayisha say something?" It was the only explanation I had.

To my surprise, he seemed almost embarrassed. "No. I . . ." He actually blushed. ". . . overheard you last night, when you were having a chat with your mother."

Oh. I briefly closed my eyes and curled my lips inward. Biting down hard. *Crap.*

"I didn't mean to overhear," he went on. "I was on my way upstairs from the kitchen and wanted to say a proper good night to you both. I didn't realize your conversation was so intense until I'd drawn closer . . ."

He let his words trail off.

"How much did you hear?" I asked, trying to recall everything that had been said.

"Only a bit. Including the part about not returning to Barrington. Because there's nothing for you there."

My body slumped. The worst part for him to overhear. "I'm failing, Arthur," I said quietly. Wanting him to understand, to not hate me. "At everything."

"Finley." His beautiful dark eyes softened the tiniest bit. "Barrington is your first foray into a private boarding school, yes?" I nodded. "Then of course you're failing. Those places are gladiator pits. Positively wretched. I've been in them from the beginning and I don't think I figured out how to survive until I was somewhere in Year Five." He saw my confusion and clarified, "When I was nine. And one could make the argument that I in fact did *not* survive, hence my studying in America. And you. Coming from a place like Christmas?" He gestured to the surroundings. "No wonder you weren't prepared. And for the record, Finley. You may not have been the roaring success right out of the gate I suspect you'd envisioned for yourself, but you were far from a failure."

"Tell that to Bronwyn," I muttered, indulging in a pity-party wallow that wasn't remotely attractive.

Bronwyn is awful. Everyone knows that." He pointed at me. "But *you* let her get inside your head too much, too early, and far too often. That's on you."

Which was entirely accurate. Every school had their mean girls. It was unfortunate that the one at Barrington chose me to be her target. It was even worse that I'd allowed it.

Arthur glanced over his shoulder at the Hummer, and Esha, who was watching us now. Though a good twenty yards separated us, I read the tension in her expression from here. However, despite whatever it was she was feeling, she still managed a small smile and nod for me.

I nodded back.

"Listen," he said. "I've got to get going."

"What happened between Esha and my grandmother?"

He hesitated then shook his head. "It wouldn't be right. I'm sorry."

I nodded, respecting his respect, even as I grappled with all the abrupt changes that had transpired in the span of my lunch with my dad.

"Arthur? Is . . . Would it be okay if, if I texted you? Sometime?"

There was a long pause and what I wouldn't give to have

some magic device to allow me to know what it was he was thinking because I didn't have the first clue.

"I don't mean to be rude," he said at last. "But I'd really rather you didn't." He shrugged one shoulder, apologetic. "I've been down that road before."

I swallowed and bit back the swell of emotion that was threatening.

"Finley?" I looked up and found him watching me intently, as if there was more he wanted to say. But whatever it might have been, he changed his mind and instead smiled, a real smile, not big and cheerful, but nonetheless sincere. And it brought about the adorable cheek dimple that was my Kryptonite as he simply wished me a "Happy Christmas."

Twenty-Four

Grandma Jo looked like shit.

We stared at each other without saying a word for a good ten seconds before she waved for me to come all the way inside her cottage, which I did. She closed the door behind me and followed me into her living room, which, for the record, looked like a Pottery Barn showroom done up for Christmas.

I'd debated a while after Arthur left before I came over to her cottage, intending to let her know that I'd seen her and Esha the night before, that I knew . . . well, something. I wasn't sure exactly how far into identity politics I wanted to go with my grandmother.

This already felt like the world's most awkward minefield.

But the moment she opened the door and our eyes met, I knew that she knew that I knew. What came next, I did *not* know.

I stood by the fireplace mantel, like I had with my mother. Grandma Jo was by her own Christmas tree, which was elegantly beautiful, her hands on her slim hips and her face unnaturally wan. The true giveaway, however, was her hair. Grandma Jo's hair was always perfect. It was important for her to look polished and professional. Now, though, it seemed as if she had run her hands through it without thought, strands going in every direction.

I bit my lip and laced my fingers behind my back.

"Well," she said at last, her voice haggard. "This conversation is a long time coming."

It took every ounce of self-restraint not to respond with an extremely sarcastic *Ya think?!* But she already seemed so demoralized and hurt. I wanted to hug her but I sensed she needed to say some things first.

She cleared her throat. "First of all," she began stiffly, "I'm sorry. I should have been forthcoming with you a long time ago."

That made me feel a thousand times better. And yet . . .

"Grandma, you can't possibly think I'd care."

"No. But . . ." She shrugged, unconsciously rubbing her wrist. "It would make you see me differently."

"It'd let me see you as you really are." It struck me anew about how much of my grandmother I apparently didn't know, what she must've gone through over the years, all of which she kept away from me. It stung a little, even though a part of me understood why. I mean, what if one day I had a grandchild? How much about myself would I really want them to know? Especially if it was deeply personal, like this. I'm thinking not a lot. Maybe my grandmother and I were more alike than I realized.

Her expression relaxed the tiniest bit. "I'm sorry for not telling you. It's hard sometimes to remember that your generation's view is different on these things. At least outside of this town."

She had a point. Connecticut's perspective on sexuality and

gender identity and everything in that range of discussion was significantly different than what one could find in wide swaths of Middle America, but that didn't mean there hadn't been changes over the past few decades. There had been. Even I saw them. And, sure, our small town was conservative overall, but there were good people here who loved each other just as they were.

"Have you tried?" I asked. "You know, telling folks in Christmas?"

She shot me that piercing look, the one with the raised eyebrow that always made me shrink back.

"Finley, I've heard people talk my whole life." Her hazel eyes sharpened. "Starting with GGB. She made her feelings for 'those people' very clear. And I'm aware the environment in parts of the country is better, but there are parts where it's the same as when I was your age."

"You've known since you were my age?"

"Essentially."

Grandma Jo moved to sit down in the cream-colored armchair and I took that as my cue to do the same on the sofa opposite her.

"And . . . Dad?" *Might as well go there*, I thought.

She linked her hands in her lap, her spine straight enough even Arthur would approve. "When I was younger, I attempted to deny my feelings by proving they weren't real." That was a heckuva euphemism. It made Mom's "life happened" seem so tame. "They were real. Obviously. But being a single mother, and running this inn, I could pretend they weren't far longer than I should have."

"So, I mean. You don't have to tell me, but what happened? Why did Arthur and Esha leave?"

Her jaw clenched. "Because I fucked up again."

Aaaand my grandmother dropped the F-bomb. That happened. Then I zeroed in on "Again?"

She absently picked up a brushed-nickel decorative owl from an end table, and looked at it. "Do you remember Ms. Brooke from Dallas?"

I closed one eye in a squint as the faint image of a woman with intense makeup and white-blonde hair like a TV anchorwoman appeared in my mind. She'd been nice.

"Your personal-shopper friend?"

I got an arched brow. "She was not my personal shopper."

And another awkward bomb. "*Ohhh . . .*" When I got some time, I was going to have to go over a lot of what I thought I knew. I had a sneaking suspicion there were many things I'd missed along the way. At which point it occurred to me, "You haven't, um . . . shopped with her in while."

"Six years. Which was my fault. Brooke and I started dating after GGB passed. It was long-distance at first so she was okay that I wasn't out to anyone."

"Even Dad?"

She nodded. "That didn't occur until a few years ago."

Whoa. I could not fathom that. Dad and Grandma Jo were always close. I thought that was one of the reasons I was bonded with both my parents, that Dad had used his relationship with Grandma Jo as a sort of paradigm. If I'd been gay, I was pretty sure both of my folks would have known before I did. It made me all the more grateful for them, knowing that they would always love me no matter what and never make me feel like GGB had made Grandma Jo feel. Like she had to live in two different worlds.

"How did you come out to Dad?"

"Brooke gave me an ultimatum—tell at least Skip or it's over. She said four years of hiding was long enough. And she was right."

"Okay, so you told Dad . . ."

"No." Off my surprise, she squirmed. "I didn't think she was serious; I thought we could keep going like we were."

I balked. "For how long?"

She cringed. "Forever?"

"Grandma!"

I was genuinely shocked. My grandmother planned everything down to the tiniest detail. Always. She said it was because she was a Virgo. The idea that she had no plan to come out and was content to do nothing was incongruous with everything I knew about her.

"Admittedly, it wasn't the best strategy," she said dryly, as if reading my thoughts.

"Grandma, you would never let me get away with something like that."

For the first time in my life, I watched my grandmother look abashed. "Because it's foolish. *I* was foolish. Brooke broke up with me and by the time I realized it was real, it was also too late. She'd met someone else in Fort Worth. They're married now."

She set the owl back down.

"When did Dad find out?"

"When I had a borderline breakdown. He found me in a weepy mess and I told him everything, and he sent me to Hawaii for a month."

My eyes grew wide. "*That's* why you went to Hawaii for a month?"

I remembered now. My parents had had to step up to watch

the Hoyden in her absence, which was a rarity. Grandma Jo hardly ever took time off, let alone a whole month. They had played it off like she was taking a much-needed vacation.

She nodded. "I was a mess." She ran a hand through her hair. "Not unlike I am now."

"And Esha?"

"Is someone I like. Very much," she said quietly.

"In only a few days?"

To be honest, that was more about me and what I was feeling for Arthur. What if it wasn't real? What if it was only because of the holidays?

"Well." She reached up to lightly stroke the front of her throat as a flush darkened her cheeks. "It's a little longer than that. She called personally to book their rooms. We got to talking, then, to my surprise, flirting and . . ." She caught herself, becoming aware I was still there, listening. She shifted in her chair. "And I like her."

I thought about updating Arthur with this new information, but then I remembered I couldn't. And I felt as deflated as my grandmother looked.

"Then why did they check out? And why did she seem upset?" I asked.

"Because Esha learned you didn't know about me. It was one thing to not tell Dean, whose approval on the building board I need in order to get that spa built. It's quite another to not tell your own granddaughter. And Esha's had too much experience with dating people who aren't truthful to risk going down that road again. I don't blame her."

"But you've told me now. I know. Everyone can know, right?"

I watched her shoulders, so much broader than mine will

likely ever be, droop. "Finley, I'm not sure I'll ever be that brave," she almost-whispered in self-directed disappointment.

I slumped back against the sofa, dismayed by her answer. I watched her throat bob as she swallowed some emotion and her gaze grew hazy and unfocused. I felt the urge to go over to her and grab her by those drooped shoulders and shake her, tell her, *You can be that brave. I've seen you be brave a million times.* But I was in no position to lecture anyone about that, about bravery.

The room was quiet for several minutes and the logs in the fireplace crackled. I swung back to one of the things she'd said.

"Hold up, Grandma. Are you saying you've been stringing along Dr. Raymond to get the spa built?"

She half rolled her eyes and waved me off. "Dean plays the numbers. He's flirting with at least seven other women as we speak." She snorted. "There's practically a Facebook group for us."

"Seriously?"

She nodded, relieved, I suspected, to be able to find humor in something, if only for a moment. "My money's on Frannie Taft over in Purcell, though Mitzi is a bit of a dark horse."

I blinked about fifty times in rapid succession, my brain spinning like the Wheel of Fortune in terms of issues that should be addressed, and landed on, "But Mitzi bakes with so much sugar!"

She shot me a knowing look. "Oh, honey. Don't let Dean fool you. That man is a total sugar *fiend*."

I swear to God, this was the weirdest Christmas ever.

Twenty-Five

The Tuck house was rocking, even from where I stood on the curb. Music thumped a deep bass—*boom-boom-boom*—and despite the dropping late-December temperatures that came with sundown, there were at least three clusters of partygoers scattered around the red Solo cup–littered front lawn, chatting and drinking.

I assumed Brody's parents were in Vail, where they had a timeshare and where they went this time each year. Which meant Brody's December parties were the stuff of legend. At least around here.

What was new, however, was the wide white sign out front that read: MERRY CHRISTMAS EVE EVE, Y'ALL!!!

In red letters. If I wasn't mistaken, the sign was made out of vinyl, attached to two wooden posts stretched beneath the front windows of the two-story, faux ski lodge–style house.

That had to be Mia's doing. Someone had balanced an empty Jack Daniel's bottle on top of one of the posts. This party was already well on its way to being a shit show. I'd seen it before.

It hadn't been my intention to come here. I'd forgotten to

respond to Mia's text, which was an oversight, not a slight. (There was no chance she would ever believe me.)

After my conversation with my grandmother, preceded by my conversation with Arthur, preceded by my conversation with Dad, I went out for a long walk. I figured if I got away from the inn, by myself, there would be less chance of being roped into a new, unexpected, emotionally draining revelation. There'd been enough of those.

As I walked, I noticed it was much colder than it had been the past few days and the light from the occasional streetlamp reflected off the tumbling arrival of low clouds. Since I'd been in Connecticut, I'd gotten out of the habit of regularly checking the weather, which was something you learned to do from an early age in Oklahoma, because while other parts of the country treated weather like a conversation starter, here it could kill you.

For the moment, however, it was merely cold. But I knew from experience it was about to turn freezing. The way things were going, it would probably start snowing the second Arthur's plane back to Connecticut took off on Christmas morning.

Grandma Jo had told me that was when they were headed out. Clearly, they wanted to leave as soon as possible. Why else travel on the actual holiday? Arthur's magic credit card could easily buy them a longer hotel stay. But that wasn't what they wanted.

They wanted to blow this Popsicle stand.

Deuces.

Peace on Earth on the way outta town.

I couldn't blame it all on Grandma Jo, either. I knew I played a part. I also knew Arthur well enough by now, and even his aunt to a degree, to know that if either of them had expressed even the slightest interest in staying, whether it was in Oklahoma itself or the Hoyden specifically, the other would have given in at once. I liked that about them, how they supported each other.

But it was obvious neither had done that. And so I would likely never see Arthur again. Not if I stayed here. In Christmas.

I'd been standing outside for close to ten minutes, my hands in my coat pockets, my red knit cap pulled down over my ears. I had on a scarf and gloves, but my shoes were just basic Adidas and my socks only slightly thicker than average so my toes were already icicles.

It's what broke me from my inertia to finally go inside.

Along the way I passed a few familiar faces, but though my time away hadn't been long in the grand scheme of things, it took a few extra beats for their names to click. Kimmy Bunting's little sister was in the middle of chugging a bottle of Bacardi 151. Her parents were gonna love that.

I only got some waves and head bobs, which I returned in kind before entering the blessedly warm house.

I knew this house. Brody and I used to come here all the time less than a year ago. God, was it really that recent? It felt like an eternity.

Nothing had changed. The foyer was still lined with framed photos of him, his parents, and his older brothers. Benton and Bryson.

It smelled the same, too, despite the overwhelming pungency of spilled beer and booze, pot, and cigarettes. Mrs. Tuck always liked to keep bowls of potpourri stashed around the house, which she would change with each season. Spring was roses, summer was lavender, autumn was cloves and oranges, and winter was pine. I could make out the hints of pine, buried beneath it all.

The noise level was overwhelming. The living room was crammed with people, shout-talking, laughing, smoking, lotta dancing. In the minute since I'd walked in, the temperature had gone up by forty degrees, but I didn't unbutton my coat.

Someone handed me a cup of red liquid then kept going. There was exactly zero chance I'd be drinking that for about a thousand reasons. I set it down behind one of Mrs. Tuck's ornate decorative displays on a shelf where it would have the least chance of getting knocked over as the night wore on. I hoped.

Going in farther, I spotted Brody in the corner. He was in the middle of a handstand on a keg as another guy—Toby Killian?—poured beer from the nozzle into his mouth. Neat. At least he still had his shirt on, but the night was young.

A dozen other kids around my age, one way or the other, cheered him on.

I stood apart and watched them. Unnoticed. Until I heard a familiar voice above the din loudly say, "Holy shit! You came?"

I turned to see Mia standing by an entrance I knew led to the kitchen.

She wore a cropped red Christmas sweater with the words **SLEIGHIN' THESE HOS**. In her hand was a red cup, her name (**MIA'S CUP!**) written in green puff paint on the side. Her expression was both wary and, if I wasn't mistaken, almost pleased. But more wary.

"Yeah," I shouted back while nodding.

She stepped closer and yelled back at me: "I didn't think you were gonna."

That makes two of us, I nearly said but refrained.

Someone bumped me from behind as they headed toward the kitchen, and I realized I was standing in the way. Mia saw the same thing. She grabbed me by the shoulder and hauled me into the adjacent mudroom and shut the door. It was cooler and quieter and I was grateful.

Mia leaned her back against the door and eyed me. I noticed her cup was now gone.

"You okay?" she asked. "You look kinda, I dunno. Freaked, maybe?"

For all her inherent narcissism, Mia could be unnervingly perceptive. A good many of our talks over the years had begun with her noticing something was bothering me before I said anything, sometimes before I noticed myself.

"Yeah." I rubbed my forehead against the tension. "It's just been a really . . . challenging Christmas," I admitted, opting for understatement.

She bit her lower lip. "Is that cuz of me and Brody?"

"No, Mia. It has nothing to do with you and Brody." But then I cocked my head to one side and decided, what the heck. I *did* have some questions on the matter. "Although, now that you bring it up, why didn't you tell me about you guys?"

She shrugged and her sweater slipped off one shoulder. "I mean, what was I supposed to say? Me and Brody, we're a thing now?"

I stared at her. "Yes. Yes, that is exactly what you should have said. Those very words would have worked."

"But you and I were barely talking." Her eyes darkened. "You disappeared, Finley. Poof!" She made an accompanying gesture with her fingers.

"I went to another school in another state—"

I was about to tell her about how I'd mucked it up there, how I wasn't going back, but the words stuck. *Why can't I just say it?* I felt like Grandma Jo, in a way. Caught between two worlds, unable to commit to either one.

Mia couldn't have known any of that, of course. She interpreted what she heard through her own special filter and what I got in response was an actual foot stomp, complete with both fists clenched.

"Everything's always all about you and that stupid school! Finley's so smart, Finley's going to the fancy school, Finley gets the boy! Well, *I* liked the boy first! I liked him ever since him and Tanner played on Junior Varsity together!" Tanner was Mia's older brother, who was now a freshman at Utica Community College.

"You never said anything."

"What was I supposed to say? I never thought Brody'd like someone like you or me and then he did but it was *you* instead of *me*? It's always you. I'm always just your satellite, you know?"

"No, I don't know. You've never said *any* of this before." She hadn't even hinted.

"Well, it's true," she pouted. "People here notice me now that you're gone. Brody noticed me."

Something occurred to me then. "Is that why you told me to break up with him?"

Her eyes widened. "I didn't *make* you do anything!"

"That's not what I said—"

"You're in charge of your own life, Finley. Don't be blaming me for anything."

"I never—"

"It's so typical. And you know what? I'm *glad* you left. I'm *glad* we're not friends anymore. Now I can finally have the spotlight. It's Mia Time!"

I snort-laughed. Which was the exact worst thing I could have done.

"Fuck you, Finley," she said, flipping me off, then she opened the door from the mudroom back into the main house and slammed it as hard as she could behind her.

I probably stood in the mudroom for a full five minutes, absorbing the finality of our friendship. Which on some level I knew was a good thing. Healthy, even.

But I'd never lost a friend before. Not like this. And for all of her many faults, Mia and I had a lot of history. I suppose I shouldn't be surprised that a part of me wanted to go after her and tell her to listen to me, that I wasn't saying *any* of what she just accused me of saying.

I turned around instead. Opened the door to the outside and stepped into the cold.

The mudroom led to the side of the house where it was still shadowy, and I followed the narrow cement pathway around to the front, where even more people were gathered. Word must have gotten out to the surrounding counties.

"Didn't expect to see you here."

I glanced to my left and saw Ayisha there, standing under a tree, dressed in black jeans and boots and her emerald-green coat. Her braids were fully down around her shoulders and she was by herself, too, which surprised me. When I saw her out and about, she usually had at least two friends with her. I envied that.

"Same," I said, wandering closer. "I mean, not expecting to see you. Here."

She exhaled, her breath visible in the night air. "Yeah, well. Not a lot else to do, is there?" She took a sip of whatever was in her Solo cup. "It's Diet Coke. Straight," she volunteered. "Mamma let me borrow the car tonight."

No more need be said; I knew what a big deal that was. The Lewis household had one car, a burgundy Honda Accord, and Ms. Lewis was adamant about keeping it in perfect working condition. Ayisha being allowed to drive it alone was a sign of trust, one she wouldn't violate by drinking and driving. I'd heard a story once about her kicking a friend to the curb when she lit up a cigarette, and I mean the *actual* curb. Pulled over and told her to get out.

She glanced around. "Where's Arthur?"

I felt my stomach wrench at the reminder. "Gone."

She seemed puzzled. "Gone?"

I nodded and went to tuck my hair over my ear, only to be reminded I was wearing a knit cap and that wasn't actually necessary.

"His aunt, um, decided to change their reservation. They drove to Norman earlier today, and they fly out in the morning, day after tomorrow."

"That's Christmas Day."

"Yep."

"Why?"

I bit my upper lip.

Ayisha tipped her head to one side. "Did you two break up?"

I made a face. "We were never a couple."

"Not officially."

A quiver of irritation started to form. "Or unofficially."

"Gonna call bullshit on that. The looks you gave me when you thought he and I were flirting . . ." She smirked and I felt a habitual wave of annoyance start to rise up. But then it stopped and receded almost as quickly as it appeared.

I simply did not have it in me anymore.

She sensed it and dropped the teasing. "You'll figure it out once you get back to Hogwarts."

I bit my lip and she seemed to guess what that meant—that I still hadn't made up my mind about returning.

"Oh, come *on*!" Ayisha walked three feet away from me before turning around, giving me a good look at her pissed-off expression. "What is wrong with you? Are you stupid?"

"Sometimes," I muttered.

"Finley, why would you throw away this opportunity?"

"Because it's not mine in the first place."

"I'm going to stop you right there. Do *not* go down the martyr route. That's obnoxious. You got into Barrington because your grades were good and I'm guessing you wrote a great essay. Don't you dare throw it away like it's nothing. It's *not* nothing. It's someone's dream and you earned it, so act like it. Respect it."

"What about you?"

"What about me?"

"It's your dream, too."

She shoved her hands into her coat pockets. "I'm fine."

"I don't believe you."

"I don't need you to believe me."

"Listen, Ayisha." I was getting excited. "I think you should follow up after Christmas. Reapply or whatever else you need to do to get back in."

"That's foolishness."

"No, it isn't."

"It is, Finley. Mamma needs me here."

"Not anymore. Billie and Linda won't be in Christmas. You can go now."

For a moment there was a flash of hopefulness in her dark

eyes. But it faded almost as quickly. "It's too late," she said. "I'm a junior now."

"So am I. What does that have to do with anything?"

"It's already becoming time to start applying to colleges. I missed my shot."

"Now *I'm* going to stop *you*. You can still maybe get into the school and you know darn well it'd look good to colleges, even if it's only a year."

"I don't know that they'd still want me."

"So, find out."

"How?"

"Arthur's aunt can ask Ms. Martinez. They're friends. Ms. Martinez is on the admissions board. Here."

I took my phone out of my coat pocket and found Ayisha's number, which I'd put in once years ago and never deleted. Sadly, because I needed as many numbers in there as possible for when someone grabbed my phone to act like an asshole (it had happened). I didn't want anyone shouting, *Finley's only got thirty numbers and most of them are old people she's related to.* (That hadn't happened to me, but Shane Gowdy did it once to Lyndy Decker and it was humiliating.)

I typed her a text with Arthur's number. Decorum dictated I should have asked his permission first, however I didn't have that luxury anymore since he asked me not to text him.

"Okay. I just sent you Arthur's contact info. Check in with him and see if his aunt or any of their contacts can find out your status."

She glanced at her phone, where I saw my text had arrived. Then she frowned at me. "Why would he help me?"

"Because that's Arthur," I said simply, and my heart grew warm. I saw the image of the time he helped Steve and so many other moments. "He's kind. And we've already kind of talked about you going there."

She stared at me for a moment. Then to my shock, she deleted my text. "No."

"What? Why?"

"Because I'm not going to take your place."

"Why not? I took yours."

"We can't know that for sure."

"I didn't get in the first time, only after someone"—I pointed at her—"dropped out."

"Whatever. I'm not changing my mind on this."

She started walking away from me so I shouted: "I'm not the only person not coming back next semester!"

Double negative notwithstanding, this stopped her.

She waited then rolled her arm. "Go on."

"Thea Selsky. My roommate. Or ex-roommate. She's pregnant and apparently dropping out. Which means there's at least one opening other than my own."

Ayisha's eyes widened. "Seriously?"

"Super seriously. Fully knocked up. By a guy named Beaux. With an 'x'."

"That's unfortunate."

"You're talking about the 'x' part."

The corner of her mouth twitched. "I am."

I smiled like I was on the verge of getting admission to some sort of long-sought club. Before she could utter a single syllable, I texted her Arthur's information a second time. "There. There's no reason for you not to check your status." I could feel her resolve starting to shift. "You got in once before. You should at least try again."

She stared down at the second text. Then looked back up at me. "What about you? Are you going to try again?"

"What do you mean?"

"You failed there, right?"

"Well, I mean, my GPA is 2.8, so not *technically* failing. More like, I feel like a failure."

"Then you'd better work harder next time. Because if I get in and I whip your ass, I don't want to hear any of your stupid whiny excuses about shit being *so hard*."

"But—"

"Nope." Her thumb hovered over the delete button a second time.

"Don't!"

"Then you'd better get your ass back there, because if I *do* get into that super-prestigious boarding school and I have to deal with a bunch of white girls named Muffy and Buffy, I am *not* doing this alone. Got it?" When I didn't immediately respond she stepped closer and poked me in my sternum with her index finger. "I said, 'Got it?'"

I wasn't sure if I wanted to laugh or cry. I chose to nod. "Yep."

She nodded, too, then glanced over her shoulder when a bare-chested Brody ran out of the front of the house in pursuit of one of his football buddies, who held his plaid button-up shirt high.

Brody yelled, "Give it back, Parker!"

"Make me!" was the response.

"Suck my dick!"

"Jesus. I can't believe we both dated him," Ayisha said with rueful dismay.

Feeling bad about bagging on Brody, I offered, "He does smell nice."

"It's Old Spice."

That truly shocked me. "I thought he had some super-expensive aftershave from New York."

"Nah. He pours Old Spice into an old bottle of Tom Ford that he stole from his dad's trash can. I was there when he did it."

"Huh."

She set her red cup on the flat top of the low-rise brick fence that marked the outer perimeter of the Tuck yard. "I'm heading home now. I have a big day tomorrow at your grandmother's Christmas Eve party and I don't want to be tired." She looked at me then tilted her head in the direction of her car. "You want a ride?" When I pointed at my chest, she shook her head. "You're gonna be annoying, I can tell."

I laughed.

Then I gave one last glance back at the Tuck front yard, where many of my old peers were gathered—from the front porch, Mia shouted at Brody to get back in before he caught pneumonia; Kimmy Bunting's little sister was puking in some shrubs; two drunk boys I didn't know were in the middle of shoving each other, chests puffed, soon to start fighting—and I realized I didn't belong there.

Not anymore.

My heart ached with a kind of melancholy as I realized this, but at the same time I felt strangely at peace.

"Yeah," I said, as I joined Ayisha. "Thanks."

And together we left the party, right as it started to snow.

Twenty-Six

By the time Ayisha dropped me off at the inn, there was at least a half inch of white on the ground. We didn't chat much. The snow was already too intense, which made for tricky driving and I didn't want to distract her. Besides, we knew we'd see each other tomorrow for the party.

When I slipped in through the inn's back door, I paused to kick the snow off my sneakers and it occurred to me in a flash that the reindeer must be thrilled with this weather development.

Naturally the thought of reindeer made me think about Arthur. Which both made me smile, because it was a dorky association, and feel a slice of sadness that he wasn't here.

I sighed. All I wanted at that moment was a cup of peppermint tea, which was kept in the kitchen, so I headed that way. But as I got closer, I heard voices—very familiar voices—and I stopped, out of sight.

"What are you doing?" It was my mother.

"Making a sandwich." That was my father. He sounded mildly perturbed.

"Pimento cheese, Skip? Really?" I had to side with Mom on this one.

"It's delicious."

"It's made of mayonnaise."

"Not entirely. There's cheese. And pimentos."

"Have you been eating like this the entire time I've been away?"

There was a pause. "Maybe."

I heard my mother make a sound of irritation. "Give me that." More noises followed, including plates and cutlery and the refrigerator door opening.

"This is why you have high cholesterol," she continued.

"Some of that's good cholesterol," he countered.

"Not as much as you think." The refrigerator alarm started to softly ping. "Do you want turkey or tuna fish?"

"The turkey's for tomorrow."

"There's a ton here, they won't miss enough for one sandwich."

"I'm not telling Mrs. Buzzard."

"Chicken." She sounded teasing. "And if you say—"

"She's a Buzzard, not a chicken!"

Oh, Dad.

"Oh, Skip."

The alarm kept pinging. It carried a surprising distance for something that's intended to be subtle.

"There," Mom said. "I covered it up. No one will be the wiser."

I heard the fridge door close. More cutlery noises.

"Where do you suppose she is?" Dad asked. "Mom said they talked hours ago."

"Jo told me she wasn't upset."

"Like we knew she wouldn't be."

"I wish Jo had listened to us earlier."

"Everyone's gotta come to their decisions in their own way."

Mom's tone dropped. "I agree." And I knew they weren't talking about my grandmother anymore.

"Do you?"

"Yes, Skip. I *told* you so. You're the one who's been keeping me away. I had one moment of confusion, of wondering what it would be like to be somewhere else. And then I realized I wanted to come home. I feel like you're punishing me."

"I'm not. I promise. I *promise*." Quiet for several beats, then Dad said, "It's really coming down out there."

"I've texted her twice. Did you text her?"

"No. I figured yours were enough." All sounds of sandwich-making ceased. A long beat of silence. "I'll text her."

The text notification on my phone—a bell—went off. Loudly. I bit my lip. Oh, look. I *did* have two outstanding texts from my mom. And now one from my dad.

"Finley?"

Busted. Dammit.

I came around the corner and plastered on a smile. "Hey."

Mom was at the center island with, as expected, a loaf of multigrain bread, turkey, lettuce, and tomato. Dad was tidying up behind her. It felt remarkably normal. Except they were in the inn's kitchen because Dad had moved into a cottage.

"Where have you been?" Mom demanded as soon as she saw me.

"I went for a walk and wound up at Brody's house."

Mom frowned. "By yourself?"

Dad scowled. "In the snow?"

I directed my first reply to Mom. "Ayisha drove me back." And my second reply to Dad. "It only started snowing twenty minutes ago."

Dad pointed to the window over the sink where thick white flurries of snow flew past, visible despite the interior lighting. "It's really coming down out there."

I almost said, *I heard you the first time*. "I know." I took a piece of turkey. Mom was not amused. "Do you think this means folks won't come to Grandma Jo's party tomorrow?"

"No one misses your grandmother's Christmas Eve party," Mom said, adding more turkey to the sandwiches. I noticed she was making two.

Interesting.

Dad nodded. "It's true." Then he cleared his throat. "Speaking of your grandmother, she told us you two had a talk earlier today."

"A *much*-needed talk." Mom emphasized, putting the bread tops on the sandwiches.

"Which," Dad continued, "for the record I encouraged—"

"We."

"—we encouraged her to have a long time ago."

"Years." Mom pointed the knife in my direction for emphasis.

I leaned a hip against the island and crossed my arms. "Are you two, of all people, dunking on Grandma Jo for not telling me something deeply personal and important? For *hiding* things from me?"

They exchanged glances and had the grace to look uncomfortable.

Dad muttered, "You had to make a smart baby."

Mom cut the one sandwich at an angle so the halves formed triangles. "I had help." Then she handed Dad the sandwich and cut her own in half, down the middle, like a sane person. "Finley, do you want a sandwich?"

"No, thanks." For once, I was surprisingly not hungry.

Dad looked down at his plate for a long moment. Then looked at Mom. Then back down at his plate. He picked up one half of the turkey sandwich shaped like a triangle and took a bite, from the corner's end. Like he always did. I thought I saw the tiniest loosening of his posture. And for the first time since I'd been home, a genuine lightness began to creep back into his expression.

Mom missed it as she brushed her crumb-covered hands over the sink but kept her eyes on me. "Do you want to talk about it?"

"Grandma Jo's gay. Or lesbian. Or, whatever she wants to be. There. We talked about it."

"How does that make you feel?"

I groaned. "Please. I beg you. No more talking. Just for tonight, okay? Between all the talking I've done in the past twenty-four hours with you two and Grandma and Mia and Ayisha and Arthur, I'm heavy-talked out. I just want to lie on a sofa and watch a fluffy Christmas movie and then watch the snow come down."

Mom smiled. "That sounds like a lovely evening, honey."

Dad nodded. "I have a few saved on my DVR in the cottage."

She and I both shifted to look at him. "Who are you?" she said.

And I added, "You hate those movies."

"Some are better than others." He chewed another bite. "They've been making me feel better lately."

Mom regarded him, now curious. "Which ones do you have saved?"

"*While You Were Sleeping* and *Christmas in Connecticut*."

She positively melted. "Those are my favorites."

Their eyes met. "I know."

Their eyes held longer than necessary, and I knew they'd forgotten about me, which didn't bother me at all. In fact, a bloom of hope started to form and I knew instantly what I needed to do.

I yawned.

Broadly. Full arms extended in the air, eyes closed, head shaken, all for the dramatic effect. Then I added droopy eyes, to sell it.

"You guys go ahead," I said, with a weariness that was only a slight exaggeration. "I'm headed upstairs to bed."

My parents refocused on me in surprise. "You just said you wanted to watch a movie."

"Tell me how it ends."

Dad said, "Which one?"

I shrugged. "Whichever." Then I kissed both their cheeks, said, "Love you," and got out of the way as fast as I could.

I didn't bother with the peppermint tea. I didn't even wait around to eavesdrop. Just booked it up the backstairs to my temporary room and made a silent prayer for those two crazy kids to figure it out. *Please, please* figure it out . . .

Later, once I was in my sleep sweats and warm, dry socks, I stared out the window at the snow falling like mad. The weather app said it was going to be whiteout conditions all night and all day tomorrow, with the chance of it stopping sometime on Christmas Day. Over an inch of snow had accumulated by this point and you could tell it was just getting started.

Of course.

Excellent timing now that Arthur "All Perfect American Christmases Have Snow" Chakrabarti Watercress had left. At least I knew he was in Norman right then, which meant he was close enough to be seeing this, too. And maybe he was staring out a window at the same time I was, seeing the snow, and wishing . . .

On impulse, I grabbed my phone and checked Arthur's Instagram before I could stop myself. And right there was a recent post, from thirty-two minutes ago. A video clip. Of the snow falling. With the caption: *Almost perfect.*

I frowned, wondering what he meant by "almost." Hadn't he requested—no, wait, *demanded*—snow on Christmas? Well, here it was. Lots of it. What more did he want?

I was tempted to leave a comment asking that very question, though I didn't.

Then I noticed the time on my phone was 12:09 a.m., which reminded me that I needed to get some sleep. Christmas Eve would be a long day.

Who knew what it would bring?

I stood and crossed back to the bed, sidestepping a small pile of my clothes on the floor that I would deal with tomorrow, or possibly the day after, and the soft arch of my right foot landed painfully on something small, round, and very hard.

I looked down to see a dark item on the floor, caught in the beams of light reflected off the snow.

I reached to pick it up.

The conker.

Small and silly, with Arthur's shoestring dangling.

I remembered then how embarrassed he'd been at the accidental double entendre. How he'd blushed. And how the energy between us had changed, and I knew he felt it, too.

I was seized by the impulse to take a picture and text it to him—*look what I found!* But I had given him a promise not to.

Because he'd been down that road before. With Astrid. Whom he liked very much. His crush. The one he liked enough to get him into his big mess.

A tingle went up my spine then. Not of concern, like this morning at breakfast, but of growing awareness.

Did that mean Arthur thought of me like he thought of Astrid? Like his crush?

Oh.

Oh, wow.

That one sure had taken its sweet time to seep in and I felt a surge of pure happiness.

But I promptly came right back down again. He was still gone and still about to depart Oklahoma.

All I wanted to do right then was let him know that I *wasn't* Astrid. I wouldn't play with his heart. I wanted him to believe me. But at the same time, he'd set up a boundary. Which deserved respect. It would be easy to text him a photo, or call him under the flimsy work-around of *You said text, you didn't say anything about calling.*

Or maybe leaving a comment? Under his Instagram post?

But no. I couldn't do either of those. I knew what he'd meant.

So, I didn't text him and I didn't leave a comment. Instead, I put the conker under my pillow, wanting to laugh at myself.

Then I snuggled beneath the comforter, pulled up to my nose, and watched the snow pour past my window, to create the bright white tableau that would be awaiting me in the morning.

Twenty-Seven

That little conker came with me everywhere the whole next day, tucked in my jeans pocket, ready for when I'd reach in to grasp it in my palm, feeling somehow closer to Arthur each time.

Not that I *had* time.

My part of the Christmas Eve party prep began at eight a.m. sharp, which meant today was a minimum twelve-hour day. Thankfully Grandma Jo paid overtime to her employees, including me, which wound up being a generous chunk of change.

For the first four hours, I joined Ayisha, Val, Mrs. Buzzard, Reggie, and Lloyd in getting the inn ready. This meant removing furniture from rooms—no small task when the sofas in the lobby had to be hauled into storage, which was thankfully on the first floor. It would have been nice to have had help from Dad, whose car was still in the parking lot so I knew he was there, but he failed to make an appearance. Which I was hoping had something to do with my mom's car *also* still being in the parking lot, the only sign she was still around.

And that meant I didn't complain with all the furniture schlepping. But it did make me ravenously hungry, especially with all the delicious smells coming out of the kitchen.

By noon I couldn't take it anymore and headed for the kitchen, the wrath of Mrs. Buzzard at my intrusion be damned, and encountered Steve, who was on his way out. He had completed a CK grocery delivery, so he wasn't wearing the entire elf outfit, merely the coat and scarf. His shoes were a well-worn pair of brown waffle-stomper boots and his headgear a green, furry aviator cap, pulled down around his ears.

"Hey, Finley," he said in his raspy voice, with a cheerful wave.

I waved back. "Hey, Steve."

He paused. "Where's my man Arthur?"

I bit my lip at the painful reminder. "He and his aunt checked out and went to a hotel in Norman."

Steve frowned. "Something happen?"

"No. They just decided to make a change."

"Are they gonna be here for the party tonight?"

"No."

His thin frame deflated. "Oh, that's a shame."

It really was.

"Tell him I said howdy if you see him."

I promised I would. Then my stomach gurgled loudly enough for Steve to hear and make a "whoa" face and I entered the kitchen.

All day there had been a plethora of aromas swirling, but one stood out. It was spicy in a different way and I followed my nose to the stove when Mrs. Buzzard wasn't looking and discovered the source was a reddish, lumpy, soup-like concoction simmering in a pot on the back burner.

Mrs. Buzzard turned and caught me so I pointed. "That's new."

"Eh?!"

"That's NEW."

"Indian stew!"

I leaned in closer. "Smells nice."

"That's the tumor!"

I blinked.

Steve swung inside the kitchen with a new box of tomatoes and clarified, "Turmeric."

"Ah."

Mrs. Buzzard shouted: "Daal!"

Steve and I exchanged looks. Steve shrugged and boogied right out of the kitchen. He was no fool.

"It means stew!" Mrs. Buzzard pointed at the pot. "Lentils, coconut, cinnamon, something called 'ghee'? And a buncha other stuff! Daal! Here!"

Before I realized her intent, she'd scooped up a spoonful and held it up to my lips, leaving me no option but to taste. And while I didn't have anything to compare it to, never before having had daal, it was undeniably delicious.

Mrs. Buzzard seemed pleased by my reaction.

"Good, huh?!" she asked.

"It's fantastic."

I reached for the spoon, hoping for another bite but I got my hand slapped instead. Then she filled a small bowl and practically shoved it into my hands.

To my surprise, she turned back to the pot and said in a normal voice, "Your grandmama added that to the menu for those Indian folks. Asked me to make it even though they left. Poor thing." She shook her head, but in a way that I knew she at least had some inkling of my grandmother's motivation, and, to my relief, she seemed sad *for* Grandma.

And so was I.

My heart ached not merely for myself, at Arthur's absence, but for Grandma Jo's loss, too.

A week ago, she had told me with a sparkle in her eyes how she had ordered the ingredients for traditional Indian meals and had even learned to prepare some herself. I wondered now if she had planned to make them for Esha and their dinner that never happened.

On impulse, I took out my phone and snapped a few pics, which earned me a glower from Mrs. Buzzard, who resumed shouting.

"Eat it, don't snap it!"

Impulse hit again and I took a picture of Mrs. Buzzard. Her scowl turned more ferocious and she opened her mouth to yell at me until I said, "You look cute."

And showed her the photo. Which was at the very important higher angle and caught her blue eyes behind her thick glasses.

She stared, but when I asked her if she wanted me to send her a copy, she grunted in a way that I was pretty sure was affirmative.

Stepping off to the side, I quickly scarfed down the bowl of daal and put the dish in the dishwasher. When I started to exit, Mrs. Buzzard yelled: "Wait!"

I turned.

"You dropped your nut!" she said, holding up my conker.

That was the first time anyone had ever said that to me.

I swiped the conker, thanked her, and made my way to the front lobby, still clutching it and thinking about Arthur, which was when I almost collided with:

"Brody?"

Brody turned and smiled bashfully, rubbing the back of his head. "Hey, Fin."

"What brings you by?"

"Uh, do you have a sec?" He glanced at Val, who was working the front desk with her typical level of invisible enthusiasm.

I nodded and we went to the library, which was empty. It reminded me of Arthur. Brody seemed out of place here. And uncomfortable. His hands were tucked in the back pockets of his jeans and both his amazing hair and heavy winter coat were still dusted with melting snow.

"Mia said you came by the party last night," he said.

"I did. I'm sorry I didn't say hi, but you seemed busy."

His head bobbed. "Yeah, I got pretty wasted. Been pounding pressed juices all morning." We both nodded; I was familiar with his hangover remedies. "Um, I just wanted to say, you know, I'm real sorry. 'Bout wiggin' out the other night, at the parade. It was uncool."

My heart softened. One of Brody's biggest attributes—besides his looks—was his willingness to own up to his mistakes. He had other good, non-physical qualities, but I think I appreciated this one the most.

"It's okay," I said, my smile soothing. "These things are weird."

"Yeah, I just, you know, didn't expect to see you with someone else."

"Back atcha."

His chin dipped. "Sorry." he murmured, chagrined. "I shoulda told you 'bout that, too."

"It's fine, don't worry." I reached out to give his arm a reassuring squeeze. "And Mia really likes you a lot. I can tell."

"I like her, too." He cringed. "Hope that's okay to say."

"It is. We're broken up."

"I kinda always knew I was never supposed to be your guy anyhow. We don't . . ." He mimed his two hands missing each other. ". . . fit. But, me and Mia, we do."

He was right, they really did fit. For how long? That was anyone's guess. But for now, at this point in their lives, they made sense in a way he and I never had and never would.

His gaze dropped as he noticed something. "What's that?" he asked, pointing to my hand.

He had spotted the string and chestnut I had yet to return to my pocket and I laughed, rubbing one eyebrow in embarrassment.

"It's a conker." When he looked understandably confused, I explained. "It's a British game where two people take chestnuts on strings and try to hit their opponent's as hard as they can."

"Why?"

A very sound question.

"To break the shell." I'd done a quick read-up on the rules via my phone last night.

Brody considered this and I could tell his natural competitive side was working out the gist. "What if it doesn't break?"

"You keep trying. Over and over and over, until . . ." My words trailed off as I started to feel something simple and honest and true go from tickling the back of my mind to the forefront with such ease it felt as if it had been there all along. And maybe it had. Maybe I simply needed to come upon it in my own way. My answer. Clear and straightforward. ". . . until it breaks open."

"And it's called a conker?"

"Yeah. But with a 'k,' not 'qu.' Though, conquer is part of it. Conquer the other person's chestnut, conquer your fears of not getting it right the first time or the second or the ninth. You keep swinging and swinging and swinging until eventually, that nut breaks." I put the conker in my pocket as my chest started to feel like it was filling with sunshine and certainty. "Brody, I have to go."

"Okay, Fin," he said, hands jammed deeper in his coat pockets. "I just wanted to make sure you and me were, you know, cool."

"Yeah. We're cool. Thanks." I stood up on my toes and quickly kissed his cheek. "Merry Christmas, Brody Tuck. And thanks for making sure we're good."

I hurried out of the library, in search of Mom and Dad. I wanted to talk with them, share what I was feeling. But then I remembered they may be in the middle of their own revelation and changed direction, winding up by Grandma Jo's office.

The door was half open.

Grandma Jo stood beside her desk, reading glasses on, reviewing papers. The window behind her desk brought in the light of the snowy outdoors and I got a clearer look at how drawn she seemed. She'd dressed nicely for the day, though I knew she would change into her Christmas party outfit later.

But what stood out was that she had forgotten to apply her lipstick, which never happened. Lipstick was like my grandmother's one constant. Typically dark red, though not *too* dark, with pencil lining that must be blended and never allowed to be noticed, with a hint of gloss to give it a shine that didn't veer into gloopy. For her to forget to *apply* was unheard of.

I tapped on her door. At the noise, she looked over her glasses at me.

"Yes?"

"Hi." I stepped inside. "I thought I'd check in, see how you're doing? With, you know, everything."

"Fine. Busy," she said in a clipped tone.

But then Grandma Jo seemed to hear herself and stopped. She set the papers down then leaned against her desk and took off her reading glasses. She gazed at me in a way she hadn't before, her guard lowered.

I asked again, gentler, "How are you, Grandma?"

She swallowed and her eyes took on an unfocused quality. "I'm sad," she admitted, in a voice echoing the emotion. "And angry at myself."

I bit the inside of my lip. "I saw Mrs. Buzzard making daal."

She nodded. "I was going to surprise Esha with it." A small shrug followed by a wry pull of her lips. "No reason to waste the ingredients so I asked Mrs. B to go ahead with the dish." I didn't think that was the only reason, which she confirmed. "And it reminded me of her."

I crossed to hug her because she clearly needed it, and when her arms came around me, I knew I needed it, too.

A few days ago, she had told me we were all in our own process of evolution, or words to that effect. I better understood that now. Growing up, adults always seemed to have the answers, never made mistakes, were on the right path. But that was an illusion. Grandma was as confused and disappointed and frustrated as I was, which was hard to realize—would it ever get easier?—but also a relief in its own way. I wasn't some massive screwup because I didn't know everything exactly as I should *when* I should.

But I did know one thing.

I pulled back from our hug to look at her.

"Grandma," I said with resolve. "I'm going back to Barrington."

Her expression brightened. "You decided?"

"I did—hold on." I frowned. "I don't think I told you I was thinking about *not* going back."

"Your father told me."

"I don't think I told him, either."

"Your mother told him."

I rolled my eyes in frustration. "Okay, new family pact? We tell each other"—I waved between us—"the important things. Which includes telling *me*."

A smile tugged at the corner of her lipstick-free mouth. "Deal." She sized me up. "What made you change your mind?"

"More like, finally make up my mind. And you'll laugh."

"I won't."

I held up the conker by its string.

"That?" Her face was practically a question mark.

"It's a conker."

She snort-laughed.

"Grandma!"

"Sorry," she murmured contritely, then nodded to it. "Explain to me."

So, I explained to her the rules of the game and how it applied to me making the biggest decision of my life. "You keep swinging, over and over, until you get the desired result," I said. "Which in this case is a cracked chestnut. But with me, I need to keep swinging, too. Until I get what I want."

"Do you know what you want?" she asked reasonably.

"Not yet. But I think I'll figure it out."

She cupped my cheek. "I'm very proud of you, Finley Brown."

"You could do it, too," I said earnestly.

She seemed puzzled. "What do you mean?"

"With Esha? You could try again. If you really want to."

Her expression closed back up then. "I wish it was that easy." She moved back to stand behind her desk. "But she doesn't live here."

"That didn't bother you before."

Grandma Jo made a noise under her breath and pinched the bridge of her nose. "She's leaving for England tomorrow. And I have the party . . ."

"England?" A stab of concern sliced through me. "Arthur, too?"

"I don't know." Her eyes met mine. "I'm sorry, Finley, but she didn't say where he was going, only that they were both leaving Oklahoma first thing in the morning."

I found Ayisha helping Reggie move some tables around the perimeter of the lobby. As soon as Reggie returned to the kitchen, I made a beeline for Ayisha.

"Hey! I need you to do me a favor."

The look she shot me stopped me in my tracks. "Oh? Now it's I *need* to do you a favor?"

I held up a single finger. "Let me rephrase that."

"Good idea."

"Ayisha." I put my hands together. "Would you possibly consider texting Arthur a photo?" Ayisha leaned back, decidedly wary, and I caught on. "Not *that* kind of photo. A pic of daal."

"Doll?"

"It's an Indian dish. See?"

I showed her my phone with the pic I'd snapped earlier. "Oh, that dish Mrs. B's making."

"Exactly. I think Arthur and his aunt should know about it, and especially that Grandma Jo had it made for them, in case they changed their minds and stopped by for the party."

Ayisha raised an eyebrow. "There's a blizzard outside. I don't think they're coming back for a party."

A sense of defeat washed over me. Of course she was right. Why would they possibly leave the safe, warm confines of whatever hotel it was they were staying at to brave the elements to come to a party at an inn they left only the day before? The notion had been half-baked at best, but when confronted by common sense, it became nonsense. And depressing.

She cocked her head to one side. "Did Ms. Brown break up with Arthur's aunt?"

My mouth dropped. "Am I the only one who didn't know about my grandmother?"

"You didn't know?" Her brown eyes danced with amusement.

"Oh, come on!" I threw my hands up in the air dramatically, which caused Ayisha to laugh.

She shoved my shoulder. "This is too easy. I didn't know either until I caught her and the aunt a few nights ago out in the courtyard. Don't worry, it was strictly PG-13."

"Can we concentrate on something less mentally unnerving?"

"Why can't you text Arthur the food pic?"

"I promised I wouldn't text him, and yes, this is a total work-around, which I was trying to avoid, but honestly? Grandma Jo is so sad."

That resonated for Ayisha. She bit her lower lip. "Yeah, I could tell something was off. She forgot lipstick."

"Right?"

Ayisha held up her phone. "Text me the foodie pic."

"You don't think it's a stupid idea?"

"I do. But stupid ideas are all we have at the moment."

Fair enough. And I was ridiculously happy she'd said "we."

I sent her the pic. "I know it might be awkward texting Arthur out of the blue like this—"

"Oh, we're already texting."

My back went rigid. "What?"

She held her hands palms up. "You gave me his number!"

"*Last night!*"

"I don't waste time." She grinned. "You should see your face right now." Then she patted my shoulder. "Don't worry your pretty blonde head. He's not my type. And besides, you're the one he likes."

I full-on gulped at the nervous excitement that evoked. "Did . . . he say something?"

"Nah. I can just tell." Her thumbs moved over her phone's keyboard with lightning speed. "There. Sent."

A trickle of relief went down my spine, despite the likelihood that nothing would come of it. "Thank you."

"You two better get back to texting directly before I get to school with ya because I am not playing your go-between."

"I like your confidence."

"Me too."

We shared a smile. Then she nodded to the other three folded tables leaning up against the wall. "Your turn to help."

Twenty-Eight

Mom was right. No amount of snowfall was going to keep the townsfolk of Christmas away from Grandma Jo's Christmas Eve party.

The lobby was filled with people by four thirty, which, considering the event wasn't officially supposed to begin until five, was a big tell that tonight was going to be very, very long indeed.

My parents still hadn't made an appearance and I'd give them another hour before I started sending them "where are you??" texts. See how *they* liked it.

I'd changed out of my work clothes and into my official Christmas outfit for the evening, which consisted of black wool pants, low-heeled dress boots I seldom wore, and a red sweater. Grandma Jo's aesthetic leaned toward elegant, which meant she would never ask anyone to wear a gaudy holiday sweater, even for fun.

However, that sentiment was not held by most of the other townsfolk who took pride in wearing some truly obnoxious outfits. There were at least three sweaters with working lightbulbs, a white suit made of fabric with red Santa heads, someone dressed in a Christmas tree costume. And Mitzi in her favorite gingerbread-Swiss-Miss-hybrid outfit that was ill-advised on anyone who didn't resemble Scarlett Johansson. Which Mitzi did not.

But no one had a green sweater with a reindeer vomiting ornaments.

Mitzi held court by the table holding the collection of her desserts from the Gingerbread Café and I couldn't help noticing Dr. Raymond was nearby, sharing secret glances.

But he doled out the bulk of his attention to Grandma Jo—wearing a beautiful A-line, red velvet dress, with full lipstick now in place—when she wandered by. I heard him suggest they go outside to the courtyard to her enough times that I knew he was hoping to spring a mistletoe trap, but she would send him a "ha, ha, no" look and then flit off to chat with another guest.

Ms. Lewis was there, along with Billie and Linda, all three in their holiday best with the twins in matching green velvet pinafore dresses and Ms. Lewis in a dark burgundy pantsuit, also velvet. Ayisha—who had somehow found time to sweep her braids into an immaculate topknot—mainly took care of them and I saw her shoot her twin sisters looks each time they wandered near the piano. At one point she stage-whispered, "This isn't one of your recitals!"

Which earned her dual pouts in return, but also a small smile from her mother.

It reminded me of what Mom had said, about how Ms. Lewis had to raise three kids by herself. Clearly she was doing an amazing job, but I knew I'd never fully understand the sacrifices made along the way. By her, and by Ayisha.

My job during the Christmas Eve party was to carry around platters of appetizers, which were always a careful balance between sophisticated and edgy for this part of the country (gluten-free guacamole cups with a cherry on top and caprese bites on skewers) and comfort food (snowman cheese balls and all manner of things wrapped in bacon). Few people tried the daal, even when Reggie labeled it "chili surprise." Their loss.

These parties were never my favorite thing to do at the inn, though I had to say this year was particularly difficult to get through. My eyes kept drifting to the front doors with some illogical hope that at least one Chakrabarti would step through with the proclamation that seeing evidence of the daal that was clearly made for them was all the proof they needed of Grandma Jo's good intentions and wounded heart. That they, the Chakrabartis, were truly missed. At which point I would tell Arthur about my intent to return to Barrington, to take another swing.

But that didn't happen.

In the kitchen, I grabbed a fresh platter of hors d'oeuvres at the same time Ayisha arrived to drop off her empty platter.

Our eyes connected. I opened my mouth to sp—

She pointed at me. "If you ask me one more time if I've heard from Arthur, I'll make you bring the bourbon mini–hot dogs to the tipsy housewives and listen to them juggle euphemisms."

That was an involved and very specific threat, but I closed my mouth just the same.

Back in the lobby, I saw Mrs. Gowdy holding a generous glass of mulled wine and laughing with too much enthusiasm to her cohorts while holding a mini-wiener on a toothpick and, yeesh.

"Howdy, Finley."

I turned to find none other than Mayor Bobby Jim Slaughter waving at me.

He was wearing his best (read: only) pine-green corduroy jacket with red elbow patches, which at last year's Christmas Eve party he told me made him seem festive *and* intellectual. It should be noted he told me this while he was also chewing a BBQ-meatball skewer with his mouth open, so I'm pretty sure the effect was a wash.

"Hello, Mr. Mayor," I replied with a smile.

"Looks like your gramma's got y'all real busy."

"Yes, sir." I proffered a silver plate. "Cranberry crostini?" I'd grabbed one of the "sophisticated" options.

He squinted at it longer than necessary.

"Those look crunchy."

"They're cranberry and ricotta cheese on tiny toasted rosemary baguettes."

I was pretty sure his mouth watered. As warranted. They were damn tasty. But then Mayor Slaughter's brows furrowed in concern.

"I don't suppose you got anything softer? Gotta be careful with the newly capped tooth." He opened his mouth and pointed. I set my gaze past him because that was a sight I did not need. "'An 'oo 'ell?"

"I'm sorry?"

He closed his mouth. "Can you tell which tooth got capped?"

"No, sir."

He beamed. "Dean's a wizard."

I suggested, "How about I get you some Santa's Eggs?" Which were basically green deviled eggs with red tomato specks. "They're soft."

"Hell yes!" He looked skyward. "Sorry, Jesus."

He did that about three times a conversation back when I was interning at city hall. Grandma Jo once said he might as well be Catholic since he cussed and prayed for forgiveness in the same breath.

Sixty seconds later I had crossed back into the kitchen and switched platters, returning with the eggs. He put five on his plate, ate two, then filled the empty space on his plate with three more. I wondered what *his* cholesterol was like.

Before I could move on to other guests, though, Mayor Slaughter stopped me.

"Oh, and while I got your attention, Finley, I been meanin' to say thank you."

I frowned. "Thank me?"

He nodded vigorously. "For making all those changes to the town's website."

Oh, fuckity fuck! (Sorry, Jesus.) I had completely forgotten!

"Changes?" My voice squeaked but at least I managed to not drop the platter.

He kept nodding. Vigorously. "Yup! I saw 'em right away, and at first I wasn't real sure whatcha were doin'." *I was sweating was what I was doing.* "But then I started lookin' at the new pictures . . ." *I also wanted to curl up and die.* ". . . and I thought, 'I betcha she's makin' it look good for those folks at that school she's at.' "

Aaaand now I blinked. A lot. Flummoxed. "Uh, actually, yes. That's—that's exactly what I was doing."

He slapped the hand not holding his plate with the mountain of eggs against his thigh. "I knew it! And by golly, it worked! Christmas hasn't looked that good since that evil basta— sorry—that piece of—sorry—since Ralph Tater-Hall stole all the money and left us capped at the knees. But our town looks awesome! At least on the site."

"Oh. Well, I'm, um, so—"

He kept grinning. "Obviously you did a little 'mbelishment here and there." I held up my finger and thumb—*very close*. "But that's okay." *Thank God.* "I showed it to some of the other folks on the council and we decided it was divine inspiration." *Hmmmmm.* "We got some extra cash off beer sales when the Sonic Santas nearly won state in basketball thanks to Brody"—*Of course*—"and we'd been tryin' to find a way to spend it and realized, why not start findin' ways to fix it up 'round here? But start kinda small to see how it'd go over."

"Small?"

"The parade!"

"The . . . parade?" My voice squeaked again.

"Yep! I'ma tell you what, the stuff you put on the site looked *real* nice, like that snowman balloon. The lights! And the goats were cutie pies! So we went lookin' to get things like you imagined."

"Me?" If my voice got any higher it would only be canine-audible.

"Yep. Figured it'd be easier than tryin' to change the site since none of us are great with big website stuff. And it worked! Got a real nice write-up in the *Norman Transcript*. Print and website. Kicked up some real interest. Folks are already talkin' about what we can do *next* year, when we got more time to plan."

I legitimately didn't know what to say.

"Feel free to lemme know if you get any other ideas."

"Yes, sir."

"Although, I changed the password on the site so you'll have to email me directly." He winked, then noticed Dr. Raymond across the room. "Gonna go talk shop with Dean. See ya, Finley. And good job."

He successfully maneuvered his way through the crowd to

join Dr. Raymond by the Christmas tree, making sure to say hello to everyone along the way like a true politician, and I realized it might not be the tailgate beer sales alone that helped get him reelected.

I also realized something else: I had made a difference. Admittedly it was an accidental difference and I was lucky Mayor Slaughter had a good sense of humor about my appropriating the town's website. But the point was I had taken action that created changes that would be felt by others.

It made me want to do more. To take further action.

When I saw Grandma Jo's gaze get snagged on the lonely pot of daal, I got an idea.

I knew I wanted her to be happy, to see Esha again. To get her a second chance. And obviously I wanted to see Arthur. I was missing him terribly, which sort of amazed me. It had only been a day, but it felt so much longer.

However, Ayisha sending him random photos of food was probably not going to cut it. I had to be bolder. I had to do this in person so there were no mistakes.

With that in mind, I slipped away from the party and into the kitchen amid the still-swirling—though starting to wind down somewhat—chaos of the party prep.

I located Ayisha in the back, swapping out platters.

"Hey. Can you drive me to Norman?" I asked, sans preamble.

She was impressively unfazed. "When?"

"Now?"

"See," she said, continuing to add new toasted turkey turnovers with apricots and almonds to her platter, "I know you know there's a blizzard going on because you have eyes and everyone's talking about it, so I also know you don't really mean now."

"I kinda mean now?"

She slowly turned to face me. "Okay, one: that's crazy. And two: Mamma drove so I think you already know the answer she'd give. But feel free to ask her."

We both knew I wouldn't.

I sighed in frustration. "I have to get to Arthur and Esha before they leave the state and maybe the country, and that can only happen if I go *to* them now."

"I feel like there are other, less potentially lethal options."

"Like texting Arthur?" I was hoping maybe for some sort of neutral judgment on her part to tell me that breaking my promise to Arthur was permissible.

"Actually, no. I think his phone is off."

My jaw went sideways. "How often *are* you two texting?"

"Down, girl. I wanted to see if he'd gotten your food pic so you'd stop bugging me."

"Oh. And?"

"Calls go straight to voicemail and my follow-up text bounced."

"Do you think he blocked you?"

She shot me a look. "No one blocks me. I think there's a freaking blizzard going on outside and it's affecting reception."

"Even more reason I have to go to them."

"Totally the opposite, but you seem determined. Can you get one of your parents to drive you?"

"Normally, yes. But I think they're kinda, um . . . reconciling."

She held up a hand. "Go no further."

I chewed on my lower lip. "Mrs. Buzzard offered me the keys to her car yesterday."

"Do you really want to drive solo in these conditions?"

"No."

"First sensible thing you've said since you walked in here. What you need is someone with a car who'll drive you to Norman."

A raspy man's voice said, "Hey there!"

Ayisha and I turned in unison to see a snow-dusted Steve enter the kitchen with a cardboard box of groceries from CK and set them on a back counter.

"Done!" he proclaimed. "What a day, huh?"

Then he turned as he wiped his brow and grinned widely at us.

And I was pretty certain I was looking at a Christmas miracle.

Twenty-Nine

Twenty minutes later, that certainty about a miracle was wearing off.

Steve and I had successfully made it out of the neighborhood in his green El Camino. But the farther we got from the inn, the more concerned I grew. It occurred to me as I glanced out of the corner of my eye at Steve, hunched forward over the steering wheel, peering through the half-de-iced windshield and his own yellow-lensed night-driving visor, that I hadn't actually thought this through.

I wasn't worried about Steve. Everyone knew him and knew he was eccentric, not criminal. It was more about the weather and the sheets of snow that were still falling, accompanied by stronger wind than I'd realized, which reduced the visibility to maybe fifty feet beyond the front of the car.

We were on our way toward U.S. 77, which was a two-lane route to Norman. Thankfully the roads were almost completely empty, other than the occasional oncoming eighteen-wheeler that appeared out of the hazy winter wall of snow like a monster from the mist.

Folks still talked about the Christmas Eve blizzard of 2009

that dumped fourteen inches of snow on Oklahoma in twenty-four hours. No one ever thought that would happen again. However, the farther out into this mess we got, the more I was starting to think it just might.

And I was out in it. On a quest. Like an idiot.

"Steve, are you sure you're cool with this?" I asked, hoping I had disguised the concern from my voice.

He looked over at me then pointed at the driving visor. "Oh, yeah. This thing's a wonder. I was starting to think I was having a brain aneurysm the way my eyesight was dimming at night but this cleared it right up." He tapped the yellow visor for emphasis.

"Speaking of eyes . . ." I nodded to the front windshield, which he hadn't faced once for the past ten seconds.

He laughed a single, hard cough-laugh, which seemed to have dislodged something from his lungs. He rolled down his manual window, bringing in a freezing blast of air, then forgot the lyrics of a Jim Croce song and spit into the wind, which, yep, came right back into his visor. The attempt to wipe it off made matters worse.

"Now it's blurry!" he shouted over the din of the swirling wind.

"Roll up the window!" I shouted back, hugging my coat closer to my body.

He rolled up the window.

Or made the attempt.

Unfortunately, it jammed midway.

He then tried to counter the arctic onslaught by turning up the heater to the max, but that feature was soon revealed to not be the strongest in this particular automobile.

Great.

I dipped my nose behind my scarf and tucked my gloved hands under my armpits for heat, discreetly checking my phone as best I could under the circumstances. Ayisha had agreed to give me updates with any important information, either about the party or about contact with Arthur. So far, bupkis. However, I was thinking it might be time to send her an SOS if things kept going the way they were going.

Unfortunately, they did.

"Arthur's a real cool guy!" Steve shouted, smiling his approval toward me. "He brought me breakfast two days in a row."

I sat up straighter, pleased. "He did?"

"Yeah. Blueberry muffins! Didn't have the heart to tell him I'm allergic to berries, but the shits were totally worth it. Thanks for asking me to go fetch him with ya."

"Thank you for driving." *I think.* Still up for debate. Especially since the windshield wipers did an admirable job on the snow hitting the windshield from the outside, but apparently the car either didn't have a defroster or it was broken because it froze quickly.

Steve pointed to the glove box. "Can you get the ice scraper?!"

I did as he requested and retrieved a cheap plastic handheld ice scraper.

"Thanks!" he shouted, then I watched him drive with one hand and scrape the inside of the windshield with the other. "You know what this all needs?"

"Triple A?" I responded.

"Music!"

He took his hand off the steering wheel long enough to both terrify me and punch the on button for the radio. Which was when I learned where Steve put the bulk of his money for the El Camino: the sound system.

It was a marvel!

Hall and Oates's version of "Jingle Bell Rock" easily blasted over the wind and surrounded us like a loving embrace of holiday cheer interwoven smoothly with the constant danger of freezing conditions and storm-limited visibility.

Steve sang with unbridled energy, and it really says a lot about the power of that song because in a matter of seconds I was hesitantly bopping my head, too, and whisper-singing. Not as zealously as Steve, but I had to admit, I was momentarily caught up.

Until disaster struck.

Instinctively sensing danger, I looked forward—

"Aaaaahhh!"

—and saw another vehicle headed in the opposite direction toward us.

In our lane!

"Aaaaaahhh!!"

Steve saw it, too.

"Aaaaaaahhh!!!"

That car's lights were high and wide, like the eyes of a dragon emerging from the dark, and in an instant, I knew if we collided, the El Camino would definitely lose.

Steve took his hands off the wheel and prayed.

I grabbed the wheel and jerked it hard right.

The other vehicle went left.

We started spinning wildly.

Steve started praying louder.

I remembered enough of my mother's "ice driving" lectures to know to turn the wheel *into* the spin.

Which worked!

But we still slid off the road, into a drainage ditch, rear end–first.

And stopped.

Hard.

God bless the seat belt.

The radio played on. In the moments after we ceased moving, I knew we had dodged a major accident. My heart was hammering.

"Are you okay?" I breathlessly asked Steve, whose yellow visor was cracked in four places but otherwise seemed okay.

He nodded, dazed.

I looked closer, but other than blinking rapidly, he did seem fine.

What about the other car??

I opened the door and slid out of the passenger's seat, regained my balance, scrambling up the three-foot incline out of the icy ditch to the roadside, snow still coming down like God had a Celestial Snow Doodad and was having Himself far too much fun.

Other than my own rapid breathing, harsh and shallow, it was surprisingly quiet.

In the dark, I could make out the shape of the other vehicle—a large SUV of some sort—stopped across the road, which itself seemed empty but for our two cars. The SUV's headlights illuminated an impressive distance despite the weather.

The passenger's-side door opened and a figure hopped out.

I squinted.

The figure started jogging across the road in our direction and as he got closer, a warm feeling inside me started to stir wildly because I knew that gait, I knew that puffy green jacket, and I knew the way he held himself upright, like a member of the royal guard. Because I knew:

"Arthur!"

Thirty

"Finley?!"

There was enough light for me to be able to see the utter astonishment that raced across Arthur's face.

I didn't think. I launched myself to hug him tightly. For a moment, I felt his surprise, then he reached a single arm around my waist and relaxed.

"You're here," I whispered.

"As are you," he said in disbelief.

I pulled back to look up at him and saw that disbelief mingled with delight and confusion in his eyes. All completely understandable. I felt them, too. Then his gaze slid from my eyes to my mouth and back again and a *stillness* fell over both of us. I knew right then and there, standing in the center of an empty, snow-covered road, he wanted to kiss me and I wanted nothing more than to kiss him back. It seemed inevitable, it felt destined, it—

"My man!"

Dammit!

Arthur and I blinked and stepped away from each other as Steve—who had broken free from his post-crash daze to exit the car—pulled Arthur into a hug.

"Guy, we were goin' lookin' for you, but then we almost got run over by this tank that came outta freakin' nowhere!"

"Not a tank," Arthur clarified, turning to point back at the Hummer where Esha now stood, watching us.

"Did you forget which side of the road to drive on?" I teased.

He arched a single brow. "*I* did not."

"I did," Esha called out to us. "And I think now would be an excellent time for the three of you to get out of the middle of the road."

As if on cue, we all heard the unmistakable sound of a fast-approaching car.

Arthur, Steve, and I hustled to join Esha moments before a small, dark pickup truck zoomed by, so fast I could barely make out the four people crammed in the cab, laughing and not paying attention, including the driver, Kimmy Bunting's little sister, who never paid attention to anything anyway and very likely shouldn't have been driving. And it hit me in that moment that if *they* had been the ones to encounter the wrong-lane Hummer there was almost no chance they would have reacted fast enough to avoid a collision. It could have been, would have been, a very different outcome.

My gaze met Arthur's own wide eyes and I knew he'd had the same realization.

"We should get going," Esha said, turning to Steve. "Are you all right to drive?"

Steve pointed to his own chest. "In general? I mean, mostly. But I just scarfed an edible after that wreck to get my"—he made a terrified face—"down and then my night visor got all busted all up and—"

"So, no, then."

"No."

Esha turned to me. "Then it's up to you, Finley."

I did a double take. "Me? But what about Arthur?"

Arthur held up his left hand. "I actually slipped on some ice while refueling the Humvee to come here and my wrist is possibly sprained, or at the very least unhappy with me." I noticed a small, fresh cut and some swelling around the base of his hand.

"Hence my turn behind the wheel," Esha clarified. "Which I believe we can all agree should not be repeated."

Concern rippled through me. "Are you okay?" I asked Arthur, stepping closer.

"Do you need an edible?" Steve held up a small Ziplock with what appeared to be cookies. "They're legal here now."

"No, thank you. Very kind." He met my eyes and I saw them grow gentler. "I will be fine after it's iced and rested."

"But he cannot drive in these conditions," Esha said. "Which means you have to get us back to the inn."

It felt strangely biblical when she said it like that. On Christmas Eve, in the middle of a snowstorm. And also terrifying, which must have shown on my expression.

"You can do it, Finley," Esha said kindly. "I have faith in you."

She placed the keys in my hand and I felt an enormous responsibility. But I met her dark eyes and a calmness settled over me. And a deep regret.

I hugged her tightly. "I'm sorry."

"Oh, darling, whatever for?" She sounded amused but also pleased.

I pulled back to look at her. "Just trust me on this."

I smiled, which she returned. Then we all entered the Hummer, Steve and Esha in the back, Arthur in the passenger's seat. With me as the driver. During an evening snowstorm. Mom would have a heart attack.

Which reminded me.

"Can you text Ayisha to tell her we're on our way back to the inn?"

Arthur squirmed. "I can't, actually. I may have, ah, dropped my phone in the loo."

Esha chuckled.

I reached into my coat pocket and handed him my phone. He managed to adroitly text with his right hand.

From the back I heard, "Hi, I'm Steve, by the way."

"Esha Chakrabarti, pleasure to meet you."

"You are so pretty."

Arthur's eyes never left my phone. "She's a lesbian, Steve," he said, still texting.

"Oh, okay."

Arthur glanced over at me, smug, his voice lower. "*Now* it's germane to the conversation."

I rolled my eyes and started the ignition.

I heard Steve say, "You're still pretty."

"Thank you," Esha murmured.

The knobs for things like heating and defrost were easily marked and I activated both, rubbing my gloved yet still half-frozen hands. Sitting there like this, I felt a bit like Alice in Wonderland after she shrinks. Everything was just so big.

Now Arthur focused on me. "It really is remarkably easy to drive. Other than its obvious enormity, terrible fuel efficiency, and the awkwardness of the turns."

"Is that all?" I quipped.

"And the gear shift tends to be a bit sticky." *Fantastic.* He leaned across the massive center console as he pointed to the light switches. "There's the lights. I can say from experience, there's no need for brights."

Was I slightly distracted to have Arthur closer to me? Yes, yes I was. But it was important for me to keep my wits about me. I took a deep breath—my grip on the steering wheel deathlike, my back upright, my eyes forward, my heart an entire percussion band in my chest—and pulled the gear shift down into "D," which did take more effort than I anticipated.

"Excellent," Arthur cheered.

Foot on the accelerator.

"Release the parking brake."

I released the parking brake. The Hummer rolled forward about an inch.

"Now you should depress the accelerator."

Oh, right.

I pressed down on the accelerator and the Hummer smoothly rolled forward. I turned the wheel to aim us back onto the road itself, automatically hitting the left turn signal even though there were no other cars around because I'd heard both my grandmother and mother endlessly complain about people not bothering to do that.

We merged onto the road.

And I was driving.

The first five minutes were a blur of fear-induced adrenaline. But after that, it slowly started to become easier. Granted, I drove possibly twenty miles an hour, sometimes less, and we only passed one other car the whole way back. It still counted, though.

Arthur stayed leaning in toward me, being quietly encouraging. The snowfall started to lessen, too, becoming less murder-blizzard and more "isn't this charming."

I heard my phone buzz.

Arthur shifted back into the passenger's seat to properly check it.

"Ayisha texted back," he informed me.

"Would you read it to me?"

"'Cool.'" He nodded approvingly. "Succinct. Ah, wait. Here's another." He read, "'Your parents finally made it to the party. Yeah, they've been totally doin' it.' Oh." He glanced at me. "Relations have improved, I take it?"

"Mom cut his sandwich the way he likes it and Dad saved her favorite Christmas movies."

"Makes perfect sense. Here's another text: 'They're asking where you are.'"

"Tell them—"

"'And don't even think I'm going to lie for you.'"

"Oh my God, I wouldn't!" I said, and he started to text. "Don't send that." He backtracked. "Tell them the truth"— Arthur typed with his one thumb—"and that we should be back soon. Wait, very soon. It'll make Mom feel better."

"Send?"

"Send."

He hit send.

"New text. 'Now your grandma wants to know where you are.'" Arthur typed his own reply while vocalizing it for me. "'Arthur here. Does Ms. Brown know who is returning with Finley?'" He waited a moment for the reply to arrive. "'Nope. I thought the surprise would be fun.' How romantic. Ah, wait. One more. She could give Bronwyn a run for her money in terms of texting speed."

I shot him a look. "Don't ever compare Ayisha to Bronwyn."

He didn't bother to try to defend himself. "Understood. And the new text reads: 'Mamma and your mom are talking.

I heard them say Barrington at one point. I have questions!' "

Hearing that sent a shot of excitement through me. Arthur also seemed pleased.

"Is she coming to join us?" he asked.

"Hope so."

Esha's voice piped up from the back seat. "Is this regarding Ayisha getting in touch with Sonya?"

"Yes, Mashi."

"Well, let her know I've sent a message to Sonya," Esha continued. "I should imagine if Ayisha has already been accepted once that she meets their requirements. Getting her in a second time shouldn't prove too difficult, particularly if your pregnant roommate drops out."

I looked at Arthur. "I thought you were against gossip."

"It was pertinent!" he defended.

"Thank you for helping," I redirected back to Esha.

I glanced in the rearview mirror and caught Esha's nod before her attention drifted back to the window. She bit her lip as a cloud of uncertainty drifted over her expression and I thought about how she was taking a risk, too. With her heart. For my grandmother. She was private about it, but still brave.

"What made you want to return to Christmas?" I asked Arthur.

He chuckled. "That sounds like a holiday tune."

Which Steve heard. He quickly leaned forward in the space between the front seats.

"Tunes! Can we listen to Christmas music, huh? It'll make everything sooooo much cooler."

Boy, is he high.

Arthur said, "Only if it's not a distraction for Finley."

I shook my head, already feeling considerably more comfortable. "Go for it."

Steve cheered.

Arthur turned on the radio, and while the sound system couldn't hold a candle to the customized El Camino, it got the job done. It was Christmas Eve and that meant whichever station you tuned into was playing Christmas songs. We wound up listening to one of the countless versions of "Carol of the Bells," which was enough to satisfy Steve, who sat back again and closed his eyes.

With a glance toward his aunt, Arthur leaned closer to me. "To answer your question, after everything had calmed down, we both realized we'd acted rather hastily."

I chuckled. "Was it the daal?" I asked.

"Yes," Esha said from the back.

I looked in the rearview mirror again. "Seriously?"

"Bengali chana daal is my favorite," she said, still nervous, but now with the barest hint of a smile. "I told Jo that in passing. I wouldn't have thought she would remember."

Arthur nodded, adding, "She loves chana daal." And murmured, "Which is not a euphemism." I bit my lip to not laugh and he grinned. "Possibly a euphemism."

"I cannot hear what you are saying," Esha called out. "But I think by your expression it must be naughty."

"I love you, Mashi," he told her with a big smile.

"Very naughty, then," she said dryly.

We all laughed.

When Arthur turned back, I asked him, "Does this mean you're only returning for your aunt?" and held my breath.

His smile faded as he stared at me intently. "No," he said, with a slight shake of his head. "I have my own reasons."

Goose bumps danced along my skin and it took all of my concentration to make the turn onto Merry Street without plowing into a lamppost.

But then we saw the sight before us and I felt a breath catch.

There was snow everywhere! Covering all the imperfections, hiding all signs of aging, and bringing a hush that was felt as much as heard.

I had never really seen my town like this before. It's possible that was what Merry Street of Christmas, Oklahoma, always looked like when it snowed, but not that I could recall. It was like something out of a postcard or a snow globe.

Or a stolen photo on a website.

It was magical.

At that same moment, the first strings of "Happy Xmas (War Is Over)" began to play and Steve bravely decided to join in with John Lennon. Let's just say Yoko did it better. But then to my surprise, Esha joined in as well. Arthur laughed. Then his eyes met mine and we both began to sing along, too. And, despite everything that got us here, for all its random weirdness and near-death experience, it was as close to a perfect Christmas moment as I'd ever had. I would remember it forever.

The final voices of the Harlem Community Choir were fading as I pulled the Hummer into the lone empty spot at the front of the inn and parked.

Safely.

"Well done, Finley," Esha said in warm approval.

"Woot-woot!" came from Steve.

Arthur smiled and held my gaze. "Perfect," he said so only I could hear.

The four of us exited the Hummer into the snowfall and Steve gave a salute.

"Thank ya for the adventure, folks. Merry Christmas!"

"Hold up, Steve," I told him. "You're not leaving."

"Absolutely not," Arthur affirmed.

I saw Steve start to blush. "There's a party going on," he said, pointing to the windows where loads of people were visible.

"You're staying here tonight," I told him. "At the inn." Even if it meant he took my tiny room and I slept on a lobby sofa (once we got it out of storage).

"It's snowing," Arthur said to him. "Besides, we have to get your car back."

"Y'all sure?" he asked, hesitant.

I took his hand and affected a moderately decent British accent. "Absolutely." After all, I owed him. Big time.

He smiled. "Well, okay!"

The four of us went up the steps and through the front doors and we entered the party.

The entire town wasn't there, obviously. But the important people were, the ones who had known our family for years, and the ones who got things done.

As we stood at the threshold between the entry and the lobby lounge, Ayisha appeared by my side. "Took you long enough," she stage-whispered, nodding hi to Arthur, who stood behind me. He waved back.

"I drove a Hummer H2!" I stage-whispered back, then squeezed her hand to convey my thanks. She shook her head at me, and smiled. An indulgent smile, sure, but it wasn't a smirk. I would update her later about Sonya Martinez.

Because right then it was as if the crowd sensed our arrival and there was a subconscious parting. And though it wasn't quite a record-scratch moment, it was darned close.

A quick glimpse and I located my parents by the fireplace, holding hands. Dad was chatting with Mayor Slaughter and Mitzi and Dr. Raymond. While Mom was having a far more engaged conversation with Ms. Lewis and my heart swelled with hope for my friend's future.

Somewhat off by herself, however, was the person for whom I'd done all this.

Grandma Jo.

Who at first appeared upset when she saw me and I had no doubt that she and my parents would have worked in tandem to give me the lecture of a lifetime about doing something incredibly foolish—even without knowing the full extent of what had happened—except her focus then shifted from me to Arthur.

And from Arthur to Esha.

Grandma Jo's anger vanished at once. It was replaced by a gasp of shock followed by profound relief and a swift array of emotions that were still quite new for me to witness from her. Was it possible she had tears in her eyes? I couldn't tell because Grandma Jo was suddenly striding across the crowded lobby of her beloved Hoyden Inn. And then, in front of the people of Christmas, family, friend, and folk alike, she took Esha Chakrabarti's smiling face between her hands and kissed her into next Sunday.

And she didn't even need a mistletoe trap.

Thirty-One

The snow stopped falling by around ten p.m. and less than an hour later, the sky was a pristine blanket of stars.

The Christmas Eve party was well past the official conclusion, having finally wound down close to eight thirty, and made me want to start grabbing coats for people so they would get the hint.

The good news was the townsfolk didn't bail after Grandma Jo's display of romantic courage. Heck, it might have made them stay longer, just for the gossip of it all.

But as I returned to offering appetizers to the guests (much to Arthur's amusement), I was able to overhear most of the chatter. I might have been related to the subject of their conversations, but I was also there in a service capacity and people tend to forget who's who while they're choosing between a smoked-salmon/cucumber finger sandwich and a bacon-wrapped jalapeno, all while gossiping.

Still, they weren't judging. Not that I heard. At least at this point. Some of that would inevitably happen later, because change can come easily for some, yet take longer for others. Grandma Jo understood that. I was just glad she finally stopped letting it shape her.

One person who wasn't judging was Dr. Raymond. I have to give it up for the good dentist. As soon as he saw Grandma Jo and Esha kiss, he said, "Oh, okay," then turned all of his focus to a triumphant Mitzi, who offered him some Christmas bark and a dazzling smile, both of which he merrily accepted.

Mom and Dad cornered me not long after my return to let me know that what I did was irresponsible and danger-ous, both of which were fair assessments. And that was before they'd heard about the crash. But they were also happy that Esha was back since it meant Grandma Jo was beaming like a kid, something neither my parents nor I could ever recall hap-pening. That had never been my grandmother's style. Maybe now it would be.

Dad said the whole thing was a huge relief. And more than anything he wanted his mom to be happy, which she clearly was. Time would tell if Grandma Jo and Esha were in for the long haul or if this was a holiday romance. I had my suspicions on where I thought they'd land.

And Mom and Dad were happy, too.

Their stay at the party lasted about an hour before they gave me a hug and a kiss, grabbed some extra sandwiches, wished me a merry Christmas, then retreated to Dad's cottage before I could ask what Mom'd talked about with Ms. Lewis. There were times when they seemed so old to me, usually when I was getting in trouble for something. But there were other times when I remembered they were actually crazy young, all things considered, and this Christmas had been a big reminder.

Steve went up to his room for the evening, where he could stay for as long as the weather was brutal, or he wanted it, which we all knew wasn't long. He hated being cooped up. It simply wasn't his bag.

I was with Arthur when he told Steve that he would arrange to have the El Camino towed to the Santa's Sleigh Repair as soon as possible and then have everything taken care of. Gratis, since, if nothing else, they could have easily killed him with the driving mistake. Steve was blown away. But he was also tired. After an elaborate handshake that Arthur could only follow in part, Steve retired for the night.

Once he was gone, Arthur asked me, "Do you think it would be presumptuous for me to buy him a camper?"

It said a lot about the evolution of our relationship that the question didn't faze me.

Somewhere around the time the snow was stopping, I lost track of Arthur. He'd been in the corner of my eye for most of the night, but once I joined Ayisha in the kitchen for clean-up duty, I couldn't keep him in my sights anymore.

Ayisha waited until we had loaded both dishwashers and hand-washed all the rest before she grabbed a towel to dry her hands and casually said, "I talked to Mamma about Barrington."

I stopped what I was doing at once. "And?" I asked, barely able to contain my nervous anticipation.

She took her time folding the towel and placing it in the laundry hamper off to the side. "And she thought you made a good point about Billie and Linda. Also, turns out, our moms have been talking for a while, not just tonight. They've been conspiring to get the Wonder Twins into the arts school."

"So you can be free for Barrington!" I was both thrilled and impressed with our mothers. Sneaky! But also perfect.

"That's the hope," she said, playing it cool.

My energy surged and I started bouncing on the tips of my toes like Dr. Raymond. "You're going, aren't you?" It was more a statement than a question.

"We'll see," she hedged, but I knew that was more about self-protection.

I grinned. "I feel like it's going to happen."

She grinned despite herself. "We'll see," she repeated. "But Mamma supports the idea now."

Which was huge! Something I wouldn't have been able to appreciate before. Unable to contain my excitement, I hugged her, which she was not expecting.

"Okay, whoa, slow down," she said, even as she was laughing. "You're like a Labrador puppy."

"You'll be my roommate," I proclaimed when I stepped back, almost giddy. The look of mild horror only made my smile grow. "You will."

"We'll see." She pointed at me. "But if I do, you'd better watch out. Muffy and Buffy aren't the only ones who are gonna have to step it up if I get there."

I laughed. "I'll be prepared."

Then she smiled at me, and headed out to the front of the inn where her mother and sleepy sisters were waiting to drive her home.

By eleven thirty, I was done.

There would be plenty of work left for the morning, like moving the furniture back (Dad wasn't getting out of it this time), but the guests were gone and most of the lights shut off, except for the ones on the tree by the window. Those stayed on, like a beacon.

The rest of the inn was quiet, and my loved ones were on to their happily-ever-afters, in whichever form they would ultimately take.

And I wanted my turn.

But after searching for Arthur for fifteen minutes, I was

starting to think maybe he'd gone upstairs to his room. Which was disappointing. I knew we could talk tomorrow, on Christmas Day. Yet . . .

I decided to try outside, in the back courtyard, and wouldn't you know it? That's where he was, the lunatic. By the firepit. Bundled up in his green jacket and knit hat and gloves and scarf. A heavy woolen blanket was wrapped around his legs and he had appropriated one of the inn's wrought iron fireplace shovels, which he was holding over the flames for some reason.

"Hey," I said, keeping my voice on the softer side. There was something about the snowy quiet of a late December night that made people want to whisper.

When he saw me, he smiled. "Hello."

I crossed over to him and felt the heat from the fire warm my cheeks.

"I've been looking for you. What are you doing out here?"

"Roasting chestnuts, of course." He grinned. "It's one of the final things to do on my wish list."

"I seem to recall something about that."

He patted the seat beside him and with a shimmer of excitement, I moved to the spot. He draped the blanket over my legs for shared warmth.

"Have you had one?" He nodded to the plate of cooked chestnuts perched on the edge of the brick firepit.

"I haven't."

Setting the fireplace shovel to the side, he picked up the plate of roasted chestnuts with his good hand and held it out to me. "You have to peel them, like an egg."

I chose one. "You like to give out instructions, have you noticed that?"

He blushed. "I do, don't I?" I nodded. "Does that bother you?"

"Not lately."

Our eyes met and held. Then I started to peel the chestnut but stopped and frowned.

"What is it?" he prompted.

"I think I'm anthropomorphizing the chestnut."

His brows drew together. "Quite possibly the last thing I expected you to say."

I chuckled. "That's me, keeping you on your toes."

"At which you are quite good," he murmured. Then nodded to the chestnut. "Now, why are you giving Nutty here feelings?"

Fishing in my front pocket, I withdrew—

"The conker!" His dark brown eyes danced with delight as he plucked it from my hand.

"I found it last night. Stepped on it, actually."

"Brilliant! Tomorrow we'll have to break it in with a match."

"No." I shook my head.

"No?"

"This conker is my talisman. I don't want it broken." He stared at me, the corners of his beautiful mouth twitching. "Go ahead, laugh, but it's true."

Instead, he shook his head. "No. We shall employ other chestnuts for our match." He handed it back to me. "Clearly this one is special."

"It is." I put it in my pocket. "It helped me realize that I want to come back to Barrington in January. I want to keep trying."

Arthur's eyes widened in hopeful surprise. "Really?"

"Even though I didn't do as well as I thought I would the first semester, I have to keep trying, don't I?"

"Yes." He grinned.

"I think it'll be better this time. I won't be alone. Ayisha will hopefully be there." My eyes met his and I swallowed. "And you'll be there, too." It came out more like a question.

"I will," he assured me. "I'll be there whenever you wish. And I'm delighted by your decision."

"Are you?" I grew hopeful.

"Very much." He grinned again, looking light and happy. "Now, here. Try that perfectly non-emotional roasted chestnut you're holding by way of reward, and tell me what you think."

He indicated the roasted chestnut. I resumed peeling it then took a bite. To my surprise, the texture reminded me of a mushroom and it had a buttery flavor.

"And?" he asked, curious.

I made a face as I tried to determine what this reminded me of. "It tastes like . . . a sweet potato? Which wasn't what I was expecting."

"Not as good as the Jammie Dodgers you left for me."

"You got them!" He nodded and I felt a mixture of pleasure and embarrassment. "They were going to be my Christmas present to you, but you were leaving . . ."

"It was a bit of an eye-opener when I saw them. Astrid would never have thought of something like that, found something I liked, and brought it to me." He watched me closely.

"I guess we Brown women like to use food as bait," I said lightly, but almost at once realized that it was pretty forward and not at all like me.

I looked away from him, registering the blanket of snow around the courtyard. Which reminded me. "Why 'almost'?"

He frowned. "Is this a Finley-ism? Where you start in the middle of a subject and expect others to understand?"

"Yep." I nodded. "On your Instagram last night, you wrote 'Almost perfect' about the snow. Why 'almost'? How isn't this the perfect white Christmas you requested?" I indicated our surroundings.

"Isn't it obvious?" he asked. I shook my head. "Because I wasn't with you."

My eyes grew wide. For a moment I didn't know what to say, I was too surprised, too happy. Then I told him the first thing in my heart. "I missed you last night. When it started snowing, I wished I could be with you, see your reaction, talk with you . . ." I bit my lip.

He relaxed and smiled and I wondered how I could have ever thought of him as anything other than the cutest boy I'd ever seen. "Then we are of the same mind," he said. "Because I missed you, too."

I leaned in closer. "I'm glad you came here, to Christmas for your terrible Christmas." I said softly. Sincerely. "It turned out to be my favorite Christmas."

"I have to confess something," he said quietly, but with a hint of nervousness just below the surface. "I . . . I didn't want to come here to Christmas merely because the website made it look impossibly charming."

"You didn't?" My voice was barely above a whisper.

He shook his head. "I wanted to come . . . because *you* were here." He turned to look at me and gave a shy shrug. "I hope that doesn't come across wrong. Everything else about why I wanted to bring my auntie here is entirely accurate, I assure you. I simply left out that one little tidbit."

"That's not a tidbit, Arthur. That's huge."

He blushed.

"It is rather, isn't it?" He tugged on his earlobe. "I imagine that was a big part of why I reacted so poorly when I got here and found out the website was a fabrication. It reminded me of Astrid and how I'd liked her and trusted her and got hurt when she lied. Once I calmed down and got to know you, and this town called Christmas, I realized how silly I was behaving. You and Astrid are so different." He shook his head. "Thank God."

"You came to Christmas for me?" I whispered.

He nodded. His dark eyes were wide and vulnerable.

Giddiness danced in my heart. "I didn't think you even liked me," I told him.

"I like you very much. From the moment you took my favorite seat in class."

"Since then?" I was incredulous.

He nodded again. "What other girl would wade into a freezing pond in December to save a tiny bee?"

"No one sane."

"No one so extraordinary."

I reached over and took his hand. It was warm and felt as perfect now as it had in the sleigh. "You hid the liking really well."

"I thought myself rather obvious."

I shook my head. "No. But I'm starting to learn how to read you better."

I placed my hand against his chest and didn't think twice as I leaned forward and kissed him. His lips were warm and gentle. The smoke from the fire mixed with the roasted chestnuts and the distinctive amber woodsy scent I'd come to associate with Arthur Chakrabarti Watercress. My head swam.

I drew back enough to whisper in his ear, "Merry Christmas, Arthur."

He slowly smiled, a sense of relief coming over him. Beneath the warm blanket, he squeezed my hand and leaned forward to kiss me a second time and a third and then I forgot to count. When we finally did stop, we smiled at each other and snuggled under the wool blanket, an endless array of stars shining overhead.

"Happy Christmas, Finley," he said, pulling me close beside him.

It *had* been a happy Christmas after all, despite how it had started, and the several bumpy points along the way. And as I sat by the fire, Arthur's arms around me, listening to his heartbeat, I had a feeling the new year was also going to be very interesting once I returned to school. *Our* school. There would be challenges, of course. Some I anticipated, like Bronwyn, and others I wouldn't see coming.

But that was still over a week away.

And right now, I had this moment. With this boy. Which was all I needed.

My heart was full.

So, I kissed him again.

Turn the page for a first look at Finley and Arthur's adventures at Barrington Academy in

One

I regretted my decision immediately.

As I stood in the open front doorway of the Airbnb two-story mini-mansion rented by my classmate Bronwyn, I saw my new schoolmates dressed in attire that rivaled something out of a Hollywood costume party and I felt the plunge of dread.

They were audacious.

And impressive.

And I . . . was not.

I had come dressed as a burglar. Which was an outfit that required all the creativity of grabbing black jeans, a black turtleneck, black boots, black knit cap and gloves, and a five-dollar felt mask I'd ordered from Amazon so I could go low-key cheap for this event.

Which I had.

What I hadn't even done was grab a pillowcase stuffed with fake cash, because I only have two and they're both floral—which kind of throws off the whole "burglar" vibe—and I hadn't wanted anything to happen because Target didn't carry that set anymore.

It wasn't that I didn't care I had finally been invited to one of Bronwyn Campbell's famous parties, because I did.

A lot.

I also hadn't wanted to *look* like I cared. I mean, what if I'd shown up in some insanely elaborate costume—like, say, the throne from *Game of Thrones*—only to find myself faced with a sea of snobby expressions as my costume-free classmates sneered at my faux pas because dressing up for Halloween was for children and we were upperclassmen at the prestigious Barrington Academy. That meant we were *not* children. Even if I was still a few weeks shy of turning sixteen.

So, I'd fallen back on the tried-and-true strategy of "don't look like you're trying too hard," which had always served me well in the past.

Not tonight.

Because these people were dressed like they were at the freakin' Met Gala.

And I was one felt mask away from wearing an outfit already in my normal rotation.

Major miscalculation.

Not that anyone noticed.

No one paid me more than the most cursory glance before they returned to whatever it was they were doing, even if they weren't doing anything.

Was that a good thing? TBD.

My stomach roiled slightly and my second regrettable decision of the evening—sneaking a tiny bottle of pinot grigio from my roommate Thea's curiously impressive airplane wine collection, which she kept in the square fridge tucked in her closet—started to make its presence known.

She'd told me the first week of school that I could have one if I wanted, so technically it wasn't sneaking. In the ensuing weeks since then the subject had never been raised again and our interactions had dwindled to polite greetings on the rare occasions we encountered each other, so I couldn't be 100 percent certain. But I really wanted a dose of liquid courage before coming.

So, I grabbed one.

I'd only been at the Connecticut prep school since June, but my attention had been so firmly on trying not to fail any of my classes, both over the summer and now in the fall, that I hadn't made socializing a priority.

As a result, five months in, I didn't really have any friends, and I had to admit, I was more than a little lonely. Tonight was supposed to be my attempt to change that. After all, I'd received an emailed invite from Bronwyn, which was a first.

People didn't say no to Bronwyn.

At least not that I'd been able to witness.

She was the daughter of a wealthy real estate mogul, and she considered herself an aspiring beauty influencer with, as she liked to remind people, over twelve thousand followers. "And *counting*!"

I, on the other hand, last posted on Instagram two months ago. About my breakfast. It got four likes, including my mom's.

Sweat was starting to break out across my chest as my heart thundered with anxiety.

My eyes darted around the expansive living room, not quite sure where to land because there was so much going on. Noise from the deafening music. Smoke from a variety of cigarettes, some legal.

And the costumes. *Oof.*

I spied Josie Sutton in a shiny gold flapper dress with fringe galore, a headband, and a long cigarette holder drunkenly chatting with my mostly MIA roommate, Thea, and her boyfriend, Beaux, who were dressed like Claire and Jamie from *Outlander*. That astronaut costume sported by Gaines Alder looked potentially authentic, and, oh, God. I think Landon Sinclaire really *was* dressed like the throne from *Game of Thrones*.

What was I thinking? I felt like a child attempting to migrate to the adult table.

If I turned around right now and left, no one would know I'd ever come. I could give the whole "be more social" thing a try another time, when there was less pressure.

Like graduation.

"Hello, Finley."

I spun in the direction of whoever'd said my name and found myself face-to-face with—

I squinted.

"Arthur?"

At least, I *think* it was Arthur Chakrabarti Watercress? Unlike many of our other classmates, Arthur was dressed more sedately in a formfitting tuxedo that likely cost a pretty penny, his inky-dark hair tightly slicked back to the point of shining, giving him a very different vibe than I was used to seeing in our two shared classes or around our campus.

"Bond," he replied, utterly deadpan. An unlit cigarette dangled from his pouty lips and the faint scent of wine wafted off him, which surprised me. I'd never considered him to be the party type. More studious, like me. Then again, we were both at a party and I was already feeling the effects of the tiny bottle of wine, so I was in *no* position to judge.

"What?" I shouted in confusion above the thumpy music.

He pointed at himself and repeated, "James Bond. The Sean Connery version. From *Dr. No*, specifically. All others are imitations."

I almost rolled my eyes. What a dork.

Although, now that I allowed a second glance, he actually looked kinda—

"Arthur! *There* you are!"

He and I turned in synch and my stomach dropped because

Queen Bronwyn herself was descending on us like a pterosaur in a perfect recreation of the Lily James version of *Cinderella*, right down to the blond wig over her gorgeous auburn hair and post–Fairy Godmother transformation blue dress.

Damn. She looked fantastic.

And she barely flicked a glance in my direction because her focus was securely on Arthur.

She handed him a chilled martini glass with a clear liquid and a curly slice of lime peel at the bottom.

"Shaken, *not* stirred," she said, smiling broadly. "As requested."

I arched a brow. *What service.* Which was curious, because Arthur was hardly the social butterfly. At least that I'd observed. Not that I kept track of his comings and goings, because I didn't.

But now I had to wonder: *Was something going on between them?*

Last I'd heard, Bronwyn was together with some guy named Prescott, who was at Mayo Prep in Upstate New York, and the only reason I knew that personal tidbit about her was because she managed to work it into every third conversation I'd ever overheard her have. ("Prescott tells me he won't go to Lancaster Mountain to ski anymore, not since he's been to the ski resorts in *New York*." "Prescott sent me this box of candy from *Belgium*. Isn't it *amazing*?" "Prescott met *Drake*! At his *concert*! He sent me *a selfie!*")

"Many thanks," Arthur said, taking the glass from her. "Cheers." He took a sip. Nodded. "That's quite excellent." His crisp English accent lent an air of authenticity to his would-be Bond persona.

Bronwyn's smile grew coquettish. "Prescott says I make the *best* vodka martinis."

Ah. *There* he was. Good ol' Prescott.

Arthur turned to me, held up the glass. "Do you want to try a sip?" he asked, and if he hadn't been looking directly at me, I would have assumed he meant someone else. Arthur and I hadn't had many interactions these past few months. Well, other than him scowling at me because I took his favorite seat in class that first week.

I smiled politely. "No, thank you." The pinot grigio aside, I barely drank and wasn't going to dive into the deep end via vodka tonight.

He shrugged and took another sip.

Bronwyn was now looking at me, her blue eyes like lasers. "Finley?" I nodded. "I didn't recognize you."

My mind went blank with anxiety, but I knew I needed to reply, so I pointed to my head. "I hid my hair." Not the most insightful response, but at least it was accurate. My most recognizable feature—long blond hair—was indeed tucked away beneath the knit cap. There was also the cheap mask I was wearing, which suddenly itched.

"I see that." She returned her attention to Arthur and smiled. "You look *great*."

He nodded once and repeated, "Many thanks."

She drew in a breath to say something else when Flapper Josie swooped in, grabbing Bronwyn by the upper arm, to Bronwyn's annoyance. Josie was too tipsy to notice.

"Come do shots!" she shouted at her BFF.

Bronwyn looked on the verge of shrugging her off when Astronaut Gaines and a boy dressed as the Mad Hatter who I was fairly certain was named Hawley Chen also appeared to pull her away, deeper into the house. All shouting, "Shots! Shots! Shots!"